THE FEDERATION

A HANDBOOK OF INFORMATION ON THE UNITED FEDERATION OF PLANETS

THE FEDERATION

Design and Writing
 Bernard Edward Menke
 Rick David Stuart
Timeline Assistance
 John Theisen

Editorial Staff
Editor-In-Chief
 L. Ross Babcock III
Senior Editor
 Donna Ippolito
Editor
 Todd Huettel

Production Staff
Production Managers
 Jordan K. Weisman
 Karen Van Der Mey
Art Director
 Dana Knutson
Cover Art
 David R. Deitrick
Illustration
 Todd F. Marsh
 John C. Tylk
 Bob Eggleton
 Daniel E. Carroll
 Jay Harris
Typesetting and Layout
 Tara Gallagher
Pasteup
 Todd F. Marsh
 Dana Knutson

Dedication: To those individuals who gave their lives pursuing the dream of a united humanity among the stars.

With Special Thanks to Lieutenant William Gaiser and Michael Cornish

Copyright © 1966, 1986 Paramount Pictures Corporation.
All Rights Reserved.
STAR TREK is a registered trademark of Paramount Pictures Corporation.

Published by FASA Corporation
P.O. Box 6930
Chicago, IL 60680
Printed in the United States of America

TABLE OF CONTENTS

INTRODUCTION 7
   Scope of this Book 7
   Summary of Contents 7
ORIGINS OF THE FEDERATION 9
   The Articles of Federation 10
   Membership in the Federation 13
   The Cultural Spectrum 14
      The Founding Members 14
      A Diversity of Cultures 16
PLANETARY SYSTEMS 19
   Map of the Federation 20
   Inhabited Worlds 24
   Starship Construction Facilities 33
   Places To Go, Things To Do 34
      Quadrant One 34
      Quadrant Two 34
      Quadrant Three 35
      Quadrant Four 35
   Creatures of Interest 35
MAJOR WORLDS 39
TIMELINE 73
CURRENT DIPLOMATIC RELATIONS 85
   The Klingon Empire 85
   The Romulan Star Empire 85
   The Orion Free States 85
   The Gorn Alliance 85
   The Tholian Assembly 85
   Other Considerations 86
   Current Treaties 86
      Dannon's Treaty 86
      The Treaty of Axanar 87
      The Organian Peace Treaty 87
GOVERNMENTAL STRUCTURE 88
   The Federation Council 89
   The Federation Assembly 90
   The Federation Security Council 90
   **The Federation Economic and
      Social Council** 90
   The Federation Judioiary 91
      The Federation Tribunal 91
      Quadrant Courts 91
   The Federation Secretariat 92
      Department of Star Fleet 92
      Department of Interstellar Relations 92
      Department of Interstellar Trade and
         Commerce 92
      Department of Colonization 93
      Department of Planetary Development . .93
      Department of Scientific Research and
         Development 93
      Department of Justice 94
      Department of Education 94
      Department of Finance 94
      Department of The Interior 94

POLITICS 95
   Issues 95
   Interest Groups and Political Parties . . .95
      The Outer Systems Party 95
      The Associates Union Party 96
      The Independent Systems
         Movement Party 96
      The Star Fleet Advocates Assembly 96
      The Amalgamation of
         Federation Scientists 96
ECONOMICS 97
   Monetary Systems 97
      The Federation Credit Exchange 97
      Letters of Exchange 97
      Subspace Transfer of Funds 97
      Guaranteed Exchanges in Kind 97
      Emergency Funding 97
   Major Corporations 98
   The Federation Stock Exchange 110
   The Federation Commodities Market . . .111
KEEPING THE PEACE 112
   Federation–Star Fleet Relations 112
   Funding the Fleet 113
      UFP Budgetary Contribution 113
      Customs Duties and Related Expenses . .113
      Star Base Production 113
      Planets for Sale 113
      Commerce Protection 113
      Private Contributions 113
   General Orders to Star Fleet 114
SELECTED PERSONALTIES 116
THE FUTURE OF THE FEDERATION 126
   Cultural Assimilation 126
   The Price of Freedom 126
   Home is Where You Make It 126
   The Graduating Class of 2/37 126

THE FUNDAMENTAL DECLARATION OF SENTIENT RIGHTS

**Section II of the Statutes of Alpha III
Adopted as the Preamble to the
Articles of Federation
Stardate 0/8706.05**

It being determined that sentient beings possess sufficient intelligence to permit self-awareness, they are to be accorded specific inherent rights, regardless of their origin, biological condition, or social and cultural identification. These rights include:

1. The right to live one's life without fear or oppression to the fullest possible extent, qualitatively and chronologically.
2. The right to acquire knowledge, unhindered by prejudice or deliberate obstruction.
3. The right to select for oneself without individual or collective interference those ethical and moral values by which one determines proper conduct.
4. The right to use one's natural and acquired abilities to pursue personal and cultural objectives unfettered by the limitations of outside forces.
5. The right to affiliate with other sentient beings to the mutual benefit of all concerned.

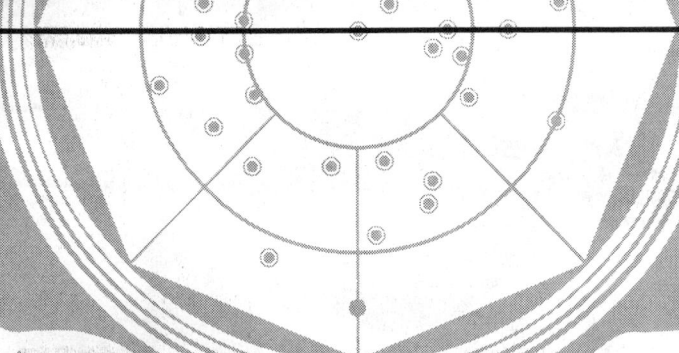

THE PRIME DIRECTIVE

As the right of each sentient species to live in accordance with its normal cultural evolution is considered sacred, no Star Fleet personnel may interfere with the healthy development of alien life and culture. Such interference includes the introduction of superior knowledge, strength, or technology to a world whose society is incapable of handling such advantages wisely. Star Fleet personnel may not violate this Prime Directive, even to save their lives and/or their ship, unless they are acting to right an earlier violation or an accidental contamination of said culture. This directive takes precedence over any and all other considerations, and carries with it the highest moral obligation.

INTRODUCTION

SCOPE OF THIS BOOK

The following information illustrates the interstellar political organization known as the United Federation of Planets. Both players and gamemasters may use this **STAR TREK Role Playing Game** supplement as a reference source on matters pertaining to the Federation when roleplaying adventure modules or in creating campaigns. Whenever necessary, conflicting information from various sources has been reconciled to conform to FASA's *STAR TREK* universe. Readers will also discover an abundance of new information on the worlds and people making up the United Federation of Planets.

CONTENTS OF THIS BOOK

The section entitled **Origins of the Federation** gives background information on the formation of the Federation, a description of the major civilizations within it, and how newly discovered planets can apply for membership. A section on **Federation Planetary Systems** presents a list of most of the inhabited worlds in Federation space, world logs for the major Federation worlds, as well as descriptions of numerous cultural events and points of interest within Federation space. The **Timeline** presents a complete chronology of major events in Federation history. **Current Diplomatic Relations** outlines the Federation's relationship with the other interstellar powers in the region and summarizes a few treaties signed by the UFP. **Governmental Structure** illustrates the organization of the Federation's bureaucratic and diplomatic offices. The Federation's political system and descriptions of several political parties are in the **Federation Politics and Political Interests** section. **Economic Aspects of the Federation** describes the various economic policies and procedures by which the Federation conducts trade among the stars. It also presents information on the larger interstellar corporations operating in Federation space. **Keeping The Peace** outlines the relationship between Star Fleet Command and the Federation government, how Star Fleet is funded, and the Federation's General Orders to Star Fleet Command. **Selected Personalities** presents biographical information on major individuals who have contributed either positively or negatively to Federation history. Some possibilities concerning the future of the UFP are discussed in the section entitled **The Future of the Federation**.

ORIGINS OF THE FEDERATION

The universe belongs to those brave enough to share it in peace.

Harmon Axelrod, President of the Federation Council
Stardate 0/8801.07

The United Federation of Planets is the largest economic, political, and social organization in recorded history. Sphere-shaped and with a diameter of over 180 parsecs, it spans more than half the known spiral of the Milky Way galaxy. The Federation currently maintains over 500 member worlds, supported by a fully developed bureaucratic infrastructure and defended by the most powerful collection of starships ever to span the stars.

More importantly, the United Federation of Planets represents the galaxy's most successful attempt to protect the individual freedoms and rights of sentient beings, regardless of their biological origin or social affiliation. In a universe where cultures often dedicate themselves to domination and ruthless expansionism, the Federation advances the knowledge and economic and social progress of every member world. In addition, it upholds the right of individual worlds to govern themselves as each sees fit.

The United Federation of Planets is the product of the combined efforts of hundreds of statesmen and politicians, soldiers and diplomats, and Humans and Humanoids originating from five highly distinct civilizations. They all shared a common dream: given the opportunity, sentient creatures among the stars can exist and prosper in mutual harmony and peace. Having overcome the threat of cultural extinction (often by only a narrow margin of safety), these five cultures shared the profound desire to seek out others like themselves with whom to share the universe.

Following a series of almost disastrous global wars in their 20th century, Terrans began to migrate to the neighboring worlds of their own system and then to the nearest star system. The labors of these early explorers were rewarded in the year 2042, with the discovery of the culturally and scientifically advanced civilization of Alpha Centauri. Cultural exchanges resulted in peace accords, which were largely possible due to the surprisingly similar physical characteristics of the two races.

Combining the Alpha Centauran Zephram Cochrane's principles of spacial warp displacement with Human engineering ingenuity resulted in many early colonization efforts, bringing the two races even closer together. A chance encounter with Vulcans in the year 2065 might easily have ended in unnecessary hostility were it not for the quick thinking and restraint shown by both sides. Their reactions are surprising, considering the Vulcans were not only distinctly alien in their physical appearance, but also alien in their emotional (or non-emotional) makeup as well.

Not all unexpected contacts ended so pleasantly. Between 2070 and 2085, these three starfaring races were forced to deal with the last vestiges of the Vegan Tyranny. The presence of a common foe united the three powers and planted the seeds of the Federation. Despite the threat of this mysterious enemy, the twelve-year period between 2075 and 2087 has often been called Terra's Golden Age. During this period, contact with the Tellarites ended in peaceful cooperation and mutual benefit. Also, the first wave of Human and Human-Centauran colonial efforts began to bear fruit. It was a time when the vast richness of the Orion Homeworlds was discovered and when the existence of Romulan and Klingon savagery was yet unimagined.

Toward the end of the century, these races made contact with the Andorian civilization, which would later become a founding member of the Federation. In this instance, the allied races' overt bluffing and aggressive postering helped defuse a potentially hostile situation. The Andorians were a much older race, and their space exploration pre-dated both Alpha Centauran and Human efforts. They had more than sufficient reason to be wary of alien contact, given their previous encounters with the remnants of the Vegan Tyranny. Nevertheless, the advantages of mutual alliance outweighed the dubious gains of hard-to-hold conquests, and the Andorians joined the informal alliance.

Many Terran textbooks credit Humans as being the driving force behind creation of the Federation. This is about as true as saying that the attempts to form such an interstellar body met with positive responses and unparalleled success. Actually, it was the Alpha Centauri statesman Zorafran Stallamaine who first suggested forming a political union of the Five Primary Worlds, as Alpha Centauri, Andor, Tellar, Terra, and Vulcan were then known. Similarly, the first serious discussion of political union, which took place on Alpha Centauri in 2077, ended in disaffection and discord, due primarily to the inability to define the specific goals and objectives of the new, experimental governmental order.

It was the Vulcans who, during the period from 2077 to 2082, worked with fellow delegates to keep the hope of a Federation alive. Their contributions, more than any other, culminated in a second conference on Vulcan in 2082. At this meeting, many of the objections and disagreements that had surfaced on Alpha Centauri five years earlier were overcome by compromise and by applying the principles from the famous Statutes of Alpha III. Nevertheless, so great were the cultural differences between the Five Primary Worlds that an additional five years of effort remained before delegates assembled on the neutral planetoid of Babel. In 2087, they adopted the Articles of Federation and established a lasting governmental body to maintain peace throughout the galaxy.

THE ARTICLES OF FEDERATION

The driving force behind the United Federation of Planets is a philosphical and political document known as the Articles of Federation. Established on Stardate 0/8706.06, the Articles of Federation serve both as a statement of mutual understanding and unity and as a collection of guidelines to be applied rigorously. They represent the democratic ideals of each of its founding members' civilizations and their commitment to the preservation of galactic peace and security. Documents such as the United Earth Constitution, the Centauri Concordium, the Andorian Pledge of Triumphant Security, the Statutes of Alpha III, and the Fundamental Declaration of the Martian Colonies helped form the underlying principles drafted into the Articles.

The Federation's charter is composed of 109 articles divided into 16 separate chapters. As it is impossible to consider each individual article here, following is a summary of their provisions and specifications. The summary is taken directly from the text of the original document currently on display at Memory Alpha.

CHAPTER ONE, ARTICLES 1–2:
THE PURPOSE AND PRINCIPLES OF THE FEDERATION

That these member races are joining together in political and social union reflects their desire for mutual security as well as their sincere belief that they can advance the conditions of life for all sentient life forms throughout the galaxy. To this end, the United Federation of Planets is hereby established to preserve interstellar peace, to coordinate galactic exploration, to deter would-be aggressors, and to lend mutual support for the advancement of all member races without distinction or qualification.

CHAPTER TWO, ARTICLES 3–6:
MEMBERSHIP

Membership is extended to the original founding members as of this Stardate 0/8706.06. In addition, membership shall be open to any and all societies willing to abide by the conditions of federation specified herein, contingent on the decision of the Federation Assembly and at the recommendation of the Federation Council. The Assembly may suspend membership for a civilization at the request of the Council and may impose permanent expulsion if necessary.

CHAPTER THREE, ARTICLES 7–8:
UFP AFFILIATIONS

The principle organizational bodies of the Federation shall include the following: the Federation Assembly, the Federation Council, provision for a Federation Economic and Social Development Organization, a Trusteeship Council, a supreme judicial system, a secretariat made up of individual governmental departments, and a military body known as Star Fleet Command, to be composed of each member planet's navies for purposes of mutual defense. Additional organizations or agencies may be designated as the need arises. There shall be no restrictions with respect to gender or social origin for eligibility in any of these Federation-affiliated bodies.

CHAPTER FOUR, ARTICLES 9–22:
THE FEDERATION ASSEMBLY

The Federation Assembly shall be open to all members of the Federation and shall hold discussions on any question pertaining to the safety and/or welfare of member races within the Federation or of the Federation itself. Each member planet shall have one vote, and all proposals of the Assembly will require a two-thirds majority vote to be enacted. The Assembly shall also require the Federation Secretariat to report to the Assembly on matters of concern at periodic intervals. The Assembly has the authority to make recommendations to the Federation Council when such recommendations advance interstellar cooperation and ensure individual rights of Federation citizens. The Assembly is empowered to approve or to reject the Federation's budget and shall decree the amount of financial responsibility each member planet shall receive. Should such financial responsibilities not be met, the Assembly may, by a majority vote, act to suspend temporarily that member's right to vote on matters before the Assembly. The Assembly shall meet at specific intervals or as circumstances may require. This body is also empowered to authorize the formation of organizational bodies not previously established by a majority vote.

CHAPTER FIVE, ARTICLES 23–32:
THE FEDERATION COUNCIL

The Federation Council shall consist of eleven members, five of which are permanent members and the rest being non-permanent members sitting on the Council for a period of three years. Each council member shall have one vote. The permanent members will consist of one representative from each of the original founding members. The remainder are to be elected by the Assembly. The head of the Council will be selected from among his peers and will receive the title of President of the Council. The Federation Council will be responsible for maintaining the peace and security of the Federation, and may pass resolutions with the full weight of Federation law as necessary to ensure the safety of the Federation. A majority vote is required to implement any decision by the Council. Unlike the Federation Assembly, the Federation Council is to be in continuous session and may meet at any location as may be required. Like the Assembly, the Council can, by majority vote, establish other organizations or governmental bodies as the need arises.

**CHAPTER SIX, ARTICLES 33–38:
SETTLING DISPUTES**

The Articles of Federation recognizes the likelihood of major disputes arising between Federation members or between members and non-members, either of which may threaten the peace and security of the Federation. In such cases, any member or non-member may bring such matters to either the Federation Council or Assembly for mediation, given that those involved agree in advance to accept the Federation's impartial resolution of the affair. If necessary, such matters may be referred to the Federation Judiciary for further arbitration. Should the Federation Assembly be called upon to hear said dispute, the Assembly can make formal recommendations to the Council for a final disposition of the matter. Upon due impartial consideration, the Council shall make a final disposition of the dispute, which shall be binding on all parties.

**CHAPTER SEVEN, ARTICLES 39–51:
CONCERNING ACTS OF AGGRESSION**

Whenever there is clear evidence of hostile acts being carried out against one or more members of the Federation, the Federation Council is empowered to decide what actions are appropriate to deal with the situation, short of using armed force. The Council's response may include, but is not limited to, the imposition of economic sanctions and the interruption of trade and/or cultural exchange between member worlds. If such actions are considered inadequate to the existing threat, the Federation Council may then call upon Star Fleet Command to restore peace and security. In the event a Federation member is the originator of such aggression, no use of force shall be employed, unless said member forfeits the opportunity to negotiate a settlement before the Federation Assembly.

**CHAPTER EIGHT, ARTICLES 52–54:
STAR FLEET COMMAND**

Given the need for a common defense, Star Fleet Command is hereby created to coordinate the armed forces of the Federation, subject to the control of the Federation Council. This force shall consist of contributions of personnel and materiel from the original member worlds. A central training center will be established to supply the ongoing needs of the fleet. Further expansions of the fleet will be consistent with the needs of the Federation, and will include considerations of exploration and scientific inquiry as well as the maintenance of a strong military presence.

**CHAPTER NINE, ARTICLES 55–60:
ECONOMIC AND SOCIAL COOPERATION**

In addition to maintaining internal peace and security from external threats, one of the Federation's aims shall be the economic stability and social advancement of its members. To this end, the members of the Federation pledge themselves to pursue the following goals: the recognition of the rights of individual sentient beings throughout the galaxy, the economic, educational, and social progress of fellow members, and the continued understanding and respect for racial differences.

**CHAPTER TEN, ARTICLES 61–74:
THE FEDERATION ECONOMIC AND SOCIAL COUNCIL**

Pursuant to the aims expressed in the preceding articles, the Federation government shall establish a council that shall evaluate economic and social conditions on member and non-member planets within the Federation. This council shall coordinate actions with other governmental organizations to promote economic and social welfare of the Federation, with particular emphasis given to upholding individual rights. In the event of clear evidence of individual or collective violation of such rights, this council may make recommendations to the Assembly to correct such conditions whenever and wherever they may occur.

**CHAPTER ELEVEN, ARTICLES 73–74:
CONCERNING UNCHARTED REGIONS OF SPACE**

The Federation recognizes the need for interstellar exploration and expansion, as well as the common desire to seek out and contact undiscovered civilizations and sentient life forms. To this end, the Federation accepts responsibility for administering those regions of space adjacent to established Federation zones of influence.

CHAPTER TWELVE, ARTICLES 75–85:
FEDERATION TRUSTEESHIP

In the interests of interstellar peace and economic and social evolution, when sentient races are discovered in adjoining regions of space and if said races have not yet attained a competent measure of self-government for whatever reason, the Federation has the right to defend and protect such races. Any such action will be in accordance with the provisions of the Articles of Federation, ensuring due respect for other life forms. [Ed. Note: This chapter serves as the philosophical basis for granting protectorate status to various worlds whenever that world's normal development is threatened.]

CHAPTER THIRTEEN: ARTICLES 86–96
THE TRUSTEESHIP COUNCIL

In cases where a given world or society is under the specifications of the Prime Directive or quarantined due to protectorate status, such worlds shall be administered by a special Federation council of trustees designated by the Federation Assembly. The trustees will oversee the development of such worlds over an extended period of time, periodically visit the planet in question, and report on local conditions to the Federation Assembly at periodic intervals, with recommendations as to the continuing disposition of such worlds. Whenever more than one planet is designated as a protectorate or is otherwise protected under the provisions of the Prime Directive, a separate trusteeship council shall be established to administer each world accordingly.

CHAPTER FOURTEEN: ARTCLES 97–101
THE FEDERATION SECRETARIAT

In the interests of bureaucratic efficiency, the principal administrative obligations of the Federation shall be divided among various departmental bodies, each headed by a duly appointed director, which shall collectively constitute the Federation Secretariat. Each individual department is responsible for reporting to the Federation Assembly on matters pertaining to their specific areas and in such instances where special circumstances may warrant. Each department may in turn recommend to the Federation Assembly or the Council the creation of subordinate bodies under their control to maximize governmental efficiency and/or to deal with specific problems or conditions as may arise.

CHAPTER FIFTEEN: ARTICLES 102–105
MISCELLANEOUS CONSIDERATIONS

Whenever there arises a conflict of interests between individual Federation members, the provisions and specifications of the Articles of Federation shall take precedence. To exercise their official functions freely, representatives of member worlds to the Federation Assembly or Council shall have diplomatic immunity from local prosecution if and when said representatives incur infractions of local statutes.

CHAPTER SIXTEEN: ARTICLE 106
AMENDMENTS TO THE ARTICLES OF FEDERATION

Amendments to the existing Articles of Federation shall come into effect only after formal proposal of said amendment before the Federation Assembly and the support of a two-thirds of all full-status members of the Assembly.

[Ed. Note: To date, there has only been one amendment to the Articles. Effective Stardate 2/0103.13, this amendment effectively banned the presence of slaves and the practice of slavery anywhere within Federation space. It also gave the Federation the right to act as necessary to abolish the practice of slavery anywhere within the Federation sphere of influence.]

MEMBERSHIP IN THE FEDERATION

Membership in the United Federation of Planets is open to any sentient species willing to abide by the conditions and obligations described in the Articles of Federation and the statutes constituting Federation law. In practice, whenever such a race displays a sufficiently high degree of cultural advancement and has demonstrated its peaceful intentions, the Federation's Department of Interstellar Relations contacts the candidate. Specific criteria used to gauge a world's suitability for membership can include a high degree of literacy among the planet's inhabitants, scientific progress sufficiently advanced to accept the existence of other sentient beings, application of the sciences to solve cultural problems or disadvantages, the existence of a cultural philosophy that values individual life, and an acceptance of cultural differences within the makeup of the social order. Though there is no single prerequisite for admission to the Federation, the above-mentioned conditions are among the major considerations.

Once a planet is determined to be ready for contact, representatives of the Federation journey to the prospective world and, taking care to avoid unnecessary cultural shock, make their presence known to the local planetary inhabitants. After establishing themselves as peaceful emissaries, the Federation's diplomatic representatives acquaint their counterparts with Federation history, cultural heritage, and political freedoms, and offer to establish friendly relations with them.

If the planet's populace accepts such overtures, there follows a period of cultural exchange between Federation members and the newly contacted world (typically one to three years), allowing each side to learn about the other. Unless otherwise decreed by a special vote of the Federation Assembly, technological and scientific exchanges are kept to a minimum. Following this trial period, the Department of Interstellar Relations makes a final recommendation to a joint session of the Federation Council and Assembly. Those assembled then vote to accept or reject the candidate world's application for membership.

If the new civilization is accepted into the Federation, it receives either full or associate member status within the Federation's governmental system. Full-member worlds are accorded the right to place a representative on the Federation Assembly, thus granting them an equal voice in the drafting and passage of Federation legislation. Full-status members may also join the Federation Security Council and be elected to administrative and legislative positions within the Federation government, including the Federation Council. Full-status members must make regular contributions to the Federation Treasury, the exact amount being determined beforehand by members of the Department of Finance. In addition, full-status members are requested to contribute to financial appropriations voted by the Assembly in times of emergency.

For cultural, political, or philosophical reasons, a member civilization may sometimes object to contributing funds that might, directly or indirectly, be used for military purposes. In such case, that civilization receives associate-member status. Associate-member status is also given automatically to all Federation colonies with populations of over one million inhabitants. In the Federation government, associate members have representatives in the Federation Assembly, but these representatives cannot be elected to the Federation Council. Associate members may vote on issues pertaining to the Assembly in general, and their representatives may hold positions within the Judiciary or on special committees, but they have less influence than full members.

Whether full member or associate member, the newly admitted civilization is subject to and protected by the laws governing the Federation, as determined by the Federation Assembly and ratified by the Federation Council. The society is likewise entitled to Star Fleet protection and any economic and cultural advantages bestowed by membership. Most important, the world maintains the right of self-government, the right to determine its own cultural future, and the right to live in accordance with its own laws and customs, free from external interference or coercion.

Occasionally, a society or culture not advanced enough to qualify for formal admission will require special consideration by the Federation. The most recent case in point is that of Coridan, a planet whose inhabitants suffered greatly from unrestricted mining operations (what some would call depredations) by various Federation members as well as Orion independents. In such cases, the Assembly may vote to grant Protectorate Status to the planet, in effect placing a hands-off sign on the world. Often, this status is applied to newly emerging civilizations under the doctrine of the Prime Directive. The intention is to protect the natural and orderly cultural development of a given world from outside interference or 'contamination'.

Although offering numerous advantages, membership in the United Federation of Planets must be taken seriously. In accepting the advantages of Federation benevolence, member worlds admittedly do so at a price. They cannot develop an interstellar navy, but they may support a local, in-system fleet. Member worlds must adopt established Federation economic standards when dealing with worlds outside their own systems. Not only does this include incorporating standardized weights and measures, specific monetary systems, and customs procedures, but also economic restrictions and sanctions against other worlds. An example is the refusal to permit trade in Orion slaves anywhere within Federation space. Although Star Fleet is pledged never to use coercive force against a Federation member nor to allow aggression between members, member worlds whose internal policies do not agree with those of the majority may be subject to economic and cultural sanctions, whose result might seem oppressive.

For these reasons, many eligible planets within the Federation's sphere of influence choose to remain independent. Similarly, Federation representatives have not attempted to incorporate worlds from the Triangle Zone, even though many of these qualify for membership. The Federation tolerates these independent worlds as long as their government's policies do not conflict with those of the Federation. Commercial and cultural relations are maintained only if the civilization in question respects Federation economic, political, and military interests. Delegations to independent worlds are dispatched periodically to renew ties of friendship, to monitor cultural progress, or to renew offers of formal membership. Under no circumstances will the Federation ever attempt to impose membership forcibly on a government that cannot or will not accept the obligations of membership.

Theoretically, a member world may withdraw from the Federation when that world deems such action to be in its best interests. The first amendment to the Articles of Federation specifically dictates that any alteration of membership status requires a formal request for dissolution of membership and a two-thirds vote of the Federation Assembly.

THE CULTURAL SPECTRUM

In infinite diversity, there are infinite combinations.
In infinite diversity, we find infinite strength.
Surak of Vulcan, Stardate –3/08

Any political organization is only as strong and viable as the sum of its parts. This is especially true of the Federation, with its thousands of inhabited worlds and hundreds of unique civilizations. Although this book cannot describe all these worlds, following is a brief discussion of the major cultures that contribute significantly to Federation policy and advancement. These civilizations represent the wide diversity and cultural richness that, more than anything else, sets the Federation apart from its rivals.

THE FOUNDING MEMBERS

The United Federation of Planets originally consisted of five members: Alpha Centauri, Andor, Tellar, Terra, and Vulcan. Each of these senior members retains considerable influence in the formation of Federation policy and contributes significantly to the advancement of Federation ideals.

Alpha Centauri

The origins of the Centauri race remain shrouded in mystery and speculation to the present day. Some Centauran scientists believe that the civilization of the Al Rijil system may not be native to their planet. In truth, the physiological characteristics of Centaurans and Humans are practically identical. Also, the ruins of early Centauran civilization mirror those along the Mediterranean basin on Terra during its fifth century B.C.. Most important of all, no written records or oral traditions from Centauran history reach back more than 2,500 years. These facts have led scholars to suggest that the Centaurans may be transplanted Humans taken from Terra and 'seeded' on Alpha Centauri by the race of beings known as the Preservers.

Whatever the truth, Centauran civilization is one of the most advanced in the Federation, second only to Terra itself. It is a democratic civilization based on fundamental political principles similar to those of early Greece on Terra. Alpha Centauri's ordered climate provides an abundance of goods, which decreases the need for intercultural competition. Thus, the Centauran civilization developed a practical system of interplanetary travel that pre-dates Human efforts. Taking advantage of the solar winds from their three primary suns, the Centaurans invented an interplanetary solar-sail about the time that Terran civilization was experiencing its Industrial Revolution. (Centauran sun-jamming races remain a popular sport to this day.) By the time they made contact with the first emissaries from Earth, the Centaurans had already colonized a second Class M planet as well as several smaller satellites within their system.

The practical experience they gained in these colonization efforts led to the formation of the first representative form of interstellar government, the Alpha Centauri Concordium of Planets. This political confederation served as the model for what would later become the United Federation of Planets. Although Alpha Centauri is typically remembered as the birthplace of Zephram Cochrane, the celebrated inventor of the warp drive system, it is equally true that Centaurans provided the political impetus that led to the creation of the Federation.

Andor

The Andorian race predates Humanity by about 3,000 years. The planet Andor is covered with ice and snow except at its equator, where surface temperatures can reach 50° C. The large polar regions experience temperatures ranging from -20° to -45° C. Andorians are partially endothermic beings who have difficulty functioning in warmer climates. They are immediately recognizable by their bluish skin and pure white hair. The former is due to the presence of high levels of cobalt in Andorian blood. In addition, Andorians have antennae that serve as sensory organs, much like the sensory apparatus of the Terran bat.

Theories about Andorian prehistory speculate that small, nomadic, tribal groups originated in the polar regions. With the development of agriculture and cities, Andorians acquired a highly developed sense of territoriality. This, combined with a biological aggressiveness in warmer summer periods, led to organized warfare and the first nation-states. Eventual advances in technology led to the first practical system of planet-wide climate control, which was the decisive factor in establishing a permanent civilization on Andor.

Although they managed to deflect their aggressiveness before destroying themselves, the Andorian race still required an outlet for their natural ferocity. The first successful manned efforts at interstellar flight provided this release approximately 50 years before Humans made similar attempts. A period of eager expansionism followed, fueled in part by overpopulation that occurred for the first time in Andorian history.

The result of this space exploration was the establishment of the Andorian Empire, approximately 75 years before the formation of the United Federation of Planets. It was this collection of 13 inhabited worlds that bore the brunt of the Vegan Tyranny as that race tried to reestablish galactic dominion.

For all its willful aggressiveness, the Andorian civilization has much to offer fellow beings. For example, Andorian philosophy has produced a unique form of symbolic logic that recognizes the intrinsic value of emotions. Other Andorian contributions include noteworthy studies in controlling mental illnesses, some of the Federation's finest architecture, and excellent shipbuilding designs. Though ready for a fight at a moment's notice, the typical Andorian is as eager to build and create as he is to damage and destroy.

Tellar

The Tellarite civilization has the unique distinction of being the only subterranian culture ever to attain space flight. The Tellarites are the 'youngest' of the five founding members, having achieved cultural and social unification around the time of the first Human-Centauran contact. However, the Tellarites extended themselves farther and faster than any of their companion races. Motivated by hopes of locating new mineral resources, Tellarite traders were the first to discover the vast resources of the Orion Homeworlds and the first to begin trading with various Orion trading houses. The Tellarites' imperative for trade and barter stems from the need to deal with their twin problems of native overpopulation and a scarcity of mineral reserves within Tellar's home system.

The Tellarites' squat and hairy appearance adds much to their reputation for being pugnacious, quarrelsome, and generally ill-tempered. Although Tellarites possess a strong territorial sense, which extends to considerations of personal rights, they are no more quarrelsome or ill-mannered than any other sentient being conscious of his own planet's welfare. Socially, Tellarites are protective of their young and have a strong sense of family and extended social obligations. In addition, they have a distinct love of argument and conversation. Combined with their high intelligence, their enjoyment of risk-taking makes them natural diplomats, explorers, and gamblers.

Terra

Originating on the planet Sol III (also known as Earth), Terran civilization has proven itself to be the technological and cultural leader of the original five Federation members. Humans prize this distinction highly and strive earnestly to maintain it. Actually a collection of racial groups rather than a single social entity, Humanity very nearly ceased to exist before it could develop space flight. With a long history of cultural aggression (which differs from the Andorian biological aggressiveness), Humans endured centuries of conflict over territory and natural resources, culminating in three global wars in its 20th century.

The last and most ruthless of the three, known as the Eugenics Wars, began when misguided scientists attempted to use genetic engineering to accomplish what political imperialism and social ideology had failed to achieve: the forceful imposition of world peace. The planet was nearly devastated by the generous use of nuclear weapons. The conflict ended at the close of the century with less than one-fourth of the planet's inhabitants left alive to count themselves as 'victors'.

From out of this mass extermination came the impetus for creating a representative world government. With this government came the need to form a stable social order that valued individual life above all other considerations. This social rebirth rekindled mankind's interest first in interplanetary and then in interstellar exploration. Humans developed a practical fusion-drive system in their early 21st century, and launched their first manned interstellar vessel, the *Icarus*, toward their nearest neighbor, Alpha Centauri. This resulted in the discovery of the Centauran civilization and the formal establishment of social/diplomatic relations between the two civilizations in 2059.

After the Federation was established, Terra became the primary economic and military contributor to the fledgling government. Terran representatives in Star Fleet Command led the exploration of new frontiers while Terran corporations collectively donated the largest economic share of any founding world to the Federation Treasury.

In addition, Terra coordinated the development of numerous colony worlds, which eventually became highly prosperous Federation members. When the Romulan War began, Terran volunteers made up the majority of the forces that served in the bloody conflict. Today, Terra continues to maintain its cultural, political, and scientific leadership in a Federation that exceeds 500 members.

Vulcan

The Vulcan race predates the rise of Humanity by almost 10,000 years. Originating in the desert wastelands of a Class M planet in the Epsilon Eridani system, the Vulcan race is presently the second most widely represented race in the Federation. Their ancestors are presumed to have also been the forebears of the Romulan race.

At one time, Vulcan society was violent, emotional, even savage in nature. Vulcans warred constantly for a period lasting almost 800 years. Then, several thousand years before the rise of classical civilization on Terra, rival power blocks on Vulcan faced the very real prospect of mutual extinction. At this juncture, the scientist-philosopher Surak boldly proposed a complete cultural restructuring of Vulcan society, with well-defined, ordered, ethical doctrines based on empirical logic replacing personal expression of emotions. As they had exhausted all other cultural options, the Vulcans completely reorganized their cultural system within two generations. Also during this period, Vulcan ceased to be ruled by a male-dominated elite and became the progressive matriarchy based on social equality that it is today.

Vulcans are physically easy to distinguish from other Humanoids, given their generally tall and slender appearance. They have arched eyebrows and delicately pointed ears that angle upwards. The latter are a result of evolution, but tend to give the average Vulcan a pronounced demonic air. Vulcans are physically stronger than their Human counterparts, though the Vulcan's lack of overt violence usually belies this attribute. This strength is due in part to the climate on Vulcan (which combines extreme heat as well as a thin atmosphere) and in part to the rigid conditioning every Vulcan endures from childhood on.

It is often mistakenly believed that Vulcans do not have feelings. Actually, Vulcans have always possessed the capacity for understanding and dealing with emotions, but they simply choose not to do so. Once the typical Vulcan child is deemed old enough, family, class, and social influences are geared toward the total suppression of emotion in the child. In reality, few Vulcans can ever completely divest themselves of emotional responses. As a case in point, consider that Vulcan philosophy has as yet failed to completely subordinate the recurring mating-cycle that each Vulcan must endure every seven years. During this period, the individual undergoes emotional and physiological imbalances, each contributing to a powerful mating drive. Only the few who have completed the grueling mental and physical requirements of the Kolinahr discipline have ever approached this ultimate goal. Though Vulcans living among other races may become somewhat emotional, such outbreaks would be socially unacceptable among other Vulcans.

However alien and artificial it may appear, the Vulcan philosophy of non-emotion has produced some of the finest scientists, scholars, mathematicians, military experts, politicians, and poets in Federation history. Whatever else one might say of this energetic, though emotionally controlled race of beings, credit must be given where it is due.

A DIVERSITY OF CULTURES

The Federation is rich in social and cultural diversity due to its hundreds of member worlds. Many of these unique civilizations have made significant contributions to the Federation over the years. Following is a brief summary of those cultures and races that have added in one way or another to the advancement of Federation social and economic progress.

Arcturan

An advanced humanoid culture, Arcturans model their various customs and dress on those of Terra's late Elizabethan period of 17th-century England. Arcturans are noted for their immense love of self-expression as well as their casual acceptance of different racial/cultural beliefs. Politically, the Arcturans are the leaders of the Federation's moderate faction.

Argelian

Since their Great Awakening two centuries ago, this humanoid culture has been universally known for its friendliness and hospitality. Though not as technologically advanced as other major races, Argelians make up for this in their warmth and genuine pleasure in meeting visitors from other planets. They have totally rejected all forms of violence and have developed a cultural dislike for negative emotions such as hatred and jealousy.

Caitian

One of the newer non-humanoid races to join the Federation, the Caitians evolved from creatures resembling Terran felines rather than from primates. Caitians generally range from two to three meters in height and have tan to reddish-tan fur and manipulative forepaws. The adult Caitian voice resembles the purring of a Terran cat. Despite their striking similarity to Earth predators, most Caitians are not carnivorous, preferring instead a balanced and nutritious vegetarian diet. Caitian culture emphasizes the love of beauty and personal loyalty. This is due to the interlocking individual and clan relationships underlying their culture. Indeed, Caitians prize loyalty in themselves and others above all other considerations.

Cygnian

Cygnet XIV is a female-dominated society in which males are only semi-literate (the reverse of the situation in the Orion colonies). Cygnian culture is technologically advanced, especially in cybernetics and computer sciences. Star Fleet crews and private research institutions are particularly anxious to have Cygnian females on their teams of computer specialists.

After the Vulcans, Cygnians are the strongest physically of all Federation members. The expression "bright-eyed and bushy-tailed" may well have been coined with a Cygnian in mind. Though humanoid in appearance, Cygnians retain certain features vaguely similar to Terran equestrians: i.e., long tails and long, flowing hair along the central raised spine. With their sharp, green-colored eyes, this race has a particularly exotic image.

Deltan

The Deltans are a race of pacifistic Humanoids who have concentrated on social and personal development. Devotion to studies in racial and social interactions has given them an understanding of a wide range of mental disciplines. Deltans of both genders naturally produce a high level of chemical pheromones that act as a highly potent sexual stimulant to other Humanoids. Not too surprisingly, Deltans are highly advanced in their understanding of humanoid sexual relations.. Deltans serving in Star Fleet must take an oath of celebacy to avoid social complications arising from their latent abilities.

Edoan

Sometimes incorrectly referred to as Saurians, the Edoans are a race of peaceful, sentient reptiles who have dedicated themselves to the fine arts of mathematics and wine production. Edo is a densely populated jungle planet that, paradoxically, produces some of the richest wine in the Federation. Many experts consider Edo's Saurian brandy to be among the finest vintages on the interstellar commodities exchange. Edoans have contributed significantly to specialized areas of mathematics such as sub-spacial geometry and four-dimensional calculus. Edoan scientists are noted for their accuracy and dedication. Within Star Fleet, Edoan navigators are second only to the Medusans in ability.

Izaran

The most fiercely independent of all Federation cultures, the Izarans are descendents of one of the joint Human-Centauran colonization efforts made in the early days of interstellar exploration. Today, Izar is a self-sustaining member of the Federation. Izarans prize personal liberties above all other social or political considerations. Though peaceful by nature, they are not above fighting for a just cause. Izar has produced some of the finest military leaders in Federation history.

Joridian

The Joridians are a race of humanoid telepaths who have developed an advanced culture based on philosophical inquiry. Joridians typically avoid contact with outside races, preferring their own culture to those with 'lesser philosophies', but will carry out their obligations to other Federation members when called upon to do so. A peaceful and productive race, Joridians are often found in areas where their legal and philosophical expertise can be used to the fullest. They are often selected to make initial contact with newly discovered civilizations, and many serve in the Federation judiciary.

Kaferian

A race of intelligent insectoids, Kaferians maintain a closely knit, hierarchical social structure largely devoted to agricultural and biochemical pursuits. They are famous throughout the Federation as chemists, and Kaferian research has contributed much to a basic understanding of biochemical processes among numerous non-humanoid races.

Medusan

The Medusans are a race of non-corporeal beings whose physics and mathematics are the most advanced of any Federation culture. Clearly the oldest surviving civilization in the Federation, Medusans were once Humanoid in appearance, but evolved beyond the need for physical form long ago. In their natural state, Medusans resemble the Organians, creatures of pure energy and intelligence. Unlike the Organians, however, the sight of a Medusan is disturbing enough to cause severe psychological damage or even permanent brain damage and madness in Humanoids. To avoid accidental exposure, Medusans seldom leave their planetary system, and then only under the strictest conditions.

New Parisian

The Human inhabitants of New Paris have one of the most cultured societies in the Federation. Modeled on the principles that formed the French Republic of Terra in its 18th century, New Parisian society is famous for its many achievements in art, literature, and music. Over the last hundred years, many of the Federation's most critically acclaimed art works have originated in New Paris.

Tiburon

Tiburons are a humanoid race believed by many to be the descendants of a lost Terran expedition that departed Terra shortly after the end of the Eugenics Wars. Though Human in appearance, Tiburons show evidence of genetic mutation, which may be due to long-term exposure to high radiation levels. Tiburons can alter their physical appearance in a limited manner, effectively changing their gender at will. In this, they are similar to the Antosians (who can alter their molecular shape and density), though the Antosians' ability appears to be acquired rather than genetic. Not surprisingly, Tiburon society makes no gender-oriented distinctions, either socially or politically. They are vegetarian by nature, and maintain a deep respect for all living organisms. Tiburons are noted for their administrative and organizational abilities; there are few Federation governmental agencies that do not employ numerous Tiburon natives.

DIVERSITY OF CULTURES

CAITIAN

TELLARITE

KAFERIAN

JORIDIAN

DELTAN

EDOAN

CYGNIAN

ANDORIAN

PLANETARY SYSTEMS

The following section provides information on planetary systems within the Federation sphere of influence. Note that the following material does not include disputed worlds within the Organian or Romulan Neutral Zone, nor the various independent worlds of the Triangle Zone.

MAP OF THE FEDERATION

The United Federation of Planets is astrographically divided into four distinct areas referred to as quadrants, although this designation is more traditional than mathematically precise. Quadrants One through Four mark the furthest extent of Federation influence to the Northwest, Northeast, Southeast, and Southwest.

The following map displays the major worlds and significant colony worlds of the Federation as of 2/2306.01. Major planetary systems are designated by a darkened circle, and colony worlds are designated by a hollow circle. The map also delineates the original boundaries of the Federation as of Stardate 0/87, which contained the planetary systems of the founding members of the UFP.

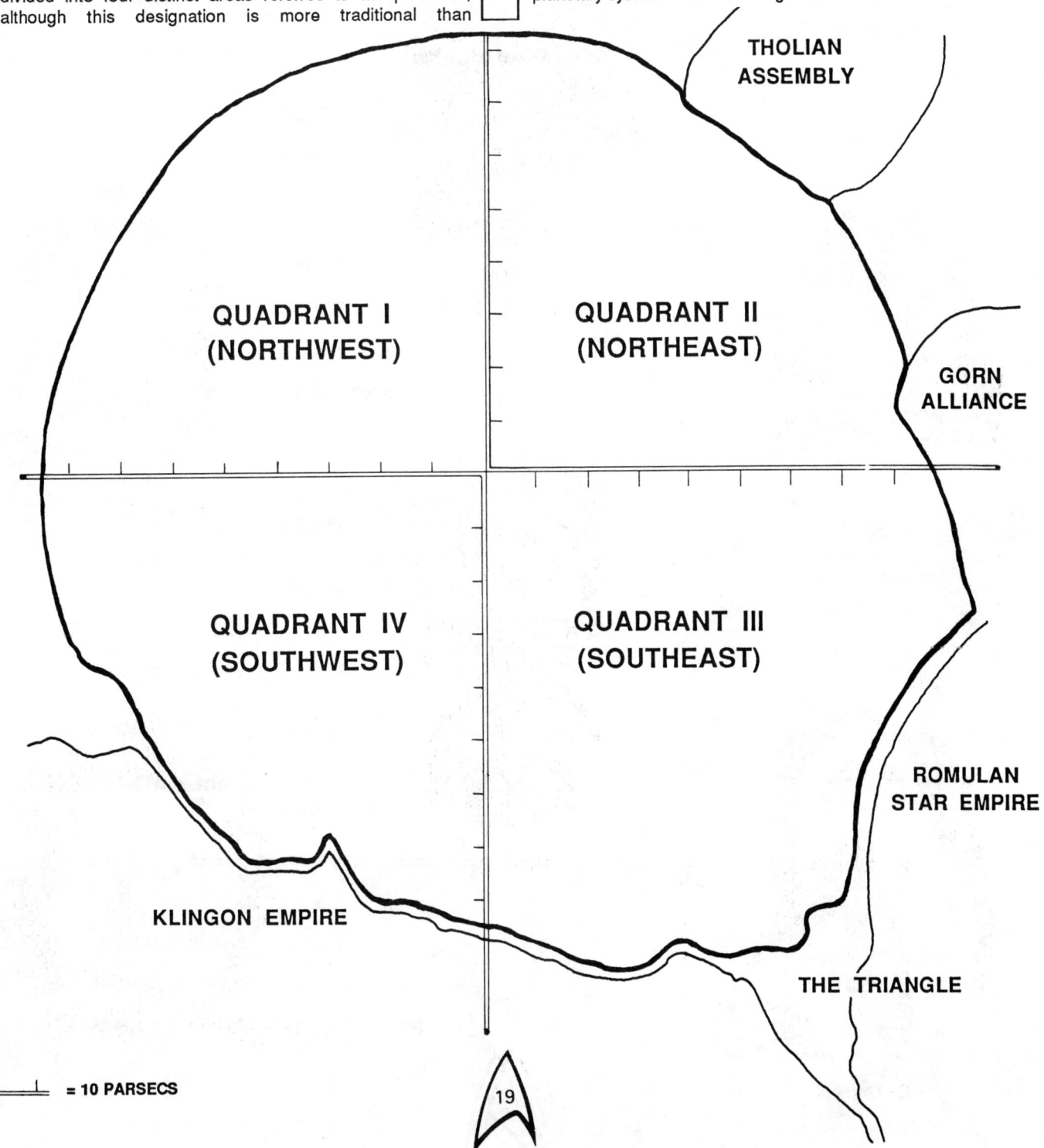

MAP OF THE FEDERATION
QUADRANT I (NORTHWEST)

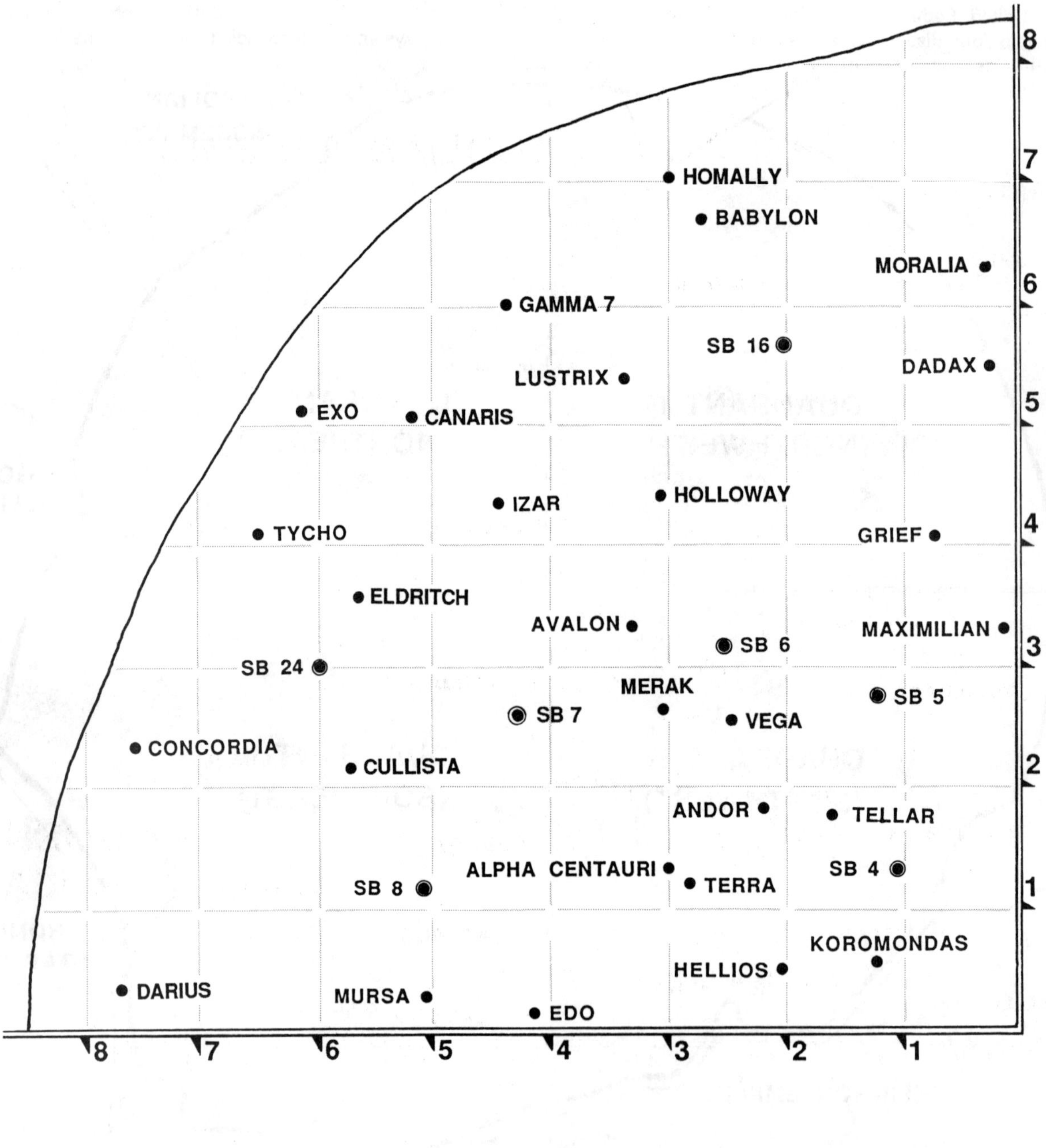

EACH SQUARE = 10 PARSECS

MAP OF THE FEDERATION
QUADRANT II (NORTHEAST)

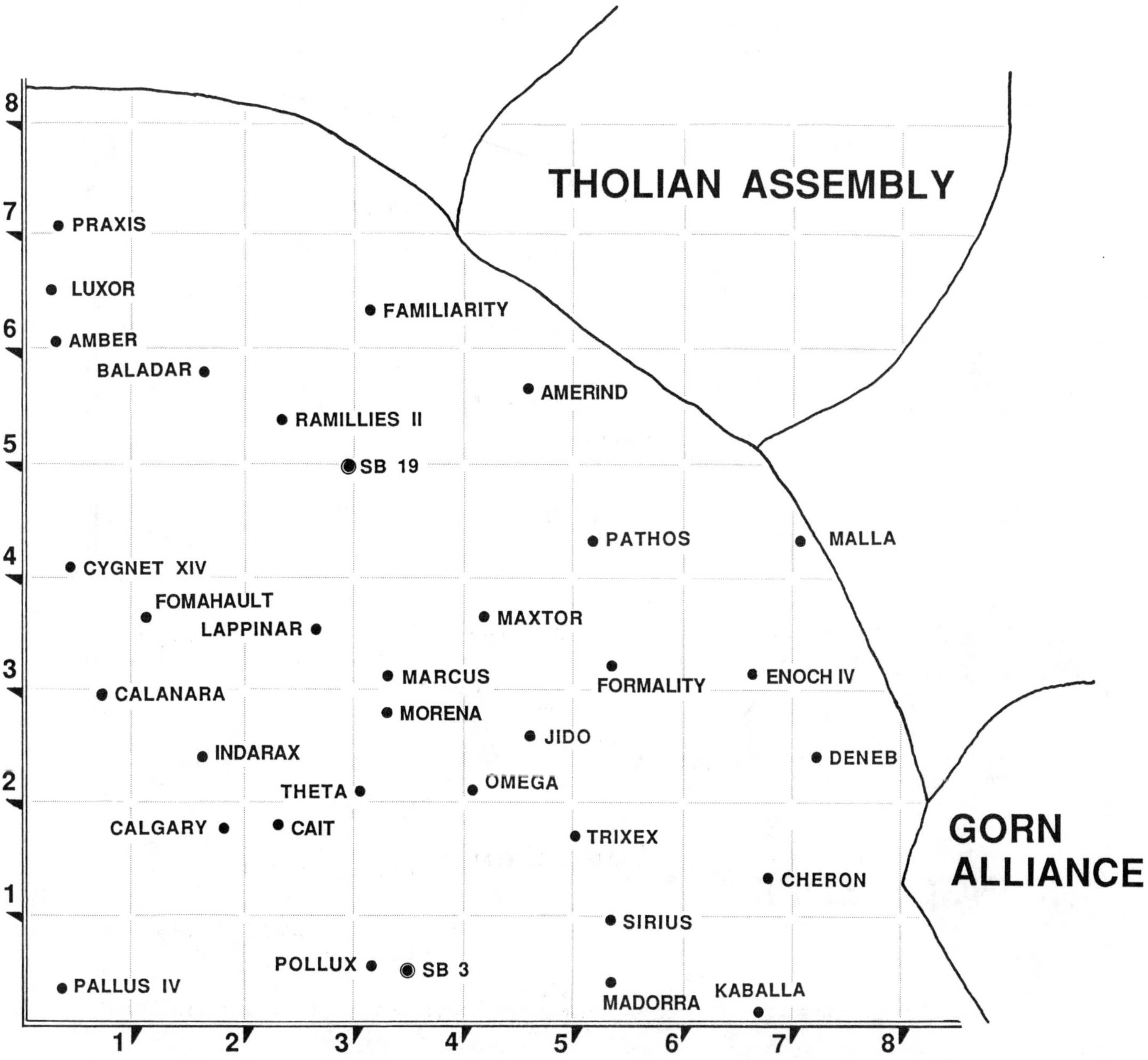

EACH SQUARE = 10 PARSECS

MAP OF THE FEDERATION
QUADRANT IV (SOUTHWEST)

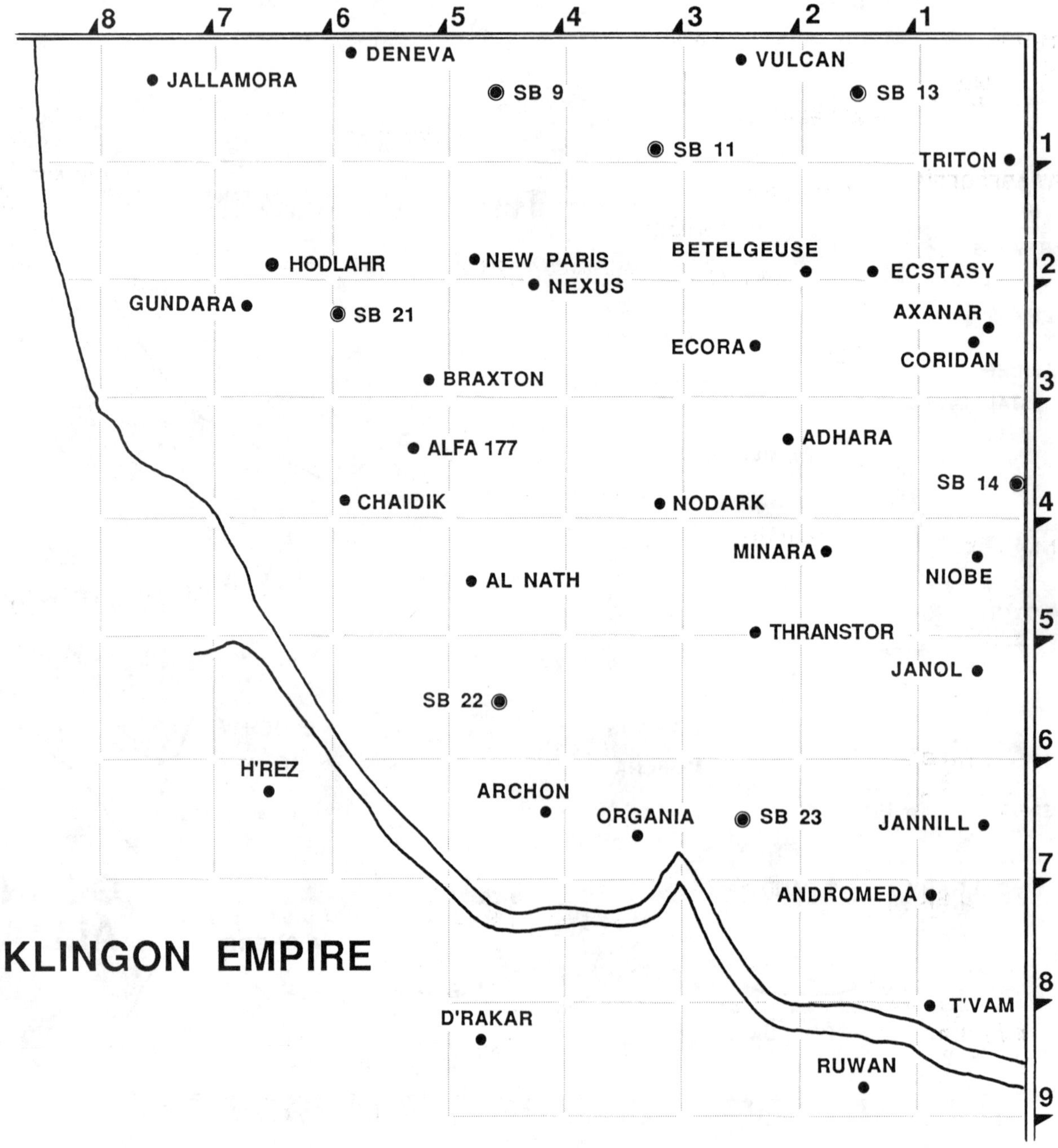

EACH SQUARE = 10 PARSECS

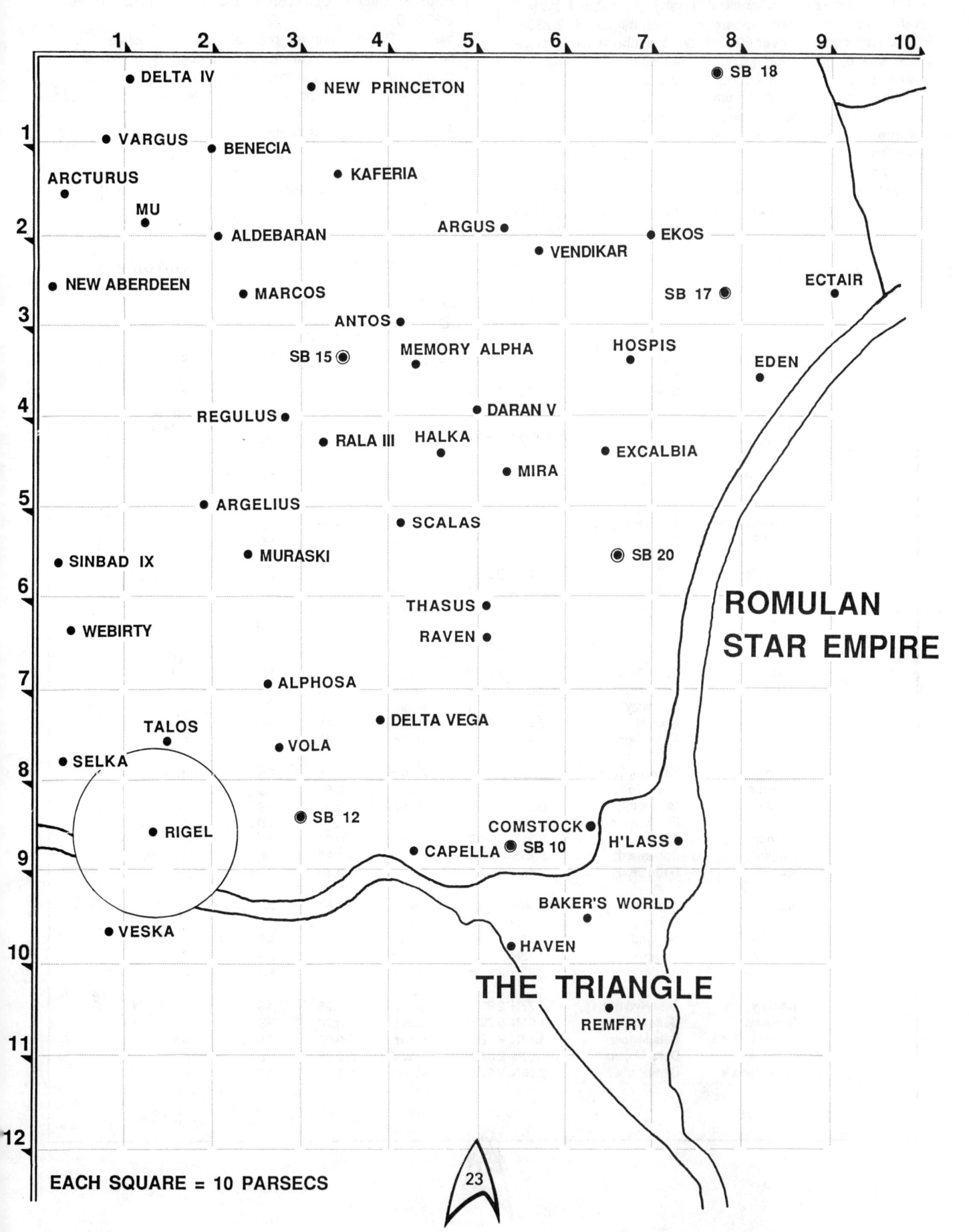

INHABITED WORLDS

Following is an alphabetical registry of inhabited planets within the Federation sphere of influence as of 2/2306. There are currently over 600 inhabited worlds within Federation space, not including worlds currently within disputed areas of control (such as in the Organian Neutral Zone) or colony worlds chartered after 2/2306.01. Information on each inhabited planet includes the following specifications:

Name: The world's proper name.
System: The name of the planetary system in which the world resides.
Location: System's map coordinates.
Race: Predominant racial type [Andorian (Andor), Caitan (Cait), Alpha Centauri (Cent), Cygnian (Cygn), Deltan, Edoan, Human or Humanoid, Mixed, Non-Humanoid (NHum), Tellarite (Tellar), or Vulcan].
Pop: Estimated population in billions of inhabitants as of 2/2306.01.
Status: Planet's current political status [associate Federation member (AS), full-status member (FS), Federation colony world (Col), independent world (Indep), quarantined world (Quar), or protected world under the Prime Directive (PDir)].
Profile: Major planetary concerns [agriculture (Ag), entertainment (En), cultural (Cl), industry (In), mining (Mn), naval support base for Star Fleet (Nv), shipbuilding (Sh), science (Sc), trade center (Tr), or other special or unknown considerations (X)].

FEDERATION PLANETARY SYSTEMS
INHABITED WORLDS

World Name	System Name	Location	Race	Pop	Status	Profile
Abyss	Abyss Alpha	3.72S 5.53W	Vulcan	1.10	AS	Ag Sc
Adhara	Epsilon Canaris	3.53S 2.26W	Human	4.30	Indep	Sc
Adoss	Gamma Emerata	2.21N 2.37E	Vulcan	0.25	Col	Ag Sc
Aesa IX	Aesa	3.77N 3.26E	Vulcan	1.35	AS	In Sc Tr
Albireo	Beta Cygni	3.27N 1.97W	Human	6.50	FS	Ag In
Aldebaran	Alpha Tauri	2.01S 2.01E	Human	7.25	FS	Cl In
Alfa 177	Alpha Honorus	3.51S 5.26W	Human	0.04	AS	Cl In Sc Tr
Alpha III	Alpha Canaris	0.93N 1.62W	Human	6.56	FS	Cl In Tr
Alpha Majoris II	Alpha Majoris	2.82N 0.97W	Human	5.50	FS	Cl Tr
Alpha Proxima II	Dnoces	0.21S 2.49W	Human	0.03	FS	Cl Sc Tr
Alpha Centauri	Al Rijil	1.27N 2.92W	Cent	21.50	FS	Cl Sc Sh Tr
Altair	Alpha Aquilae	3.02N 0.99E	Human	7.00	FS	Cl In Tr
Amber	Beta Rigalia	6.05N 0.27E	Cent	2.25	AS	Ag Nv Tr
Amerind	Epsilon Beta	5.78N 4.52E	Human	0.05	PDir	X
Anchor	Beta Hydra 378	5.90N 3.27E	Tellar	0.37	AS	Ag Nv Tr
Andor	Epsilon Indi	1.82N 2.22W	Andor	10.17	FS	Cl Nv Sh Tr
Antares	Alpha Scorpii	2.02N 1.79E	Human	4.00	FS	Cl Nv Tr
Antipathy IV	Antipathy	1.91N 2.25W	Andor	2.48	Col	Ag
Antos	Socratii	2.99N 4.12E	Human	5.00	Indep	Sc
Apollonia	Alpha Sigma	4.44N 6.37E	Mixed	1.38	Col	Ag IN
Aplithin	Pithecus Majorus	7.16S 2.40W	NHum	2.75	FS	Nv Sh Tr
Arcturus	Alpha Bootis	1.48S 0.39E	Human	8.50	FS	Cl In Nv Tr
Ardana	Mu Leonis	0.98N 6.12E	Human	2.25	FS	Cl Tr
Argelius	Rho Magnin	5.18S 1.97E	Human	1.75	AS	Cl En Nv Tr
Ariannus	Arianna	2.33N 3.39E	Human	0.01	AS	Cl Tr
Avalon	Ceberhardt	3.25N 3.25W	Human	1.25	AS	Ag In Nv
Axanar	Delta Orcus	2.46S 0.47W	Human	0.10	PDir	X
Babel	Wolf 424	3.98S 3.18E	Human	0.01	AS	X
Babylon	Babylus	6.70N 2.75W	Mixed	0.0001	Col	In Nv Tr
Baladar	Beta Indi	5.82N 1.77E	Andor	0.37	AS	Ag In Tr
Barabas	Baran	4.42N 0.29E	Andor	7.59	FS	Cl Tr
Bardex III	Bardex	2.02N 3.21W	Mixed	4.58	FS	Ag Cl Nv Tr
Barrony	Zeta Hydra 281	4.77N 2.92E	Mixed	1.26	AS	Ag Mn Nv Tr
Barsoom	Delta Gamma	1.01N 5.79W	Mixed	0.20	FS	Ag Mn Nv Tr
Baxter's World	Beta Minora	3.47N 2.22E	Tellar	0.02	Col	Ag Mn
Benecia	Delta Majoris	1.01S 2.01E	Mixed	0.27	FS	Ag Tr
Berengaria V	Berengaria	2.98N 2.27E	Mixed	1.50	AS	Mn

FEDERATION PLANETARY SYSTEM – INHABITED WORLDS (Continued)

World Name	System Name	Location	Race	Pop	Status	Profile
Beta III	6-11	6.18S 4.82W	Human	6.00	AS	Tr
Beta Prime	Beta Leonis	1.81N 2.73W	Andor	0.04	AS	Ag In Mn Tr
Blackart	Alpha Vergoris	6.27N 3.52E	Tellar	0.01	Col	Mn
Blithinia	Boron 437	6.02N 2.99E	Tellar	0.01	Col	Mn
Bonanza	Aegis Aquilia	4.45N 4.47W	Mixed	0.35	AS	In Mn Nv Tr
Borigris	Borigrass	2.07S 3.82W	Mixed	2.48	AS	In Mn Tr
Borom	Alpha Quarram	1.83S 4.22W	Andor	5.87	FS	Cl In Tr
Braxton	Zeta Minoris	2.89S 5.17W	Andor	2.91	Col	Ag In Mn
Cait	Caitia	1.80N 2.16E	Cait	7.65	FS	Cl In Sh Tr
Callista	Beta Aurigae	2.07N 5.82W	Vulcan	4.75	FS	Ag Tr
Calsa	Wolf 346	1.77S 2.28W	Vulcan	3.25	FS	Ag In Tr
Camus	Beta Tauri	1.07S 0.89E	Human	1.25	FS	In Nv
Calanara	Beta Leonis	2.95N 0.77E	Vulcan	1.01	FS	In Nv
Calgary	Griswald 3489	1.75N 1.88E	Mixed	2.47	FS	Ag Nv Tr
Canaris	Scorpi Maxima	5.05N 5.22W	Andor	2.00	FS	Ag Mn
Candide	Candida	2.05N 6.14W	Human	0.75	Col	Mn Tr
Canopus	Beta Geminorum	3.30N 1.27E	Andor	10.01	FS	Cl In Nv Tr
Capella	Alpha Aurigae	8.75S 4.25E	Human	1.03	FS	In Nv
Castor Fields	Castora	0.64N 6.15E	Mixed	1.00	AS	Cl En Tr
Castrola IX	Castrola	1.02N 5.89E	Mixed	0.78	AS	Ag Mn
Cavala	Beta Forminia	3.72N 4.21W	Andor	5.33	FS	Ag Tr
Cavalier	Calka	1.67S 0.51E	Human	0.12	AS	Ag Cl En
Ceopus	Aecupus	5.09N 1.12W	Human	2.25	FS	Cl Tr
Cestus III	Cestus	3.29N 8.54E	Mixed	1.01	FS	Mn Tr
Charlemagne	Aquilla Scorpi	2.63N 7.66E	Human	1.15	FS	In Nv Tr
Cheleb	Beta Ophiuchi	1.22N 4.27E	Tellar	4.01	FS	In Mn
Cheron VI	Cheron	1.27N 6.78E	Human	1.00	FS	Ag Mn Tr
Cochrane I	Zeta Riguli	2.73S 5.23W	Mixed	2.83	FS	Cl In Tr
Cochrane II	Gamma Delta 125	2.77N 3.36W	Mixed	1.48	FS	Ag Cl Nv
Cochrane III	Delta Canarus	4.54N 4.73W	Andor	2.46	FS	Cl Tr
Commissariate	Beta Trianguli	5.07N 2.25W	Mixed	1.56	AS	Ag
Concordia	Gamma Palabus	2.36N 7.53W	Mixed	2.35	FS	Ag Cl Tr
Coromindas	Corom	3.78N 3.22W	Tellar	2.33	FS	Ag Nv
Coridan	Danthos	2.70S 0.91W	Human	0.10	PDir	X
Covdival	Cordival	7.22N 0.21E	Human	1.49	AS	Nv Tr
Crassenia	Crovala 173	2.68S 2.44W	Tellar	2.00	AS	Mn
Crassus	Ambiphon	2.78N 5.32W	Human	2.99	FS	Nv Tr
Crater's World	Gamma Zeta IV	4.45S 6.01W	Human	0.01	AS	Sc
Cremindas	Beta Rigala	4.31N 4.22E	Deltan	1.10	AS	Cl Sc
Crimilak	Alpha Coranda	3.77N 4.77E	Deltan	2.29	FS	Cl In Sc
Cromidia	Gamma Ophiuchi	1.17N 6.91E	Human	1.12	FS	Mn Nv
Curiosity	Pharos 625	2.47N 5.55E	Deltan	2.37	FS	Cl Sc
Cyclopus	Verigus K	8.00S 6.82E	Human	0.12	AS	AG
Cygnet XIV	Cygnus	4.05N 0.41E	Cygn	4.25	FS	Cl In Sc
Dadax	Dextera 273	5.47N 0.25W	Mixed	2.00	FS	Sc Tr
Daidaem	Gamma Hydra 371	4.55N 0.78E	Mixed	3.25	FS	Cl Sc Tr
Dalanda V	Dalanda	6.58N 1.72E	Mixed	1.37	AS	Mn Tr
Danton Major	Danton	2.47N 4.32E	Deltan	2.38	FS	Cl In Sc Tr
Daran V	Daran	3.88S 4.93E	Mixed	4.50	FS	Cl In Nv Sc
Darius III	Delta Darius	0.34N 7.78W	Deltan	7.25	FS	Cl En
Darmal	Darmius	0.66N 3.69E	Mixed	3.48	AS	En X
Dartanian	Ti Che	4.68S 3.39E	Mixed	4.28	AS	Nv X
Delta IV	Delta Principius	0.21S 1.02E	Deltan	8.52	FS	Cl
Delta Vega	Trimordidion	7.27S 4.02E	Human	0.07	AS	In Mn Tr

FEDERATION PLANETARY SYSTEM – INHABITED WORLDS (Continued)

World Name	System Name	Location	Race	Pop	Status	Profile
Democritus	Demos 372 Alpha	3.58S 3.74W	Human	2.48	FS	Cl In Nv
Demoiselle II	Demoiselle	3.22N 2.28E	Mixed	2.38	AS	Cl In
Deneb	Alpha Cygni	2.38N 7.22E	Mixed	5.50	FS	Cl Sc Tr
Deneva	Beta Darius	0.23S 5.79W	Mixed	2.50	FS	Cl In Cs Tr
Determination	Demarcation	0.37N 4.27W	Mixed	2.48	AS	Cl
Dimorus III	Dimorus	1.23N 3.27E	NHum	1.00	Indep	X
Diomede	Beta Aquilae	2.07N 2.98W	Mixed	2.48	FS	Nv Tr
Divestment	Formindas 743	2.38N 5.84W	Mixed	0.05	Col	Mn
D'livian VI	D'livian	1.48S 4.37W	Mixed	1.82	AS	In Tr
Doxi	Darlovan 277	2.81N 4.22E	Mixed	0.03	Col	En
Dundas	Ursula Apha 26	2.73N 3.77W	Mixed	1.38	FS	Cl Mn Tr
Dundee II	Dundee	3.28N 4.37W	Andor	2.17	FS	Nv Sc Tr
Duo III	Duosetel	2.11S 3.27E	Deltan	4.93	AS	Sc Tr
Earl Minor	Demos Majoris	2.43S 4.55W	Mixed	5.00	FS	Cl Sc
Ecora	Delta Vara	2.62S 2.33W	Cygn	2.46	FS	Tr
Ecstasy	Hydra Impora	1.92S 1.32W	Mixed	1.00	AS	En
Edo	Epsilon Minora	0.15N 4.11W	Edoan	7.87	FS	Cl In Tr
Egaran II	Egara 172	3.73N 3.72W	Cent	2.29	AS	Cl
Egross	Alpha Vega 272	1.37N 3.22E	Mixed	2.19	AS	In Tr
Ekos	M43 Alpha	2.02S 6.95E	Human	6.50	PDir	X
Elas	Tellun	8.58S 4.98E	Human	12.56	AS	Cl X
Elba	Quarius Nova	1.37N 6.69E	Mixed	0.0001	AS	X
Eldamas	Eldamas 344	2.47S 4.69W	Mixed	2.19	AS	Mn Tr
Eldorado	Eldamas 344	2.47S 4.69W	Mixed	1.00	AS	Mn Nv Tr
Eldritch	Delta Corondis	3.58N 5.58W	Tellar	2.92	FS	Cl En
Elevation	Epsilon Zeta	4.46N 4.46W	Human	2.88	AS	Cl Sc
Elorex	Eloras 375	2.32S 7.36W	Andor	0.19	Col	In Mn
Eminiar VII	Eminiar	2.15S 5.77E	Human	5.50	FS	Cl In Tr
Enarrom	Parsus Indi	3.45S 2.62W	Cent	3.27	FS	Cl Sc Tr
Enas	Gamma Minora 12	4.33S 5.67E	Cygn	4.37	FS	Cl Sc
Enasatar	Geminorum Pala	2.47N 4.61E	Tellar	0.01	Col	Mn
Enid VI	Vega Majoris	3.45N 6.55E	Mixed	1.57	AS	In
Enoch IV	Vega Majoris	3.45N 6.55E	Mixed	2.37	AS	In Tr
Escara	Delta Indi 668	3.22N 3.81E	Cygn	1.99	FS	Cl Sc Tr
Eternity	Alpha Eridani	4.55N 6.02E	Mixed	0.0018	AS	X
Etrolopar	Alpha Carinna 17	3.99N 5.97E	Cygn	2.11	AS	Sc
Etross	Menaras 222	3.55N 4.75W	Human	3.98	FS	In Tr
Europa	Sol	1.23N 2.79W	Human	0.20	FS	Sh
Existence Point	Honora Minoris	5.53N 5.50W	Mixed	2.19	Indep	Cl
Falas	Danara 5986	4.77N 3.33E	Cygn	5.50	FS	Cl Tr
Falorin	Alpha Parsis 25	3.79S 4.51W	Mixed	2.33	AS	In Sc
Familiarity	Beta Maxim 437	6.31N 3.22E	Mixed	2.46	AS	Cl Sc Tr
Fellowship	Beta Maxim 437	6.31N 3.22E	Mixed	2.02	AS	Cl
Femininity II	Beta Maxim 437	6.31N 3.22E	Mixed	1.37	AS	Cl
Fenbly VII	Sigma Minoris	5.33S 1.07E	Human	2.38	FS	Cl In
Findesa	Gamma Dinara	4.57N 1.75W	Mixed	2.98	AS	Cl En
Finlorra	Gamma Leonis	5.05N 1.22W	Tellar	1.00	AS	Mn Tr
Finlax	Delta Paruli	4.88N 5.77E	Human	2.22	FS	In Sc Tr
Fomahault	Alpha Piscis Austrini	3.77N 1.29E	Mixed	3.57	FS	Cl
Formality	Gamma Eta Dara	3.22N 5.27E	Andor	4.48	FS	Sc Tr
Fullman	Ursu Geminorum	4.27N 0.77E	Human	4.22	AS	Nv
Fullsome Park	Ursu Geminorum	4.27N 0.77E	Mixed	2.99	AS	En Tr
Function	Foram Canara	5.36S 5.66W	Mixed	1.92	AS	Sc
Gaggle Point	Luris Eta	3.57S 6.01W	Cent	2.31	AS	En
Gamadrine	Danara 5986	4.77N 3.33E	Tellar	0.89	FS	Mn
Gamma Hydra IV	Gamma Hydra	5.91S 5.96E	Mixed	0.0001	Col	Mn Tr
Gamma Vertis	Virgo Tacritus	2.02N 7.26E	Human	1.60	FS	In Nv Tr
Gammorah	Ceta 503	7.02N 2.24W	Human	0.36	AS	Cl Mn Tr

FEDERATION PLANETARY SYSTEM – INHABITED WORLDS (Continued)

World Name	System Name	Location	Race	Pop	Status	Profile
Geo	Alpa Baratis	2.48S 7.05W	Mixed	1.00	FS	Cl
Gideon	Delta Dorado	3.57S 2.35E	Human	12.00	Indep	Cl
Gissen V	Gissen 986	3.03N 2.48W	Mixed	3.57	FS	Cl Sc Tr
Grammen Park	Alpha Piscis Austrini	3.77N 1.29E	Mixed	1.95	AS	En
Gravenworld	Maven Parsis	4.56N 0.45W	Cent	3.22	FS	Cl Sc Tr
Greensward	Sigma Valara	1.44N 4.98E	Human	0.04	Col	Tr
Greenwald	Alpha Trimora	1.59N 5.99E	Human	1.50	FS	Cl Tr
Grief	Tahniva 311	4.02N 0.77W	Cygn	1.00	AS	Cl
Grinnidas	Darmala Beta	0.85N 5.02W	Mixed	3.98	FS	Cl In Tr
Grissom's World	Grissom 6678	0.78S 4.78W	Human	2.99	FS	Cl In Sc Tr
Grix	Delta Eridana	0.99S 6.75W	Edoan	0.01	Col	Cl Tr
Grossex	Delta Eridana	0.99S 6.75W	Edoan	0.01	Col	Cl Tr
Gundara	Zeta Ophiuchi	2.47S 6.66W	Mixed	3.22	FS	Cl In Tr
Habrenn	Arabenn	4.57N 1.12W	Cent	3.01	FS	Cl In
Hadley II	Hadley 557	0.89N 0.88E	Mixed	7.47	FS	Cl In Nv Tr
Halador	Sigma Zeta 477	0.91N 7.39E	Human	0.02	Col	Mn
Halcyon	Alpha Baratis	2.48S 7.05W	Human	0.01	Col	Mn
Haldraine	Alpha Nimorra	3.78N 2.11E	Mixed	1.32	AS	Cl
Halka	Nola Boradne	4.27S 4.58E	Human	1.57	Indep	Cl Mn
Hannamore	Darmala Beta	0.85N 5.02W	Mixed	2.22	FS	Cl Tr
Hanson's World	Beta Hydra	0.91N 2.78E	NHum	0.20	PDir	X
Hardin's World	Delta Panaras	2.46N 5.33W	Human	1.32	FS	In Mn Tr
Harmony	Harridane 226	5.27N 3.89E	Vulcan	2.37	FS	En In Nv Sc
Harpie	Kelvolara 688	3.45N 0.26W	Human	0.02	Col	Mn
Hastings	Alpha Piscis Austrini	3.77N 1.29E	Mixed	3.46	FS	In Nv Tr
Havelind	Caracore	3.57S 2.69W	Cait	4.77	FS	Cl In
Haxwren	Caracore	3.57S 2.69W	Mixed	3.46	FS	Cl In Tr
Hellios	Sigma Wyrenex	0.48N 2.02W	Mixed	4.72	FS	Cl
Heprinala	Bornelli 709	1.32N 0.86W	Vulcan	3.57	FS	Cl Sc
Heristis	Bornelli 709	1.32N 0.86W	Vulcan	3.00	FS	Ag Cl
Heuristic	Rexenox	5.37S 0.22W	Mixed	2.45	AS	Ag Sc
Hexentrex	Beta Triaran	6.44S 2.97W	Vulcan	4.57	FS	Ag Cl
Hochlor IV	Hochlor	2.17S 3.47E	Cait	5.43	FS	Cl In Tr
Hodlahr	Sigma Indus 462	1.88S 6.42W	Human	2.99	FS	Nv Tr
Hollow Way	Gypsem Zeta 703	4.57N 3.24W	Mixed	2.43	FS	Ag
Homally	Zeta Niobe	7.01N 3.21W	Human	1.00	FS	Ag Cl
Honoria	Lura Voris 747	3.47N 3.55E	Mixed	4.47	FS	Ag Cl In Tr
Hospis	Sigma Tricali	3.34S 6.77E	Mixed	1.00	AS	Ag
Hospitality II	Havidar	0.25N 5.07E	Mixed	2.47	AS	En
Hostoria	Luxor 867	2.46N 2.22E	Vulcan	3.47	FS	Cl In Sc
Hurlin	Zeta Paor	5.68N 6.33W	Vulcan	4.77	FS	Ag Cl Sc
Icarus	Al Rijil	1.27N 2.92W	Cent	18.56	FS	Ag In Sc Tr
Idara	Megolar	4.67N 0.26E	Cent	4.73	FS	In Tr
Idiom	Valen's Star	5.38N 0.42E	Mixed	3.57	AS	Ag Cl
Idix	Duviniax	2.47N 4.43E	Vulvan	3.99	FS	Cl Sc
Idoxar	Sigma Exat	3.57N 6.44W	Edoan	2.17	FS	Ag Cl In
Imagination	Metriunn 867	3.33N 3.82W	Mixed	1.47	AS	En Tr
Importunity	Hutchinsen 866	5.57N 0.36E	Mixed	3.57	FS	Tr
Indarax	Epsilon Indar	2.51N 1.52E	Andor	2.34	FS	X
Ingraham B	Ingraham	1.48S 5.02E	Human	4.25	FS	Ag In Tr Sc
Ioma	Iomegas	0.02N 0.37W	Mixed	5.50	FS	Ag Tr
Iotia	Sigma Iotia	6.78S 4.55W	Human	4.75	AS	Tr
Iparassen	Delta Zeta 785	5.68S 4.77E	Human	4.68	FS	Tr
Ipicran	Delta Zeta 785	5.68S 4.77E	Tellar	0.001	Col	Mn Tr
Izar	Epsilon Bootis	4.37N 4.44W	Human	16.75	FS	Cl In Tr

FEDERATION PLANETARY SYSTEM – INHABITED WORLDS (Continued)

World Name	System Name	Location	Race	Pop	Status	Profile
Jalinitir	Valar Majoris	3.22N 0.26W	Vulcan	5.60	FS	Cl In Sc
Jallamora	Trasenn 685	0.36S 7.46W	Human	0.0001	Col	Mn
Jallimass	Zeta Bevarra	0.88N 6.35E	Mixed	3.47	FS	Ag Cl
Jamison's World	Epsilon Keva	3.72N 3.12W	Andor	12.57	FS	Ag Nv Tr
Jammolora	Tau Tauri	2.47N 2.22W	Andor	10.46	FS	Ag Nv Sc Tr
Janus	Gamma Major	3.78S 0.22W	Human	0.01	AS	Mn
Jarovalla VI	Jarovalla	3.76N 1.53E	Andor	3.00	FS	Ag Tr
Javlinador	Beta Kurissa	4.37N 2.24E	Mixed	3.29	FS	Ag Cl In
Javora	Gamma Tauri	4.02N 3.49W	Mixed	2.47	FS	Ag
Jaxsen III	Jaxsen	0.27N 2.21E	Andor	1.37	FS	Ag Cl In
Jido	Jidop	2.58N 4.72E	Andor	2.00	FS	Tr
Jorindas	Beta Vertis	0.99S 4.27W	Human	1.50	FS	Nv Tr
Julietta	Juris	0.87N 2.28E	Cygn	4.40	FS	In Sc
Jungar	Epsilon Ballara	2.17S 2.11W	Vulcan	2.85	FS	Cl In
Jurisa	Juris	0.87N 2.28E	Vulcan	2.00	FS	In Sc Tr
Justinia	Juris	0.87N 2.28E	Vulcan	1.60	FS	In
Kaballa	Nimori Ceti	0.11N 6.77E	NHum	Unkwn	PDir	X
Kadacohr	Kadass	1.44N 3.41W	Andor	2.00	AS	Ag Nv
Kaferia	Tau Ceti	1.27S 3.56E	NHum	4.45	FS	Ag
Kamadarc	Kalamar	1.37N 4.27W	Tellar	2.75	FS	Mn Nv Tr
Kamandas	Burkid	0.22S 3.28W	Tellar	1.45	FS	Mn Tr
Katan III	Tau Abir	0.46N 2.47W	Human	2.72	AS	Ag
Katar VI	Katar	3.52S 4.01E	Human	3.47	FS	Ag In
Kavatala Superior	Kavatala	3.47N 3.78E	Mixed	4.50	FS	Cl In Tr
Kol's Orchard	Kolitor	0.52N 1.08W	Cent	4.01	FS	Ag Cl
Koromond	Koromandas	0.54N 1.24W	Mixed	12.47	FS	Ag Cl In Tr
Labarinth	Tau Zeta	1.89N 3.72W	Tellar	5.17	FS	In Mn
Labiarn V	Labiarn	5.02N 0.46E	Human	2.73	FS	In Tr
Lakeland	Purlii	8.20S 6.42E	Mixed	0.114	AS	En
Lamentation	Hedrox 576	3.22S 0.21E	Mixed	0.001	Col	Ag
Lao T'Shin	Gemini Dentos	2.27S 1.57W	Tellar	1.00	FS	Mn Tr
Lappax II	Lappax	3.04N 3.87W	Human	2.47	FS	In Sc
Lappinar	Laxes Alpha	3.55N 2.77E	Cent	3.55	FS	In Tr
Lasur Funop	Lasur	6.06S 3.62W	Tellar	2.75	FS	Mn Sc Tr
Laura's World	Laurison 294	2.44S 3.75W	Mixed	0.001	Col	Cl
Laxaren	Lacorby 192	5.03N 4.44E	Vulcan	1.99	FS	Cl Sc
Lecorak	Chelikbar	3.57N 2.67W	Tellar	3.77	FS	In Sc Tr
Lecroutex	Lecrotox	4.27N 6.33E	Mixed	2.25	AS	Ag Mn
Lexinisar	Menitrom 799	2.47N 3.55W	Mixed	1.47	AS	Ag
Lexor VII	Lexor	2.36N 3.22W	Vulcan	3.57	FS	Ag Cl Sc
Listra Principis	Listra	6.44N 0.33E	Human	2.88	FS	Cl In Sc
Live Again	Oroness	3.28S 0.27W	Mixed	0.0001	Col	Ag
Livenix	Illex	2.84N 2.22E	Cent	0.0002	Col	Ag Sc
Lixis XI	Lixis	3.57S 2.57E	Vulcan	12.47	FS	Sc Sh Tr
Lochabahr	Lochnarle	6.44N 3.22W	Human	0.90	AS	Ag Tr
Lochlar	Lojar	2.47N 6.87E	Human	7.37	FS	Ag Sc Sh
Loki	K'Kronn	3.57S 2.51W	Andor	11.27	FS	Mn Tr
Lone Node	Alpha Demetrius	3.44N 3.77E	Human	0.001	Col	Mn
Lustralva	Merellion Sigma	4.78N 6.02E	Deltan	7.84	FS	Cl In Tr
Lustrix	Remusa 885	5.37N 3.33W	Andor	4.43	AS	Cl Mn
Luxor	Terrilepton	6.59N 0.39E	Human	3.28	FS	Ag
Mabarra V	Mabarra	3.32N 4.28W	Mixed	5.33	FS	Ag
Macadarna	Giordin 275	2.57N 4.36E	Cait	1.88	AS	Cl In
Machelvi	Valtrax	1.37N 2.36E	Human	13.39	FS	Ag Cl In Tr
Madacarax	Valtrax	1.37N 2.36E	Mixed	0.004	Col	Ag
Madistra	Sigma Geminis	3.79S 2.35W	Mixed	3.44	FS	Cl In Mn

FEDERATION PLANETARY SYSTEM – INHABITED WORLDS (Continued)

World Name	System Name	Location	Race	Pop	Status	Profile
Madorra	Madorax	0.47N 5.32E	Deltan	2.16	FS	Cl Sc
Magister	Magesty	3.77N 0.11E	Human	12.47	FS	Ag In Tr
Majority	Luris Maxcinis	5.02N 3.17E	Human	7.47	FS	In Tr
Maklin VIII	Maklin	0.27S 2.34E	Vulcan	2.38	FS	Ag Sc
Makus III	Makus	2.18S 0.33E	Vulcan	10.01	FS	Cl In Tr
Malawren	Malas	3.88N 0.22E	Mixed	3.22	AS	Ag
Malla	Maurex 782	4.23N 7.01E	Human	1.23	AS	Ag Mn
Malarhone	Minarcis Alpha	5.37N 1.44E	Cent	3.37	FS	Cl In Tr
Maluria	Omega Cygni	0.59S 5.23E	Mixed	7.01	FS	In Mn Tr
Manark II	Manark	1.07N 2.47E	Human	10.01	FS	In Tr
Marac Polis	Marac	2.47N 0.97E	Human	1.00	AS	In Sc Tr
Marcos	Marcios	2.55S 2.27E	Mixed	1.50	AS	In
Marcus	6-23	3.07N 3.28E	Vulcan	2.25	FS	Sc
Maren	Maren Alpha	2.19N 1.09E	Human	1.25	AS	Ag In Mn Tr
Mars	Sol	1.23N 2.79W	Human	15.74	FS	In Nv Sh Tr
Maxima Prime	Maxim	2.94N 4.52E	Human	3.20	FS	Sc
Maximilian	Zeta Geminorum	3.28N 0.11W	Mixed	1.00	AS	In Mn Tr
Maxtor	Mirith	3.88N 4.22E	Vulcan	2.75	FS	Sc
Medusa	Rhys	5.57S 6.37E	NHum	5.00	FS	Sc
Melkot	Melka	5.99S 6.69E	NHum	2.25	Indep	X
Memory Alpha	Kam Sim	3.31S 4.25E	Mixed	0.01	AS	Sc
Memoxa	Mirith	2.33N 2.44E	Vulcan	3.75	FS	Sc
Merak	Latis Cyrtiva	2.77N 3.22W	Vulcan	0.12	FS	In Mn Sh Tr
Mercury	Sol	1.23N 2.79W	Human	0.22	FS	In Sh
Mexas II	Mexas	5.14N 0.22E	Mixed	2.34	AS	Ag
Mindara XII	Mindara	4.22S 4.02E	Mixed	2.11	AS	Ag Mn
Midos Principius	Midos	3.05N 3.22E	Cent	11.20	FS	Cl In
Minidine IV	Minidine	2.02S 4.22E	Vulcan	5.22	FS	Cl Sc Tr
Minis	Dayliss	3.40N 0.34E	Mixed	3.33	FS	Cl Tr
Minora	6-15	2.11N 2.76W	Vulcan	9.22	FS	Cl In Sc
Mira	Omicron Ceti	4.57S 5.33E	Human	1.10	AS	Ag
Miri's World	Beta Persei	5.48S 6.02E	Human	0.001	PDir	X
Molitor	Molitus	2.37N 1.23W	Mixed	21.22	FS	Ag
Monarch II	Monarch Alpha	4.38N 2.11E	Human	1.20	AS	Ag
Moralia V	Moralia	6.38N 0.22W	Human	0.0001	Col	Ag
Morena	Eridani Gamma	2.88N 3.12E	Human	10.10	FS	Nv Sh
Moxen	Moxenalus	3.68N 2.11E	Cent	1.28	AS	In
Mu	Leoxa	1.83S 1.21E	Cent	2.10	FS	Ag Tr
Mudd's World	Beta Aurigae	4.22S 5.32E	NHum	0.001	Quar	X
Mursa	Tau Anacritus	0.22N 5.02W	Andor	12.11	FS	Sc Sh
Nagrond	Naxor 599	5.32S 6.04W	NHum	0.27	PDir	X
Namorra	Namor	0.23N 1.37W	Human	1.37	AS	Ag
Narcissus III	Narcissus	4.08N 4.44E	Vulcan	2.19	AS	Cl Sc
Narval	Narvox	3.27N 2.11E	Cait	2.45	FS	Cl
Naxis	Naxion	5.52N 2.96E	Mixed	8.55	FS	Cl In Tr
Necturop	Nekusa	4.25N 2.08E	Mixed	1.25	AS	Ag Tr
Neural	Zeta Bootis	3.23S 3.39W	NHum	0.01	PDir	X
New Aberdeen	Phi Galatius	2.41S 0.21E	Mixed	11.37	FS	In Sh Tr
New Brisbane	Pagora	3.55N 3.12E	Human	1.37	FS	In
New Bristol	Ceti Reguli	0.33N 2.43E	Human	2.12	FS	In Tr
New Dublin	Ceti Reguli	0.33N 2.43E	Human	1.55	FS	Ag In Tr
New Horizon	Gamma Quadratis	0.47N 1.46W	Mixed	0.18	AS	Ag
New Kensington	Beta Aleph 703	0.11N 6.02W	Human	1.00	AS	Ag Mn Tr
New Paris	Omega Aurigae	1.78S 4.78W	Human	1.26	FS	Cl In Tr
New Princeton	Delta Leonis	0.28S 3.11E	Mixed	2.25	FS	Cl
New Victoria	Nova Dimora	2.68N 2.44E	Vulcan	2.89	FS	Cl Sc
Nexus	Vilius Serpentus	5.14N 0.23W	Mixed	4.22	FS	Cl Tr
Niobe	Gamma Indus 552	4.28S 0.45W	Andor	2.21	AS	Cl

FEDERATION PLANETARY SYSTEM – INHABITED WORLDS (Continued)

World Name	System Name	Location	Race	Pop	Status	Profile
Nodark	Nadarkis	3.89S 3.11W	NHum	0.23	PDir	X
Norassil	Norassen	2.67N 2.77E	Vulcan	1.00	AS	Ag Cl
Normality	Keldanar 383	1.88N 2.62W	Human	2.17	FS	Ag In
Nostravis	Nestor Prime	3.17S 0.46E	Mixed	6.75	FS	Ag Cl In Tr
Oloss	Olossa	3.47S 5.05E	Mixed	2.39	AS	Ag En
Omegon	Omega	2.02N 4.06E	Human	5.55	PDir	X
Omicron Delta	Narble Qyx	1.22S 3.42E	Mixed	0.11	Indep	X
Ontara Prime	Sigma Quadratis	5.37N 0.27E	Mixed	1.26	AS	Ag Cl
Orontes	Oroness	3.27S 2.54W	Cent	2.11	FS	Ag Cl Sc
Osiris VII	Osiris	4.35N 0.22E	Cent	2.22	AS	Ag
Othello	Jarvis Alpha	4.37N 3.17E	Human	2.00	FS	Ag
Ovid	Parnellus	2.19S 5.18W	Human	0.0001	Col	Ag Cl
Ovlon II	Ovlon	4.27N 2.88W	Mixed	2.50	AS	Ag
Pallas Prime	Pallas 785	2.33S 7.04E	Mixed	0.0011	Col	Mn
Pallus IV	Pallus	0.27N 0.35E	Deltan	3.35	FS	Cl Sc Tr
Pallatrine	Gamma Omicron	3.04N 4.22E	Mixed	5.22	FS	Cl In Sh
Pampilia	Gamma Omicron	3.04N 4.22E	Mixed	1.37	AS	Ag
Pana	Panasa	3.72N 0.28W	Tellar	4.22	FS	In Mn
Paradimdas	Paradox	2.59N 1.33E	Mixed	3.25	FS	Ag In
Paradira	Beta Rosa	0.26N 0.88E	Andor	1.08	AS	Ag Tr
Parmentex	Parim 758	3.54N 0.33E	Andor	11.47	FS	Ag In Mn Sc
Passgate	Alpha Geminorum	2.07S 2.16E	Mixed	1.75	AS	Nv Tr
Pathos	Paradigm	4.22N 5.18E	Human	1.99	AS	Cl
Patric's Planet	Paramindas 575	3.22S 0.12W	Mixed	2.17	FS	Ag Cl In
Persistence	Nova Persis 288	0.69S 2.16E	Human	0.05	Col	Ag
Pike's Planet	Pitcara Prime	2.07N 0.15W	Mixed	1.36	AS	Ag
Pillum	Pillas Minora	6.32N 3.11E	Cent	1.35	FS	Cl In Sc
Piram III	Piram	0.88N 2.14E	Cent	2.25	FS	Ag Sc Tr
Placidity	Panasa	3.72N 0.28W	Tellar	5.27	FS	Mn
Platonius	Helios	2.04N 5.93E	Human	0.0001	Quar	X
Pollux	Beta Geminorum	0.51N 3.19E	Human	0.12	AS	Ag Mn
Posititas	Posara	3.16S 0.19W	Tellar	1.47	FS	Mn Tr
Praxis	Praxis Verdantis	7.01N 0.35E	Human	0.0001	Col	Mn
Precipice	Brightstar	9.11S 4.61E	Human	1.01	AS	Tr
Primidara II	Primidara	1.88N 3.22E	Vulcan	3.17	FS	Sc Tr
Primavera	Piras Zeta	1.47N 3.12W	Vulcan	2.42	FS	Cl Sc
Principius	Princip	6.42S 2.87E	Cent	6.04	AS	Ag Cl In
Proxima Centauri	Al Rijil	1.27N 2.92W	Cent	4.47	FS	Cl In Sh Tr
Quadrix II	Quadrix	0.77N 2.02W	Cent	5.01	FS	Ag Cl
Quarrel	Wolf 515	4.22S 0.12W	Mixed	6.36	FS	Sc
Questar	Boron 667	2.17N 0.12E	Human	2.45	FS	Ag
Raballex	Raballa	5.57N 3.22E	Human	5.22	FS	Cl In
Rala III	Rala	4.22S 3.21E	Human	2.57	FS	Ag In
Raman	Beta Lyra	5.37S 6.33E	Mixed	4.00	FS	Ag Cl
Ramillies II	Ramillies	5.37N 2.35E	Human	1.25	FS	Nv Tr
Rashile	Ungethiem	8.81S 6.02E	Human	0.002	AS	Ag
Raven	Gamma Lyrai	6.37S 5.05E	Mixed	3.26	FS	Nv Sc
Ravenna	Alpha Marak 272	6.02N 3.49E	Mixed	2.98	FS	Ag
Regulus	Alpha Leonis	3.99S 2.81E	Mixed	5.57	FS	Cl In Tr
Resolution	Posara	3.16N 0.13E	Vulcan	2.25	FS	Nv Tr
Revanche	Zeta Loris	5.36N 0.23W	Mixed	2.47	FS	In Mn
Rider's End	Ridix	0.34N 0.21W	Cent	4.24	FS	Ag
Rivala Two	Rivala	1.36N 4.21E	Deltan	0.0001	Col	Ag
Riviera	Ochs	2.22N 1.79E	Mixed	0.01	AS	En
Rover Prime	Sigma Barana	5.27N 1.33E	Mixed	1.22	AS	Ag In
Roxan	Ampolis	0.44N 0.45E	Mixed	2.52	AS	In Nv
R'Riss	Zeta Kiladen	0.98N 0.35E	NHum	3.75	PDir	X

FEDERATION PLANETARY SYSTEM – INHABITED WORLDS (Continued)

World Name	System Name	Location	Race	Pop	Status	Profile
Sadora	Sadora Rex	3.12N 3.19E	Deltan	6.22	FS	Cl In
Salazaar	Karnor	3.77S 3.31E	Mixed	15.75	FS	In Sh Sc Tr
San Sorella	Alpha Marak 272	6.02N 3.49E	Mixed	5.27	FS	In Mn
Scandha'	Zeta Perseus	0.34N 3.12E	Human	2.01	AS	Mn
Second Chance	Proxima Canaris	0.43S 2.71E	Human	0.58	AS	Ag Tr
Sigma Draconis	Sigma Beta 443	2.02N 5.22E	Vulcan	2.25	FS	Cl In Nv
Silicasca	Silicasa	3.78N 2.08W	Vulcan	3.65	FS	Cl
Silivis	Silivar	6.01N 0.32W	Vulcan	3.59	FS	In Nv
Sinbad IV	Scheherazad	5.60S 0.20E	Human	1.38	FS	Tr
Sind	Sindarius	0.16N 0.55E	Deltan	2.25	FS	Tr
Singularity II	Singularity	0.32N 3.55E	Cent	3.58	FS	In Tr
Sirius	Alpha Canus Majoris	0.97N 5.39E	Cent	4.67	FS	Cl In Tr
Socrata	Rho Drunir	1.77N 3.51W	Mixed	2.42	FS	Mn
Sojourn	Servitrix	2.19N 2.57E	Vulcan	0.002	Col	In
Spica	Juris Canopus	0.35N 0.12E	Mixed	0.0001	Col	Mn
Springboard	Alpha Canaris	0.47S 5.22W	Cent	1.48	FS	Nv Tr
S'Sleen	Beta Virgilis	0.35S 2.08E	NHum	1.00	PDir	X
S'Sliss	Beta Virgilis	0.35S 2.08E	NHum	1.00	PDir	X
St Cyr	Wolf 672	1.25N 3.03E	Human	0.0001	Col	Ag
Surak I	Filtra	2.32N 1.71E	Vulcan	3.75	FS	Cl In Sc
Surak II	Filtra	2.32N 1.71E	Vulcan	3.11	FS	Cl In Sc
Succour	Zeta Maximus	2.46N 4.38W	Human	0.0001	Col	Cl
Sustenance	Sestarci 124	0.07N 0.34E	Cent	1.99	FS	Ag
Sympathy	Hydra Geminorum	5.21S 0.22W	Human	0.0001	Col	Cl
Synchrinity	Gamma Trixis	2.49N 0.32E	Human	0.0001	Col	Ag
Talos IV	Talos	7.49S 1.48E	NHum	0.01	Quar	X
Tamarind	Tamaros	3.99N 3.27E	Human	0.0001	Col	Ag Mn
Tamerlane	Tamaros	3.99N 3.27E	Human	0.0001	Col	Ag
Tanalorne	Alpha Vegetis	0.56N 2.94E	Mixed	0.15	Col	Ag Sc
Tantalus V	Tantalus	2.77N 4.04E	Mixed	0.0001	Quar	X
Tarry Awhile	Carmara 712	4.24N 2.02E	Human	0.0021	AS	Ag Tr
Tarletus II	Tarletus	2.19N 4.44E	Cent	2.17	FS	Tr
Tarsus	Tarsis	3.89N 3.11E	Mixed	2.23	FS	Ag
Taryton	Wolf 698	0.32N 4.21E	Tellar	3.56	FS	Mn Tr
Telcos	Telcosus	2.57N 0.29W	Andor	10.46	FS	Ag Mn
Tellamarkus	61 Cygni	1.49N 1.91W	Tellar	12.45	FS	Cl In Tr
Tellar	61 Cygni	1.49N 1.91W	Tellar	15.75	FS	Cl In Sc Tr
Temelicus	Molinus	0.44S 3.26W	Cent	4.11	FS	Cl Sc
Termala	Molinus	0.44S 3.26W	Cent	2.67	FS	Cl In Sc
Terra	Sol	1.23N 2.79W	Human	25.00	FS	Cl In Sh Sc
Terra Four	Barnard 183	2.18N 0.24E	Human	13.56	FS	Cl In Sc
Terra Five	Eta Seratorn	0.26S 2.17W	Human	5.58	FS	Cl In
Testament	Sigma Cygni 57	5.81N 0.31E	Mixed	4.25	FS	Mn Tr
Th'allt	Thalak	5.02N 0.65E	Andor	1.99	AS	Mn Tr
Thasus IV	Thasus	6.02S 5.07E	NHum	Unknwn	Quar	X
Thesalla	Tharsis	5.26N 3.46W	Andor	3.16	FS	Cl Mn
Theta VII	Theta Gamma	2.09N 3.05E	Mixed	0.30	FS	Ag Mn
Thoris	Equess	0.72N 5.68E	Human	0.0001	Col	Ag
Thranstor IV	Thranstor	4.97S 2.23W	Mixed	4.26	FS	Cl In Tr
Thraxis	Thrax	0.54N 6.03W	NHum	0.12	AS	Cl
Tiburon	Beta Theseus	6.02N 5.79E	Human	15.00	FS	Cl In Tr
Time Planet	Alpha Zeta	4.05N 6.68E	NHum	Unknwn	Quar	X
Timidity	Molinus	0.44S 3.26W	Human	0.0001	Col	Ag
Titan	Sol	1.23N 2.79W	Human	0.11	FS	Sh
Triacus	Alpha Lyrae	2.66N 2.48W	Human	0.16	AS	Ag

FEDERATION PLANETARY SYSTEM – INHABITED WORLDS (Continued)

World Name	System Name	Location	Race	Pop	Status	Profile
T'Rillan	T'Rill	3.26S 4.05E	Vulcan	12.20	FS	Ag
Trimarka	Draco Minora	2.67S 0.94E	Vulcan	2.47	FS	Cl Sc
Trinity	Boristar	2.55S 0.36E	Mixed	0.0001	Col	Ag Mn
Triskelion	M24 Alpha	0.75N 0.19E	Mixed	0.01	PDir	X
Triton	Draco Ursula	1.01S 0.22W	Tellar	2.59	FS	Cl Mn
Trixex	Beta Corvela	1.71N 5.02E	Mixed	3.71	FS	Cl
Troyius	Tellun	8.58S 4.98E	Human	3.58	AS	Cl
Twilight Base	Draco Omega 371	4.02S 2.22W	Human	1.01	Indep	X
Typerias	Gamma Persei	4.38S 4.01E	Vulcan	7.50	FS	Cl Sc
Tyrst	Barnard 392	0.24N 5.55W	Mixed	0.0001	Col	Ag Cl
Unity	F'rhircch	0.36S 5.20E	Human	4.89	FS	Ag Cl In
Ursula	Beta Norab	4.02N 0.76E	Vulcan	3.75	FS	Ag Sc
Vandalia IV	Vandalia	0.13N 3.29E	Mixed	10.37	FS	Cl In Tr
Vandalora	Vandalia	0.13N 3.29E	Mixed	11.47	FS	Cl In Tr
Vargus	Theta Majoris	0.98S 0.75E	Tellar	2.75	FS	Cl Mn
Vega	Alpha Lyrae	2.66N 2.48W	Human	5.76	FS	Cl En Tr
Vendikar	Eminiar	2.15S 5.77E	Human	14.82	AS	Cl
Venus	Sol	1.23N 2.79W	Human	2.57	FS	Ag
Videtu	Videtti	7.61S 2.39E	Deltan	11.47	FS	Ag Tr
Virtue	M67 Alpha	6.02N 2.02W	Mixed	0.0003	Col	Cl
Vistil Major	Vistil	5.04N 2.67W	Vulcan	1.01	FS	Cl Sc Tr
Voltaire	Vandalia	0.48N 3.29E	Mixed	2.08	FS	Cl
Vulcan	40 Eridani	0.09N 2.31W	Vulcan	12.50	FS	Cl In Sc Sh
Wall	Bahr	8.92S 5.31E	Human	1.25	AS	Mn
Wanderlust	Sigma Borella	0.98N 3.13E	Mixed	0.0001	Col	Cl
William's Pit	Pasara Majoris	1.04N 4.22E	Human	0.0001	Col	Ag
Wrigley's Plt	Sol	1.23N 2.79W	Mixed	0.0010	AS	En
Xerxes	Golumbin 699	2.29N 5.38W	Mixed	0.0012	Col	Mn
Zacarious	Golumbin 699	2.29N 5.38W	Human	0.0001	Col	Ag
Zarus	Zarus Thustra	2.38N 2.17E	Human	1.84	FS	Ag In
Zeon	M43 Alpha	2.02S 6.95E	Human	3.59	PDir	Cl In Sc Tr
Zorn I	Theta Rill	2.09S 5.26W	Human	3.01	FS	Ag Cl
Zorn II	Theta Rill	2.09S 5.26W	Human	2.44	FS	Ag Cl

Star Base	Location
Star Base 1	1.23N 2.79W
Star Base 3	0.51N 3.50E
Star Base 4	1.23N 0.98W
Star Base 5	2.74N 1.23W
Star Base 6	3.23N 2.54W
Star Base 7	2.74N 4.26W
Star Base 8	1.23N 4.98W
Star Base 9	0.51N 4.53W
Star Base 10	8.55S 5.60E
Star Base 11	0.93S 3.18W
Star Base 12	8.34S 3.00E
Star Base 13	0.42S 1.46W
Star Base 14	3.74S 0.02W
Star Base 15	3.77S 3.31E
Star Base 16	5.70N 2.00W
Star Base 17	2.61S 7.89E
Star Base 18	0.22S 7.76E
Star Base 19	5.00N 3.00E
Star Base 20	5.45S 6.46E
Star Base 21	2.32S 5.93W
Star Base 22	5.56S 4.53W
Star Base 23	6.49S 2.50W
Star Base 24	3.00N 6.00W
Star Base 27	8.03S 0.42W

STARSHIP CONSTRUCTION FACILITIES

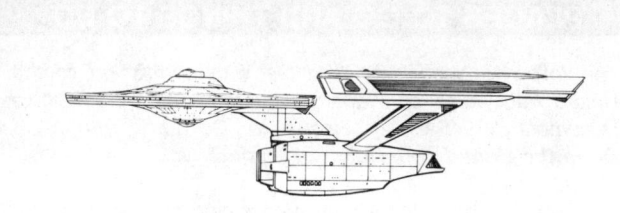

Within the Federation, there are currently 16 major civilian and military shipyards, accounting for over 95 percent of all starships constructed annually. At present, these yards produce a total of over 4,500 warp-driven vessels each year. The following is a breakdown of average starship construction by vessel type and location.

AVERAGE ANNUAL PRODUCTION RATES OF MILITARY AND COMMERCIAL VESSELS

Planetary System	AS	BB	CR	CT	CV	DD	ES	FR	MN	SC	FR	TN	TR	WP	COM
Alpha Centauri	–	–	–	13	–	–	–	–	2	–	–	–	–	40	236
Andor	–	–	14	–	–	–	8	–	–	–	–	–	–	47	122
Arcanis	–	–	–	–	–	–	–	–	–	–	–	–	–	–	275
Cait	–	–	4	–	–	–	30	–	–	–	18	–	7	47	18
Lasur	–	–	–	–	–	–	–	–	–	–	–	–	–	–	124
Lixis	–	–	–	–	–	–	–	–	–	–	–	–	–	–	98
Lochlar	–	–	–	–	–	–	–	–	–	–	–	–	–	–	76
Merak	–	–	–	6	–	–	–	15	–	–	–	4	–	47	4
Morena	–	–	4	6	90	8	24	8	–	4	8	–	6	40	16
Mursa	–	–	–	–	–	–	–	–	–	–	–	–	–	–	48
New Aberdeen	–	–	–	–	–	–	–	–	–	–	–	–	–	–	240
Pallatrine	–	–	–	–	–	–	–	–	–	–	–	–	–	–	110
Proxima Centauri	–	–	–	–	–	–	–	–	–	4	10	–	–	–	–
Salazaar	7	–	34	19	90	63	–	9	–	4	–	2	7	47	222
Sol II (Venus)	12	–	14	–	–	–	8	–	–	–	–	–	–	95	–
Sol III (Terra)	–	1	2	–	–	–	–	–	–	–	–	2	–	40	750
Sol IV (Mars)	–	1	6	–	–	13	28	–	–	4	–	–	–	–	28
Sol V (Europa)	–	–	–	–	–	–	–	–	–	4	–	–	6	40	–
Sol VI (Titan)	–	–	–	–	–	–	40	–	–	–	–	–	13	47	–
Tellar	7	–	–	–	–	–	–	–	–	–	18	–	7	47	525
Vulcan	–	–	–	–	–	–	–	–	–	–	–	–	–	20	400
Wall	–	–	–	–	–	–	–	–	–	–	–	–	–	–	184
Annual Totals:	26	2	78	44	180	84	130	40	2	20	54	8	46	557	3476

Grand Total: 4747

Abbreviations
- **AS:** Assault Ships
- **BB:** *Excelsior* Class Battleships (projected construction levels)
- **CR:** Cruisers
- **CT:** Cutters
- **CV:** Corvettes
- **DD:** Destroyers
- **ES:** Escort Ships
- **FR:** Frigates
- **MN:** Monitors (sub-light craft)
- **SC:** Scouts
- **FR:** Cargo Carriers (all types used by Star Fleet)
- **TN:** Tenders
- **TR:** Personnel transports (all types used by Star Fleet)
- **WP:** Warp Shuttles and Courier ships
- **COM:** Civilian and commercial vessels

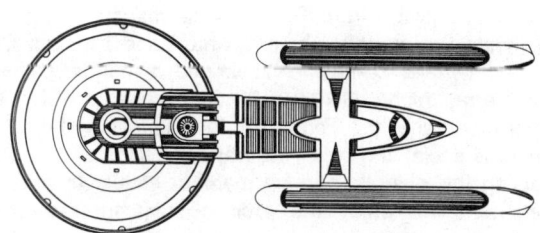

PLACES TO GO AND THINGS TO DO

The following section is reprinted with permission of the United Federation of Planet's Government Printing Office Document 37945AJ-32, **Places to Go and Things to Do in the United Federation of Planets.**

If nothing else, the United Federation of Planets is an exciting place in which to live. Its hundreds of inhabited worlds and dozens of major tourist and amusement centers offer visitors myriad exciting possibilities. The Federation boasts enough sights and delights, be they natural or manufactured, real or imaginary, to satisfy any special interest or particular desire. Indeed, anyone can find what they are looking for in the UFP, as long as they do not mind the travel time! The followng is only a brief list of some of the more popular attractions the Federation has to offer.

QUADRANT ONE

Quadrant One encompasses the original boundaries of the Federation as established in 0/8706, containing the five original member civilizations of the UFP: Alpha Centauri, Andor, Tellar, Terra, and Vulcan. This region is one of the richest tourist and recreational centers of the Federation. An estimated seven billion Humanoid and non-Humanoid visitors vacation in this part of the Federation every year.

Small wonder! Beginning with Terra, there is a wide variety of sights and entertainments available. Terra remains one of the most alluring worlds in the entire Federation. Much of the beauty and old-world style that was the hallmark of Terran civilization before the Eugenics War has been completely restored. Aside from its landscapes, Terra boasts Star Fleet Command headquarters in San Francisco, and in Terran orbit are the largest civilian and Star Fleet starship construction centers in the entire UFP. Though security measures prohibit the general public from viewing much of the work conducted by Star Fleet, the *USS Republic*, a decommissioned *Constitution* Class starship, is open to tourists near the New Xanith Orbital Recreation Center. Also in the Sol system is Wrigley's Pleasure Planet, an entire planet devoted to delighting young and old for a modest price.

Moving outward from Terra, the nearest star system, Al Rijil, hosts the planets Alpha Centauri and Proxima Centauri, both major centers of advanced humanoid cultures. After Terra, Alpha Centauri is the largest cultural and scientific center in the Federation, and tourists will discover numerous social and cross-cultural exhibitions and displays reflecting the planet's primary member status. In addition, sports fans will enjoy the exciting sunjammer solar-sail races held between these two worlds each year. Students of history will be inspired by the Cochrane Memorial and the Federation Historical Institute on Alpha Centauri and the Federation Peace Studies Institute on Proxima Centauri. In addition, both worlds are well-known for their huge expanses of unspoiled wilderness, areas rivalling even the famed Benecian outback.

Sports lovers will enjoy the year-round skiing on Andor, which offers some of the best slopes in the quadrant. For those seeking the strange and unusual, visit Alpha Majoris, home of the Melitus cloud creature, or stop at Avalon, which presents visitors with a spectacle of knights in armor and fair damsels in the capitol city of Camelot. For those seeking entertainment on a grander scale, the planet Imagination has hundreds of special theme parks and picturesque preserves recreating dozens of specialized cultures and time frames from across the galaxy.

Lovers of fine wine will want to stop off at Edo, home of some of the galaxy's most prestigious wines and liqueurs. After stocking up there, one can visit the central courts of the Federation judiciary on Alpha III, which also maintains several major firms that practice interstellar law.

QUADRANT TWO

Though not as populated as its neighbors, this particular Federation quadrant has much to offer the dedicated sightseer. For instance, Altair is famous for the medicinal properties of its native waters. Millions flock to this warm and sunny planet each year to 'take the cure' for whatever ails them. For the bargain hunter, the planet Anchor offers the finest in local pottery and glasswear, while Antares is a trader's delight. With no port-of-call restrictions, literally anything can be found in the thousands of bazaars making up Antarian society. For those interested in the finer things, Ardana's capital city in the clouds possesses some of the finest art and literature found anywhere in the Federation. Those interested in science will marvel at the cybernetic and computer-oriented technologies displayed on Cygnet XIV. Gamblers should enjoy pausing in Castor Fields to play the planet's magnificent horse races, which are conducted with due pomp and ceremony. Investors may want to pause on Demoiselle II, whose craftswomen are renowned for their excellent gems and precious stones. Make it a point to tarry for a moment on Eternity, the poignant and beautiful resting place of those who have died in defense of the Federation. One can also stroll along the wide, sandy beaches on tropical Cait, home of the Federation's only intelligent feline race.

QUADRANT THREE

Seekers of the exotic will not want to miss a chance to visit Aldebaran, famous for its amazing variety of plant life, rare wines, and other delicacies. Ingraham B likewise boasts some of the finest floral species in the known universe, many of which are for sale and are sure to appreciate rapidly in value. For those looking for a change from our modern technological age, step onto Arcturus and into Terra's past, where each day is the 16th century. Similarly, the planet Cyclopus presents visitors with the grandeur of Terra's ancient Rome in the modern age. History buffs will enjoy a visit to the Star Fleet Museum on Memory Alpha. Capella will test a hunter's mettle with its famous power cats, among the most elusive and intelligent of all carnivorous prey. Romantics will want to take their loved ones on a visit to Laura's World at least once in their lifetime. Simple and undisturbed, this entire planet is devoted to lovers. If sandy white beaches are desired, stop by Lakeland. The fashion-conscious will be enraptured with Daran V's fine textiles and silks.

QUADRANT FOUR

Seafood lovers will fall in love with Alpha Proxima II, home of one of the Federation's largest sea-farming concerns and suppliers of rare culinary extravaganzas. In the eyes of many, Deneva is second only to Terra and Alpha Centauri as a cultural capitol. A visit to this warm and friendly planet will be well worth the time spent, considering its vast array of classical and modern arts and entertainments. Make it a point to see the planet Aplithin, home of the Federation's intelligent avians. One tour of this world's lofty eyries and majestic mountain cities will make anyone want to return again and again.

CREATURES OF INTEREST

In addition to various places of interest, the Federation claims numerous creatures that should intrigue the average tourist. The Vulcan Science Academy, Department of Exobiology and Planetary Zoology, lists a total of 735,452 identifiably unique classifications of life-forms currently existing within the confines of Federation space. In addition, estimates predict a greater variety of living organisms existing on uncharted worlds within the Federation. Various Federation worlds attract tourists curious about the intelligent and semi-intelligent creatures abiding there. Following is a selection of the noteworthy alien creatures to be found on planets in Federation space.

ALIEN CREATURE RECORD: CAPELLAN POWER CAT

Life Form: Mammal
  Size: Large
  Feeding Habits: Carnivore
Average Attributes:
  STR — 75
  END — 72
  DEX — 48
  MENT — 9
Tactical Movement and Combat Statistics:
  AP: 9
  Combat Skill Rating: 88
  Damage: 2D10+9
  Armor: 7

General Description:

The Capellan power cat is a large, tawny-colored carnivore found in the northern deserts of the planet Capella. Noted for its viciousness, especially during its early summer mating season, the power cat has the unique ability to store electromagnetic energy from natural and artificial sources of energy. This animal's defensive reflexes cause an electrical discharge of considerable strength upon contact (2D10 points of damage). Aggressive and extremely protective of its young, the power cat is not afraid of Humanoids, though it will attack only if provoked.

ALIEN CREATURE RECORD: DENEBIAN SLIME DEVIL

- **Life Form:** Amphibian
- **Size:** Large
- **Feeding Habits:** Carnivorous
- **Average Attributes:**
  - STR — 68
  - END — 58
  - DEX — 68
  - MENT — 6
- **Tactical Movement and Combat Statistics:**
  - AP: 14/10
  - Combat Skill Rating: 75
  - Damage: 2D10+4
  - Armor: 5

General Description:

The Denebian slime devil is a particularly loathsome creature that inhabits the numerous swamps and freshwater lakes of Deneb. Like most Denebian life forms, it is carnivorous, requiring large amounts of protein in its daily diet. Measuring between five and six meters in length, the amphibian slime devil is amazingly agile on dry land as well as in water (14 AP on land and 10 AP in water). It attacks anything within ten meters, constricting its prey with its multiple, sucker-lined tentacles. Nocturnal by nature, the slime devil prefers to rest on the muddy bottoms of swamps, rivers, and ponds until nightfall.

ALIEN CREATURE RECORD: DRACONIAN AIR DRAGON

- **Life Form:** Avian
- **Size:** Large
- **Feeding Habits:** Omnivorous
- **Average Attributes:**
  - STR — 75
  - END — 62
  - DEX — 58
  - MENT — 7
- **Tactical Movement and Combat Statistics:**
  - AP: 13
  - Combat Skill Rating: 60
  - Damage: 2D10+4
  - Armor: 6

General Description:

A native of the planet Sigma Draconis, the Draconian air dragon is the largest of the planet's many avian species. A nocturnal hunter, the creature inhabits the mountain ranges of the planet's southern hemisphere. Though avian in its use of multiple pairs of wings to fly, the air dragon is also covered with tough scales, which lend the beast its name. Though not aggressive toward Humanoid life forms, this animal is not above attacking Humanoid settlements when it experiences acute food shortages. Some Vulcans claim to have used their psionic abilities to domesticate these wild creatures, though no air dragon has ever survived for long in captivity.

ALIEN CREATURE RECORD: HORTA

- **Life Form:** Mammal
- **Size:** Large
- **Feeding Habits:** Special
- **Average Attributes:**
  - STR — 100
  - END — 100
  - DEX — 50
  - MENT — 9
- **Tactical Movement and Combat Statistics:**
  - AP: 8
  - Combat Skill Rating: 50
  - Damage: Special
  - Armor: 10

General Description:

The horta is a native of Janus IV, a Federation mining colony that produces pergium. This silicon-based life form lives in the interior of the planet and can move through solid rock by excreting a highly corrosive acid. It derives its sustenance by digesting the mineral content of the liquified ores through which it moves. As contact with its acid excretions is highly dangerous (treat as 6D10+2 points of damage), exposure to the horta should be avoided. Despite its potential danger, the horta is a highly intelligent sentient being. It can exist in an oxygen-nitrogen atmosphere for limited periods of time. If its eggs or hatchlings are not disturbed, the horta are pacifistic and benevolent creatures.

ALIEN CREATURE RECORD: MELLITUS CLOUD CREATURE

- **Life Form:** Amorphous
- **Size:** Medium
- **Feeding Habits:** Omnivore
- **Average Attributes:**
  - STR — 35
  - END — 90
  - DEX — 84
  - MENT — 5
- **Tactical Movement and Combat Statistics:**
  - AP: 12
  - Combat Skill Rating: 62
  - Damage: 2D10+1
  - Armor: 2

General Description:

Native to the planet Alpha Majoris, this timid creature is often mistaken for the vampire cloud creature that once inhabited the planets of the Tycho system. Unlike that predatory creature, which consumes hemoglobin from its victim's blood, the Mellitus cloud creature is an omnivorous scavenger that ingests proteins from non-living organisms and some mosses and plants. It can assume different shapes, depending on its reaction to the environment. When frightened or in motion, it assumes a bluish-green gaseous form. When at rest, it is a grayish solid mass.

ALIEN CREATURE RECORD: MORENAN TREE BEAR
- **Life Form:** Mammal
- **Size:** Small
- **Feeding Habits:** Special
- **Average Attributes:**
  - STR – 30
  - END – 45
  - DEX – 48
  - MENT – 7
- **Tactical Movement and Combat Statistics:**
  - AP: 10
  - Combat Skill Rating: 12
  - Damage: 1D10
  - Armor: 2

General Description:
A timid creature resembling a furry Terran kangaroo, the Morenan tree bear inhabits the forests of Morena's southern continent. This creature does not eat, in the usual sense of the word. Instead, it subsists on energy emitted from positive emotions such as affection and love that other life forms give off. By a process still not entirely understood, the tree bear forms a symbiotic relationship with its host, returning sensations of calm and peacefulness for those sensations it receives. For this reason, Morenan tree bears are highly prized as pets.

ALIEN CREATURE RECORD: MUGATU (VARIOUS NAMES)
- **Life Form:** Mammal
- **Size:** Medium
- **Feeding Habits:** Carnivorous
- **Average Attributes:**
  - STR – 52
  - END – 55
  - DEX – 56
  - MENT – 6
- **Tactical Movement and Combat Statistics:**
  - AP: 10
  - Combat Skill Rating: 55
  - Damage: 3D10+2
  - Armor: 5

General Description:
The actual origin of the Mugatu is unknown. Distinctly similar species of this animal have been found on many planets inhabited by Humanoids. The beast is a furry anthropoid standing some two-and-a-half meters high, with a curved horn protruding from its forehead. The real threat of the Mugatu is its poisonous fangs, which inflict a debilitating paralysis on its victim, causing death in hours unless an antitoxin is administered. Scientists are presently at a loss to explain how similar species of this creature appeared on different worlds. One theory holds that the creature, like some Humanoid cultures, was transplanted by a race of beings similar to the Preservers. As yet, there is no proof to confirm or refute this speculation.

ALIEN CREATURE RECORD: SEHLAT
- **Life Form:** Mammal
- **Size:** Large
- **Feeding Habits:** Omnivorous
- **Average Attributes:**
  - STR – 70
  - END – 65
  - DEX – 58
  - MENT – 7
- **Tactical Movement and Combat Statistics:**
  - AP: 10
  - Combat Skill Rating: 55
  - Damage: 2D10+3
  - Armor: 6

General Description:
The Vulcan sehlat is a large furry mammal often described as an enormous teddy bear with fangs. In ancient days, Vulcans domesticated sehlats to serve as sentries and personal bodyguards. This animal has the ability to forge strong mental links with its owner. In these more civilized times, the sehlat has been reduced to the role of a pet. However, it is still more than capable of defending Vulcans from predators that remain in the planet's hinterlands.

ALIEN CREATURE RECORD: TRIBBLE
- **Life Form:** Mammal
- **Size:** Very Small
- **Feeding Habits:** Herbivore
- **Average Attributes:**
  - STR – 8
  - END – 7
  - DEX – 24
  - MENT – 4
- **Tactical Movement and Combat Statistics:**
  - AP: 6
  - Combat Skill Rating: 2
  - Damage: 1D10
  - Armor: None

General Description:
A life form native to the planet Jorindas, the tribble is one of the most inoffensive creatures in the galaxy. Tribbles resemble small, fur-covered puff balls, ranging in size from one to 20 centimeters wide. Though plant-eaters in their native environment, they are somewhat partial to cereals and grains. A tribble's metabolic system is geared toward reproduction, which can be accelerated to dangerously high levels when food sources are abundant. They are unique in their ability to sense Humanoid emotional states, responding negatively to displays of hostility or aggression and positively to expressions of affection. If shown affection, they produce a wide range of low-pitched vocal tones that have a soothing affect on Humanoid nervous systems. For this reason, tribbles (in small quantities) are often in demand as pets.

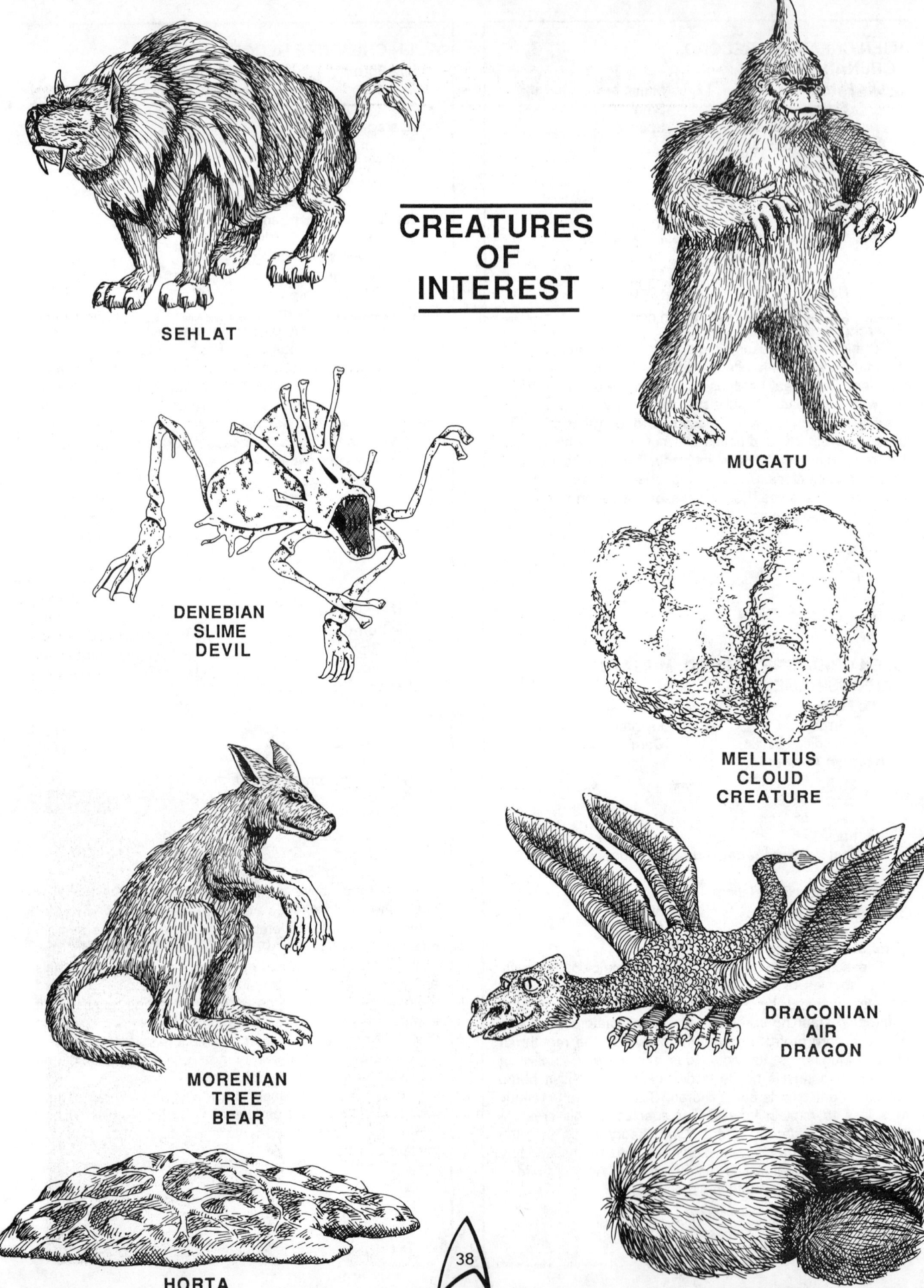

MAJOR WORLDS OF THE FEDERATION

Although this book cannot catalog every planet within Federation space, certain worlds have a special significance and should be examined in closer detail. The following section provides information on the 100 planets constituting the major cultural, economic, and political centers in the Federation. The following world logs also illustrate the wide variety of cultural and racial differences existing within the 4,000,000 square parsecs of space controlled by the United Federation of Planets.

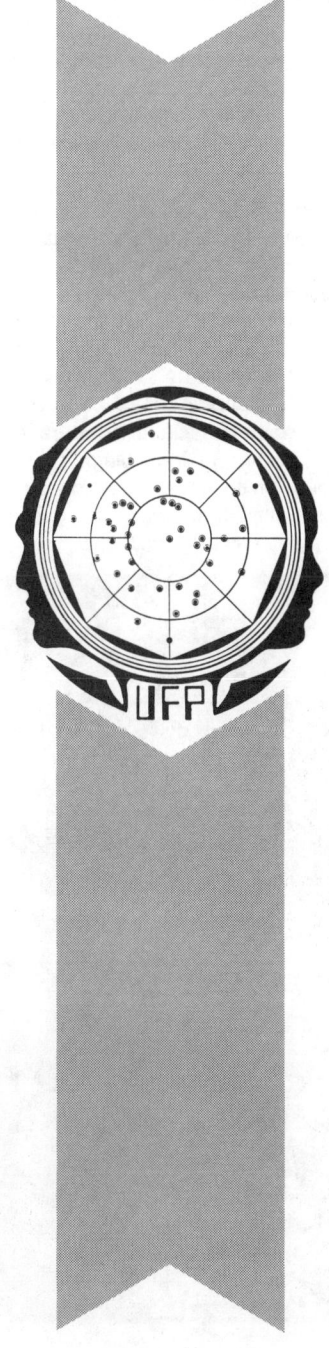

World Log: ALBIREO
System Data
    System Name: Beta Cygni
        Map Coordinates: 3.27N 1.97W
    Number Of Class M Present: 1
Planetary Data
    Position In System: II
    Number Of Satellites: 1
    Planetary Gravity: .85g
    Planetary Size
        Diameter: 17,000 km
        Equatorial Circumference: 52,000 km
        Total Surface Area: 620,000,000 sq km
        Percent Land Mass: 40%
        Total Land Area: 248,000,000 sq km
    Planetary Conditions
        Length Of Day: 25 hrs
        Atmospheric Density: Terrestrial
        General Climate: Warm Temperate
    Mineral Content
        Normal Metals: 60%
        Radioactives: 10%
        Gemstones: 10%
        Industrial Crystals: 10%
        Special Minerals: Trace
Cultural Data
    Dominant Life Form: Human
    Technological/
    Sociopolitical Index: 787455–77
    Planetary Trade Profile: CCDBECC/C (C)

Albireo is the second in a six-planet triple-star system. The Federation colony on this world was established toward the end of the last century. The high levels of solar radiation generated by the suns create a wide range of climactic conditions on Albireo.

As the weather made it almost impossible to farm, the colonists manufactured synthetic foodstuffs to support the planet's two billion people. After food productivity increased, the world began exporting their synthetic foodstuffs, which eventually became the principle economic staple of the planet.

Albireo is noted for its beautiful aurora displays at the end of each winter season, which draw tourists from all parts of the Federation.

World Log: ALDEBARAN
System Data
    System Name: Alpha Tauri
        Map Coordinates: 2.01S 2.01E
    Number Of Class M Present: 1
Planetary Data
    Position In System: III
    Number Of Satellites: 6
    Planetary Gravity: 1.2g
    Planetary Size
        Diameter: 15,500 km
        Equatorial Circumference: 49,000 km
        Total Surface Area: 575,000,000 sq km
        Percent Land Mass: 30%
        Total Land Area: 172,500,000 sq km
    Planetary Conditions
        Length Of Day: 27 hrs
        Atmospheric Density: Thin
        General Climate: Cool Temperate
    Mineral Content
        Normal Metals: 40%
        Radioactives: 10%
        Gemstones: 25%
        Industrial Crystals: 20%
        Special Minerals: Trace
Cultural Data
    Dominant Life Form: Human
    Technological/
    Sociopolitical Index: 778998–76
    Planetary Trade Profile: BCBACBC/B(B)

Aldebaran is a major Federation port and administrative and supply center. Beyond this, it is also noted for its many floral varieties and unspoiled wilderness. A very popular tourist attraction and vacation spot, Aldebaran boasts a wide variety of exotic foods and wines found nowhere else in the galaxy. After Arcturus, it is the largest center of corporate holdings outside the original boundaries of the Federation.

World Log: ALFA 177

System Data
- System Name: Alpha Honorus
- Map Coordinates: 3.51S 5.26W
- Number Of Class M Present: 1

Planetary Data
- Position In System: 2
- Number Of Satellites: 1
- Planetary Gravity: .95g

Planetary Size
- Diameter: 17,500,000 km
- Equatorial Circumference: 46,000 km
- Total Surface Area: 480,000,000 sq km
- Percent Land Mass: 90%
- Total Land Area: 432,000,000 sq km

Planetary Conditions
- Length Of Day: 37 hrs
- Atmospheric Density: Thin
- General Climate: Cold Temperate

Mineral Content
- Normal Metals: 70%
- Radioactives: 05%
- Gemstones: 05%
- Industrial Crystals: Trace
- Special Minerals: Trace

A marginal Class M planet, Alfa 177's thin atmosphere and distance from its parent sun drop temperatures below −107° C. at night. Despite this hazard, various life-forms have managed to evolve on the planet. In particular, a species of horned canine has adapted especially well to its climate. Alfa 177 is also noted for its rare mineral ores, which contain unusual magnetic properties. Such ores have an adverse effect on transporter operations, and caution should be observed when beaming to or from this planet.

World Log: ALPHA III

System Data
- System Name: Alpha Canaris
- Map Coordinates: 0.93N 1.62W
- Number Of Class M Present: 2

Planetary Data
- Position In System: 4
- Number Of Satellites: 7
- Planetary Gravity: 1.2g

Planetary Size
- Diameter: 10,200 km
- Equatorial Circumference: 36,800 km
- Total Surface Area: 370,000,000 sq km
- Percent Land Mass: 40%
- Total Land Area: 148,000,000 sq km

Planetary Conditions
- Length Of Day: 22 hrs
- Atmospheric Density: Terrestrial
- General Climate: Warm Temperate

Mineral Content
- Normal Metals: 70%
- Radioactives: 20%
- Gemstones: 05%
- Industrial Crystals: Trace
- Special Minerals: Trace

Cultural Data
- Dominant Life Form: Human
- Technological/Sociopolitical Index: 885753–88
- Planetary Trade Profile: BCBDBBC/C (B)

Colonized in Terra's 22nd century as Terra Four, Alpha III is now one of the major cultural and administrative centers of the Federation, and one of the seven members of the Federation Security Council. Alpha III is noted in Federation history as the birthplace of the famous *Statutes of Alpha III*, considered one of the most important political documents ever written. These statutes created a republic based on the ancient Terran Platonic system, and have served as a model for other political systems ever since.

World Log: ALPHA MAJORIS II

System Data
- System Name: Alpha Majoris
- Map Coordinates: 2.82N 0.97W
- Number Of Class M Present: 2

Planetary Data
- Position In System: II
- Number Of Satellites: 1
- Planetary Gravity: .7g

Planetary Size
- Diameter: 15,000 km
- Equatorial Circumference: 38,000 km
- Total Surface Area: 478,000,000 sq km
- Percent Land Mass: 40%
- Total Land Area: 191,200,000 sq km

Planetary Conditions
- Length Of Day: 25 hrs
- Atmospheric Density: Terrestrial
- General Climate: Warm Terrestrial

Mineral Content
- Normal Metals: 50%
- Radioactives: 10%
- Gemstones: 25%
- Industrial Crystals: Trace
- Special Minerals: Trace

Cultural Data
- Dominant Life Form: Human
- Technological/Sociopolitical Index: 787785–77
- Planetary Trade Profile: CDDDCDD/C(D)

One of two planets orbiting a red giant sun, Alpha Majoris II was settled by a Human colonial team shortly after the Federation was formed. It is the home of the Mellitus creature, a semi-intelligent plasma-based creature discovered in Stardate 2/15. (This peaceful creature should not be confused with the vampire-like cloud creature of the Tycho system.) Alpha Majoris II is also famous for its many rare and beautiful gems prized throughout the galaxy for their purity and elegance.

World Log: ALPHA PROXIMA II
System Data
- System Name: Dnoces
- Map Coordinates: 0.21S 2.49W
- Number Of Class M Present: 1

Planetary Data
- Position In System: II
- Number Of Satellites: 7
- Planetary Gravity: 1.1g

Planetary Size
- Diameter: 21,000 km
- Equatorial Circumference: 53,000 km
- Total Surface Area: 520,000,000 sq km
- Percent Land Mass: 60%
- Total Land Area: 312,000,000 sq km

Planetary Conditions
- Length Of Day: 27 hrs
- Atmospheric Density: Thick
- General Climate: Warm Terrestrial

Mineral Content
- Normal Metals: 40%
- Radioactives: 30%
- Gemstones: Trace
- Industrial Crystals: Trace
- Special Minerals: Trace

Cultural Data
- Dominant Life Form: Human
- Technological/Sociopolitical Index: 8887886–97
- Planetary Trade Profile: BBAABCC/B(B)

World Log: ALPHA CENTAURI
System Data
- System Name: Al Rijil
- Map Coordinates: 1.27N 2.92W
- Number Of Class M Present: 3

Planetary Data
- Position In System: VII
- Number Of Satellites: 2
- Planetary Gravity: .86g

Planetary Size
- Diameter: 18,000 km
- Equatorial Circumference: 22,000 km
- Total Surface Area: 425,000,000 sq km
- Percent Land Mass: 30%
- Total Land Area: 127,500,000 sq km

Planetary Conditions
- Length Of Day: 25 hrs
- Atmospheric Density: Terrestrial
- General Climate: Tropical

Mineral Content
- Normal Metals: 60%
- Radioactives: 10%
- Gemstones: 10%
- Industrial Crystals: 10%
- Special Minerals: Trace

Cultural Data
- Dominant Life Form: Alpha Centauri
- Technological/Sociopolitical Index: 999998–98
- Planetary Trade Profile: AABAABB/A(B)

World Log: ALTAIR
System Data
- System Name: Alpha Aquilae
- Map Coordinates: 3.02N 0.99E
- Number Of Class M Present: 2

Planetary Data
- Position In System: VI
- Number Of Satellites: 2
- Planetary Gravity: 1.5g

Planetary Size
- Diameter: 20,500 km
- Equatorial Circumference: 24,000 km
- Total Surface Area: 520,000,000 sq km
- Percent Land Mass: 60%
- Total Land Area: 312,000,000 sq km

Planetary Conditions
- Length Of Day: 22 hrs
- Atmospheric Density: Terrestrial
- General Climate: Terrestrial

Mineral Content
- Normal Metals: 65%
- Radioactives: 15%
- Gemstones: 05%
- Industrial Crystals: Trace
- Special Minerals: Trace

Cultural Data
- Dominant Life Form: Human
- Technological/Sociopolitical Index: 677857–77
- Planetary Trade Profile: BCCBDBC/B(C)

Alpha Proxima was one of the first Human out-system colonies. Major local industries include radioactives mining and widespread agriculture. Alpha Proxima also claims one of the largest sea-farming concerns in the Federation. Over 180,000 square kilometers are used for off-shore foodstuffs production.

Al Rijil is a triple-star system that supports life on its fourth, fifth, and seventh planets. The first two are colonies of Alpha Centauri proper. The considerable similarities between Humans and Alpha Centaurans have led some exobiologists to suggest that the latter may be Humans transplanted from Terra around the third century B.C., although this has never been proven. Alpha Centauri was the home of Zephram Cochrane, the inventor of the warp drive. Currently, it ranks as one of the major cultural and scientific centers in the Federation, second only to Terra. One of the five founding members of the Federation, Alpha Centauri also has permanent representation on the Federation Council. This lush tropical world presently supports a population of 20 billion inhabitants.

Humans currently inhabit two Class M planets in the Alpha Aquilae system. Relics on Altair show the existence of an ancient civilization that pre-dates Human occupation of the planet. Some believe these ruins may belong to the Preservers' culture, while others suggest a connection to the Vegan Tyranny. Current archeological evidence is inconclusive. Altair is also known for the medicinal properties of its mineral-rich waters. Millions of Federation citizens come to Altair each year to 'take the waters', which has created a lucrative tourist trade.

Altair's colony world, Alpha Aquilae IV, recently declared itself independent, sparking a brief but inconclusive interplanetary conflict that was terminated by Federation peace-keeping forces. The government on Altair currently governs both worlds while a Federation diplomatic team attempts to negotiate a resolution to the political crisis.

World Log: AMBER
System Data
- System Name: Beta Rigalia
- Map Coordinates: 6.05N 0.27E
- Number Of Class M Present: 1

Planetary Data
- Position In System: V
- Number Of Satellites: 3
- Planetary Gravity: 0.78g

Planetary Size
- Diameter: 12,500 km
- Equatorial Circumference: 22,250 km
- Total Surface Area: 275,000,000 sq km
- Percent Land Mass: 44%
- Total Land Area: 121,000,000 sq km

Planetary Conditions
- Length Of Day: 21 hrs
- Atmospheric Density: Thin
- General Climate: Cool Temperate

Mineral Content
- Normal Metals: 40%
- Radioactives: Trace
- Gemstones: Trace
- Industrial Crystals: Trace
- Special Minerals: Trace

Cultural Data
- Dominant Life Form: Alpha Centauri
- Technological/Sociopolitical Index: 676666–66
- Planetary Trade Profile: CCDDCDE/C(C)

World Log: AMERIND
System Data
- System Name: Epsilon Beta
- Map Coordinates: 5.78N 4.52E
- Number Of Class M Present: 1

Planetary Data
- Position In System: 2
- Number Of Satellites: 0
- Planetary Gravity: 1.05g

Planetary Size
- Diameter: 14,250 km
- Equatorial Circumference: 18,750 km
- Total Surface Area: 285,000,000 sq km
- Percent Land Mass: 50%
- Total Land Area: 142,500,000 sq km

Planetary Conditions
- Length Of Day: 25 hrs
- Atmospheric Density: Terrestrial
- General Climate: Warm Temperate

Mineral Content
- Normal Metals: 40%
- Radioactives: Trace
- Gemstones: 15%
- Industrial Crystals: Trace
- Special Minerals: Trace

Cultural Data
- Dominant Life Form: Amerind
- Technological/Sociopolitical Index: 343342–43
- Planetary Trade Profile: None

World Log: ANCHOR
System Data
- System Name: Beta Hydra 378
- Map Coordinates: 5.90N 3.27E
- Number Of Class M Present: 1

Planetary Data
- Position In System: II
- Number Of Satellites: 1
- Planetary Gravity: 0.97g

Planetary Size
- Diameter: 8,900 km
- Equatorial Circumference: 12,200 km
- Total Surface Area: 279,000,000 sq km
- Percent Land Mass: 55%
- Total Land Area: 153,450,000 sq km

Planetary Conditions
- Length Of Day: 23 hours
- Atmospheric Density: Thick
- General Climate: Warm Temperate

Mineral Content
- Normal Metals: 44%
- Radioactives: 10%
- Gemstones: Trace
- Industrial Crystals: Trace
- Special Minerals: Trace

Cultural Data
- Dominant Life Form: Tellarite
- Technological/Sociopolitical Index: 776566–74
- Planetary Trade Profile: CCDCECC/B(C)

This pleasant world was named for the distinctive color of its sunsets, due to its cooler, Type K sun. Amber is important as a major supplier of hybrid grains to many portions of the Federation. Though not extensively mined, the planet has many easily accessible copper deposits, making it a valuable trading center. Amberites permit offworlders to mine copper in exchange for offworld goods and services. A Star Fleet cadet training center is also located here.

A Federation protectorate under the Prime Directive, the Amerind culture appears to have been planted here several thousand years ago by the mysterious Preservers. The presence of a modern, automated deflector system on the planet as well as the near-perfect similarity between the Amerinds and ancient Terra's North American Indians support this fact. When last contacted, the Amerinds were in an early tribal stage, peaceful and prosperous, though not overly developed culturally. The Federation is planning to send a cultural observation team to the planet in the near future.

Envisioned as a major mining/supply point between Federation worlds and colonial settlements, Anchor has been passed by as the Federation turns its attention to more strategic regions of space. Anchorites subsist in a modest feudal system, although several southern cities continue to trade locally produced glass and pottery with other systems. Within the last decade, Star Fleet has built a repair facility in orbit around the planet, and many trust that the influx of Star Fleet personnel will revive the planet's industy.

World Log: ANDOR
- **System Data**
  - System Name: Epsilon Indi
  - Map Coordinates: 1.82N 2.22W
  - Number Of Class M Present: 2
- **Planetary Data**
  - Position In System: VIII
  - Number Of Satellites: 3
  - Planetary Gravity: 1.2g
  - **Planetary Size**
    - Diameter: 18,000 km
    - Equatorial Circumference: 24,000 km
    - Total Surface Area: 470,000,000 sq km
    - Percent Land Mass: 80%
    - Total Land Area: 316,000,000 sq km
  - **Planetary Conditions**
    - Length Of Day: 21 hrs
    - Atmospheric Density: Thin
    - General Climate: Cold
  - **Mineral Content**
    - Normal Metals: 40%
    - Radioactives: 20%
    - Gemstones: 10%
    - Industrial Crystals: Trace
    - Special Minerals: Trace
- **Cultural Data**
  - Dominant Life Form: Andorian
  - Technological/Sociopolitical Index: 999997–88
  - Planetary Trade Profile: AFGEABE/D(C)

World Log: ANTARES
- **System Data**
  - System Name: Alpha Scorpii
  - Map Coordinates: 2.02N 1.79E
  - Number Of Class M Present: 1
- **Planetary Data**
  - Position In System: 2
  - Number Of Satellites: 3
  - Planetary Gravity: 1.1g
  - **Planetary Size**
    - Diameter: 10,200 km
    - Equatorial Circumference: 17,500 km
    - Total Surface Area: 305,000,000 sq km
    - Percent Land Mass: 50%
    - Total Land Area: 152,500,000 sq km
  - **Planetary Conditions**
    - Length Of Day: 25 hrs
    - Atmospheric Density: Terrestrial
    - General Climate: Warm Temperate
  - **Mineral Content**
    - Normal Metals: 30%
    - Radioactives: 10%
    - Gemstones: 30%
    - Industrial Crystals: Trace
    - Special Minerals: Trace
- **Cultural Data**
  - Dominant Life Form: Human
  - Technological/Sociopolitical Index: 888887–77
  - Planetary Trade Profile: AABBAAB/A(B)

World Log: ANTOS
- **System Data**
  - System Name: Socratii
  - Map Coordinates: 2.99S 4.12E
  - Number Of Class M Present: 1
- **Planetary Data**
  - Position In System: 7
  - Number Of Satellites: 5
  - Planetary Gravity: 0.9g
  - **Planetary Size**
    - Diameter: 8,750 km
    - Equatorial Circumference: 14,500 km
    - Total Surface Area: 280,200,000 sq km
    - Percent Land Mass: 30%
    - Total Land Area: 84,060,000 sq km
  - **Planetary Conditions**
    - Length Of Day: 18 hrs
    - Atmospheric Density: Terrestrial
    - General Climate: Warm Temperate
  - **Mineral Content**
    - Normal Metals: 60%
    - Radioactives: Trace
    - Gemstones: 20%
    - Industrial Crystals: Trace
    - Special Minerals: Trace
- **Cultural Data**
  - Dominant Life Form: Antosian
  - Technological/Sociopolitical Index: 667685–67
  - Planetary Trade Profile: None

The home of a race of blue-skinned Humanoids, Andor was one of the founding members of the Federation. Andorians are quickly distinguished by their natural skin coloring and their antennae, which act as an additional sense organ. They are known for their aggressiveness, though this tendency is often over-exaggerated. Andor currently has a population of over 20 million inhabitants. As one of the most advanced races in the Federation, Andorians maintain a permanent seat on the Federation Council.

The largest interstellar trade center outside the Rigel system, Antares is the commercial and financial capital of the Federation. This is due in large part to Antares' central location and to the cultural predominance of Antaren business scientists. Many say that if a commodity exists anywhere in the galaxy, one can find it on Antares. With the exception of slave trade, Antares has no port-of-call restrictions regarding the nature of goods imported to the planet.

A humanoid race discovered shortly before the Romulan War, the Antosians are a peaceful race with no interest in affairs outside their own world. Having declined formal membership in the Federation, they nevertheless retain peaceful relations with their interstellar neighbors. Native Antosians have learned cellular metamorphosis, allowing them to alter their physical appearance while maintaining their general shape and mass. This has been a well-kept secret among the Antosians for centuries. They have shared this knowledge only with Captain Kelvar Garth of Izar, in an effort to save his life after a deep-space accident left him horribly burned and disfigured.

World Log: APLITHIN

System Data
- System Name: Arcanis Majoris
- Map Coordinates: 7.16S 2.40W
- Number Of Class M Present: None

Planetary Data
- Position In System: 4
- Number Of Satellites: 2
- Planetary Gravity: .70g

Planetary Size
- Diameter: 8,245 km
- Equatorial Circumference: 13,470 sq km
- Total Surface Area: 285,000,000 sq km
- Percent Land Mass: 40%
- Total Land Area: 114,000,000 sq km

Planetary Conditions
- Length Of Day: 17 hrs
- Atmospheric Density: Terrestrial
- General Climate: Cool Temperate

Mineral Content
- Normal Metals: 30%
- Radioactives: Trace
- Gemstones: Trace
- Industrial Crystals: Trace
- Special Minerals: Trace

Cultural Data
- Dominant Life Form: Arcanian
- Technological/Sociopolitical Index: 776783–66
- Planetary Trade Profile: BBDCDCC/C(C)

Lying near the Organian Neutral Zone, Aplithin is one of the more distant members of the Federation. This class K planet is noteworthy as the home of an intelligent species of avians, bipedal creatures standing about two-and-a-half meters tall with a feathery wingspan of over five meters. The world's low gravity and tenuous atmosphere give the inhabitants the power of controlled flight. Not surprisingly, Aplithinian cultural centers are located in the mountain ranges of the northern hemisphere. Since their contact with the Federation over a century ago, Aplithin has become a full UFP member and supports a large Federation research installation.

World Log: ARCTURUS

System Data
- System Name: Alpha Bootis
- Map Coordinates: 1.48S 0.39E
- Number Of Class M Present: 1

Planetary Data
- Position In System: IV
- Number Of Satellites: 7
- Planetary Gravity: .78g

Planetary Size
- Diameter: 10,200 km
- Equatorial Circumference: 17,300 km
- Total Surface Area: 320,000,000 sq km
- Percent Land Mass: 60%
- Total Land Area: 192,000,000 sq km

Planetary Conditions
- Length Of Day: 25 hrs
- Atmospheric Density: Terrestrial
- General Climate: Warm Temperate

Mineral Content
- Normal Metals: 40%
- Radioactives: 10%
- Gemstones: 20%
- Industrial Crystals: Trace
- Special Minerals: Trace

Cultural Data
- Dominant Life Form: Human
- Technological/Sociopolitical Index: 776877–67
- Planetary Trade Profile: AABACBB/B(B)

A major cultural and commercial center, Arcturus maintains a Human culture comparable to that of Terra's Elizabethan England. The Arcturans are very influential among Federation members, many of whom have adopted their mode of dress and cultural styles. Arcturus currently has a representative on the Federation Council.

World Log: ARDANA

System Data
- System Name: Mu Leonis
- Map Coordinates: 0.98N 6.12E
- Number Of Class M Present: 1

Planetary Data
- Position In System: III
- Number Of Satellites: 1
- Planetary Gravity: 1.2g

Planetary Size
- Diameter: 10,200 km
- Equatorial Circumference: 16,400 km
- Total Surface Area: 310,000,000 sq km
- Percent Land Mass: 80%
- Total Land Area: 248,000,000 sq km

Planetary Conditions
- Length Of Day: 27 hrs
- Atmospheric Density: Terrestrial
- General Climate: Cool Temperate

Mineral Content
- Normal Metals: 40%
- Radioactives: 10%
- Gemstones: 10%
- Industrial Crystals: Trace
- Special Minerals: 30%

Cultural Data
- Dominant Life Form: Ardani
- Technological/Sociopolitical Index: 767878–88
- Planetary Trade Profile: BAABCBC/C(D)

One of the newest Federation members, Ardana supports a humanoid culture split between two social classes: the ground-dwelling troglytes, who serve as cavern-miners, and the more culturally advanced inhabitants of the anti-gravity city Stratos, literally a city in the clouds. Stratos supports approximately 700,000 inhabitants, although an accurate census of the troglytes has never been taken. Ardana is important not only for its many cultural and artistic achievements, but also for its extensive subterranean zienite mines. Social differences between the social orders are being eliminated as a result of a Federation Council resolution.

World Log: ARGELIUS II

System Data
- System Name: Argelius
- Map Coordinates: 5.18S 1.97E
- Number Of Class M Present: 1

Planetary Data
- Position In System: II
- Number Of Satellites: 1
- Planetary Gravity: 1.1g

Planetary Size
- Diameter: 11,500 km
- Equatorial Circumference: 17,500 km
- Total Surface Area: 310,000,000 sq km
- Percent Land Mass: 50%
- Total Land Area: 155,000,000 sq km

Planetary Conditions
- Length Of Day: 25 hrs
- Atmospheric Density: Terrestrial
- General Climate: Cool Temperate

Mineral Content
- Normal Metals: 60%
- Radioactives: Trace
- Gemstones: 20%
- Industrial Crystals: Trace
- Special Minerals: Trace

Cultural Data
- Dominant Life Form: Argelian
- Technological/Sociopolitical Index: 888788–76
- Planetary Trade Profile: AABCBCB/A(B)

A major port facility, Argelius is a cultural and artistic nexus renowned for the friendliness and hospitality of its people. Since their Great Awakening two centuries ago, the Argelians have adopted a totally pacifistic social order, deploring all forms of violence. The current population of Argelius is about two billion.

World Log: AVALON

System Data
- System Name: Ceberhardt
- Map Coordinates: 3.25N 3.25W
- Number Of Class M Present: 1

Planetary Data
- Position In System: III
- Number Of Satellites: 2
- Planetary Gravity: 1.05g

Planetary Size
- Diameter: 10,200 km
- Equatorial Circumference: 17,250 km
- Total Surface Area: 315,600,000 sq km
- Percent Land Mass: 70%
- Total Land Area: 220,092,00 sq km

Planetary Conditions
- Length Of Day: 25
- Atmospheric Density: Terrestrial
- General Climate: Controlled Terrestrial

Mineral Content
- Normal Metals: 70%
- Radioactives: 10%
- Gemstones: 10%
- Industrial Crystals: Trace
- Special Minerals: Trace

Cultural Data
- Dominant Life Form: Human
- Technological/Sociopolitical Index: 542453–34
- Planetary Trade Profile: DDDCEED/A(B)

The first planet outside the Sol system to be terraformed by Humans, Avalon was settled by several thousand Humans who wished to return to ancient Terran codes of chivalry and feudal society. Adopting the name of a mythical habitation on Earth, the original settlers adapted the ancient feudal customs and privileges of their ancestors. Avalon retains this quixotic ideal to the present day, remaining over 80 percent feudal-agricultural. However, the recent construction and leasing of a Star Fleet support facility on Avalon has introduced a limited amount of industrial and technological potential to this world. The current population of the planet numbers over one billion inhabitants, with over two million in the capital city of Camelot.

World Log: AXANAR

System Data
- System Name: Delta Orcus
- Map Coordinates: 2.46S 0.47W
- Number Of Class M Present: 1

Planetary Data
- Position In System: I
- Number Of Satellites: 0
- Planetary Gravity: 1.12g

Planetary Size
- Diameter: 14,330 km
- Equatorial Circumference: 50,420 km
- Total Surface Area: 645,124,000 sq km
- Percent Land Mass: 11%
- Total Land Area: 70,963,000 sq km

Planetary Conditions
- Length Of Day: 27 hrs
- Atmospheric Density: Terrestrial
- General Climate: Arctic

Mineral Content
- Normal Metals: 10%
- Radioactives: 9%
- Gemstones: Trace
- Industrial Crystals: Trace
- Special Minerals: 12%

Cultural Data
- Dominant Life Form: Axanorian
- Technological/Sociopolitical Index: 677663–46
- Planetary Trade Profile: DDBFEEE/D(D)

A planet containing an intelligent though primitive Humanoid race, Axanar was the scene of the first engagements of the Four Years War. In Stardate 1/9408, Captain Kelvar Garth of Izar led a Federation squadron against a Klingon task force to prevent the Klingons from maintaining their foothold on the planet. Later, he commanded the forces that sieged the planetary system and defeated the Klingon forces on Axanar. Following the war, Axanar became a Federation Protectorate, and still maintains a Cultural Observation Mission to mend the harm that the Klingons caused the local inhabitants.

World Log: BABEL
System Data
    System Name: Wolf 424
        Map Coordinates: 3.98S 3.18E
    Number Of Class M Present: 1
Planetary Data
    Position In System: XII
    Number Of Satellites: 8
    Planetary Gravity: .77g
    Planetary Size
        Diameter: 8700 km
        Equatorial Circumference: 12,500 km
        Total Surface Area: 280,000,000 sq km
        Percent Land Mass: 90%
        Total Land Area: 252,000,000 sq km
    Planetary Conditions
        Length Of Day: 18 hrs
        Atmospheric Density: Thin
        General Climate: Cold Arid
    Mineral Content
        Normal Metals: 80%
        Radioactives: Trace
        Gemstones: Trace
        Industrial Crystals: Trace
        Special Minerals: Trace

An otherwise barren and unimportant planetoid, Babel has been the site of many major Federation conferences, beginning with the signing of the Articles of Federation. Terraformed for Humanoid habitation, Babel has added a major library and cultural support center to its conference facilities.

World Log: BARRONY
System Data
    System Name: Zeta Hydra 281
        Map Coordinates: 4.77N 2.92E
    Number Of Class M Present: 1
Planetary Data
    Position In System: III
    Number Of Satellites: 2
    Planetary Gravity: 0.89g
    Planetary Size
        Diameter: 12,700 km
        Equatorial Circumference: 17,700 km
        Total Surface Area: 285,000,000 sq km
        Percent Land Mass: 50%
        Total Land Area: 142,500,000 sq km
    Planetary Conditions
        Length Of Day: 22 hrs
        Atmospheric Density: Terrestrial
        General Climate: Warm Temperate
    Mineral Content
        Normal Metals: 30%
        Radioactives: Trace
        Gemstones: Trace
        Industrial Crystals: Trace
        Special Minerals: Trace
    Cultural Data
        Dominant Life Form: 40% Human
                                          60% Other
        Technological/
        Sociopolitical Index: 888887–98
        Planetary Trade Profile: CCDCDDC/C(D)

Barrony was the home planet of the late Maximus O'Connor until he purchased the planet Laura's World. It is currently the private abode of O'Connor's heir, who has made the planet a safe haven for escaped Orion slaves and other individuals seeking political sanctuary. Through an arrangement with Star Fleet Command, portions of Barrony are leased to Star Fleet for commercial and military use. Only those with Security Clearance 5 or higher know what price Star Fleet pays in exhange.

World Log: BARSOOM
System Data
    System Name: Delta Gamma
        Map Coordinates: 1.01N 5.79W
    Number Of Class M Present: 1
Planetary Data
    Position In System: IV
    Number Of Satellites: 5
    Planetary Gravity: 1.25g
    Planetary Size
        Diameter: 9,000 km
        Equatorial Circumference: 14,800 km
        Total Surface Area: 300,000,000 sq km
        Percent Land Mass: 60%
        Total Land Area: 180,000,000 sq km
    Planetary Conditions
        Length Of Day: 19 hrs
        Atmospheric Density: Thin
        General Climate: Cool Temperate
    Mineral Content
        Normal Metals: 20%
        Radioactives: 10%
        Gemstones: 30%
        Industrial Crystals: 20%
        Special Minerals: 20%
    Cultural Data
        Dominant Life Form: 75% Tellarite
                                          25% Human
        Technological/
        Sociopolitical Index: 767688–68
        Planetary Trade Profile: BBBCBBB/B(C)

Barsoom is a geologist's dream, having an abundance of different precious metals and ores. Colonized over 100 years ago by both Human and Tellarite settlers, Barsoom has become one of the richest mining and industrial worlds in the Federation. The planet also maintains the largest Tellarite population (over 5 million inhabitants) outside the Tellar homeworld system.

World Log: BENECIA

System Data
- System Name: Delta Majoris
  - Map Coordinates: 1.01S 2.01E
- Number Of Class M Present: 1

Planetary Data
- Position In System: III
- Number Of Satellites: 12
- Planetary Gravity: .98g
- Planetary Size
  - Diameter: 10,200 km
  - Equatorial Circumference: 15,700 km
  - Total Surface Area: 308,000,000 sq km
  - Percent Land Mass: 70%
  - Total Land Area: 215,600,000 sq km
- Planetary Conditions
  - Length Of Day: 23 hrs
  - Atmospheric Density: Terrestrial
  - General Climate: Terrestrial
- Mineral Content
  - Normal Metals: 70%
  - Radioactives: 20%
  - Gemstones: Trace
  - Industrial Crystals: Trace
  - Special Minerals: Trace

Cultural Data
- Dominant Life Form: 65% Alpha Centauri / 35% Human
- Technological/Sociopolitical Index: 876666–88
- Planetary Trade Profile: BCCCDDD/C(D)

World Log: BETA III

System Data
- System Name: 6-11
  - Map Coordinates: 6.18S 4.82W
- Number Of Class M Present: 1

Planetary Data
- Position In System: VI
- Number Of Satellites: 2
- Planetary Gravity: 1.1g
- Planetary Size
  - Diameter: 9,700 km
  - Equatorial Circumference: 18,000 km
  - Total Surface Area: 265,000,000 sq km
  - Percent Land Mass: 42%
  - Total Land Area: 111,300,000 sq km
- Planetary Conditions
  - Length Of Day: 24 hrs
  - Atmospheric Density: Terrestrial
  - General Climate: Warm Temperate
- Mineral Content
  - Normal Metals: 35%
  - Radioactives: Trace
  - Gemstones: Trace
  - Industrial Crystals: Trace
  - Special Minerals: Trace

Cultural Data
- Dominant Life Form: Landrusian
- Technological/Sociopolitical Index: 455552–77
- Planetary Trade Profile: CCDCCDD/D(D)

World Log: BLACKART

System Data
- System Name: Alpha Vergoris
  - Map Coordinates: 6.27N 3.52E
- Number Of Class M Present: 1

Planetary Data
- Position In System: VIII
- Number Of Satellites: 3
- Planetary Gravity: .87g
- Planetary Size
  - Diameter: 19,700 km
  - Equatorial Circumference: 59,500 km
  - Total Surface Area: 725,000,000 sq km
  - Percent Land Mass: 40%
  - Total Land Area: 290,000,000 sq km
- Planetary Conditions
  - Length Of Day: 25 hrs
  - Atmospheric Density: Thin
  - General Climate: Arid
- Mineral Content
  - Normal Metals: 10%
  - Radioactives: 15%
  - Gemstones: 10%
  - Industrial Crystals: 25%
  - Special Minerals: Trace

Cultural Data
- Dominant Life Form: Tellarite
- Technological/Sociopolitical Index: 889973–58
- Planetary Trade Profile: BCEDCEC/C(C)

Founded after the Romulan War by a joint Human-Alpha Centauri colonial mission, Benecia remains a vast wilderness planet, only one-quarter of which has ever been explored. Local industries include forestry and processing native raw minerals. The local inhabitants have resisted the importation of excessive technology, with an eye toward disturbing the local environment as little as possible. Benecia was also the home of the Back-to-Earth movement, which had a widespread following until it collapsed after the second Babel Conference. Current Benecian population is less than 25,000.

Beta III's advanced Humanoid civilization was managed for several hundred years by a massive central computer complex built by the planet's leading philosopher/scientist Landru. When an investigation team from the *USS Enterprise* discovered the social stagnation produced by this computer, they induced the master computer to self-destruct to free the planet's populace. Since that time, the civilization has returned to a normal path of social evolution and is currently an associate member of the Federation.

A major Tellarite mining concern, Blackart is a planet rich in natural resources. It is also suspected of being one of the largest black market centers in the galaxy. Control of the planet is currently in dispute, due to various corporate rivalries. There are even unconfirmed reports that wealthy industrialists on Blackart maintain Orion female slaves. The Federation regional courts are taking the matter seriously, and are considering using Star Fleet resources to inspect all incoming and outgoing traffic in the Alpha Vergoris system.

World Log: BONANZA
System Data
- System Name: Aegis Aquilia
  - Map Coordinates: 4.45N 4.47W
- Number Of Class M Present: 1

Planetary Data
- Position In System: IV
- Number Of Satellites: 2
- Planetary Gravity: 1.2g

Planetary Size
- Diameter: 7,800 km
- Equatorial Circumference: 12,850 km
- Total Surface Area: 225,000,000 sq km
- Percent Land Mass: 95%
- Total Land Area: 213,750,000 sq km

Planetary Conditions
- Length Of Day: 27 hrs
- Atmospheric Density: Thin
- General Climate: Arctic

Mineral Content
- Normal Metals: 42%
- Radioactives: Trace
- Gemstones: Trace
- Industrial Crystals: 45%
- Special Minerals: Trace

Cultural Data
- Dominant Life Form: 40% Human
  - 40% Tellarite
  - 10% Vulcan
- Technological/Sociopolitical Index: 778887–78
- Planetary Trade Profile: BBCDCCD/D(D)

A frigid icy rock, inhospitable and virtually featureless, Bonanza is an important planet due to the planet's considerable sub-surface gold and diamond deposits. With a large population of offworld miners living under pressurized domes, Bonanza has steadily increased in value since its discovery two decades ago. Geologists estimate that the gold and diamond reserves will not be depleted for at least another century. Star Fleet maintains a small orbital defense installation supporting large monitors and numerous corvettes to guard the system from unauthorized intrusion.

World Log: CAIT
System Data
- System Name: Caitia
  - Map Coordinates: 1.80N 2.16E
- Number Of Class M Present: 1

Planetary Data
- Position In System: 4
- Number Of Satellites: 2
- Planetary Gravity: 1.25

Planetary Size
- Diameter: 10,100 km
- Equatorial Circumference: 17,200 km
- Total Surface Area: 311,000,000 sq km
- Percent Land Mass: 50%
- Total Land Area: 155,000,000 sq km

Planetary Conditions
- Length Of Day: 27 hrs
- Atmospheric Density: Thick
- General Climate: Warm Tropical

Mineral Content
- Normal Metals: 40%
- Radioactives: 20%
- Gemstones: 20%
- Industrial Crystals: Trace
- Special Minerals: Trace

Cultural Data
- Dominant Life Form: Caitians
- Technological/Sociopolitical Index: 887865–76
- Planetary Trade Profile: BEFCDEG/B(C)

Cait is a lush, tropical world, whose race of intelligent felinoids is among the newest races to join the Federation. Resembling Terran felines, Caitians are thick-furred beings, light gold to dark brown in color. When first contacted, the Caitian civilization was considerably advanced, with an emphasis in the physical and biomedical sciences, even though Caitians had never ventured beyond their own planet. Despite their predatory appearance, Caitians are extremely peaceful and have strong individual and group loyalties. Cait maintains a large starship construction facility capable of producing a wide range of military and commercial craft each year. The planet is currently represented in the Federation Council.

World Log: CALANARA
System Data
- System Name: Beta Leonis
  - Map Coordinates: 2.95N 0.77E
- Number Of Class M Present: 1

Planetary Data
- Position In System: VIII
- Number Of Satellites: 6
- Planetary Gravity: 1.22g

Planetary Size
- Diameter: 17,500 km
- Equatorial Circumference: 24,000 km
- Total Surface Area: 292,000,000 sq km
- Percent Land Mass: 60%
- Total Land Area: 157,200,000 sq km

Planetary Conditions
- Length Of Day: 25%
- Atmospheric Density: Thin
- General Climate: Warm Temperate

Mineral Content
- Normal Metals: 25%
- Radioactives: Trace
- Gemstones: Trace
- Industrial Crystals: Trace
- Special Minerals: Trace

Cultural Data
- Dominant Life Form: Vulcan
- Technological/Sociopolitical Index: 888899–98
- Planetary Trade Profile: DDCCCCC/B(C)

One of the first planets ever colonized by Vulcans, Calanara is a private preserve for distinguished Vulcan citizens, past and present. The majority of the planet has been parcelled into large tracts that the Vulcan government awards to individuals on the basis of scientific and social achievement. Located in the planet's northern hemisphere is a special memorial center, housing the state-owned burial grounds for Vulcan's honored dead. Among those interred there is Surak, Vulcan's most esteemed philosopher, whose remains were transported from Vulcan following Calanara's colonization.

World Log: CANOPUS

System Data
- System Name: Beta Geminorum
- Map Coordinates: 3.30N 1.27E
- Number Of Class M Present: 1

Planetary Data
- Position In System: II
- Number Of Satellites: 3
- Planetary Gravity: .84g

Planetary Size
- Diameter: 16,500 km
- Equatorial Circumference: 51,000 km
- Total Surface Area: 625,000,000 sq km
- Percent Land Mass: 25%
- Total Land Area: 156,250,000 sq km

Planetary Conditions
- Length Of Day: 22 hrs
- Atmospheric Density: Thin
- General Climate: Arctic

Mineral Content
- Normal Metals: 30%
- Radioactives: 10%
- Gemstones: 10%
- Industrial Crystals: Trace
- Special Minerals: Trace

Cultural Data
- Dominant Life Form: Andorian
- Technological/Sociopolitical Index: 998998-77
- Planetary Trade Profile: BEFCDEG/B(C)

Canopus supports a large industry that produces heavy equipment and durable goods for colonial expeditions throughout the entire Federation. Subsidiary concerns also manufacture a wide array of equipment used to construct permanent settlements on newly colonized planets. Canopus is the largest center of Andorian culture outside their home system. A Star Fleet support facility is located on Canopus as well.

World Log: CAPELLA

System Data
- System Name: Alpha Aurigae
- Map Coordinates: 8.75S 4.25E
- Number Of Class M Present: 1

Planetary Data
- Position In System: IV
- Number Of Satellites: 1
- Planetary Gravity: 1.5g

Planetary Size
- Diameter: 18,200 km
- Equatorial Circumference: 56,000 km
- Total Surface Area: 710,000,000 sq km
- Percent Land Mass: 70%
- Total Land Area: 497,000,000 sq km

Planetary Conditions
- Length Of Day: 22 hrs
- Atmospheric Density: Terrestrial
- General Climate: Desert

Mineral Content
- Normal Metals: 40%
- Radioactives: 20%
- Gemstones: Trace
- Industrial Crystals: 20%
- Special Minerals: Trace

Cultural Data
- Dominant Life Form: Capellan
- Technological/Sociopolitical Index: 467555-56
- Planetary Trade Profile: None

Capella is a desert world populated by Humanoid nomads who may be the descendants of a lost Terran expedition. Their loose tribal organization is only beginning to take on cohesive political unity. The planet is valuable for its various industrial grade crystals and other ores. The Federation has negotiated a temporary trade agreement with the Capellans, although trade has not yet officially begun. The planet is also known for its indigenous life forms, including the Capellan power cat.

World Log: CASTOR FIELDS

System Data
- System Name: Castora
- Map Coordinates: 0.64N 6.15E
- Number Of Class M Present: 1

Planetary Data
- Position In System: II
- Number Of Satellites: 2
- Planetary Gravity: .88g

Planetary Size
- Diameter: 13,750 km
- Equatorial Circumference: 29,000 km
- Total Surface Area: 222,000,000 sq km
- Percent Land Mass: 60%
- Total Land Area: 133,200,000 sq km

Planetary Conditions
- Length Of Day: 23 hrs
- Atmospheric Density: Terrestrial
- General Climate: Warm Temperate

Mineral Content
- Normal Metals: 22%
- Radioactives: Trace
- Gemstones: Trace
- Industrial Crystals: Trace
- Special Minerals: Trace

Cultural Data
- Dominant Life Form: 50% Human, 10% Vulcan, 40% Other
- Technological/Sociopolitical Index: 889998-76
- Planetary Trade Profile: BAABCAD/B(C)

This remote planet is owned and operated by a consortium of Federation citizens who use it solely for breeding and training numerous strains of Terran racing horses. Racing events held during the latter part of the year attract millions of enthusiasts annually. The sale of pure-bred stock produces planetary revenues in the hundreds of billions of credits. Currently, close to a billion inhabitants of Castor Fields are involved directly or indirectly in this commercial concern.

World Log: CAVALIER
System Data
- System Name: Calka
- Map Coordinates: 1.67S 0.51E
- Number Of Class M Present: 1

Planetary Data
- Position In System: IV
- Number Of Satellites: 4
- Planetary Gravity: .87g

Planetary Size
- Diameter: 9,600 km
- Equatorial Circumference: 14,700 km
- Total Surface Area: 300,500,000 sq km
- Percent Land Mass: 50%
- Total Land Area: 150,250,000 sq km

Planetary Conditions
- Length Of Day: 22 hrs
- Atmospheric Density: Terrestrial
- General Climate: Cool Temperate

Mineral Content
- Normal Metals: 40%
- Radioactives: 10%
- Gemstones: 20%
- Industrial Crystals: 10%
- Special Minerals: Trace

Cultural Data
- Dominant Life Form: Human
- Technological/Sociopolitical Index: 656565–67
- Planetary Trade Profile: BCCBDCC/A(B)

World Log: CESTUS III
System Data
- System Name: Cestus
- Map Coordinates: 3.29N 8.54E
- Number Of Class M Present: 1

Planetary Data
- Position In System: III
- Number Of Satellites: 1
- Planetary Gravity: .95G

Planetary Size
- Diameter: 14,300 km
- Equatorial Circumference: 45,000 km
- Total Surface Area: 555,000,000 sq km
- Percent Land Mass: 80%
- Total Land Area: 44,000,000 sq km

Planetary Conditions
- Length Of Day: 21 hrs
- Atmospheric Density: Terrestrial
- General Climate: Warm Temperate

Mineral Content
- Normal Metals: 25%
- Radioactives: 10%
- Gemstones: Trace
- Industrial Crystals: Trace
- Special Minerals: Trace

Cultural Data
- Dominant Life Form: 40% Human / 60% Tellarite
- Technological/Sociopolitical Index: 898876–77
- Planetary Trade Profile: DDDCDED/D(D)

World Log: CHARLEMAGNE
System Data
- System Name: Aquilla Scorpi
- Map Coordinates: 2.63N 7.66E
- Number Of Class M Present: 1

Planetary Data
- Position In System: IV
- Number Of Satellites: 2
- Planetary Gravity: 1.3g

Planetary Size
- Diameter: 9,700 km
- Equatorial Circumference: 17,000 km
- Total Surface Area: 370,000,000 sq km
- Percent Land Mass: 60%
- Total Land Area: 222,000,000 sq km

Planetary Conditions
- Length Of Day: 30 hrs
- Atmospheric Density: Terrestrial
- General Climate: Warm Terrestrial

Mineral Content
- Normal Metals: Trace
- Radioactives: 10%
- Gemstones: 10%
- Industrial Crystals: Trace
- Special Minerals: Trace

Cultural Data
- Dominant Life Form: Human
- Technological/Sociopolitical Index: 777677–75
- Planetary Trade Profile: CCCDCDE/B(C)

Cavalier is an Arcturan colony world that was established two generations ago. Like their Arcturan ancestors, the inhabitants of Cavalier have adopted ancient Terran customs and dress, emulating the society and class structure of the English Empire of approximately 1640-1680. Largely an agricultural planet, Cavalier also derives revenues from large numbers of offworld tourists who come to visit each year. Not only do visitors enjoy the Cavalier lifestyle, but they can also relax at the numerous corporate entertainment centers on the planet's southern continent.

Having unknowingly settled within Gorn-claimed space, the original 125-person colony on Cestus III was killed in an unanticipated Gorn attack. Subsequent negotiations with the Gorns averted full-scale war once both sides realized the misunderstanding. Thereafter, Cestus III was granted to the Federation under an agreement that limited both governments' expansion in the area. After 15 years, the original colony has been rebuilt, and is valuable both for mining and for trade with Gorns. This latter aspect is only marginal, however, as resentment over the death of the first colonists still remains.

Charlemagne was settled a century ago by dissidents who rejected the Federation's peace treaty with the Romulans. The inhabitants of the planet based their own government on Terran monarchy from Europe in 800 A.D.. Unlike other 'copy-cat' worlds in the Federation, Charlemagne's inhabitants have rejected none of present-day technological advantages. However, because they strictly limit imports to encourage local industry, they usually go without recent Federation innovations. Star Fleet maintains a small support/repair facility on the planet, and many of the planet's inhabitants are affiliated with Star Fleet in some capacity.

World Log: COCHRANE I
System Data
    System Name: Zeta Riguli
        Map Coordinates: 2.73S 5.23W
    Number Of Class M Present: 1
Planetary Data
    Position In System: VII
    Number Of Satellites: 3
    Planetary Gravity: 1.15g
    Planetary Size
        Diameter: 17,500 km
        Equatorial Circumference: 24,000 km
        Total Surface Area: 185,000,000 sq km
        Percent Land Mass: 55%
        Total Land Area: 101,750,000 sq km
    Planetary Conditions
        Length Of Day: 20.5 Hours
        Atmospheric Density: Terrestrial
        General Climate: Cool Temperate
    Mineral Content
        Normal Metals: 35%
        Radioactives: 10%
        Gemstones: Trace
        Industrial Crystals: Trace
        Special Minerals: 22%
Cultural Data
    Dominant Life Form: 60% Alpha Centauri
        40% Human
    Technological/
    Sociopolitical Index: 889999-98
    Planetary Trade Profile: BAABBA/B(B)

Settled by Humans and Alpha Centaurans following the disappearance of Zephram Cochrane, Cochrane I is a thriving industrial planet rich in dilithium and radioactives. It also hosts the central administrative center for the Federation's Department of Colonization and numerous subsidiary agencies and organizations. The planet's Cochrane University is one of the most heavily attended in the quadrant.

World Log: COMMISSARIATE
System Data
    System Name: Beta Trianguli
        Map Coordinates: 5.07N 2.25W
    Number Of Class M Present: 1
Planetary Data
    Position In System: III
    Number Of Satellites: 3
    Planetary Gravity: 1.2g
    Planetary Size
        Diameter: 7,800 km
        Equatorial Circumference: 25,500 km
        Total Surface Area: 315,000,000 sq km
        Percent Land Mass: 100%
        Total Land Area: 315,000,000 sq km
    Planetary Conditions
        Length Of Day: 22 Hours
        Atmospheric Density: Thin
        General Climate: Cool Temperate
    Mineral Content
        Normal Metals: 20%
        Radioactives: 10%
        Gemstones: Trace
        Industrial Crystals: Trace
        Special Minerals: Trace
Cultural Data
    Dominant Life Form: 35% Andorian
        20% Vulcan
        15% Human
        15% Caitian
        15% Other
    Technological/
    Sociopolitical Index: 898985-78
    Planetary Trade Profile: BEECCCC/B(C)

The largest center of underground farming in the Federation, Commissariate supports over one-and-a-half billion inhabitants in subterranean farm complexes for most of its year. Due to the lack of sunlight and the psychological problems associated with living underground, most people living on this planet are agricultural specialists working here only for limited durations. Despite this constant turnover in personnel, Commissariate maintains one of the highest food production rates of all agricultural planets.

World Log: CORIDAN
System Data
    System Name: Danthos
        Map Coordinates: 2.70S 0.91 W
    Number Of Class M Present: 1
Planetary Data
    Position In System: IV
    Number Of Satellites: 1
    Planetary Gravity: 1.29g
    Planetary Size
        Diameter: 15,600 km
        Equatorial Circumference: 48,000 km
        Total Surface Area: 522,000,000 sq km
        Percent Land Mass: 95%
        Total Land Area: 496,500,000 sq km
    Planetary Conditions
        Length Of Day: 25 Hours
        Atmospheric Density: Thin
        General Climate: Cool Temperate
    Mineral Content
        Normal Metals: 32%
        Radioactives: 30%
        Gemstones: 04%
        Industrial Crystals: 09%
        Special Minerals: Trace
Cultural Data
    Dominant Life Form: Coridan
    Technological/
    Sociopolitical Index: 967594-67
    Planetary Trade Profile: FCAGDEF/B(E)

This small planet and its native humanoid population has been the subject of considerable controversy over the last three decades. Rich in natural minerals and large amounts of dilithium, Coridan was often the victim of privateering raids by commercial and even government-sponsored sectors. The Coridan Problem intensified when the local inhabitants applied for admission into the Federation, thus sparking a conference on Babel. However, their admission was narrowly denied in favor of a quarantined status.

World Log: CRASSUS

System Data
- **System Name:** Ambiphon
  - **Map Coordinates:** 2.78N 5.32W
- **Number Of Class M Present:** 2

Planetary Data
- **Position In System:** II
- **Number Of Satellites:** 0
- **Planetary Gravity:** 1.17g
- **Planetary Size**
  - **Diameter:** 19,000 km
  - **Equatorial Circumference:** 28,550 km
  - **Total Surface Area:** 275,000,000 sq km
  - **Percent Land Mass:** 42%
  - **Total Land Area:** 115,500,000 sq km
- **Planetary Conditions**
  - **Length Of Day:** 22 Hours
  - **Atmospheric Density:** Terrestrial
  - **General Climate:** Warm Temperate
- **Mineral Content**
  - **Normal Metals:** 37%
  - **Radioactives:** Trace
  - **Gemstones:** Trace
  - **Industrial Crystals:** Trace
  - **Special Minerals:** 35%

Cultural Data
- **Dominant Life Form:** Human
- **Technological/ Sociopolitical Index:** 7788793–88
- **Planetary Trade Profile:** BBBCBBB/C(C)

Crassus is noted for its abundance of natural mineral deposits, including gold iridium and titanium. Though the mineral fields are not as extensive as those found on other worlds, Crassian ores lie near the planet's surface, are easy to extract, and thus more profitable. The local Human inhabitants on Crassus do not mine their ores, but lease mining rights to offworld speculators and prospectors. Local Crassian industry centers around processing and extracting ores. Not surprisingly, the Federation's Bureau of Mining is located on Crassus. Star Fleet maintains a small in-system defense post as well as a small repair facility in orbit around the planet.

World Log: CRATER'S WORLD

System Data
- **System Name:** Gamma Zeta IV
  - **Map Coordinates:** 4.45S 6.01W
- **Number Of Class M Present:** 1

Planetary Data
- **Position In System:** II
- **Number Of Satellites:** 1
- **Planetary Gravity:** 1.1g
- **Planetary Size**
  - **Diameter:** 16,900 km
  - **Equatorial Circumference:** 52,000 km
  - **Total Surface Area:** 625,000,000 sq km
  - **Percent Land Mass:** 50%
  - **Total Land Area:** 312,500,000 sq km
- **Planetary Conditions**
  - **Length Of Day:** 27 Hours
  - **Atmospheric Density:** Terrestrial
  - **General Climate:** Arid
- **Mineral Content**
  - **Normal Metals:** 20%
  - **Radioactives:** Trace
  - **Gemstones:** Trace
  - **Industrial Crystals:** Trace
  - **Special Minerals:** Trace

Crater's World is the site of a once-prosperous civilization of aliens characterized by their biological dependence on large quantities of salt. Scientists speculate that a change in the planet's global weather patterns dried up vast salt seas, driving the race to extinction. Originally designated Planet M113, the world was later named in honor of the late Professor Crater and his wife Nancy, the first archeologists to examine the planet's archeological ruins. In the last decade, a permanent archeological base has been established on the planet to continue the Craters' work.

World Log: CYCLOPUS

System Data
- **System Name:** Verigus K
  - **Map Coordinates:** 8.00S 6.82E
- **Number Of Class M Present:** 1

Planetary Data
- **Position In System:** III
- **Number Of Satellites:** 0
- **Planetary Gravity:** 1.5g
- **Planetary Size**
  - **Diameter:** 19,500 km
  - **Equatorial Circumference:** 60,000 km
  - **Total Surface Area:** 765,000,000 sq km
  - **Percent Land Mass:** 71%
  - **Total Land Area:** 540,000,000 sq km
- **Planetary Conditions**
  - **Length Of Day:** 32 Hours
  - **Atmospheric Density:** Terrestrial
  - **General Climate:** Cool Temperate
- **Mineral Content**
  - **Normal Metals:** 38%
  - **Radioactives:** Trace
  - **Gemstones:** Trace
  - **Industrial Crystals:** Trace
  - **Special Minerals:** Trace

Cultural Data
- **Dominant Life Form:** 35% Human, 30% Andorian, 20% Alpha Centauri, 15% Other
- **Technological/ Sociopolitical Index:** 999994–95
- **Planetary Trade Profile:** ACFDDEF/A(B)

A trade world located near the border of the Triangle Zone, Cyclopus is one of the Federation's most distant associate-member worlds. It is noted for producing a hybrid grain developed from a local grass variety and a Terran wheat. Cyclopus' governmental structure is also noteworthy, as it is modeled after that of the ancient Terran Roman Empire. Cyclopian officials are friendly with the other independent worlds in the region, but steadfastly refuse to have anything to do with the Romulans.

World Log: CYGNET XIV

System Data
- System Name: Cygnus
- Map Coordinates: 4.05N 0.41E
- Number Of Class M Present: 1

Planetary Data
- Position In System: XIV
- Number Of Satellites: 3
- Planetary Gravity: 1.2g

Planetary Size
- Diameter: 19,000 km
- Equatorial Circumference: 60,000 km
- Total Surface Area: 725,000,000 sq km
- Percent Land Mass: 50%
- Total Land Area: 362,500,000 sq km

Planetary Conditions
- Length Of Day: 25 hrs
- Atmospheric Density: Terrestrial
- General Climate: Warm Temperate

Mineral Content
- Normal Metals: 70%
- Radioactives: Trace
- Gemstones: Trace
- Industrial Crystals: Trace
- Special Minerals: Trace

Cultural Data
- Dominant Life Form: Cygnian
- Technological/Sociopolitical Index: 989887–66
- Planetary Trade Profile: ABABBBA/A(B)

An elected member of the Federation Council, Cygnet XIV is a planet with a female-dominated social order. Cygnian females are highly advanced and intelligent, but their male counterparts are only semi-intelligent. In physical appearance, Cygnians are humanoid with vestigial tails and central spine formations resembling those of Terran horses. They are very technologically advanced, especially in computers and cybernetics. Cygian females are highly prized as computer specialists by both Star Fleet and the private sector.

World Log: DARAN V

System Data
- System Name: Daran
- Map Coordinates: 3.88S 4.93E
- Number Of Class M Present: 1

Planetary Data
- Position In System: V
- Number Of Satellites: 2
- Planetary Gravity: .96g

Planetary Size
- Diameter: 12,520 km
- Equatorial Circumference: 39,330 km
- Total Surface Area: 492,447,000 sq km
- Percent Land Mass: 26%
- Total Land Area: 128,036,000 sq km

Planetary Conditions
- Length Of Day: 28 Hours
- Atmospheric Density: Terrestrial
- General Climate: Warm Temperate

Mineral Content
- Normal Metals: 48%
- Radioactives: 10%
- Gemstones: 10%
- Industrial Crystals: Trace
- Special Minerals: Trace

Cultural Data
- Dominant Life Form: 65% Human / 20% Tellarite / 10% Vulcan / 5% Other

Technological/Sociopolitical Index: 998983–76
Planetary Trade Profile: CAFEBCF/G(G)

A major supply and support facility during the Romulan War, Daran V is still a major trading center and supports many descendants of veterans of that war. Daran textiles are renowned for their quality and durability, and Daran architects have created marvels on the planet. The planet's inhabitants are reputed to be among the most friendly individuals in the Federation.

World Log: DELTA IV

System Data
- System Name: Delta Principius
- Map Coordinates: 0.21S 1.02E
- Number Of Class M Present: 2

Planetary Data
- Position In System: V
- Number Of Satellites: 7
- Planetary Gravity: .95g

Planetary Size
- Diameter: 15,000 km
- Equatorial Circumference: 51,000 km
- Total Surface Area: 625,000,000 sq km
- Percent Land Mass: 60%
- Total Land Area: 375,000,000 sq km

Planetary Conditions
- Length Of Day: 20 hrs
- Atmospheric Density: Thin
- General Climate: Cool Temperate

Mineral Content
- Normal Metals: 55%
- Radioactives: 15%
- Gemstones: 10%
- Industrial Crystals: Trace
- Special Minerals: Trace

Cultural Data
- Dominant Life Form: Deltan
- Technological/Sociopolitical Index: 988767–87
- Planetary Trade Profile: ABABCCB/B(B)

Delta IV is the home of a Humanoid race known as the Deltans, an advanced and very pacifistic culture noted for their artistic achievements. Deltans resemble Humans in all outward respects except for the absence of facial and body hair. Like Orion females, all Deltans possess an unusual biochemical makeup that generates massive amounts of pheromones, which sexually stimulate members of the opposite sex. Current Deltan population is six billion.

World Log: DELTA VEGA
System Data
- System Name: Trimordidion
- Map Coordinates: 7.27S 4.02E
- Number Of Class M Present: 1

Planetary Data
- Position In System: X
- Number Of Satellites: 0
- Planetary Gravity: 1.05g

Planetary Size
- Diameter: 18,100 km
- Equatorial Circumference: 50,000 km
- Total Surface Area: 700,000,000 sq km
- Percent Land Mass: 90%
- Total Land Area: 630,000,000 sq km

Planetary Conditions
- Length Of Day: 19 Hours
- Atmospheric Density: Thin
- General Climate: Cool Temperate

Mineral Content
- Normal Metals: 10%
- Radioactives: 10%
- Gemstones: Trace
- Industrial Crystals: Trace
- Special Minerals: 40%

Cultural Data
- Dominant Life Form: Human
- Technological/Sociopolitical Index: 667768–76
- Planetary Trade Profile: CCCDCB/C(C)

World Log: DEMOISELLE II
System Data
- System Name: Demoiselle
- Map Coordinates: 3.22N 2.28E
- Number Of Class M Present: 1

Planetary Data
- Position In System: II
- Number Of Satellites: 3
- Planetary Gravity: 0.88g

Planetary Size
- Diameter: 11,700 km
- Equatorial Circumference: 35,500 km
- Total Surface Area: 425,000,000 sq km
- Percent Land Mass: 97%
- Total Land Area: 412,500,000 sq km

Planetary Conditions
- Length Of Day: 20 Hours
- Atmospheric Density: Terrestrial
- General Climate: Warm Temperature

Mineral Content
- Normal Metals: 20%
- Radioactives: Trace
- Gemstones: 45%
- Industrial Crystals: Trace
- Special Minerals: Trace

Cultural Data
- Dominant Life Form: 25% Human, 25% Cygnian, 50% Other
- Technological/Sociopolitical Index: 886778–77
- Planetary Trade Profile: CCBDEBC/C(D)

World Log: DENEB
System Data
- System Name: Alpha Cygni
- Map Coordinates: 2.38N 7.22E
- Number Of Class M Present: 1

Planetary Data
- Position In System: IV
- Number Of Satellites: 3
- Planetary Gravity: 1.1g

Planetary Size
- Diameter: 10,500 km
- Equatorial Circumference: 32,000 km
- Total Surface Area: 400,000,000 sq km
- Percent Land Mass: 15%
- Total Land Area: 60,000,000 sq km

Planetary Conditions
- Length Of Day: 19 Hours
- Atmospheric Density: Thick
- General Climate: Tropical

Mineral Content
- Normal Metals: 20%
- Radioactives: Trace
- Gemstones: Trace
- Industrial Crystals: Trace
- Special Minerals: Trace

Cultural Data
- Dominant Life Form: 60% Human, 40% Alpha Centauri
- Technological/Sociopolitical Index: 998898–67
- Planetary Trade Profile: CCBCEDE/C(C)

Delta Vega originally housed only an automated dilithium cracking station. Later reports of extensive dilithium deposits far beyond original estimates spurred numerous industrial concerns to establish permanent mining facilities on this otherwise barren and uninteresting world. In the last decade, Delta Vega has acquired over seven million Human inhabitants who have helped turn the planet into an important trade center.

One of the newer Federation colonies to gain associate-member status, Demoiselle II is ruled by a matriarchy. Its main export is gemstones, and native Demoisellians are regarded as expert gemcutters and appraisers. Diplomats and traders sometimes exchange stones unearthed from Demoiselle II with the Orions, who prize these gems highly.

A world almost completely covered by swamps and marshes, Deneb is an important source of native plants used to synthesize various pharmaceutical products. A combined population of Human and Centauri settlers have constructed a small city-capitaol near Deneb's northern ice cap. Here, rare plant and mineral resources are converted into their base chemical forms for shipment offworld. Deneb also has the distinction of being home to one of the Federation's more loathsome creatures, the Denebian slime devil.

World Log: DENEVA
System Data
  System Name: Beta Darius
  Map Coordinates: 0.23S 5.79W
  Number Of Class M Present: 1
Planetary Data
  Position In System: IV
  Number Of Satellites: 3
  Planetary Gravity: 1.15g
  Planetary Size
    Diameter: 9,700 km
    Equatorial Circumference: 14,500 km
    Total Surface Area: 300,500,000 sq km
    Percent Land Mass: 45%
    Total Land Area: 135,225,000 sq km
  Planetary Conditions
    Length Of Day: 25.5 hrs
    Atmospheric Density: Warm Temperate
    General Climate: Terrestrial
  Mineral Content
    Normal Metals: 40%
    Radioactives: 10%
    Gemstones: Trace
    Industrial Crystals: 10%
    Special Minerals: Trace
Cultural Data
  Dominant Life Form: 60% Deltan
                      20% Tellarite
                      20% Other
  Technological/
  Sociopolitical Index: 998988–88
  Planetary Trade Profile: AABAABA/A(B)

World Log: EDO
System Data
  System Name: Epsilon Minora
  Map Coordinates: 0.15N 4.11W
  Number Of Class M Present: 1
Planetary Data
  Position In System: III
  Number Of Satellites: 1
  Planetary Gravity: .85g
  Planetary Size
    Diameter: 8,520 km
    Equatorial Circumference: 12,450 km
    Total Surface Area: 220,500,000 sq km
    Percent Land Mass: 40%
    Total Land Area: 90,000,000 sq km
  Planetary Conditions
    Length Of Day: 22 hrs
    Atmospheric Density: Terrestrial
    General Climate: Tropical
  Mineral Content
    Normal Metals: 50%
    Radioactives: Trace
    Gemstones: 10%
    Industrial Crystals: Trace
    Special Minerals: Trace
Cultural Data
  Dominant Life Form: Edoan
  Technological/
  Sociopolitical Index: 766688–67
  Planetary Trade Profile: BBCBBBC/B(C)

World Log: EKOS
System Data
  System Name: M43 Alpha
  Map Coordinates: 2.02S 6.95E
  Number Of Class M Present: 2
Planetary Data
  Position In System: III
  Number Of Satellites: 1
  Planetary Gravity: 0.98g
  Planetary Size
    Diameter: 18,000 km
    Equatorial Circumference: 35,000 km
    Total Surface Area: 317,000,000 sq km
    Percent Land Mass: 45%
    Total Land Area: 142,650,000 sq km
  Planetary Conditions
    Length Of Day: 25.5 Hours
    Atmospheric Density: Terrestrial
    General Climate: Warm Temperate
  Mineral Content
    Normal Metals: 33%
    Radioactives: 12%
    Gemstones: Trace
    Industrial Crystals: Trace
    Special Minerals: Trace
Cultural Data
  Dominant Life Form: Ekosi
  Technological/
  Sociopolitical Index: 556552–77
  Planetary Trade Profile: None

Deneva is one of the Federation's major commercial and industrial centers, and has a representative on the Federation Council. Founded in Stardate 1/64 by Alpha Centaurans, Deneva served as a ship repair and resupply center in the Romulan War. After the war, numerous Human and non-Human settlers joined the Centaurans. Deneva has come to be regarded as a symbol of the Federation, a monument to the cultural advantages made through inter-racial cooperation. Its rich variety of minerals supports a vast metallurgical-industrial base. Two decades ago, Deneva's population was decimated by hundreds of flying parasites, but recent census figures show signs of recovery. Current population estimates are between four and four-and-a-half million inhabitants.

Sometimes referred to as Sauria, Edo is a small planet orbiting an orange Type K sun. It is the home of an intelligent race of reptilians, who are among the newest additions to the Federation. Edoans are tri-spacial beings, having three arms and three legs. They have a particular affinity for mathematics, and many serve on Star Fleet crews as skilled navigators. Edo itself is a warm, humid, tropical world with considerable amounts of mineral and other natural resources. It is famous for its numerous wines, which are prized by collectors and connoisseurs throughout Federation space and beyond. Current population of Edo is between four and five billion inhabitants.

Ekos supports a humanoid culture similar to that of Terra during the first half of the 20th century. Twenty years ago, Ekos was in a state of political and social upheaval due to a series of global economic problems. At that time, Dr. John Gill, the noted Federation historian, was a cultural observer on Ekos. He violated the Prime Directive by using Federation technology to raise a pseudo-Nazi party to dominance there. Dr. Gill's efforts were later subverted by party members seeking their own advancement. The subsequent intervention by an investigating party from the USS Enterprise helped narrowly avert a war between Ekos and neighboring Zeon, though Dr. Gill was killed during the resolution of the crisis. Ekos has since been protected from further contact, allowing the population of both Ekos and Zeon to work out their problems in a peaceful, cooperative manner.

World Log: ELDORADO

System Data
- System Name: Eldarnas 344
- Map Coordinates: 2.47S 4.69W
- Number Of Class M Present: 2

Planetary Data
- Position In System: III
- Number Of Satellites: 7
- Planetary Gravity: .97g

Planetary Size
- Diameter: 8,780 km
- Equatorial Circumference: 12,200 km
- Total Surface Area: 288,000,000 sq km
- Percent Land Mass: 50%
- Total Land Area: 144,00,000 sq km

Planetary Conditions
- Length Of Day: 27 hrs
- Atmospheric Density: Thin
- General Climate: Cool Terrestrial

Mineral Content
- Normal Metals: Trace
- Radioactives: 25%
- Gemstones: 20%
- Industrial Crystals: 30%
- Special Minerals: 20%

Cultural Data
- Dominant Life Form: 40% Andorian / 40% Tellarate / 20% Human

Technological/
- Sociopolitical Index: 688766–77
- Planetary Trade Profile: CCBBBBC/B(C)

A geologist's delight, Eldorado was named for its natural wealth in numerous types of rare minerals, including both radioactives and small dilithium deposits. Currently supporting a population of one billion inhabitants, Eldorado is estimated to supply two percent of the Federation's industrial crystal needs for the next decade. Star Fleet maintains a small patrol station here, with a squadron of corvettes to discourage would-be pirates and other illegal opportunists.

World Log: EMINIAR VII

System Data
- System Name: Eminiar
- Map Coordinates: 2.15S 5.77E
- Number Of Class M Present: 2

Planetary Data
- Position In System: VII
- Number Of Satellites: 1
- Planetary Gravity: 1.22g

Planetary Size
- Diameter: 13,000 km
- Equatorial Circumference: 40,000 km
- Total Surface Area: 500,000,000 sq km
- Percent Land Mass: 40%
- Total Land Area: 200,000,000 sq km

Planetary Conditions
- Length Of Day: 25 Hours
- Atmospheric Density: Terrestrial
- General Climate: Cool Temperate

Mineral Content
- Normal Metals: 10%
- Radioactives: 10%
- Gemstones: 20%
- Industrial Crystals: Trace
- Special Minerals: Trace

Cultural Data
- Dominant Life Form: Eminian

Technological/
- Sociopolitical Index: 888987–86
- Planetary Trade Profile: BBABCDD/B(B)

First contacted by Terran explorers in the first decade of Federation interstellar exploration, Eminian culture remained a mystery until contact with the *USS Enterprise* 16 years ago. Then it was determined that the Eminians had considerable technological sophistication, having developed interplanetary flight some 400 years before the Federation contacted them. Regrettably, the Eminians did not make as much progress in the social sciences as they did in the physical sciences. When Eminiar's colony world, Vendikar, declared itself independent, war erupted between the two. To preserve their way of life, both planets developed a computerized attack and defense system, enabling the two planets to continue their warfare without risking destruction of either civilization. As a result of the *Enterprise*'s visit, this arrangement was rendered obsolete, and a peaceful solution was negotiated. Today, Eminiar VII is a full-status member of the Federation in good standing.

World Log: ETERNITY

System Data
- System Name: Alpha Eridani
- Map Coordinates: 4.55N 6.02E
- Number Of Class M Present: 1

Planetary Data
- Position In System: I
- Number Of Satellites: 0
- Planetary Gravity: .95g

Planetary Size
- Diameter: 16,000 km
- Equatorial Circumference: 48,000 km
- Total Surface Area: 600,000,000 sq km
- Percent Land Mass: 75%
- Total Land Area: 450,000,000 sq km

Planetary Conditions
- Length Of Day: 22 Hours
- Atmospheric Density: Terrestrial
- General Climate: Warm Terrestrial

Mineral Content
- Normal Metals: 10%
- Radioactives: Trace
- Gemstones: Trace
- Industrial Crystals: Trace
- Special Minerals: Trace

One of the most beautiful planets in the Federation, Eternity is one of the more somber as well. It serves as Star Fleet Command's memorial to all those who died in conflicts between the Federation and foreign powers. Here lie Star Fleet personnel (and civilians) who died in the Romulan and the Four Years War, as well as persons killed in 'unofficial' or otherwise short-lived conflicts such as the Organian Conflict and the Gorn attack on Cestus III. Eternity is staffed by a permanent records team and a Star Fleet honor guard. Star Fleet supports three destroyers here, which maintain a continuous watch over Eternity.

World Log: FELLOWSHIP

System Data
- **System Name:** Beta Maxima 437
  - **Map Coordinates:** 6.31N 3.22E
- **Number Of Class M Present:** 3

Planetary Data
- **Position In System:** VII
- **Number Of Satellites:** 2
- **Planetary Gravity:** 1.15g
- **Planetary Size**
  - Diameter: 10,250 km
  - Equatorial Circumference: 17,500 km
  - Total Surface Area: 285,000,000 sq km
  - Percent Land Mass: 40%
  - Total Land Area: 114,000,000 sq km
- **Planetary Conditions**
  - Length Of Day: 22 Hours
  - Atmospheric Density: Terrestrial
  - General Climate: Cool Temperate
- **Mineral Content**
  - Normal Metals: 10%
  - Radioactives: Trace
  - Gemstones: 10%
  - Industrial Crystals: Trace
  - Special Minerals: Trace

Cultural Data
- **Dominant Life Form:** Mixed
- **Technological/Sociopolitical Index:** 343455-89
- **Planetary Trade Profile:** DDDDEDD/C(D)

The planet Fellowship is a haven for those who find themselves trapped by the growing complexities of a computerized age. The small planet was founded 40 years ago by a Terran religious organization that desired to return to a simpler way of life, devoid of technological contrivances and dependencies. Since its creation, the colony world has attracted numerous like-minded individuals, and recent census figures show a population in excess of two billion inhabitants. Citizens of Fellowship tolerate any and all philosophical positions that tolerate others in turn. They still refuse to use modern technological inventions of any kind, preferring to use their own skills. An associate-member in the Federation, Fellowship maintains contact with other worlds through their trade in local gemstones and handicrafts.

World Log: GAMMA HYDRA IV

System Data
- **System Name:** Gamma Hydra
  - **Map Coordinates:** 5.91S 5.96E
- **Number Of Class M Present:** 1

Planetary Data
- **Position In System:** IV
- **Number Of Satellites:** 2
- **Planetary Gravity:** 1.25g
- **Planetary Size**
  - Diameter: 14,250 km
  - Equatorial Circumference: 45,000 km
  - Total Surface Area: 552,000,000 sq km
  - Percent Land Mass: 70%
  - Total Land Area: 386,400,000 sq km
- **Planetary Conditions**
  - Length Of Day: 27 Hours
  - Atmospheric Density: Terrestrial
  - General Climate: Warm Temperate
- **Mineral Content**
  - Normal Metals: 20%
  - Radioactives: Trace
  - Gemstones: Trace
  - Industrial Crystals: Trace
  - Special Minerals: 45%

Cultural Data
- **Dominant Life Form:** 60% Alpha Centauri / 40% Human
- **Technological/Sociopolitical Index:** 989889-77
- **Planetary Trade Profile:** DDCDDCD/D(D)

Gamma Hydra IV is something of a 'hard luck' planet among the Federation's inhabited worlds. Little was known about the planet until after the Romulan War, and its proximity to the Romulan Neutral Zone was a deterrent to settlers for many years. Later, it was discovered that Gamma Hydra IV contained vast deposits of iridium. This discovery prompted the establishment of a small mining community some 15 years ago. Not long after the community was settled, Gamma Hydra IV's orbit took it through a rogue comet that showed traces of an unusual form of radiation. The inhabitants' radiation sickness caused them to age rapidly, eventually killing all members of the colony. The planet remained abandoned until four years ago when a second, more successful effort took root. Despite the lack of major setbacks since that time, the inhabitants of Gamma Hydra IV are beset with a reputation for having (and causing) bad luck.

World Log: GIDEON

System Data
- **System Name:** Delta Dorado
  - **Map Coordinates:** 3.57S 2.35E
- **Number Of Class M Present:** 1

Planetary Data
- **Position In System:** I
- **Number Of Satellites:** 1
- **Planetary Gravity:** 1.12g
- **Planetary Size**
  - Diameter: 15,900 km
  - Equatorial Circumference: 47,500 km
  - Total Surface Area: 611,00,000 sq km
  - Percent Land Mass: 95%
  - Total Land Area: 580,450,000 sq km
- **Planetary Conditions**
  - Length Of Day: 31 Hours
  - Atmospheric Density: Thick
  - General Climate: Warm Termperate
- **Mineral Content**
  - Normal Metals: 12%
  - Radioactives: 12%
  - Gemstones: Trace
  - Industrial Crystals: 10%
  - Special Minerals: Trace

Cultural Data
- **Dominant Life Form:** Gideon
- **Technological/Sociopolitical Index:** 499785-87
- **Planetary Trade Profile:** None

Gideon has suffered considerably from rampant overpopulation. It is an independent world that had previously avoided all contact with the Federation, fearing the cultural shock that would ensue. Fourteen years ago, the deliberate introduction of Vegan choriomeningitus into the planet's population caused the deaths of over six billion inhabitants. Though this has reduced the overpopulation problem, the Gideonites need to overcome deeper philosophical problems before they can resume contact with the rest of the Federation.

World Log: GREENSWARD
System Data
   System Name: Sigma Valara
      Map Coordinates: 1.44N 4.98E
   Number Of Class M Present: 1
Planetary Data
   Position In System: VIII
   Number Of Satellites: 2
   Planetary Gravity: 0.82g
   Planetary Size
      Diameter: 17,200 km
      Equatorial Circumference: 28,000 km
      Total Surface Area: 295,000,000 sq km
      Percent Land Mass: 33%
      Total Land Area: 97,350,000 sq km
   Planetary Conditions
      Length Of Day: 19.5 Hours
      Atmospheric Density: Terrestrial
      General Climate: Warm Terrestrial
   Mineral Content
      Normal Metals: 37%
      Radioactives: Trace
      Gemstones: Trace
      Industrial Crystals: Trace
      Special Minerals: Trace
Cultural Data
   Dominant Life Form: Human
   Technological/
   Sociopolitical Index: 998997-97
   Planetary Trade Profile: DDDEDCD/D(D)

A relatively young world, geologically speaking, Greensward is a collection of flat forest lands and long strips of coastal beach area. More importantly, it is also one of the few planets within the Federation to contain extensive ruins of an extinct advanced civilization. Scholars disagree as to whether the ruins originate from the Vegan Tyranny or are remnants of Preserver culture. Local industry centers around the careful excavation of artifacts and their resale to other archeological institutions.

World Log: HALKA
System Data
   System Name: Nola Boradne
      Map Coordinates: 4.27S 4.58E
   Number Of Class M Present: 1
Planetary Data
   Position In System: V
   Number Of Satellites: 0
   Planetary Gravity: .87g
   Planetary Size
      Diameter: 12,800 km
      Equatorial Circumference: 45,000 km
      Total Surface Area: 462,000,000 sq km
      Percent Land Mass: 45%
      Total Land Area: 207,900,000 sq km
   Planetary Conditions
      Length Of Day: 19 Hours
      Atmospheric Density: Terrestrial
      General Climate: Warm Temperature
   Mineral Content
      Normal Metals: 20%
      Radioactives: Trace
      Gemstones: 10%
      Industrial Crystals: Trace
      Special Minerals: 35%
Cultural Data
   Dominant Life Form: Halkan
   Technological/
   Sociopolitical Index: 555567–85
   Planetary Trade Profile: None

An independent world desiring no affiliation with the Federation, Halka is the home of an advanced race of Humanoids with a highly developed social philosophy. Though their planet is rich in dilithium crystal deposits, the Halkans are reluctant to trade with any members of the Federation because their native ores might, however indirectly, be used to commit acts of violence. This total trade refusal has hampered otherwise good relations with the Federation. Nevertheless, the Federation recognizes the Halkans' right to determine their own policies, and abides by their decisions. Star Fleet patrols the Nola Boradne system to discourage would-be smugglers and opportunists from attempts to mine Halkan minerals without authorization.

World Log: HARMONY
System Data
   System Name: Harridane 226
      Map Coordinates: 5.27N 3.89E
   Number Of Class M Present: 1
Planetary Data
   Position In System: II
   Number Of Satellites: 6
   Planetary Gravity: 1.2g
   Planetary Size
      Diameter: 8,900 km
      Equatorial Circumference: 14,600 km
      Total Surface Area: 295,500,000 sq km
      Percent Land Mass: 30%
      Total Land Area: 88,650,000 sq km
   Planetary Conditions
      Length Of Day: 22 Hours
      Atmospheric Density: Terrestrial
      General Climate: Warm Terrestrial
   Mineral Content
      Normal Metals: 20%
      Radioactives: Trace
      Gemstones: Trace
      Industrial Crystals: Trace
      Special Minerals: Trace
Cultural Data
   Dominant Life Form: Vulcan
   Technological/
   Sociopolitical Index: 887789–98
   Planetary Trade Profile: BBBCBBB/B(C)

Harmony is a Vulcan mixture of dissimilar economic interests molded into an efficient and profitable enterprise. Founded 70 years ago by a group of philosophers and scientists from the Vulcan Science Academy, Harmony has a pleasant environment that has attracted other Vulcan special-interest groups, including merchant traders, geologists, astrophysicists, and retired Star Fleet officers. Star Fleet maintains a small support/repair center that contributes handsomely to the planet's treasury.

World Log: HELLIOS

System Data
- System Name: Sigma Wyrenex
- Map Coordinates: 0.48N 2.02W
- Number Of Class M Present: 1

Planetary Data
- Position In System: VI
- Number Of Satellites: 2
- Planetary Gravity: 1.9g

Planetary Size
- Diameter: 10,500 km
- Equatorial Circumference: 33,000 km
- Total Surface Area: 412,000,000 sq km
- Percent Land Mass: 50%
- Total Land Area: 206,000,000 sq km

Planetary Conditions
- Length Of Day: 22 Hours
- Atmospheric Density: Terrestrial
- General Climate: Warm Temperate

Mineral Content
- Normal Metals: 25%
- Radioactives: Trace
- Gemstones: Trace
- Industrial Crystals: Trace
- Special Minerals: Trace

Cultural Data
- Dominant Life Form: 75% Alpha Centauri / 25% Human
- Technological/Sociopolitical Index: 999877-77
- Planetary Trade Profile: CCBBDCB/B(B)

Settled by Human and Alpha Centauran colonists a few years after the Federation was formed, Hellios is renowned for its agricultural production. Although newer worlds have outstripped Hellios in sheer volume of goods harvested, Hellios inhabitants pride themselves on the quality of their foods. In particular, Helliosian fruits are rare and expensive delicacies.

World Log: IMAGINATION

System Data
- System Name: Metriunn 867
- Map Coordinates: 3.33N 3.82W
- Number Of Class M Present: 1

Planetary Data
- Position In System: III
- Number Of Satellites: 3
- Planetary Gravity: 1.0g

Planetary Size
- Diameter: 8,760 km
- Equatorial Circumference: 15,400 km
- Total Surface Area: 228,000,000 sq km
- Percent Land Mass: 100%
- Total Land Area: 228,000,000 sq km

Planetary Conditions
- Length Of Day: 20 Hours
- Atmospheric Density: Terrestrial
- General Climate: Controlled Terrestrial

Mineral Content
- Normal Metals: Trace
- Radioactives: Trace
- Gemstones: Trace
- Industrial Crystals: Trace
- Special Minerals: Trace

Cultural Data
- Dominant Life Form: 30% Human / 70% Other
- Technological/Sociopolitical Index: 9999987-89
- Planetary Trade Profile: AABAABA/A(B)

This pleasure planet is actually a small planetoid, much of which has been hollowed out. Imagination serves the entertainment needs of millions of Federation tourists and vacationers each year. Though not as elaborate as similar facilities elsewhere in the Federation, Imagination is renowned for its unique collection of theme parks and period-preserves. Catering to every type of culture, past or present, this planet has earned the respect of sightseers and luxury-oriented citizens from dozens of different cultures. The saying is that if it can be imagined, it can be found on Imagination.

World Log: INDARAX

System Data
- System Name: Epsilon Indar
- Map Coordinates: 2.51N 1.52E
- Number Of Class M Present: 1

Planetary Data
- Position In System: II
- Number Of Satellites: 2
- Planetary Gravity: .79g

Planetary Size
- Diameter: 13,000 km
- Equatorial Circumference: 42,000 km
- Total Surface Area: 505,000,000 sq km
- Percent Land Mass: 42%
- Total Land Area: 212,100,000 sq km

Planetary Conditions
- Length Of Day: 20 Hours
- Atmospheric Density: Terrestrial
- General Climate: Cool Temperate

Mineral Content
- Normal Metals: 10%
- Radioactives: 10%
- Gemstones: 10%
- Industrial Crystals: Trace
- Special Minerals: Trace

Cultural Data
- Dominant Life Form: Andorian
- Technological/Sociopolitical Index: 987985-76
- Planetary Trade Profile: None

Indarax was one of the last planets to be colonized by the Andorian Empire. As such, it is slow to renounce traditional Andorian ways. True to the aggressive nature of their ancestors, Indarax maintains no natural industry. Instead, the native Andorians have turned Indarax into one gigantic center to train military personnel in various facets of the military arts. After failing to discourage this practice, the Federation recognized the right of the native Indaraxans to conduct their unusual occupation. Indaraxans saw extensive service during both the Romulan and Four Years War, earning respect and acceptance from other, more pacifistic members of the Federation. Today, Star Fleet maintains a permanent liaison/training center run by Andorians on Indarax.

World Log: INGRAHAM B

System Data
- System Name: Ingrahm
- Map Coordinates: 1.48S 5.02E
- Number Of Class M Present: 1

Planetary Data
- Position In System: II
- Number Of Satellites: 4
- Planetary Gravity: .94g

Planetary Size
- Diameter: 8,900 km
- Equatorial Circumference: 28,000 km
- Total Surface Area: 287,000,000 sq km
- Percent Land Mass: 60%
- Total Land Area: 172,200,000 sq km

Planetary Conditions
- Length Of Day: 27 Hours
- Atmospheric Density: Terrestrial
- General Climate: Tropical

Mineral Content
- Normal Metals: 25%
- Radioactives: Trace
- Gemstones: Trace
- Industrial Crystals: Trace
- Special Minerals: Trace

Cultural Data
- Dominant Life Form: Human
- Technological/Sociopolitical Index: 9888887–98
- Planetary Trade Profile: BACBBDC/A(B)

Ingraham B is noted throughout the Federation for its dazzling array of lush native flora. Botanical enthusiasts prize many of its specimens as natural works of art worth millions of credits. Some scientists believe sentient plant life may exist somewhere on Ingraham B, and a scientific research center has been established to investigate the possibility. Sixteen years ago, hordes of flying parasites almost wiped out the population, then established a symbiotic-mind control over the survivors. The inhabitants have largely recovered from that costly encounter, and maintain uninterrupted trade with the rest of the Federation. Ingraham B presently has a representative on the Federation Council.

World Log: IOTIA

System Data
- System Name: Sigma Iotia
- Map Coordinates: 6.78S 4.55W
- Number Of Class M Present: 1

Planetary Data
- Position In System: IV
- Number Of Satellites: 1
- Planetary Gravity: 1.1g

Planetary Size
- Diameter: 10,300 km
- Equatorial Circumference: 33,000 km
- Total Surface Area: 400,000,000 sq km
- Percent Land Mass: 60%
- Total Land Area: 240,000,000 sq km

Planetary Conditions
- Length Of Day: 25 Hours
- Atmospheric Density: Terrestrial
- General Climate: Terrestrial

Mineral Content
- Normal Metals: 22%
- Radioactives: 08%
- Gemstones: Trace
- Industrial Crystals: Trace
- Special Minerals: Trace

Cultural Data
- Dominant Life Form: Iotian
- Technological/Sociopolitical Index: 556675–78
- Planetary Trade Profile: CBDEECC/C(C)

Discovered early in the history of interstellar flight, the Humanoid culture of Iotia was introduced to Human social values and customs before the Federation's Prime Directive was developed. As a result of this 'contamination', the Iotians developed an aberrant culture based on an ancient Terran society that had organized criminal elements. Although this hastened the unification of the planet, it was accomplished with needless bloodshed and unnecessary misery. Since the *USS Enterprise*'s investigation of Iotia 15 years ago, Federation sociological teams have guided the Iotians to a more ethical form of government. Iotia is currently an associate member of the Federation.

World Log: IZAR

System Data
- System Name: Epsilon Bootis
- Map Coordinates: 4.37N 4.44W
- Number Of Class M Present: 1

Planetary Data
- Position In System: II
- Number Of Satellites: 1
- Planetary Gravity: 1.25g

Planetary Size
- Diameter: 15,500 km
- Equatorial Circumference: 51,500 km
- Total Surface Area: 614,000,000 sq km
- Percent Land Mass: 55%
- Total Land Area: 337,700,000 sq km

Planetary Conditions
- Length Of Day: 25 Hours
- Atmospheric Density: Terrestrial
- General Climate: Terrestrial

Mineral Content
- Normal Metals: 22%
- Radioactives: 12%
- Gemstones: Trace
- Industrial Crystals: Trace
- Special Minerals: Trace

Cultural Data
- Dominant Life Form: Izaran
- Technological/Sociopolitical Index: 998988–88
- Planetary Trade Profile: BBABBBC/A(B)

One of the original Human-Alpha Centauri colonies, Izar has long since developed into a major cultural and industrial center. Izarans are known for the high value they place on independence. Today, Izar is noted chiefly as a producer of advanced power systems and related technology, although much of the original Izaran wilderness has remained intact. This planet is also famous as the home of the Federation's most celebrated hero, Kelvar Garth, and is currently represented on the Federation Council.

World Log: JORINDAS
System Data
- System Name: Beta Vertis
- Map Coordinates: 0.99S 4.27W
- Number Of Class M Present: 1

Planetary Data
- Position In System: IV
- Number Of Satellites: 2
- Planetary Gravity: .85g

Planetary Size
- Diameter: 19,000 km
- Equatorial Circumference: 58,000 km
- Total Surface Area: 721,000,000 sq km
- Percent Land Mass: 30%
- Total Land Area: 216,300,000 sq km

Planetary Conditions
- Length Of Day: 19 hrs
- Atmospheric Density: Terrestrial
- General Climate: Cool Temperate

Mineral Content
- Normal Metals: 80%
- Radioactives: 10%
- Gemstones: Trace
- Industrial Crystals: Trace
- Special Minerals: Trace

Cultural Data
- Dominant Life Form: Joridian
- Technological/Sociopolitical Index: 987777–67
- Planetary Trade Profile: BBCBCCB/B(C)

An advanced humanoid culture, Joridians lack vocal cords, which forces them to communicate telepathically. Their average lifespan of 35 years is one of the shortest of any advanced species in the Federation. Despite a high birth rate, the population of Jorindas continues to remain at one million inhabitants. Jorindas is also noteworthy as the home planet of a unique life form known as the tribble.

World Log: KAFERIA
System Data
- System Name: Tau Ceti
- Map Coordinates: 1.27S 3.56E
- Number Of Class M Present: 1

Planetary Data
- Position In System: V
- Number Of Satellites: 2
- Planetary Gravity: 1.2g

Planetary Size
- Diameter: 20,000 km
- Equatorial Circumference: 61,000 km
- Total Surface Area: 750,000,000 sq km
- Percent Land Mass: 80%
- Total Land Area: 600,000,000 sq km

Planetary Conditions
- Length Of Day: 30 hrs
- Atmospheric Density: Terrestrial
- General Climate: Tropical

Mineral Content
- Normal Metals: 50%
- Radioactives: 30%
- Gemstones: Trace
- Industrial Crystals: Trace
- Special Minerals: Trace

Cultural Data
- Dominant Life Form: Kaferian
- Technological/Sociopolitical Index: 988767–77
- Planetary Trade Profile: ABCCCBB/A(C)

One of the first intelligent non-Humanoid races contacted by Humanity, Kaferians are insectoids who have developed an advanced civilization on a planet that resembles a gigantic rain forest. Kaferians are docile and reticent creatures. Though they have maintained trade agreements with the Federation since its inception, they have only recently applied for and received associate-member status. Kaferian culture is based on the production of native foodstuffs and local pharmaceuticals, which serve as major export items. Current population estimates place the number of Kaferian inhabitants at less than 500,000.

World Log: LAKELAND
System Data
- System Name: Purlii
- Map Coordinates: 8.20S 6.42E
- Number Of Class M Present: 1

Planetary Data
- Position In System: II
- Number Of Satellites: 2
- Planetary Gravity: .9g

Planetary Size
- Diameter: 11,500 km
- Equatorial Circumference: 36,000 km
- Total Surface Area: 460,000,000 sq km
- Percent Land Mass: 50%
- Total Land Area: 230,000,000 sq km

Planetary Conditions
- Length Of Day: 32 hrs
- Atmospheric Density: Terrestrial
- General Climate: Cool Temperate

Mineral Content
- Normal Metals: 5%
- Radioactives: Trace
- Gemstones: 4%
- Industrial Crystals: Trace
- Special Minerals: Trace

Cultural Data
- Dominant Life Form: Human
- Technological/Sociopolitical Index: 999999–97
- Planetary Trade Profile: BDDECDF/A(C)

Lakeland is a planet-wide collection of lakes and streams. One of the Federation's finest vacation spots, it is also one of the farthest, being located near the Triangle Zone. Distance notwithstanding, Lakeland enjoys a thriving tourist trade supported by innumerable fishing and aquatic sporting reserves across the planet's surface. Lakeland's government is representative, reflecting its status as a Federation colony world.

World Log: LAURA'S WORLD
System Data
- System Name: Laurison 294
- Map Coordinates: 2.44S 3.75E
- Number Of Class M Present: 1

Planetary Data
- Position In System: 1
- Number Of Satellites: 1
- Planetary Gravity: .95g

Planetary Size
- Diameter: 10,200 km
- Equatorial Circumference: 28,500 km
- Total Surface Area: 325,000,000 sq km
- Percent Land Mass: 55%
- Total Land Area: 178,750,000 sq km

Planetary Conditions
- Length Of Day: 25 Hours
- Atmospheric Density: Terrestrial
- General Climate: Controlled Terrestrial

Mineral Content
- Normal Metals: 10%
- Radioactives: Trace
- Gemstones: Trace
- Industrial Crystals: Trace
- Special Minerals: Trace

Cultural Data
- Dominant Life Form: 75% Human / 25% Other

Technological/Sociopolitical Index: 689997-77
Planetary Trade Profile: DDDEDD/C(B)

Billed as the most romantic planet in the galaxy, Laura's World is one of the few planets owned by a private citizen. Purchased shortly after its discovery some 30 years ago by the eccentric billionaire Maximus O'Connor, the planet was a wedding gift to his wife, Laura Deneuve Gamartine. Two years later, Laura died from Vegan choriomeningitus. In a state of continual grief, O'Connor retired from corporate life and turned Laura's World into a planet-wide shrine to the memory of his late wife. When O'Connor died three years later, ownership of the planet fell into the hands of his brother and only surviving heir, Paul O'Connor. Seizing on the tragic elements surrounding the planet's history, Paul turned the planet into a vast parkland. After spending vast amounts of his inheritance to complete the project, he opened Laura's World as a private, unspoiled get-away "for lovers only". O'Connor's sales pitch and the publicity surrounding his brother's eccentricity have combined to make Laura's World a unique financial success.

World Log: MAKUS III
System Data
- System Name: Makus
- Map Coordinates: 2.18S 0.33E
- Number Of Class M Present: 2

Planetary Data
- Position In System: III
- Number Of Satellites: 1
- Planetary Gravity: 1.4g

Planetary Size
- Diameter: 12,200 km
- Equatorial Circumference: 19,500 km
- Total Surface Area: 322,000,000 sq km
- Percent Land Mass: 60%
- Total Land Area: 193,200,000 sq km

Planetary Conditions
- Length Of Day: 28 hrs
- Atmospheric Density: Thick
- General Climate: Warm Terrestrial

Mineral Content
- Normal Metals: 50%
- Radioactives: 10%
- Gemstones: Trace
- Industrial Crystals: Trace
- Special Minerals: 20%

Cultural Data
- Dominant Life Form: 70% Vulcan / 30% Human

Technological/Sociopolitical Index: 887887-76
Planetary Trade Profile: BBBBCCC/B(C)

A cloudy, humid world, Makus III is a Federation member with a mixed Vulcan and Human population. Settled by Vulcan outcasts who had rejected the reforms of Surak, these individuals retain a cultural psychology with more emotional freedom than their parent world allows. Makus III later received an influx of Vegan technicians and scientists after several large dilithium deposits were discovered on the planet.

World Log: MALURIA
System Data
- System Name: Omega Cygni
- Map Coordinates: 0.59S 5.23E
- Number Of Class M Present: 1

Planetary Data
- Position In System: II
- Number Of Satellites: 6
- Planetary Gravity: .78g

Planetary Size
- Diameter: 18,200 km
- Equatorial Circumference: 62,000 km
- Total Surface Area: 715,000,000 sq km
- Percent Land Mass: 50%
- Total Land Area: 357,500,000 sq km

Planetary Conditions
- Length Of Day: 29 Hours
- Atmospheric Density: Terrestrial
- General Climate: Warm Temperate

Mineral Content
- Normal Metals: 20%
- Radioactives: 10%
- Gemstones: 10%
- Industrial Crystals: Trace
- Special Minerals: Trace

Cultural Data
- Dominant Life Form: Malurian

Technological/Sociopolitical Index: 888885-98
Planetary Trade Profile: ABCBBCC/B(B)

Maluria is a civilization on the mend. Fifteen years ago, all but a handful of its technologically advanced Humanoid natives were destroyed by a powerful space probe, later identified as the Nomad, which had been launched from Terra over a century before. The only survivors of the Malurian race were the independent traders and citizens living offplanet at the time of the disaster. As the planet's technological base itself was not disrupted (only the 'biological infestations' were removed), the task of rebuilding this once-proud Humanoid civilization has not been that difficult. The native Malurian population has risen to over one million inhabitants, due to the absence of immigration restrictions. Nevertheless, it will still take several decades for the planet to recover completely from the *Nomad* disaster.

World Log: MEDUSA
System Data
- System Name: Rhys
- Map Coordinates: 5.57S 6.37E
- Number Of Class M Present: 1

Planetary Data
- Position In System: 5
- Number Of Satellites: 2
- Planetary Gravity: 2.1g

Planetary Size
- Diameter: 12,200 km
- Equatorial Circumference: 18,500 km
- Total Surface Area: 350,200,000 sq km
- Percent Land Mass: 20%
- Total Land Area: 70,400,000 sq km

Planetary Conditions
- Length Of Day: 32 hrs
- Atmospheric Density: Thick
- General Climate: Warm Temperate

Mineral Content
- Normal Metals: 20%
- Radioactives: 25%
- Gemstones: Trace
- Industrial Crystals: Trace
- Special Minerals: Trace

Cultural Data
- Dominant Life Form: Medusan
- Technological/Sociopolitical Index: 988877–89
- Planetary Trade Profile: None

This planet is wrapped in a thick cloud layer with average surface temperatures of 38–65° C. Medusa is also the home of an ancient race that evolved beyond the need for physical bodies. Few offworlders have ever seen a Medusan, as the sight of these beings can cause serious mental disorder. Nevertheless, Medusans are a pacifistic race totally devoted to the advancement of science. In particular, they excel in interspacial geometries. They are often consulted to solve complex navigational problems for civilian and scientific interests throughout the Federation.

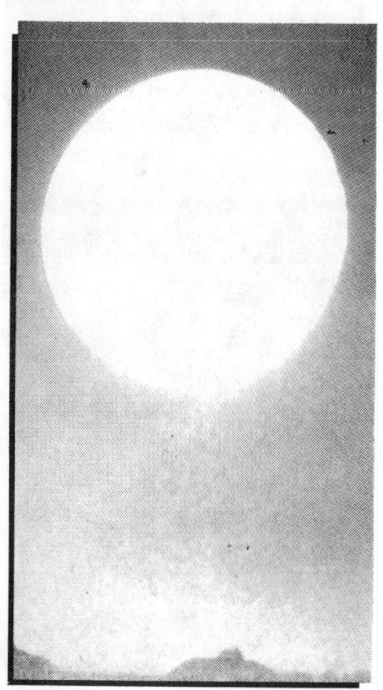

World Log: MEMORY ALPHA
System Data
- System Name: Karn Sim
- Map Coordinates: 3.31S 4.25E
- Number Of Class M Present: 1

Planetary Data
- Position In System: II
- Number Of Satellites: 0
- Planetary Gravity: 1.0g

Planetary Size
- Diameter: 14,000 km
- Equatorial Circumference: 44,000 km
- Total Surface Area: 560,000,000 sq km
- Percent Land Mass: 100%
- Total Land Area: 560,000,000 sq km

Planetary Conditions
- Length Of Day: 22 Hours
- Atmospheric Density: Terrestrial
- General Climate: Controlled Terrestrial

Mineral Content
- Normal Metals: 55%
- Radioactives: Trace
- Gemstones: Trace
- Industrial Crystals: Trace
- Special Minerals: Trace

The only redeeming feature of this barren asteroid is the Star Fleet Museum. Constructed over the last two decades, the museum is the central repository of all relevant historical, scientific, and cultural knowledge of every Federation member. This ongoing project is the central concern of the Federation Science Foundation. The main computer systems used on Memory Alpha contain the most advanced Cygnian and Terran data-processing features. Access to Memory Alpha's data banks is open and free to scholars upon request. Fourteen years ago, this installation was seriously damaged during the Lights of Zetar incident. At that time, it was feared that data loss in the main computer memory core would be irretrievable. Fortunately, the majority of the main computer's memory has been restored through the efforts of Daystrom Data Concepts Corporation.

World Log: MERAK
System Data
- System Name: Latis Cyrtiva
- Map Coordinates: 2.77N 3.22W
- Number Of Class M Present: 1

Planetary Data
- Position In System: II
- Number Of Satellites: 5
- Planetary Gravity: 1.22g

Planetary Size
- Diameter: 13,000 km
- Equatorial Circumference: 38,000 km
- Total Surface Area: 495,000,000 sq km
- Percent Land Mass: 70%
- Total Land Area: 346,500,000 sq km

Planetary Conditions
- Length Of Day: 32 Hours
- Atmospheric Density: Thick
- General Climate: Tropical

Mineral Content
- Normal Metals: 20%
- Radioactives: 25%
- Gemstones: Trace
- Industrial Crystals: Trace
- Special Minerals: Trace

Cultural Data
- Dominant Life Form: Vulcan
- Technological/Sociopolitical Index: 999879–98
- Planetary Trade Profile: AABBCBA/A(B)

One of the first worlds to be colonized by Vulcans, Merak is a tropical world rich in radioactives and industrial crystals used to run power plants. The need for increased productivity caused the colonists to eliminate much of the planet's northern rain forests to make way for newer, more advanced facilities. After the Four Years War, Merak began constructing ship-building facilities as well. It currently produces a large number of Star Fleet vessels of varying designs each year, and is also an important commercial and trade center.

World Log: MIRI'S WORLD
System Data
- System Name: Beta Persei
- Map Coordinates: 5.48S 6.02E
- Number Of Class M Present: 1

Planetary Data
- Position In System: III
- Number Of Satellites: 1
- Planetary Gravity: 1.01g

Planetary Size
- Diameter: 9,840 km
- Equatorial Circumference: 15,575 km
- Total Surface Area: 303,700,000 sq km
- Percent Land Mass: 60%
- Total Land Area: 182,220,000 sq km

Planetary Conditions
- Length Of Day: 24 hours
- Atmospheric Density: Terrestrial
- General Climate: Terrestrial

Mineral Content
- Normal Metals: 40%
- Radioactives: 10%
- Gemstones: Trace
- Industrial Crystals: Trace
- Special Minerals: Trace

Cultural Data
- Dominant Life Form: Onlie
- Technological/Sociopolitical Index: 344532-33
- Planetary Trade Profile: None

World Log: MORENA
System Data
- System Name: Eridani Gamma
- Map Coordinates: 2.88N 3.12E
- Number Of Class M Present: 1

Planetary Data
- Position In System: I
- Number Of Satellites: 0
- Planetary Gravity: 1.11g

Planetary Size
- Diameter: 14,500 km
- Equatorial Circumference: 47,000 km
- Total Surface Area: 575,000,000 sq km
- Percent Land Mass: 80%
- Total Land Area: 460,000,000 sq km

Planetary Conditions
- Length Of Day: 31 Hours
- Atmospheric Density: Terrestrial
- General Climate: Cool Temperate

Mineral Content
- Normal Metals: 5%
- Radioactives: 15%
- Gemstones: Trace
- Industrial Crystals: 10%
- Special Minerals: 10%

Cultural Data
- Dominant Life Form: Human
- Technological/Sociopolitical Index: 998997-67
- Planetary Trade Profile: AABBAAB/A(B)

World Log: MUDD'S WORLD
System Data
- System Name: Beta Aurigae
- Map Coordinates: 4.22S 5.32E
- Number Of Class M Present: 1

Planetary Data
- Position In System: 2
- Number Of Satellites: 0
- Planetary Gravity: 1.2g

Planetary Size
- Diameter: 10,600 km
- Equatorial Circumference: 17,500 km
- Total Surface Area: 280,000,000 sq km
- Percent Land Mass: 90%
- Total Land Area: 252,000,000 sq km

Planetary Conditions
- Length Of Day: 27 Hours
- Atmospheric Density: Thin
- General Climate: Cold Temperate

Mineral Content
- Normal Metals: 40%
- Radioactives: 20%
- Gemstones: Trace
- Industrial Crystals: Trace
- Special Minerals: Trace

Almost identical to Terra, Miri's World is a prime example of dual planetary evolution. The inhabitants of the planet flourished until a biological experiment into life-prolongation failed horribly, releasing a virus that killed all the adults on the planet. Though the doomed experiment did greatly expand the lifespan of the surviving children, each of these contracted the disease at the age of puberty. When the starship *Enterprise* discovered the planet about ten years ago, only a handful of survivors inhabited the planet. Since then, subsequent surveys of the planet have uncovered nearly 10,000 individuals, all under the age of twelve. Preventive serums have been successful in combatting the virus, and Federation sociological and planetary development teams are on Miri's World to guide the inhabitants until they are able to govern themselves.

Morena is the first planetary system outside the Terran-Alpha Centauri sector that Humans colonized strictly for starship construction. Though now eclipsed by more advanced production facilities on other worlds, Morena remains the most prestigious starship design and development center outside the original borders of the Federation. A featureless, barren world with little vegetation, Morena is also the home of the Morenan tree bear. This curious creature derives its sustenance not from organic compounds, but from the mental radiations generated by feelings of affection in Humanoids.

Devoid of all surface life, this cold planet is inhabited by androids. An itinerant trader named Harcourt Fenton Mudd first discovered the world. Through their interaction with Mudd, the androids learned of inherent flaws in Human behavior. Desiring to save the Human race from themselves, the androids attempted to gain control of the Federation starship *Enterprise*, but were defeated. The planet has since been quarantined. Except for authorized Federation science teams studying the androids, no outside contact is permitted with the planet.

World Log: NEW ABERDEEN

System Data
- System Name: Phi Galacius
- Map Coordinates: 2.41S 0.21E
- Number Of Class M Present: 1

Planetary Data
- Position In System: VI
- Number Of Satellites: 2
- Planetary Gravity: .86g

Planetary Size
- Diameter: 12,250 km
- Equatorial Circumference: 42,000 km
- Total Surface Area: 460,000,000 sq km
- Percent Land Mass: 40%
- Total Land Area: 180,000,000 sq km

Planetary Conditions
- Length Of Day: 28 Hours
- Atmospheric Density: Terrestrial
- General Climate: Warm Terrestrial

Mineral Content
- Normal Metals: 10%
- Radioactives: Trace
- Gemstones: 10%
- Industrial Crystals: 25%
- Special Minerals: Trace

Cultural Data
- Dominant Life Form: 50% Andorian / 25% Cygnian / 25% Human
- Technological/Sociopolitical Index: 889998–88
- Planetary Trade Profile: AABAAB/A(B)

World Log: NEW PARIS

System Data
- System Name: Omega Aurigae
- Map Coordinates: 1.78S 4.78W
- Number Of Class M Present: 1

Planetary Data
- Position In System: II
- Number Of Satellites: 4
- Planetary Gravity: .97

Planetary Size
- Diameter: 9,100 km
- Equatorial Circumference: 28,000 km
- Total Surface Area: 350,000,000 sq km
- Percent Land Mass: 80%
- Total Land Area: 280,000,000 sq km

Planetary Conditions
- Length Of Day: 25 Hours
- Atmospheric Density: Thick
- General Climate: Warm Temperate

Mineral Content
- Normal Metals: 20%
- Radioactives: 20%
- Gemstones: Trace
- Industrial Crystals: Trace
- Special Minerals: Trace

Cultural Data
- Dominant Life Form: Human
- Technological/Sociopolitical Index: 888898–97
- Planetary Trade Profile: AABBAA/A(B)

World Log: PALLAS PRIME

System Data
- System Name: Pallas 785
- Map Coordinates: 2.33S 7.04E
- Number Of Class M Present: 1

Planetary Data
- Position In System: 5
- Number Of Satellites: 2
- Planetary Gravity: .88g

Planetary Size
- Diameter: 8,750 km
- Equatorial Circumference: 12,750 km
- Total Surface Area: 285,500,000 sq km
- Percent Land Mass: 90%
- Total Land Area: 256,950,000 sq km

Planetary Conditions
- Length Of Day: 18 hrs
- Atmospheric Density: Thin
- General Climate: Desert

Mineral Content
- Normal Metals: 30%
- Radioactives: 30%
- Gemstones: Trace
- Industrial Crystals: Trace
- Special Minerals: Trace

Cultural Data
- Dominant Life Form: 60% Deltan / 20% Human / 20% Cygnian
- Technological/Sociopolitical Index: 565455–57
- Planetary Trade Profile: ACDCDDE/D(C)

A large industrial world, New Aberdeen is noteworthy for its culture, which is based on ancient Terran Scottish traditions. The planet's inhabitants are grouped into family clans, each of which sends representatives to a world-wide congress. New Aberdeen is also one of the Federation's largest manufacturers of commercial and civilian starships. Vast orbital and surface production centers produce some of the finest luxury and transport vessel designs in Federation space.

Settled in Stardate 0/9205 by Terran colonists from northern Europe, New Paris is governed by a representative system resembling that of Terra's 18th-century republican France. Inhabitants of New Paris are noted throughout the Federation for their literary and musical contributions. New Parisian fashion is also in popular demand on many of the UFP's civilized worlds. A cultural and trade leader, New Paris supports a population of over one billion inhabitants.

An arid desert world, Pallas Prime is nevertheless attractive to Federation speculators for its wealth of radioactives. Numerous small mining and trading centers have been established along the planet's northern hemisphere. However, surface conditions on the world are harsh. The planet's rapid rotation produces fierce wind storms that can last for several days. Despite this inhospitable climate, some agriculture has been successfully introduced near Pallas Prime's cooler northern ice cap, which has helped make the planet's inhabitants somewhat self-sufficient. Star Fleet maintains a training facility on the planet's southern continent for desert survival exercises.

World Log: PLATONIUS

System Data
- System Name: Helios
- Map Coordinates: 2.04N 5.93E
- Number Of Class M Present: 1

Planetary Data
- Position In System: IV
- Number Of Satellites: 1
- Planetary Gravity: .97g

Planetary Size
- Diameter: 11,800 km
- Equatorial Circumference: 37,000 km
- Total Surface Area: 460,000,000 sq km
- Percent Land Mass: 50%
- Total Land Area: 230,000,000 sq km

Planetary Conditions
- Length Of Day: 19 Hours
- Atmospheric Density: Terrestrial
- General Climate: Terrestrial

Mineral Content
- Normal Metals: 10%
- Radioactives: Trace
- Gemstones: Trace
- Industrial Crystals: Trace
- Special Minerals: 50%

Cultural Data
- Dominant Life Form: Platonian
- Technological/Sociopolitical Index: 665779–97
- Planetary Trade Profile: DDEEDED/D(X)

Platonius is inhabited by a race of Humanoids who visited ancient Terra in the fifth century B.C. after their star, Sandara, went supernova. Eventually settling on Platonius, the space explorers adopted many of the ancient Greeks' philosophical ideals. However, the Platonian race has suffered from increasing lifespans and decreasing birth rates, the result of a rare substance known as kironite, which was introduced into the Platonian food chain. When members of Star Fleet landed on the planet some 15 years ago, they determined that ingestion of this substance enhanced the psionic abilities of the individual, though with a corresponding decrease in fertility. Because the native Platonians exhibited uncontrollable desires to dominate other, less advanced groups, the Helios system has been quarantined until further notice.

World Log: PRECIPICE

System Data
- System Name: Brightstar
- Map Coordinates: 9.11S 4.61E
- Number Of Class M Present: 1

Planetary Data
- Position In System: VIII
- Number Of Satellites: 1
- Planetary Gravity: 1.1g

Planetary Size
- Diameter: 14,300 km
- Equatorial Circumference: 44,000 km
- Total Surface Area: 560,000,000 sq km
- Percent Land Mass: 94%
- Total Land Area: 530,000,000 sq km

Planetary Conditions
- Length Of Day: 25 hrs
- Atmospheric Density: Terrestrial
- General Climate: Warm Terrestrial

Mineral Content
- Normal Metals: 14%
- Radioactives: Trace
- Gemstones: Trace
- Industrial Crystals: Trace
- Special Minerals: Trace

Cultural Data
- Dominant Life Form: Human
- Technological/Sociopolitical Index: 999994–97
- Planetary Trade Profile: DDDDDEF/A(B)

The planet Precipice has the dubious distinction of being the Federation world closest to the borders of the Klingon Empire. A planet ruled by a representative democracy, Precipice has an advanced, system-wide detection system that can warn the planet's inhabitants in advance of any threat from Klingon or other hostile foes. Otherwise, there is little to boast of on Precipice.

World Log: QUARREL

System Data
- System Name: Wolf 515
- Map Coordinates: 4.22S 0.12W
- Number Of Class M Present: 1

Planetary Data
- Position In System: VIII
- Number Of Satellites: 0
- Planetary Gravity: 1.1g

Planetary Size
- Diameter: 12,400 km
- Equatorial Circumference: 38,000 km
- Total Surface Area: 450,000,000 sq km
- Percent Land Mass: 50%
- Total Land Area: 225,000,000 sq km

Planetary Conditions
- Length Of Day: 27 Hours
- Atmospheric Density: Terrestrial
- General Climate: Warm Temperate

Mineral Content
- Normal Metals: 30%
- Radioactives: Trace
- Gemstones: Trace
- Industrial Crystals: Trace
- Special Minerals: Trace

A cultural oddity among Federation worlds, Quarrel is divided into numerous private preserves where individuals and groups can resolve combat under controlled circumstances. Owned and operated by the Alpha Centauri Center for Psychological Studies, this vast experimental laboratory allows individuals to express acute anti-social and/or aggressive behavior patterns without fear of bringing actual harm to themselves or to others. The Federation Science Council has netted important results from this planet, especially in understanding Andorian hostility complexes.

World Log: RALA III
System Data
- **System Name:** Rala
- **Map Coordinates:** 4.22S 3.21E
- **Number Of Class M Present:** 1

Planetary Data
- **Position In System:** III
- **Number Of Satellites:** 2
- **Planetary Gravity:** 1.22g

Planetary Size
- **Diameter:** 18,700 km
- **Equatorial Circumference:** 64,000 km
- **Total Surface Area:** 750,000,000 sq km
- **Percent Land Mass:** 10%
- **Total Land Area:** 675,000,000 sq km

Planetary Conditions
- **Length Of Day:** 21 Hours
- **Atmospheric Density:** Terrestrial
- **General Climate:** Cool Temperate

Mineral Content
- **Normal Metals:** 30%
- **Radioactives:** Trace
- **Gemstones:** Trace
- **Industrial Crystals:** Trace
- **Special Minerals:** Trace

Cultural Data
- **Dominant Life Form:** Human
- **Technological/Sociopolitical Index:** 899985–97
- **Planetary Trade Profile:** BBDEEC/B(C)

Almost completely covered by water, this unique world has turned its natural deficit into a major advantage through automated ocean-based seafarming. Rala III currently maintains the largest concentrated seafarming project in the Federation. Annual yields of over 16 billion credits worth of seafood, grains, and mineral-rich products are harvested each year.

World Log: RASHILE
System Data
- **System Name:** Ungethiem
- **Map Coordinates:** 8.81S 6.02E
- **Number Of Class M Present:** 1

Planetary Data
- **Position In System:** IX
- **Number Of Satellites:** 1
- **Planetary Gravity:** 1.3g

Planetary Size
- **Diameter:** 16,900 km
- **Equatorial Circumference:** 52,000 km
- **Total Surface Area:** 660,000,000 sq km
- **Percent Land Mass:** 29%
- **Total Land Area:** 190,000,000 sq km

Planetary Conditions
- **Length Of Day:** 27 hrs
- **Atmospheric Density:** Terrestrial
- **General Climate:** Cool Temperate

Mineral Content
- **Normal Metals:** 2%
- **Radioactives:** 11%
- **Gemstones:** Trace
- **Industrial Crystals:** Trace
- **Special Minerals:** Trace

Cultural Data
- **Dominant Life Form:** Human
- **Technological/Sociopolitical Index:** 999993–98
- **Planetary Trade Profile:** ADDDCDE/D(C)

A Terran-like planet, Rashile is owned and operated by a Federation corporation, Rashile Gourmet Foods Incorporated, which uses the planet's rich soil for Federation-wide food production. Workers and agricultural specialists from all parts of the Federation live and work on Rashile. Their interests are represented by a participatory council reporting directly to corporate headquarters.

World Log: RIVIERA
System Data
- **System Name:** Ochs
- **Map Coordinates:** 2.22N 1.79E
- **Number Of Class M Present:** 1

Planetary Data
- **Position In System:** V
- **Number Of Satellites:** 2
- **Planetary Gravity:** .95g

Planetary Size
- **Diameter:** 13,000 km
- **Equatorial Circumference:** 41,000 km
- **Total Surface Area:** 512,000,000 sq km
- **Percent Land Mass:** 27%
- **Total Land Area:** 138,240,000 sq km

Planetary Conditions
- **Length Of Day:** 19 Hours
- **Atmospheric Density:** Terrestrial
- **General Climate:** Warm Temperate

Mineral Content
- **Normal Metals:** 26%
- **Radioactives:** Trace
- **Gemstones:** Trace
- **Industrial Crystals:** Trace
- **Special Minerals:** Trace

Cultural Data
- **Dominant Life Form:** 35% Caitian / 30% Human / 35% Other
- **Technological/Sociopolitical Index:** 888885–88
- **Planetary Trade Profile:** BBCBCDC/B(B)

A tropical world owned by General Entertainment Concepts Corporation, Riviera is a favorite vacation spot for citizens throughout the Federation. As its name implies, Riviera is famous for its extensive network of beaches, its aquatic sports, and its home-away-from-home accommodations for dozens of different cultures and life forms. Though Lakeland has more fishing spots, Riviera compensates by having a more central location within Federation space.

World Log: SALAZAAR

System Data
- System Name: Karnor
- Map Coordinates: 3.77S 3.31E
- Number Of Class M Present: 1

Planetary Data
- Position In System: III
- Number Of Satellites: 3
- Planetary Gravity: 1.12g

Planetary Size
- Diameter: 9,200 km
- Equatorial Circumference: 29,000 km
- Total Surface Area: 351,000,000 sq km
- Percent Land Mass: 82%
- Total Land Area: 287,820,000 sq km

Planetary Conditions
- Length Of Day: 28 Hours
- Atmospheric Density: Terrestrial
- General Climate: Cool Temperate

Mineral Content
- Normal Metals: 50%
- Radioactives: Trace
- Gemstones: Trace
- Industrial Crystals: Trace
- Special Minerals: Trace

Cultural Data
- Dominant Life Form: 50% Andorian / 25% Alpha Centauri / 25% Human
- Technological/Sociopolitical Index: 99998-98
- Planetary Trade Profile: AAAAAB/A(B)

The major starship design, construction, and testing center of the Federation, the orbital shipyards of Salazaar produce hundreds of military and commercial warp-driven vessels each year. This industrial and manufacturing world supports numerous Andorian, Centauran, and Terran investment companies devoted to the various facets of starship design and construction. Salazaar also maintains enormous optical and radio telescopes for galactic astronomical studies. The current population is well over 15 billion inhabitants, most of whom are contract technicians and scientists on loan from other Federation worlds.

World Log: SIGMA DRACONIS

System Data
- System Name: Sigma Beta 443
- Map Coordinates: 2.02N 5.22E
- Number Of Class M Present: 1

Planetary Data
- Position In System: V
- Number Of Satellites: 2
- Planetary Gravity: 1.25g

Planetary Size
- Diameter: 10,400 km
- Equatorial Circumference: 33,000 km
- Total Surface Area: 405,000,000 sq km
- Percent Land Mass: 70%
- Total Land Area: 283,500,000 sq km

Planetary Conditions
- Length Of Day: 26 Hours
- Atmospheric Density: Thin
- General Climate: Warm Temperate

Mineral Content
- Normal Metals: 35%
- Radioactives: Trace
- Gemstones: Trace
- Industrial Crystals: Trace
- Special Minerals: Trace

Cultural Data
- Dominant Life Form: Vulcan
- Technological/Sociopolitical Index: 888779-98
- Planetary Trade Profile: DDCCDDC/B(C)

A planet noted for its wide expanses and high surface temperatures, Sigma Draconis is also known for the variety of its avian life, the most spectacular of which is the Draconian air dragon. One of the more recent planets colonized by Vulcans, Sigma Draconis has several major cities in its southern hemisphere. It also has numerous universities and colleges devoted chiefly to the study of Vulcan and alien biologies. Star Fleet maintains a small support/repair facility on Sigma Draconis.

World Log: SPICA

System Data
- System Name: Juris Canopus
- Map Coordinates: 0.35N 0.12E
- Number Of Class M Present: 1

Planetary Data
- Position In System: 9
- Number Of Satellites: 12
- Planetary Gravity: .80g

Planetary Size
- Diameter: 7,500 km
- Equatorial Circumference: 11,500 km
- Total Surface Area: 250,000,000 sq km
- Percent Land Mass: 100%
- Total Land Area: 250,000,000 sq km

Planetary Conditions
- Length Of Day: 18 hrs
- Atmospheric Density: Thin
- General Climate: Arctic

Mineral Content
- Normal Metals: 10%
- Radioactives: 10%
- Gemstones: 50%
- Industrial Crystals: Trace
- Special Minerals: Trace

Cultural Data
- Dominant Life Form: 35% Tellarite / 20% Human / 45% Other
- Technological/Sociopolitical Index: 988985-99
- Planetary Trade Profile: BBCCDCCD(D)

A marginal Class M world, Spica is a small, insignificant planetoid. Its sole distinction is the abundance of naturally crystallized rock formations found nowhere else in the galaxy. Among these are the highly-prized Spican flamegems, small ruby-colored stones containing a liquid-mercury center. A number of Federation mining concerns prospect on Spica, which is otherwise uninhabited.

World Log: SUSTENANCE
System Data
- System Name: Sestarci 124
- Map Coordinates: 0.07N 0.34E
- Number Of Class M Present: 1

Planetary Data
- Position In System: VII
- Number Of Satellites: 1
- Planetary Gravity: 1.12g

Planetary Size
- Diameter: 10,450 km
- Equatorial Circumference: 33,550 km
- Total Surface Area: 412,000,000 sq km
- Percent Land Mass: 48%
- Total Land Area: 197,760,000 sq km

Planetary Conditions
- Length Of Day: 22 Hours
- Atmospheric Density: Terrestrial
- General Climate: Cool Terrestrial

Mineral Content
- Normal Metals: 25%
- Radioactives: Trace
- Gemstones: Trace
- Industrial Crystals: Trace
- Special Minerals: Trace

Cultural Data
- Dominant Life Form: Alpha Centauri
- Technological/Sociopolitical Index: 888987-87
- Planetary Trade Profile: BEEBDDC/B(C)

One of the Federation's major food producers, Sustenance grows the largest volume of annual crops in its quadrant. With a surface given almost entirely to mechanized farming, Sustenance grain and foodstuff sales amount to over 12 billion credits each year. It imports all its heavy machinery and technological needs in exchange for food shipments.

World Log: TALOS IV
System Data
- System Name: Talos
- Map Coordinates: 7.49S 1.48E
- Number Of Class M Present: 1

Planetary Data
- Position In System: IV
- Number Of Satellites: 0
- Planetary Gravity: .89g

Planetary Size
- Diameter: 19,200 km
- Equatorial Circumference: 60,000 km
- Total Surface Area: 665,000,000 sq km
- Percent Land Mass: 90%
- Total Land Area: 595,500,000 sq km

Planetary Conditions
- Length Of Day: 29 Hour
- Atmospheric Density: Thin
- General Climate: Cold Temerate

Mineral Content
- Normal Metals: 60%
- Radioactives: Trace
- Gemstones: Trace
- Industrial Crystals: Trace
- Special Minerals: Trace

Cultural Data
- Dominant Life Form: Talosian
- Technological/Sociopolitical Index: 49998A-99
- Planetary Trade Profile: Quarantined Planet

Discovered approximately 27 years ago, this world has not been completely surveyed, and so Star Fleet knows little about it. The results of Star Fleet's contact with the planet are classified. By order of the Secretary of Star Fleet, anyone who contacts Talos IV under any circumstances faces an automatic death penalty.

World Log: TELLAR
System Data
- System Name: 61 Cygni
- Map Coordinates: 1.49N 1.91W
- Number Of Class M Present: 1

Planetary Data
- Position In System: 5
- Number Of Satellites: 3
- Planetary Gravity: 1.25g

Planetary Size
- Diameter: 8,500 km
- Equatorial Circumference: 13,750 km
- Total Surface Area: 280,000,000 sq km
- Percent Land Mass: 50%
- Total Land Area: 140,000,000 sq km

Planetary Conditions
- Length Of Day: 20 hrs
- Atmospheric Density: Terrestrial
- General Climate: Warm Temperate

Mineral Content
- Normal Metals: 40%
- Radioactives: 20%
- Gemstones: 10%
- Industrial Crystals: 20%
- Special Minerals: Trace

Cultural Data
- Dominant Life Form: Tellarite
- Technological/Sociopolitical Index: 998989-78
- Planetary Trade Profile: EAAGADG/A(A)

Tellar is the home of one of the few non-Human races to have achieved interstellar flight. Tellarites are quarrelsome by nature, more through love of competition than aggressivness. They are also the finest gamblers in the galaxy. Tellar is a permanent member of the Federation Council, and its current population is over two billion inhabitants.

World Log: TERRA

System Data
- System Name: Sol
- Map Coordinates: 1.23N 2.79W
- Number Of Class M Present: 5

Planetary Data
- Position In System: 3
- Number Of Satellites: 1
- Planetary Gravity: 1.0g

Planetary Size
- Diameter: 9,845 km
- Equatorial Circumference: 15,465 km
- Total Surface Area: 304,517,000 sq km
- Percent Land Mass: 60%
- Total Land Area: 182,710,200 sq km

Planetary Conditions
- Length Of Day: 24 hrs
- Atmospheric Density: Terrestrial
- General Climate: Terrestrial

Mineral Content
- Normal Metals: 60%
- Radioactives: 10%
- Gemstones: 10%
- Industrial Crystals: 10%
- Special Minerals: Trace

Cultural Data
- Dominant Life Form: Human
- Technological/Sociopolitical Index: 999999–88
- Planetary Trade Profile: DDDDDDD/A(A)

This planet is the home of Humanity, and is one of the founding worlds of the Federation. It is currently the leading cultural and scientific member of the Federation. Star Fleet Command is based here, as are numerous scientific and diplomatic centers. The Sol system also supports extensive Human colonies on Sol IV (Mars), Sol II (Venus), and several moons throughout the system. Terra is a permanent member of the Federation Council. Its current population (including the Luna satellite center) is over 10 billion inhabitants.

World Log: TIBURON

System Data
- System Name: Beta Theseus
- Map Coordinates: 6.02N 5.79E
- Number Of Class M Present: 1

Planetary Data
- Position In System: 2
- Number Of Satellites: 2
- Planetary Gravity: 1.0g

Planetary Size
- Diameter: 9,700 km
- Equatorial Circumference: 14,500 km
- Total Surface Area: 280,000,000 sq km
- Percent Land Mass: 50%
- Total Land Area: 140,000,000 sq km

Planetary Conditions
- Length Of Day: 25 hrs
- Atmospheric Density: Terrestrial
- General Climate: Cool Temperate

Mineral Content
- Normal Metals: 60%
- Radioactives: 20%
- Gemstones: Trace
- Industrial Crystals: Trace
- Special Minerals:

Cultural Data
- Dominant Life Form: Tiburon
- Technological/Sociopolitical Index: 986676–67
- Planetary Trade Profile: BCBCCBC/C(C)

An associate member of the Federation, Tiburon is the home of a mutated Humanoid culture that may have escaped from Terra during the Eugenics Wars. Discovered only 60 years ago, Tiburon is a distant member of the Federation, lying near the current edge of the Federation-Gorn border. To all outward appearances, Tiburons are identical to Humans. However, Tiburons are able to change their gender at will, which is similar to the cellular metamorphosis of the Antosians. This ability may be the result of high levels of radiation from some time in the Tiberons' past. Nevertheless, their metamorphosis has produced a unique culture that views itself as a single extended family. Tiberons currently number over 700,000.

World Log: TRIACUS

System Data
- System Name: Alpha Lyrae
- Map Coordinates: 2.66N 2.48W
- Number Of Class M Present: 1

Planetary Data
- Position In System: IX
- Number Of Satellites: 7
- Planetary Gravity: 1.31g

Planetary Size
- Diameter: 18,100 km
- Equatorial Circumference: 54,200 km
- Total Surface Area: 712,000,000 sq km
- Percent Land Mass: 75%
- Total Land Area: 534,000,000 sq km

Planetary Conditions
- Length Of Day: 19 Hours
- Atmospheric Density: Thin
- General Climate: Cool Temperature

Mineral Content
- Normal Metals: 30%
- Radioactives: Trace
- Gemstones: Trace
- Industrial Crystals: Trace
- Special Minerals: Trace

Cultural Data
- Dominant Life Form: Human
- Technological/Sociopolitical Index: 776777–78
- Planetary Trade Profile: CDCDFDD/D(D)

This world was once the center of a powerful pirate empire that disappeared without a trace approximately 350 years ago. Scientists and historians are uncertain whether Triacus was the homeworld of the Vegan Tyranny or if the Vegan Tyranny absorbed the Triacans during their rise to power. Aside from the numerous ruins being excavated by planetary archeologists, Triacus is used primarily for agriculture. Today, it supports the needs of numerous neighboring systems.

World Log: TROYIUS
System Data
    System Name: Tellum
        Map Coordinates: 8.58S 4.98E
    Number Of Class M Present: 2
Planetary Data
    Position In System: V
    Number Of Satellites: 2
    Planetary Gravity: 0.92g
    Planetary Size
        Diameter: 18,200 km
        Equatorial Circumference: 45,000 km
        Total Surface Area: 385,000,000 sq km
        Percent Land Mass: 35%
        Total Land Area: 134,750,000 sq km
    Planetary Conditions
        Length Of Day: 22.75 Hours
        Atmospheric Density: Thin
        General Climate: Cool Temperate
    Mineral Content
        Normal Metals: 12%
        Radioactives: Trace
        Gemstones: Trace
        Industrial Crystals: 15%
        Special Minerals: 55%
Cultural Data
    Dominant Life Form: Troyian
    Technological/
    Sociopolitical Index: 668877–75
    Planetary Trade Profile: ABCBCCB/D(C)

Troyius, one of two planets in the Tellun system, is the home of a Humanoid culture believed to be the descendant of a lost Andorian colonial expedition. Both of these planets, Elas and Troyius, are rich in dilithium deposits, which makes them of sensitive political and military concern to both the Federation and the Klingon Empire. Troyians are blue-skinned and show pronounced aggressive tendencies when aroused, though the civilization is mostly peaceful and technologically advanced. Using its crude interplanetary spaceflight capability, Troyius fought Elas to a draw in a major interplanetary war for dominion of the star system. The Federation sent negotiators to mediate the dispute, resulting in the marriage of the Elasian ruling family's daughter Elaan to the son of Troyius' current ruler. The region is now stable, despite Klingon attempts to incite further civil disturbances in hopes of securing both worlds' stores of dilithium crystals.

World Log: VEGA
System Data
    System Name: Alpha Lyrae
        Map Coordinates: 2.66N 2.48W
    Number Of Class M Present: 1
Planetary Data
    Position In System: IV
    Number Of Satellites: 1
    Planetary Gravity: .98g
    Planetary Size
        Diameter: 9,000 km
        Equatorial Circumference: 14,400 km
        Total Surface Area: 315,000,000 sq km
        Percent Land Mass: 50%
        Total Land Area: 157,500,000 sq km
    Planetary Conditions
        Length Of Day: 23 hrs
        Atmospheric Density: Terrestrial
        General Climate: Terrestrial
    Mineral Content
        Normal Metals: 70%
        Radioactives: 05%
        Gemstones: 10%
        Industrial Crystals: Trace
        Special Minerals: Trace
Cultural Data
    Dominant Life Form: Human
    Technological/
    Sociopolitical Index: 875886–87
    Planetary Trade Profile: BCBCCB/C(C)

Once thought to be the home planet of the Vegan Tyranny (some scholars point to Triacus), Vega possesses extensive ruins belonging to some sort of sentient life. Today, Vega supports a Human population of over five billion inhabitants, and serves as a major cultural and trade nexus between neighboring star systems. Vegan nightlife is among the most festive and exciting in the entire quadrant. Much of the planet's southern continent has been left undeveloped so that archeologists can study the origins of the planet's first inhabitants.

World Log: VULCAN
System Data
    System Name: 40 Eridani
        Map Coordinates: 0.09S 2.31W
    Number Of Class M Present: 1
Planetary Data
    Position In System: III
    Number Of Satellites: 0
    Planetary Gravity: 1.15g
    Planetary Size
        Diameter: 9,700 km
        Equatorial Circumference: 14,500,000 km
        Total Surface Area: 300,200,000 sq km
        Percent Land Mass: 75%
        Total Land Area: 225,150,000 sq km
    Planetary Conditions
        Length Of Day: 27 hrs
        Atmospheric Density: Thin
        General Climate: Warm Terrestrial
    Mineral Content
        Normal Metals: 50%
        Radioactives: 20%
        Gemstones: 15%
        Industrial Crystals: Trace
        Special Minerals: Trace
Cultural Data
    Dominant Life Form: Vulcan
    Technological/
    Sociopolitical Index: 999989–98
    Planetary Trade Profile: FBECAEF/D(B)

The home of the Vulcan race, Vulcan has a very high native gravity, a thin atmosphere, and high surface temperatures that created the familiar phrase "hot as Vulcan". The Vulcan race predates the rise of Humanity and is the second most commonly encountered in the Federation. The planet is home to the famous Vulcan Science Academy, one of the most lavish experimental and theoretical research centers in the Federation. Vulcans are vegetarians by nature and are completely devoid of emotional expression. Their culture is based on a strict code of ethics that places logic and rational thought over 'Human' emotions. Vulcan is a permanent member of the Federation Council.

World Log: WALL

System Data
- System Name: Bahr
- Map Coordinates: 8.92S 5.31E
- Number Of Class M Present: 1

Planetary Data
- Position In System: VI
- Number Of Satellites: 2
- Planetary Gravity: 1.2g

Planetary Size
- Diameter: 15,600 km
- Equatorial Circumference: 48,000 km
- Total Surface Area: 610,000,000 sq km
- Percent Land Mass: 70%
- Total Land Area: 430,000,000 sq km

Planetary Conditions
- Length Of Day: 32 hrs
- Atmospheric Density: Thin
- General Climate: Warm Temperate

Mineral Content
- Normal Metals: 38%
- Radioactives: Trace
- Gemstones: Trace
- Industrial Crystals: Trace
- Special Minerals: Trace

Cultural Data
- Dominant Life Form: Human
- Technological/Sociopolitical Index: 999992–97
- Planetary Trade Profile: HBFDEEA/A(B)

A mining and manufacturing world, Wall produces some of the Federation's most dependable orbital shuttle and transport craft. Although much of Wall's resources must be imported from off-world, the sale of hundreds of transport craft each year more than makes up for this trade deficit. A representative democracy, Wall is an associate member of the Federation.

World Log: WRIGLEY'S PLEASURE PLANET

System Data
- System Name: Sol
- Map Coordinates: 1.23N 2.79W
- Number Of Class M Present: 2

Planetary Data
- Position In System: IV
- Number Of Satellites: 0
- Planetary Gravity: 1g

Planetary Size
- Diameter: 600 km
- Equatorial Circumference: 850 km
- Total Surface Area: 2,572 sq km
- Percent Land Mass: 100%
- Total Land Area: 2,572 sq km

Planetary Conditions
- Length Of Day: 24 hrs
- Atmospheric Density: Controlled Terrestrial
- General Climate: Controlled Terrestrial

Mineral Content
- Normal Metals: 90%
- Radioactives: Trace
- Gemstones: Trace
- Industrial Crystals: None
- Special Minerals: None

Cultural Data
- Dominant Life Form: 60% Human / 40% Other
- Technological/Sociopolitical Index: None
- Planetary Trade Profile: ABDBBBB/A(C)

Established in Stardate 2/02 by an interstellar cartel of entertainment directors, Wrigley's Planet is actually a stray asteroid now located in orbit around Sol IV. Hollowed out and converted into a self-contained amusement center, this asteroid contains numerous parks and special theme centers reflecting a wide range of entertainments and diversions.

TIMELINE

Following is a chronology of all major events pertaining to the United Federation of Planets.

Stardate −1/6907.20
Neil Armstrong becomes the first Human to set foot on Terra's moon, starting Human manned interplanetary exploration.

Stardate −1/8601.28
The Terran orbital transport *Challenger* explodes shortly after launch, killing all seven crew members aboard. This is the worst tragedy to date in Terra's fledgling space program.

Stardate −1/8602
Terrans launch their first permanent, orbital space station.

Stardate −1/8703
Andorians test their first prototypes of sub-light interstellar craft.

Stardate −1/9206–9609
The outbreak of the Eugenics Wars limits Terran manned space efforts as resources are turned to global war.

Stardate −1/9609
The Andorian Empire is formed with the first colonization of another world by Andorian explorers.

Stardate −1/9704.18
Terra's United States of America and Japan jointly fund the establishment of the first permanent base on Terra's moon. The Terran people re-dedicate themselves to space exploration.

Stardate 0/0001.01
January 1, 2000, the base date for the Reference Stardate system. On this date, the Science Council of Luna declares itself independent of the governments of the United States of America and Japan and requests status as a United Nations protectorate. Such status is granted, forming the first interplanetary Human government.

Stardate 0/0209
Terra's United Nations Scientific Council releases a 15-year projection estimating offworld and space-oriented industry to grow at an exponential rate.

Stardate 0/0308
Terran representatives sign the United Space Initiative in New York. This landmark agreement will focus and accelerate man's exploration of the Sol system for the benefit of all mankind.

Stardate 0/0310
Utilizing solar-sails, Alpha Centaurans begin a concerted effort to populate other planets within their own stellar system.

Stardate 0/04
Terra's Farside Moonbase begins operations, specializing in radio telescope observations.

Stardate 0/12
Marsbase 1, Terra's first interplanetary outpost, begins a thorough search for extraterrestrial life.

Stardate 0/15
Terra's first interstellar probes, the Stellar Series, are launched toward nearby stars. This probe series ends in 0/2200.

Stardate 0/2001
The Vulcan scientist Sardax proves the feasibility of interstellar travel using the base camp approach to long-range exploration. A series of supply/support colonies are later founded within a ten-light-year radius of Vulcan, with succeeding generations of colonists in turn continuing the expansion.

Stardate 0/2004
The Alpha Centauri Concordium of Planets is founded, marking the first development of an interplanetary union founded on democratic principles.

Stardate 0/2011.17
The Nomad probe is launched from Terran orbit. It is lost in space and presumed destroyed.

Stardate 0/2102
The first Tellarite experiments using a form of interstellar ramjet are begun.

Stardate 0/2207
First contact occurs between the Andorian Empire and the remnants of the Vegan Tyranny, a mysterious race of beings whose origins and physical appearance have never been determined. Some scholars suggest that the Vegan Tyranny were cybernetic rather than organic. At this time, they had lost much of their original power and influence, though it is not known how. The war between this race and the Andorians rages off and on for many years. Due to the Andorians, the Vegan Tyranny fails to regain their empire, and they all but disappear after 0/90.

Stardate 0/2210
Jackson Roykirk, designer of the Stellar Series, dies.

Stardate 0/2508
T'Sarra introduces the Kolinahr mental discipline on Vulcan.

Stardate 0/2808.12
Astronomers on Alpha Centauri pick up intelligent signals from outside their system. These signals will later be identified as originating from Vulcan.

Stardate 0/2900
Mysterious, intelligent signals are received at Terra's Farside Moonbase 2C. Emanating at 327° toward the galactic center in Sagittarius, from a distance of 15,000 light years, they are the first extraterrestrial communications ever heard by Humans.

Stardate 0/30
The inhabitants of the planet Cygnet XIV undergo a global political upheaval, resulting in the formal establishment of a dominant matriarchal system by the planet's females. Through succeeding generations, females are granted educational and other social privileges at the expense of the males. Although this system allows cybernetics and computer technology to grow, the social gap between the sexes also grows.

Stardate 0/3008.03
First contact is made between the Tellarites and Rigellian traders.

Stardate 0/3109
The Tellarites discover the fabulous wealth of the Orion Homeworlds.

Stardate 0/32
Inhabitants of the planet Edo begin to cultivate local fruits, with the goal of producing high-quality vintages. From these initial efforts will arise a planet-wide industry devoted to the production of the most sought-after wines, brandies, and liqueurs in the galaxy.

Stardate 0/3203
The United Nations commissions Solar Fleet for security and rescue purposes throughout the inhabited Sol system.

Stardate 0/35
Advanced fusion Prototype One experimental ship explodes, with all lives lost. This is a major setback for Terran interstellar travel capability. The destruction of the prototype is claimed by Colonel Green, a former United Nations Armed Forces officer. This act of sabotage begins what is now referred to as Colonel Green's War. Though the war lasts less than one year, several widespread incidents of industrial sabotage and urban terrorism show the enormous potential of such groups.

Stardate 0/3605
Terran space-time researchers find holes in the general theory of relativity, making faster-than-light communications and travel theoretically possible, though not yet an actuality. The interstellar probe *Drake* detects geon holes in the space-time fabric for the first time. These deformations are used decades later for warp communications.

Stardate 0/3805
Harmon Axelrod, first President of the Federation Council, is born.

Stardate 0/3901
Terra's Pluto Base opens. It will serve as a navigational checkpoint for out-system missions.

Stardate 0/3902.25
Preparations for the first Terran manned interstellar expedition are completed. The *UNSS Icarus* is an 8,600 metric-ton craft powered by a high-acceleration, sub-light-speed Bussard ramjet. A crowd of several thousand people watch nearby as the spaceship is launched from Luna, while billions watch live, televised coverage. Carrying a complement of 40, the *Icarus* is headed for Alpha Centauri. Its mission is to search for an inhabitable planet.

Stardate 0/4206.23
The *UNSS Icarus* arrives at Alpha Centauri. First contact occurs between Terrans and Alpha Centaurans.

Stardate 0/45
The Andorian Empire is at its height, with 13 colonized worlds outside the Andorian home system.

Stardate 0/4501
The United Nations Organization celebrates 100 years of cooperation among the peoples of Terra. People throughout the Sol system take part.

Stardate 0/4812
Alpha Centauran scientist Zephram Cochrane formulates the initial warp drive calculations that will make faster-than-light travel possible and, eventually, practical.

Stardate 0/5011
The Fourteen Clans of Cait are united under one government for the first time in their history, setting the stage for Caitian civilization as it is known today.

Stardate 0/5204
After four years, Terra receives the transmission of the Warp Drive Principle. It causes a sensation, and an intensive warp drive studies program is immediately set up.

Stardate 0/5303
Alpha Centauran biosociologist Zancmar Hodgkins publishes his Law of Parallel Planet Development, stating that similar planets develop similar life-forms with similar cultures. After careful study and approval by the Alpha Centauri Academy of Biosciences, it is transmitted to Terra, where it is received 52 months later.

Stardate 0/5409
The *Icarus* returns from its historic journey. The United Nations dispatches a mission to Alpha Centauri to open formal relations, discuss trade, and exchange knowledge of each other's history.

Stardate 0/5507–5909
The first experimental warp-driven ships are tested by Terran and Alpha Centauran research teams. The *United Nations Space Ship Bonaventure*, the first of the new ships, is commissioned. The first of the *Cochrane* Class, the *Bonaventure*, is well-armed with monochromatic high-intensity lasers, powered by the ship's fusion sub-light engine.

Stardate 0/5706
The Xenobiological Probability Study, underwritten by the University of Luna for the United Nations of Terra, is released. This study concludes mathematically that the chances of discovering any intelligent non-humanoid life forms within the next century of exploration are extremely small.

Stardate 0/59
The *Bonaventure* begins Terra's Warp Drive Era with a voyage to the Tau Ceti star system twelve light-years away.

The UN mission that left Terra in 0/54 arrives at Alpha Centauri, and diplomatic relations begin.

Stardate 0/5900 through 0/7200
Terran space forces have several violent encounters with aliens later identified as the Vegan Tyranny.

Stardate 0/6000
The warp drive ship *UNSS Powell* journeys to Alpha Centauri and is hailed as a remarkable achievement.

Stardate 0/6100
The *Powell* returns to Terra, bringing Zephram Cochrane. He is accorded all the pomp and pageantry any native Terran hero would receive.

Stardate 0/6201
The Fundamental Declaration of the Martian Colonies establishes independent government for all Terran colonies. It is used as a precedent-setting document for worlds wanting to declare governmental autonomy.

Zephram Cochrane disappears.

Stardate 0/6300

Alpha Centauri and Terra begin cultural exchanges. Their ties of friendship and cooperation continue to strengthen.

Stardate 0/6407

The *Franklin* series warp-driven message probe becomes operational. These small, unmanned probes have rudimentary astrogational equipment, and are capable of carrying a cargo of up to 0.1 metric tons in addition to several hundred recorded messages. These probes are later refitted with modern warp drives and used for the next three decades. A total of 380 are built.

Stardate 0/6507.19

While on an exploratory mission, the *UNSS Bonaventure* discovers Axanar and its intelligent but non-spacefaring Humanoid race. The discovery of this race further substantiates Hodgkins' Law, now indisputably accepted as valid.

Stardate 0/6511.12

First contact occurs with the Vulcans when a *Franklin* series warp-drive probe encounters a Vulcan colony world. As they have already developed the warp drive, Vulcan techniques substantially improve on the original design.

Stardate 0/6602

The *Bonaventure* is unaccountably lost on its third mission.

Stardate 0/6807

A delegation of Vulcan diplomats and scientists arrive on Terra to begin discussions of a formal alliance between Terra, Alpha Centauri, and Vulcan.

Stardate 0/7006–0/7210

Ten fusion-driven Space Arks are launched during this period, manned by people dissatisfied with sociopolitical and ecological conditions within the Sol system. It is later learned that the passengers of only one of these ships survived.

Stardate 0/7104 through 0/7301

An economic alliance is declared between Vulcan, Terra, and Alpha Centauri, and the first interstellar trade missions begin.

Stardate 0/7206

As a result of meetings with Vulcans and Alpha Centaurans, a detailed study is published on Terra strongly recommending a formal interstellar alliance between the three worlds.

Stardate 0/7308.20

First contact is made with the Tellarites. Under the command of Admiral Abel Niwen, a fleet of Terra's United Nations Space Force on patrol in the Sol system meets a single, intruding Tellarite ship. After an unusual confrontation, the Tellarite commander accepts an offer of peaceful coexistence between the two races.

Stardate 0/7404.17

The first successful test of warp radio between Pluto and Terra makes interstellar communication practical for the first time.

Stardate 0/7511.29

First contact with the Andorians nearly ends in disaster when an Andorian starship fires on a Terran exploratory vessel. Terra prepares for war, but cooler heads on Vulcan convince Terran leaders to negotiate with the growing Andorian Empire.

Stardate 0/7703

The First Alpha Centauri Conference preserves interstellar peace when Vulcan diplomats convince Andor that it has nothing to gain and everything to lose by fighting Terra and her allies. Andor joins the informal alliance.

Stardate 0/7801

The United Nations Space Force's *Messier* Class cruiser becomes operational. This class is the first to be equipped with the newly developed particle beam cannon. Refitted for combat duty in the Romulan War, the *Messier* Class sees extensive action in that conflict. A total of 875 are built.

Stardate 0/7907.27

Terran ships make contact with the Orion Colonies in the Rigel system after learning about their existence from Tellarite traders.

Stardate 0/8110–0/8206

The first joint scientific project between Terra, Alpha Centauri, and Vulcan shows tangible benefits when a new series of research probes are launched from all three worlds.

Stardate 0/8204

A series of meetings takes place on Vulcan, attended by delegates of the five major spacefaring governments. This attempt to establish a single, unifying government fails to receive popular support because its primary goals and policies are not adequately defined. Diplomats agree to work on defining the roles and responsibilities of the new government.

Stardate 0/8508

An unknown disease spreads through Terra's 200-man research base on Pluto, leaving no survivors. The disease is later linked to a contaminated souvenir brought in by a careless Orion trader. This is the first unpleasant incident between Terrans and Orions, and helps to set the tone for future relations.

Stardate 0/8706.06

Work begun on Vulcan five years ago leads to another series of meetings among the major starfaring races. At the First Babel Conference, all five races sign the Articles of Federation, establishing the United Federation of Planets. The original signatory powers include Terra, Alpha Centauri, Vulcan, Andor, and Tellar. The goals of the UFP include ensuring interstellar security and improving economic trade, scientific research, and galactic exploration. In conjunction with these objectives, Star Fleet Command is to be created within the next three years, providing a unified military force for exploration and common defense. The Orion Colonies offer to join the UFP, provided that they are paid ten trillion credits "in compensation". Their request is rejected, and so they remain outside the Federation.

Stardate 0/8708

In the first example of Federation military cooperation, the Alpha Centauran *Djartanna* Class destroyer enters service in the Terran United Nations Space Force. Over the next three decades, a total of 316 are constructed for the UNSF and Star Fleet Command.

Stardate 0/8804

Plans are made for a Federation-wide news-gathering and reporting agency. As a result, the Solarian News Agency merges with other planetary services, creating the United Federation of Planets Infonet.

Stardate 0/89

Space buoys are deployed to improve navigation and security within Federation boundaries.

Stardate 0/8909.14

Terran and Alpha Centauran warships are operating on a joint trading mission and war games maneuver when tragedy strikes. A misunderstanding of navigational instructions is compounded by a weapon fire-control systems failure. Two Terran destroyers are annihilated, killing 232 crewmen. This accident vividly points out the need for a single command structure and a central training facility for starship crews of all Federation members.

Stardate 0/8910.10

Star Fleet Command replaces the spacegoing forces of all member planets, and all ships are now redesignated as "United Space Ships". To discourage the possible misuse of military forces anywhere in space, General Order Number One is adopted as the most important regulation in Star Fleet.

Stardate 0/90

The UFP Patents Bureau is established to provide scientists, engineers, and inventors of all member planets galactic protection for their work.

Stardate 0/9006

Continued advances are made in communications theory and technology. Research leads to a level of near-perfect efficiency. From this point on, messages sent via warp radio, now called subspace radio, travel at the unbelievable speed of Warp 15, or 3375 times the speed of light. Over the next two years, all starships have their communications equipment modified accordingly.

Stardate 0/9109.19

Star Fleet Academy is founded on Alpha Centauri, and its first class of 300 students represents eight different Humanoid races.

Stardate 0/9211.03

The *USS Atlas*, a Federation cargo ship operating near the frontier of Federation space, is attacked and destroyed, though this is not known until the recovery of its marker/recorder buoy containing a complete transcript of the events preceding the *Atlas'* destruction.

Stardate 0/9211.17

After failing to arrive as scheduled at the Sector 5D Agricultural Colony, the *USS Atlas* is listed as missing.

Stardate 0/9302.21

A Star Fleet scout ship recovers the marker/recorder buoy from the lost cargo vessel *USS Atlas*. Tapes from the buoy reveal that the transport was not lost in space, but was fired upon by enemy aliens of unknown origin. Star Fleet Command later learns that this was the first act of violence committed by the Romulans against the Federation.

Stardate 0/9310

Star Fleet Command's *Horizon* Class cruiser becomes operational. This is the first class of warship to be jointly designed and constructed by engineers from several member systems of the new UFP. It is also the first class to be equipped with the new quasi-nuclear photon-neutron torpedoes. An excellent design, it will serve with Star Fleet's front-line units for almost five decades. More than 1,300 are built.

Stardate 0/9310.18

The *USS Amaretto*, operating within Federation-patrolled territory, is attacked by two starships of unknown configuration. The vessels are similar to those described by the commander of the *USS Atlas*. The freighter is severely damaged, but the attackers break off when a Federation four-ship destroyer squadron appears. The Star Fleet Command flagship attempts to establish communications for purposes of identification and explanation. The alien vessels fail to understand or ignore all efforts to communicate, and successfully evade pursuit.

Stardate 0/9411

A total of 32 unarmed warp-driven message probes are launched toward areas of uncharted space from starships and planets near Delta VII. Each probe contains complete symbolic instructions and messages in every known language. The messages request the establishment of diplomatic relations and the resolution of any existing dispute via peaceful means. No probe is ever regained, and all are assumed to be lost or destroyed by the pirates.

Stardate 0/9507.08

Star Fleet Engineering Command's first major construction project culminates in the activation of Star Base 1. This is the first major artificial construction, repair, and service facility built for Star Fleet Command.

Stardate 0/9511.30

The Federation Council passes a special directive to Star Fleet Command. In addition to new, massive appropriations for fleet construction, the directive orders several cruiser formations redeployed to strengthen defenses in the area where the USS Atlas was lost. A special scout squadron under the jurisdiction of Star Fleet Intelligence Command is dispatched to obtain any possible information on the pirates, and, if possible, to make diplomatic contact. The squadron consists of twelve warp-driven patrol craft, each manned by a crew of 15 volunteers. None of the craft are ever seen or heard from again.

Stardate 0/9708

Star Base 3 is completed and assumes operational status. This base is used as the primary command headquarters for Star Fleet Operations during the Romulan War. Its great distance from the front makes command, control, and communications protocols difficult to execute efficiently. For this reason, many Star Fleet squadron and group commanders are able to exert enormous personal authority, responsibility, and initiative while fighting this war.

Stardate 0/9800

Small-scale student exchange programs begin among several UFP members.

Stardate 0/9905.04

In the most tragic incident of piracy to date, the commercial passenger liner SS Diana is systematically attacked. Almost 600 passengers and crew are killed and the cargo apparently stolen. Within weeks, the Diana Lives! Foundation is established so that people do not forget the tragedy of that ship's loss.

Stardate 1/0001

Several UFP cultural exchange programs, including the Student Exchange Program and the Galactic Cultural Exchange, are postponed indefinitely. The reasons include a decreasing interest in the projects and the fear of pirates attacking shipping.

Stardate 1/0011.21

Star Fleet's 155th Combat Squadron, currently on recreational leave, is caught in a surprise attack at the site of the unfinished Outer Sector Defense Outpost 4. A major sensor failure at the outpost permits a squadron of pirate cruisers to sneak up and catch the squadron unprepared for combat. Though the pirates left the incomplete base untouched, they destroyed eleven of the squadron's twelve starships. Enemy losses are believed to be very light.

Stardate 1/0101.01

Century Day celebrations throughout colonized space are interrupted with news of the destruction at Outer Sector Defense Outpost 4. The USS Carronade, a Cavalry Class destroyer, survives to report about the sneak attack. The senior officers of the destroyer describe enemy vessels painted as giant, winged creatures that performed suicide runs with fusion-explosive missiles. Intercepted subspace radio transmissions from this battle are translated, finally giving the enemy a name—the Romulans. The UFP also obtains its first accurate bearing on Romulan-held space.

Stardate 1/0200

The USS Horizon journeys to the edge of the galaxy.

Stardate 1/0311.02

Outer Sector Defense Outpost 1, located in the Delta II system, is destroyed by a squadron of seven Romulan cruisers. Commodore Tonsum Han, commanding the 159th Combat Squadron, has his entire force out on maneuvers during the time of attack. He is subsequently court-martialed and discharged for dereliction of duty.

Stardate 1/0312.06

Star Fleet Command institutes a Mobilization Alert to bring all bases and construction facilities to combat readiness. As part of the Mobilization Alert, a Zone of Transport Escort is established in the disputed areas. Star Fleet assigns military escorts to all priority transports.

Stardate 1/0405

Star Fleet Command and several leading universities co-publish a report on the Romulan race. This study examines all available information on the Romulans and describes their threat to the Federation.

Stardate 1/0501

After several months of careful analysis and discussion, ranking Star Fleet officers at Star Base 3 report their decision. All subsectors within Sectors 5, 7, and 10 go to Code 1 War-Alert status to combat the Romulans' irregular hit-and-run tactics.

Stardate 1/0507.22

Two Romulan gunboats are surrounded and crippled in the Sexton system by units from Star Fleet's 123rd Combat Squadron. The Romulan ships self-destruct while several Federation ships maneuver close for boarding. Four UFP destroyers are lost with all hands. Star Fleet issues standing orders prohibiting its vessels from closing with even a badly damaged Romulan vessel.

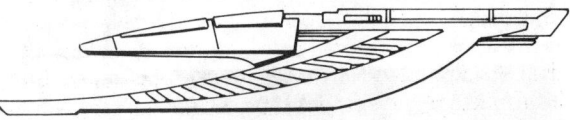

Stardate 1/0511

Star Fleet Command's Marshall Class destroyer becomes operational and is rushed into immediate full-scale production. Equipped with many of the most recent technological advances, this warship is the mainstay of the Federation's combat fleet during the latter part of the Romulan War. The Marshall remains in active service for 60 years, longer than any other major warship class before or since. A total of 2,900 ships are built.

Stardate 1/0512.09

Discussions are held at the highest echelons of the Federation and Star Fleet Command. As a result, President of the Federation Council Cristofur Thorpe issues a sealed, standing order by subspace radio to all individuals possessing the rank of Admiral, Council Secretary, or Senior Ambassador. If formal contact is made with the official Romulan government, the Federation will demand that all hostilities cease immediately, or a state of war will be declared. Any military or governmental official receiving this order has the full authority of the UFP to authorize such a declaration.

Stardate 1/0606.16

Star Fleet's 150th Combat Squadron, under the command of Admiral Rex Gunther, meets a solitary Romulan *U-13* Class cruiser near Eta Leonis VI. Instead of attacking, Admiral Gunther follows Thorpe's instructions, opens known Romulan hailing frequencies, and warns the invading ship of his orders. Gunther gives the Romulan government six months to respond. Otherwise, it means war. Though the Romulan ship does not communicate, it is permitted to depart with the warning. This marks the sole meeting of Federation and Romulan warships without bloodshed on either side.

Stardate 1/0610.14

Since Admiral Gunther issued his warning, at least one Federation warship has remained in the vicinity of Eta Leonis VI, awaiting a Romulan response. The *USS Patton*, a brand-new *Marshall* Class destroyer, is the ship on picket duty when three *U-15* Class cruisers close. While decelerating, the Romulans open fire. The *Patton*'s Captain Spadora makes one transmission before a Romulan cruiser fires a single guided missile. The torpedo hits the side of the *Patton*, totally disintegrating it. Spadora's message is received by other vessels in the area and relayed throughout the Federation. The Romulans' intentions are clear, and war is declared.

Intercepted subspace radio communications are translated and analyzed to help the UFP understand their foe. The Romulan War calls attention to the strategic importance of the Triangle.

Stardate 1/0702 through 1/0907

Scores of individual ship-versus-ship and ship-versus-outpost encounters occur throughout this period of the Romulan War. Each side wins several of these confrontations, but more often, the opposing forces successfully destroy one another.

Stardate 1/0802

Continuing their advance into Federation space, Romulan ships form 'wolf packs' to attack Federation transports. Three escorted Federation convoys are attacked and destroyed in this manner. Officials believe Romulans are hijacking the cargoes before destroying the transports. As they press deeper into Federation space, the Romulans are becoming desperately short of supplies.

Stardate 1/0805.02

Headed for the Triangle, a Romulan armada of 60 ships attacks three Federation squadrons near Gamma Hydra. Though Federation forces are outnumbered, both sides take heavy casualties. Star Fleet's new tactics match Romulan ferocity, leaving both fleets badly depleted and exhausted. However, the Romulans force a Federation retreat, and they resume course for the Triangle. The 132nd Strike Squadron, under the command of Admiral William Larson, reinforces the battered UFP forces and repulses the Romulan armada. This battle seriously weakens Star Fleet, but it also prevents the formation of a major Romulan fleet in the Triangle. Excluding isolated, small-scale engagements, the Triangle remains Romulan-free for the remainder of the war.

Stardate 1/0807.25

Four Romulan squadrons bombard Alpha Omega B with star-bomb missiles, rendering the planet uninhabitable. Two Romulan squadrons performing diversionary tactics are wiped out by local defense squadrons, but over 20,000 military and civilian personnel are killed in the main attack. This marks the Romulans' deepest penetration into Federation space.

Stardate 1/0809

Shortages of men, starships, and supplies reach critical levels for both Federation and Romulan forces, as both fleets force deep penetrations into their opposing governments' territory. Numerous raids and battle losses make it increasingly difficult for either side to form effective formations and continue the war.

Stardate 1/0811.01

While on an exploration and survey mission in the Triangle, the *USS Cavalier* is ambushed by Romulan cruisers in a newly discovered planetary system. After destroying the ship, the Romulan vessels move off without bothering to examine the system. A twelve-man landing party, under the command of Lieutenant Lawrence David Baker, is stranded there.

Stardate 1/0901.20
In his now-famous "Sighted Man of Peace" address to the Federation Council, Senior Councilman Abraham Dannon recommends offering a peace treaty to the Romulans. During the next ten days, advocates of both viewpoints hold heated discussions on the proposition.

Stardate 1/0902.01
The Federation Council votes on Councilman Dannon's proposal for a peace offer. The measure is accepted by a one-vote margin, and is immediately transmitted via subspace radio to the Romulan Star Empire.

Stardate 1/0904.28
The Federation Council receives a response from the Romulan Star Empire. According to their Imperial Senate, the treaty must contain the provisions that no members of the warring races meet face-to-face, and that no ships cross a negotiated Neutral Zone. Additional information on the exact location, dimensions, and restrictions applying to the Neutral Zone are also emphatically requested. Councilman Dannon, placed in charge of the subspace negotiations, responds within one week.

Stardate 1/0905.01
The Battle of Cheron is fought in Romulan space between two squadrons of Federation ships and remnants of four Romulan groups. The battle ends inconclusively when neither side has any combat-capable ships remaining. This battle marks the UFP's last opportunity to organize a fleet strong enough to reach the supposed location of the Romulan homeworld. It is considered a victory nevertheless, because the Romulans lost more ships than the Federation.

Stardate 1/0906.17
Stranded for seven months on what is now known as Baker's World, the crewmen from the USS Cavalier are picked up by the USS Lorelei without having suffered any casualties. For his skill and leadership, Lieutenant Lawrence David Baker receives the Star Fleet Commendation of Valor and a promotion, as well as becoming an immediate media hero.

Stardate 1/0907.28
The Romulans communicate with the Federation government and insist on additional territorial gains for the Romulan Star Empire. In exchange, they are willing to accept tighter restrictions on Neutral Zone outposts. Dannon reluctantly makes many of the necessary concessions, and Federation Council President Thorpe ratifies the completed Treaty of Peace. The treaty is transmitted to the Romulan Star Empire.

Stardate 1/0909.09
The Imperial Senate of the Romulan Star Empire broadcasts its ratification of the Treaty of Peace on all subspace frequencies. The message is picked up by Federation starships along the border, and the treaty terms go into immediate effect. After 17 years of piratical attacks and declared hostilities, the Romulan War is finally over.

Stardate 1/0909.10
Established by the Treaty of Peace, the Neutral Zone is now in effect. A period of withdrawal permitted by the treaty lasts until Stardate 1/1207. All invading Federation and Romulan forces begin retreating at maximum warp speed to their respective sides of the new boundary.

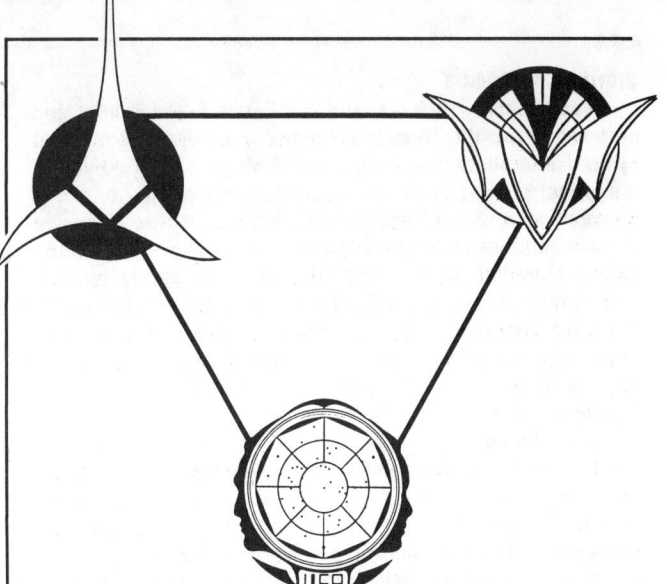

Stardate 1/0910–2412
Peace reigns, but the Orion Colonies know that the Klingon Empire will soon discover the existence of the Federation. The Colonies sign non-aggression and trade treaties with the Federation, but still remain outside the UFP.

Stardate 1/1001
With the Romulan War ended, budgetary constraints force Star Fleet Command to decommission a number of warships. The entire fleet of Messier Class cruisers is deactivated, even though the class served exceptionally well throughout the Romulan War. The Zone of Transport Escort is lifted, and galactic peace brings tremendous growth in industry, trade, and tourism.

Stardate 1/1001.05
The negotiations establishing the Romulan Neutral Zone destroy the political aspirations of Councilman Dannon. His opponents claim that he, as chief negotiator, gave away too much of the disputed area to the Romulans. Dannon is politically censured, and later, loses his position as Federation Councilman.

Stardate 1/1207
The period of withdrawal from the Neutral Zone permitted under the peace treaty is now over. From this time on, no warship may cross the Romulan Neutral Zone. All Federation cultural exchange programs resume, after having been suspended during the Romulan War. Federation officials release a public survey poll showing rising confidence in the UFP and its ability to perform its intended duties.

Stardate 1/1301
Official membership in the United Federation of Planets reaches 100.

Stardate 1/1303.21
Abraham Dannon, author of the Romulan/Federation peace treaty and chief negotiator of its provisions, is assassinated by a spectator at a political rally where he was scheduled to speak. A controversial, much-despised figure in his own time, Dannon will later be revered for his contributions to galactic peace. The Terran civilian decoration for peace, the Dannon Prize, is named for him.

Stardate 1/1803
Ships of the UFP Galactic Cultural Exchange project complete their first visit to all Federation member worlds.

Stardate 1/1804.03

Star Fleet's initial network of manned and automated outposts along the Neutral Zone becomes operational. The system is expanded and improved during the next 30 years, until most military theorists consider it impossible for a ship to cross the Zone undetected. It is assumed that the Romulans have created a similar network. This is supported by the fact that none of the 17 Federation space vessels known to have penetrated the Neutral Zone have returned.

Stardate 1/1907

A major, privately operated research station opens on Deneva and begins scientific investigations into transtater physics.

Stardate 1/2000

Well-preserved remains of the galaxy's oldest civilization, estimated to be 7.5 billion years old, are found on Planet 522-IV.

Stardate 1/2008

The USS Yardley travels to Axanar and suffers several casualties among its contact party. As a result, the planet is interdicted under the Non-Interference Directive.

Stardate 1/2106

The Star Fleet Museum on Memory Alpha is completed. This is the newest UFP repository for major scientific and historical artifacts. The facility quickly becomes a major scientific attraction for researchers from throughout the Federation. Over the next ten years, a number of famous warships are brought to the Museum and placed in tractored orbits around the planetoid.

Stardate 1/24

First evidence of extra-galactic life is discovered when an unknown probe is recovered from Sector 24.

Stardate 1/25

The UFP's major space development complex, the huge Centauri Spaceworks, opens with contracts from many member worlds.

Stardate 1/30

Captain James Smithson is dishonorably discharged from Star Fleet in the first violation of the Prime Directive.

Stardate 1/31

Growing numbers of interstellar tourists quickly make Argelius a favorite vacation spot because of its nightlife.

Stardate 1/3500

The theory of molecular reintegration achieves a major breakthrough with the first successful transmission of organic life.

Stardate 1/3612

The Federation Council refuses a funding request from Star Fleet for the development of new starships. To Star Fleet's enormous surprise, all funds previously assigned to complete the construction of Star Base 12 are "indefinitely postponed". Because construction had actually begun, the installation retains its designation, but it remains uncompleted and inoperative until after the end of the Four Years War.

Stardate 1/3802

The interplanetary war of Beta Cersus within the Romulan Neutral Zone creates tension between the Federation and the Romulan Empire. Though neither side entered the conflict, this incident loosens the Federation's purse strings for advanced class ship construction.

Stardate 1/40

The first major wave of Triangle settlements begins.

Stardate 1/4011

A new series of major antimatter refineries become available and are built at various locations in Federation territory.

Stardate 1/4104

Intelligent flying Humanoids are discovered on Alpha Virginis II, a planet located in Sector 14C.

Stardate 1/4608

Richard Daystrom, renowned physicist and developer of duotronics, is born.

Stardate 1/4705

The invention of the medical tricorder allows physicians to diagnose Rigellian plague, saving many lives.

Stardate 1/5105

First contact with the Klingon Empire leads immediately to armed conflict when the USS Sentry confronts the Klingon cruiser Devisor near Gamma Demetrius. Information obtained from spies and Klingon prisoners convinces Federation authorities that the Klingons and the Romulans have met and seem to be old and bitter foes. The "Klingon Menace" begins to overshadow conflict with the Romulans. Declaring neutrality, the Orion Colonies trade with both groups. Klingon raids on Federation shipping often masquerade as Orion-based pirates and vice-versa.

Stardate 1/5201

The Arcturus Test Range begins operations, serving as Star Fleet's newest propulsion and weaponry test facility.

Stardate 1/53

In the final year of its five-year mission to explore new worlds, the USS Valiant is lost in the vicinity of the Vendikar system.

Stardate 1/5708

The Terra-Return League is formed on Benecia Colony. It begins the Back-To-Earth movement, whose goal is to dissolve the Federation and return all Humans to the Sol system.

Stardate 1/6300

The surprising strength of the Back-to-Earth movement creates heated debate on both sides of the issue.

Stardate 1/6512

The largest spacelift in history evacuates ten million inhabitants from Bayard's Planet. The planet is in the path of the expanding Phi Puma stellar explosion, and the shock wave will destroy it.

Stardate 1/6608

Theta VII becomes the 500th member of the UFP. The Federation is becoming so large that only major grievances can be dealt with properly, a source of concern among some members.

Stardate 1/6806

To celebrate 50 years in business, the Cultural Exchange Project throws a Federation-wide fair that is long remembered.

Stardate 1/7009

Th'allt, an Andorian colony world, appeals to the Federation Council for economic protection from Tellarite merchants. The Bureau of Interstellar Trade and Commerce fails to take timely and effective action to resolve the situation.

Stardate 1/7109

Physicist Richard Daystrom shares a Nobel Prize with William Abramson for their revolutionary computer theory with duotronics, which processes information concerning every atom in the galaxy.

Stardate 1/72

Dissatisfaction with the inner workings of the Federation hierarchy creates much criticism of the UFP's Present structure among many member-worlds.

Stardate 1/7201

While conducting 'fleet maneuvers' near Th'allt as part of Operation Archimedes, Andorian Admiral Hathari fires on Tellar-registered trading ships. This reveals the Scandal of Archimedes, which emphasizes the unwieldy bureaucracy of the Federation and adds to the popularity of the Terra-Return League.

Stardate 1/7206

Richard Daystrom's revolutionary theory on computer information processing, combined with William E. Abramson's transtater physics, results in the design of the first practical, portable universal translator.

Stardate 1/7407

The materializer (later called the transporter) is invented.

Stardate 1/75

Continued discord with UFP policy cripples the Federation's economic strength and threatens its ability to provide security to all members.

Stardate 1/7603

Extensive dilithium deposits are discovered at the Rigel XII Mining Complex. The Orion colonies mine and sell the crystals to both the UFP and Klingon Empire, for use as power rectifiers in starship warp drives. Dilithium revolutionizes interstellar travel and military weapon technology.

Stardate 1/7701

The Second Babel Conference meets to address a number of issues, including the volatile issues raised by the Terra-Return League. After lengthy speeches, the vote to dissolve the United Federation of Planets fails, leaving the Federation intact. Immediately after the Conference, the Terra-Return League disbands, and its political influence ceases.

Stardate 1/8203–1/8703

Klingon activities near the Federation border decrease drastically during this period, with few Klingon warships seen and the number of routine confrontations dropping by more than 70 percent. Star Fleet Intelligence later learns from Operation Dixie that the Klingons are fighting a war with an unknown race along their coreward border.

Stardate 1/8209

Construction of the USS Constitution begins at Star Fleet's San Francisco Naval Shipyard.

Stardate 1/8402

The largest space rescue in history occurs when the USS Deerslayer recovers the 600 passengers and crew of the SS Juliana from an unexplored sector.

Stardate 1/8706

In recent years, many of the problems that have plagued the UFP have been solved. The Federation enters its second century stronger than ever. The Great Awakening begins.

Stardate 1/8801.04

Star Fleet's Constitution Class cruisers become operational with the commissioning of the USS Constitution. Less than one month later, the USS Enterprise is commissioned, under Captain Robert April.

Stardate 1/90

The USS Wells inexplicably travels through time as it returns from a three-year mission in only 33 solar days.

Stardate 1/9001

After a two-year shakedown cruise, the first five-year mission of the Enterprise begins under Captain April.

Stardate 1/9107

A study completed for the Federation Council's Office of Public Information reports that the new dilithium-powered starships will eventually permit a thorough exploration of all sectors within the Federation's sphere of influence. This finding supports Star Fleet's recent emphasis on its Galaxy Exploration Command.

Stardate 1/9209

Star Fleet Intelligence later learns that the first Axanarian task force under command of Klingon Admiral Kkorhetza left the Klingon naval base of Ruwan.

Stardate 1/9212.21

The USS Bohr is diverted from picket duty, permitting a Klingon battle force to reach the Federation-manned Arcanis IV Research Outpost. Klingon marines massacre the entire crew of this base.

Stardate 1/9301

Debris from the exploded USS Ajax is found in the form of a comet. This is the first such incident to occur. Star Fleet Intelligence later learns that the first Axanarian task force entered Federation space at this time.

Stardate 1/9302.24

The USS Irwin detects a Klingon Battle Group in the unclaimed space between the two powers. Star Fleet transfers all available warships from neighboring sectors to organize a defense.

Stardate 1/9309

Star Fleet Intelligence later learns that the first Axanarian task force arrived at Axanar at this time, with a second, reinforcing task force also on its way there.

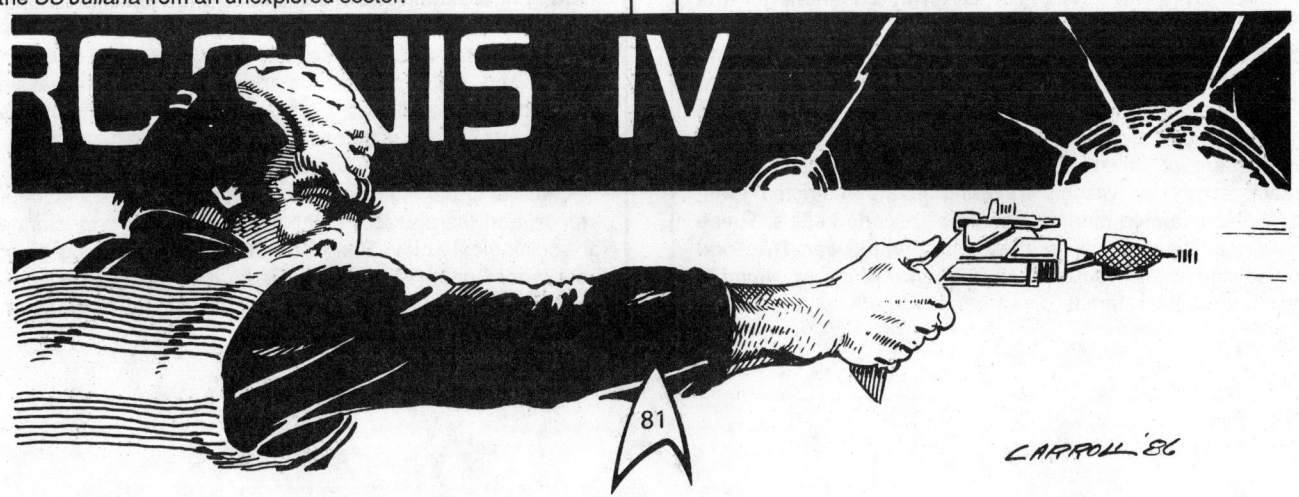

Stardate 1/9403
The USS *Gulliver*, a *Sawyer* Class scout, is sent to Axanar to evaluate the planet's sociological development.

Stardate 1/9404.01
The log later recovered from the USS *Gulliver*'s ship recorder buoy indicates that a Klingon task force met and destroyed the *Gulliver* as it entered the Axanarian system.

Stardate 1/9405.29
The USS *Xenophon*, a *Marklin* Class destroyer, encounters and disables a Klingon *D-4E* cruiser eight parsecs from Axanar. The commander of the *Xenophon* is Captain Garth of Izar.

Stardate 1/9406.05
On routine patrol, the USS *Bonhomme Richard* locates and retrieves the USS *Gulliver*'s recorder buoy, which reveals the vessel's fate. In light of the recent Arcanis massacre, the Federation Council demands that the Klingon forces at Axanar withdraw to their border under Star Fleet escort. The Klingon Admiral at Axanar is permitted four months to receive instructions from his Empire. The USS *Xenophon* is already on its way to Axanar.

Stardate 1/9407.09
Garth reaches Axanar several hours before the *Bonhomme Richard*, and so is given command of a scout squadron assigned to monitor the Klingon task force.

Stardate 1/9408.29
One of the scouts near Axanar picks up the second, incoming Klingon task force. Despite being outnumbered, Garth quickly implements a tactical plan that results in his victory at the Battle of Axanar.

Stardate 1/9409.29
In response to the Federation Council, Admiral Kkorhetza refuses to withdraw his ships from Federation territory, issuing a formal declaration of alliance with the natives on Axanar. This results in a state of war between the UFP and the Klingon Empire, and the Four Years War begins. Captain Garth defeats Kkorhetza's forces and is awarded the Federation Medal of Valor. Though tactical experts expect the Romulans to enter the war on one side or the other, they do not.

Stardate 1/9412
Researchers at HiBeam Energies, Ltd. develop the ship-mounted phaser. Hasty installation of the phasers onto Star Fleet vessels causes numerous accidents. Phasers are withdrawn from service for additional tests.

Stardate 1/9501
Captain Robert April retires from Star Fleet after quietly speaking out against certain Federation policies. He continues to serve as an ambassador-at-large.

Stardate 1/9506
Captain Christopher Pike is given command of the *Enterprise*.

Stardate 1/9509.07
As a result of the numerous ship disappearances, Star Fleet Command orders the Zone of Transport Escort for a large region of Federation space. This order restricts movement of private and commercial starships, requires naval escort for vessels travelling in the restricted area, and places armed marines aboard all escorted ships. These new regulations remain in effect until after the war. The Zone order significantly reduces the frequency of piracy attempts and unexplained starship disappearances.

Stardate 1/9601
The Battle of Sinbad IV marks the first major confrontation between ground troops of the opposing forces. The Battle of Delgon-R marks the first use of Klingon gravitic mines and the first defensive action by Klingon forces.

Stardate 1/9603
Star Fleet withdraws *Constitution* Class cruisers from front-line combat duty against Klingon forces. The class will continue to serve on other fronts in its pre-war capacities.

Stardate 1/9608
The Defense of Rudgur III marks the first use of chlortheragen, a Klingon-manufactured nerve gas. Captain Christopher Pike quarantines Talos IV under General Order Number Seven. General Order 7 states that "any transgression... shall be punishable by death," the only order ever to do so.

Stardate 1/9702
New, improved phaser weapon systems are installed in front-line ships.

Stardate 1/9709.10
The renegade Klingon Admiral Kamato and his followers establish the Imperial Klingon States in the Triangle. Initially, the IKS contains only two planets: K'Linsann (formerly Patterson's Place) and Kinarra.

Stardate 1/9801
Researchers at the Vulcan Science Academy develop a hypospray antidote to chlortheragen, the Klingon nerve gas.

Stardate 1/9802.28
Initially using captured Klingon ships, Star Fleet attacks the Klingon fleet at Grank in the largest fleet action of the war.

Stardate 1/9805.12
The Axanar Peace Mission convenes.

Stardate 1/9806.13
The Four Years War ends, with the Treaty of Axanar signed by representatives of the United Federation of Planets and the Klingon Empire. The Axanar Peace Mission negotiates the establishment of limited diplomatic channels between the two sides and obtains concessions from each to create new UFP/Klingon boundaries. The phaser and photon torpedo replace the laser and accelerator cannon as the Federation's primary shipboard weapons systems. A second colonial expansion begins into the Triangle, resulting in a trade boom unequalled in known history.

Stardate 1/9807–9904
Klingon citizens required to relocate in compliance with the Treaty of Axanar are transported to planets on their side of the newly defined Federation/Klingon border.

Stardate 1/9901–9905
No longer requiring the services of many older starships, Star Fleet decommissions or destroys large quantities of cruisers, destroyers, and scouts. All *Constitution*, *Loknar*, *Larson*, and *Nelson* Class starships, refitted with phasers and photon torpedoes, continue to serve as the Federation's first line of defense.

Stardate 1/9903
General Order Number One is specifically suspended for Axanar, and the planet is established as a UFP protectorate for sociological study. Based on the anticipated success of the Axanar Culture Mission, the Federation gives the government of Axanar the right to petition for full membership in Stardate 2/4903.

Stardate 1/9905

A full-scale research project under the Office of Star Fleet Research and Exploration confirms the underlying accuracy of the transwarp theory, later leading to the transwarp drive. The Zone of Transport Escort is lifted.

Stardate 2/0001.11

The Federation Council votes unanimously to impose harsh sanctions against Orion companies, ports, and shipping interests that participate in the Green Slave trade. UFP members boycott Orion ports, a controversial move that bankrupts a number of UFP companies dependent on Orion trade. Despite this, the boycott remains in effect, proving that the UFP can live without Orion trade.

Stardate 2/0103.13

Captain Christopher Pike of the USS Enterprise delivers a report on the Orion slave trade after an investigative mission into Orion space. Upon publication, the report shocks and outrages many. The Federation Council officially endorses the boycott of the Orion worlds, in effect telling the Orion government to ban the slave trade or face being cut off diplomatically and economically from the UFP.

Stardate 2/0105.01

The First Amendment to the Articles of Federation is passed, banning the trade in Green Slaves outside the strict confines of the Orion neutrality area. After this date, no Orion vessel operating outside the Orion colonies in the Rigel System is allowed to carry slaves. The Federation sanctions force the Orion colonies to abolish the slave trade, at least officially. Underground traffic in Green Slaves continues, though strongly interdicted in free space by Star Fleet actions.

Stardate 2/0704

After Captain Pike is promoted from *Enterprise* Captain to Fleet Captain over *Constitution* Class vessel operations, his hand-picked successor, Captain James T. Kirk, becomes the youngest man ever to command a *Constitution* Class vessel.

Stardate 2/0710.21

The vast buildup of Klingon military might has totally eclipsed all fear of the long-dormant Romulans. The complacency of Star Fleet is shattered when a Romulan vessel, using electronic cloaking to shield it from detection, destroys four Neutral Zone border outposts with a new, powerful plasma bolt weapon. The *USS Enterprise* pursues the Romulan ship into the Neutral Zone and picks up images of Romulans, revealing them to be Vulcanoid in appearance. After taking heavy damage from the *Enterprise*, the Romulan ship self-destructs.

Stardate 2/0711

The Vulcan Academy of Science allays fears of Vulcan/Romulan collusion when it publicizes its theory concerning the Romulans' Vulcan heritage. This theory postulates a race known as the Preservers, who seeded the galaxy with Humans and Humanoids.

Stardate 2/0801

The Organians prevent a second war between the Federation and the Klingons, imposing a peace treaty on both sides. The Gorns massacre the population of Cestus III. Star Fleet doubles its patrols along the Romulan Neutral Zone and establishes new, larger, more heavily armed border stations in reaction to the Romulan border attack of Stardate 2/0710.

Stardate 2/0803.21

A Star Fleet-sponsored science team rediscovers a Vulcan colony world that had been captured by Romulan forces in the Triangle Zone. When the planet's ores played out, the Romulans abandoned the mining settlement, destroying records and equipment and stranding the Vulcan inhabitants. By the time the scientists arrived, most of the Vulcans were dead. Sarek, a highly respected scientist/statesman from Vulcan, is given custody of a five-year-old Vulcan/Romulan hybrid named Saavik.

Stardate 2/0804.09
The Organian Treaty Zone is established, making important changes in the Klingon/Federation border and giving additional territory to both governments.

Stardate 2/0902
The Babel Conference on the Coridan Question is settled by the inspired oratory of Sarek of Vulcan. Coridan is made a UFP protectorate.

Stardate 2/1002
Operation Purloin begins when Captain James Kirk of the *USS Enterprise* succeeds in stealing a prototype of the cloaking device from a Romulan flagship. The *Enterprise* escapes three Romulan battlecruisers by activating the cloaking device. The Federation makes a major military gain when the device is delivered to Star Fleet headquarters.

Stardate 2/1003.01
First Federation contact with the Tholians occurs, though the Vulcans were previously aware of their existence.

Stardate 2/1004
Despite intense study by the best minds in Star Fleet, the Romulan cloaking device remains a mystery. Nevertheless, political pressure forces Star Fleet to make a public display of the stolen device. The device is installed on a Federation ship and dignitaries from all over the UFP observe the experiment from a nearby vessel. To the horror of the test's organizers and the Federation Council (who pressed for the test) the ship fitted with the cloaking device and the vessel containing the UFP dignitaries both vanish. Seconds later, there is a huge explosion. Neither ship is ever seen again, and scientists quit working on cloaking device technology.

Stardate 2/1204
The *Enterprise* returns from its five-year mission. It is the only ship remaining from the first group of early *Constitution* Class vessels. All others have been lost in service.

Stardate 2/1204
In honor of the triumphal return of the *Enterprise*, Star Fleet adopts the *Enterprise* emblem, abolishing the practice of individualized emblems for each ship.

Stardate 2/1204–1210
Admiral James Kirk is appointed to the Star Fleet's Operating Forces Board, and uses his influence and prestige to assure Star Fleet's continued vigilant, but non-militant activities in the face of increased Klingon aggression outside the Neutral Zone.

Stardate 2/1702.15
Operation Dixie departs for Klingon space to learn the fleet composition and strength of the Imperial Navy. Dixie succeeds in delivering some information, but all operatives are listed as missing in action.

Stardate 2/1704
The *Enterprise* Class heavy cruiser is established with the christening of the newly refitted *USS Enterprise*. However, the christening ceremony has to wait when a crisis sends the ship out to investigate V'ger, a huge vessel moving toward Terra and capable of incredible destruction. The *Enterprise* discovers that V'ger is the ancient Terran satellite Voyager I, and diverts it from its path toward Terra.

Stardate 2/1708
Star Fleet Intelligence dispatches Project Grey Ghost to gather information on the capacities, commitments, and deployment of forces of the Romulan Star Empire.

Stardate 2/1801.13
Gibraltar, an unwanted world in the Triangle Zone, becomes the site of a joint settlement by the UFP and the Romulan Empire for negotiations between the two powers.

Stardate 2/1808.10
Saavik, ward of Sarek of Vulcan, enters Star Fleet Academy. Sarek's family prestige heads off a storm of controversy over the admission of a 'Romulan' to the Academy. Though only half-Romulan and raised as a Vulcan, many people see Saavik as an enemy alien. Nevertheless, Saavik is a valuable resource to Star Fleet, for whom she interprets intelligence data about the Romulans. Because of her help, many myths about the Romulans are put to rest, and the Federation develops a better understanding of Romulan psychology.

Stardate 2/2206
Estimates indicate that the population of the Triangle has quintupled in the previous 22 years.

Stardate 2/2206
Project Grey Ghost returns and is heralded a complete success. Star Fleet gains important information on the nature, organization, and threat cababilities of the Romulan Star Navy.

Stardate 2/2206.01
Saavik graduates Star Fleet Academy at the top of her class. Promoted to Lieutenant, j.g., she is assigned to take her cadet cruise aboard the *Enterprise*.

Stardate 2.2206.16
Khan Noonian Singh, a dictator of Terra's Eugenics Wars who was exiled to Ceti Alpha V, captures the cruiser *USS Reliant*.

Stardate 2/2206.20
The *Reliant*, under Khan Noonian Singh's piratical command, ambushes the *USS Enterprise*, manned by Star Fleet Academy cadets on a training cruise. After a battle in the Mutara Nebula, Khan is dead, and the *Enterprise* severely damaged. Commander Spock dies saving the *Enterprise* from the detonation of the Genesis Device, which transforms inorganic matter into primitive life forms. His inert body is launched toward the world where the Genesis Effect is accelerating the growth of living things.

Stardate 2/2206.22
On the Genesis Planet, Dr. David Marcus and Lieutenant Saavik find a Vulcan baby who is growing up at a highly accelerated rate. This proves to be the regenerated body of Spock, minus his intellect and essence.

Stardate 2/2206.25
A Klingon *Bird of Prey* Class scout attacks and destroys the research vessel *USS Grissom* and cripples the *Enterprise* while it is seeking the secrets of the Genesis Device. Admiral Kirk and his companions destroy the *Enterprise* to prevent the Klingons from capturing the ship, but capture the Klingon scout. The Genesis Effect proves its instability, and the Genesis Planet disintegrates.

Stardate 2/2206.27
James Kirk and his companions bring the Klingon scoutship to Vulcan. Spock's intellect is restored by transfer of his essence, which Spock placed in Dr. McCoy just before he died.

CURRENT DIPLOMATIC RELATIONS

Following is a brief overview of the current diplomatic state of affairs existing between the United Federation of Planets and other starfaring governments.

THE KLINGON EMPIRE

Relations between the Federation and the Klingon Empire are strained at best. Since first contact with this race, the Federation has attempted to establish peaceful diplomatic relations with little or no positive results. Typically aggressive and expansionistic, the Klingons see little need to negotiate for what they can take by force of arms. However, the establishment of the Organian Treaty has forced the Klingons (at least for the moment) to consider other, less violent alternatives.

Relations between these two governments in the years following the Organian Conflict have been cool, with both sides using propaganda and their intelligence networks to wage a war of words. Although both governments have exchanged embassies in accordance with the Organian Treaty, the Klingons have been reluctant to consider any normalization of relations beyond those imposed by the Organians.

The increasing political influence of the Subaiesh family line in the *Komerex* may slowly be reversing this hard line, however. Representatives from the Klingon Diplomatic Corps (which is under Subaiesh direction) have arranged to meet with Federation diplomats to discuss easing the tensions between the two interstellar powers. Whether or not this new round of negotiations will prove fruitful remains to be seen.

Recent developments have cast doubt on whether the Organians are continuing to act as peacekeepers between the Federation and the Klingon Empire. If the Organians have lost interest in galactic politics, UFP/Klingon relations could deteriorate rapidly.

THE ROMULAN STAR EMPIRE

Currently, there are still no formal diplomatic ties between the Federation and the Romulan Star Empire. Relations between the two powers consist of armed neutrality across the Neutral Zone established when the Romulan War ended over a century ago. Federation attempts to establish additional guarantees of peace have been rebuffed by apparent Romulan indifference. The existence of at least two technological-exchange treaties between the Klingons and the Romulans makes it doubtful that the Romulans and the Federation will normalize relations in the foreseeable future. The Romulans have done nothing to allay this doubt.

THE ORION FREE STATES

Relations between the Federation and the Orions have historically been commercial rather than cultural. The Orion Free States and the Federation have repeatedly clashed over the issue of Orion slave trade within the Federation's sphere of influence. Following Federation-wide economic sanctions against them, the Orions agreed to abolish slave trade. However, evidence suggests that it continues covertly within the Triangle and in some of the more open Federation freeports.

Not every major Orion corporation or family line has agreed to Green Slave emancipation. Bitterness against this policy has led independent members of the Orion commercial cartel to conduct acts of piracy and aggression against Federation citizens. Such conditions will no doubt continue until the Orion worlds obtain a more centralized, authoritative government that can limit such activities.

THE GORN ALLIANCE

Recent relations between the Federation and the Gorn Alliance have suffered because of the lack of centralized authority over the various Gorn clans. Although the two powers have exchanged diplomatic representatives, Federation diplomats still distrust the Gorns. This is partly because of the massacre at the Cestus III outpost and partly because of the aggressive opinions expressed by various Gorn leaders at the Federation's expense. Discretion and compromise on both sides have prevented a repetition of the Cestus tragedy, but the Gorns remain openly aggressive. It will be some time before normal relations with this particular race can be achieved.

THE THOLIAN ASSEMBLY

Very little is known about the Tholian Assembly, either socially or politically, as the race does not respond to attempts at contact. They have, however, displayed a willingness (and an eagerness) to defend what they consider their territory. Unfortunately for all concerned, the boundaries of this "territory" are presently undefined.

GORN

THOLIAN

INDEPENDENT WORLDS

Other than the major diplomatic concerns outlined above, the Federation must deal with a multitude of other independent worlds and emerging political systems within Federation space, the Triangle Zone, and the Organian and Romulan Neutral Zones. The UFP seeks to maintain positive relations with as many of these systems as possible, but some of these planets' objectives are often at cross-purposes with Federation policy. Political upheaval in any one of these systems, such as the newly formed Asparaxian Confederation, could tip the delicate balance of power between the major interstellar powers unless handled appropriately. As the number of discovered worlds and civilizations in the galaxy increases every year, the Federation (and the Department of Interstellar Relations in particular) must continually renew its commitment to peaceful coexistence.

Though allowing independent worlds within the Federation to maintain their sovereignty, Federation authorities will intervene in local planetary affairs in case of conflict between two or more independents. An example is the Federation's intervention and mediation of the Troyian-Elasian War several years ago. The Articles of Federation grant it the right to maintain peace through its sphere of influence.

The Federation will defend an independent world from unwarranted intrusion or exploitation by other powers, even if those powers are members of the Federation. A prime example occurred when the Federation declared the Coridan system off-limits to prevent unlawful mining activities in that region. Such an action might not be a result of a request of the independent government.

Whenever possible, the Federation attempts to maintain friendly trade relations with independents. The corollary to this policy is that the Federation requires all independents to abide by its trade policies. An example of this was the boycott of Orion businesses by both independents and Federation members in an attempt to force abolition of the slave trade. A more subtle example is that independents must adopt Federation standards regarding weights and measures.

If an independent world possesses raw materials or products deemed essential to the continued security of the Federation, the UFP will pursue trade agreements with such powers even if the world desires to refrain from such trade. One such instance involves the 20-year negotiations between the Federation and the Halkan civilization over the latter's vast dilithium deposits, even though the Halkans oppose such trade on moral grounds.

Although the UFP would prefer that all independent worlds within its space join as full members, the Federation refrains from forcing any independent to adopt membership against its will. The UFP recognizes the rights of independents to act in accordance with their own wishes, as long as these policies do not conflict with Federation policies.

CURRENT PEACE TREATIES

The following are descriptions of the three major peace treaties that the Federation has signed within the last century or so. The first deals with the peace treaty between the Federation and the Romulan Star Empire, and the remaining two are between the Federation and the Klingon Empire. Each of the following are from Samuel T. Cogburn's *Federation Law And Diplomacy*, published Stardate 2/2102.01, reprinted with permission of the author.

DANNON'S TREATY

The name "Dannon's Treaty" refers to the peace treaty between the Federation and the Romulan Star Empire that ended the Romulan War, and it honors the senior Federation statesman Abraham Dannon. Dannon's personal support of the treaty conditions saved the lives of numerous individuals, though it cost the Federation many star systems and Dannon paid for it with both his political career and his life. Reviled as an appeaser and a traitor in his time, Dannon clearly recognized that the Federation had to grant concessions so that the Romulans would not feel they were losing honor. His understanding saved the Federation from several more years of bloody, inconclusive war.

TREATY OF PEACE BETWEEN THE ROMULAN STAR EMPIRE AND THE UNITED FEDERATION OF PLANETS

Section 1
The specific terms and conditions of this treaty being understood, the Romulan Star Empire and the United Federation of Planets agree to the immediate and bilateral cessation of all hostilities by their armed forces.

Section 2
Hereafter, a Neutral Zone will be established between the territorial integrities of both governments.

Section 3
Any intrusion by a party from either government into this zone shall be deemed an act of war, except when said intrusion can be verified to be the direct result of accident or navigational error.

THE TREATY OF AXANAR

The Treaty of Axanar is unique in Federation history because it represents the only time the Federation was able to impose its will on another foreign government without fear of immediate retaliation or rejection of terms. Following the heavy losses they suffered in the final weeks of the war, the Klingons were not in a position to argue over the terms of the treaty. In reality, they realized that the terms offered by the Federation were generous, and perhaps came to hate the Federation all the more for it.

THE PEACE TREATY OF AXANAR

Specification One
All Klingon forces remaining in space defined as within pre-war boundaries of the Federation are to withdraw immediately. Those unable to do so will be interned, but treated fairly and with due respect.

Specification Two
Upon the signing of this document, all hostilities between the United Federation of Planets and the Klingon Empire cease immediately.

Specification Three
Upon formal cessation of hostilities, both signatories will immediately begin to expedite the exchange of prisoners and other civilians currently held.

Specification Four
The Klingon Empire forthwith and forever renounces all claims to the planet known as Axanar.

Specification Five
A zone of space twelve parsecs in width from the Federation's galactic southern border shall immediately be declared sovereign Federation space. Citizens of the Klingon Empire will be accorded one standard year to relocate from this region, after which full and complete control of any and all planetary systems within this region will come under the jurisdiction of the United Federation of Planets.

THE ORGANIAN PEACE TREATY

Neither the Klingons nor the Federation had any say when the Organians drafted specific articles to end their conflict. Despite the fact that the terms issued to both sides were mild, there is little doubt that each side would have preferred harsher conditions inflicted on the enemy.

THE PEACE OF ORGANIA

Condition One
A state of peace is immediately imposed on all warring elements of the Klingon Empire and the United Federation of Planets.

Condition Two
Hereafter, an identifiable zone of 100 parsecs in length shall exist between all currently contiguous holdings of the Klingon Empire and the United Federation of Planets.

Condition Three
No display of hostile actions or use of force within this zone will be tolerated. Violators of this prohibition will be immediately rendered harmless.

Condition Four
Both parties agree to respect each other's territorial rights within their own, newly designated borders.

Condition Five
Unarmed vessels from both sides are permitted free and equal access to planets and resources within the zone of peace separating the two governments. Each will respect the other's rights and pledge to avoid violence under any circumstance when inside this zone of space.

GOVERNMENTAL STRUCTURE

As established by the Articles of Federation, the governmental structure of the United Federation of Planets is a republican system based on a centrally organized representative body. In this framework are combined executive, legislative, and judiciary powers to which each member world contributes to a greater or lesser degree. Examining the Articles of Federation shows that the founding members used considerable care and attention to create a government that would be not only efficient but also respectful of individual planets' sovereignty. Such a governing system had to allow for changes introduced by succeeding generations and had to adopt the best elements of existing political systems. Thus, the Federation government is both an amalgamation of numerous political approaches to self-government and the culmination of years of critical scrutiny and modification.

At the apex of the governmental system is the Federation Council, which is supported by the full Assembly of Federation delegates. Subordinate to the Council and the Assembly are various other governmental divisions, including the Security Council, the Federation Judiciary, and the Economic and Social Council. A complete breakdown of the Federation's governmental organization is given in the accompanying chart and described below.

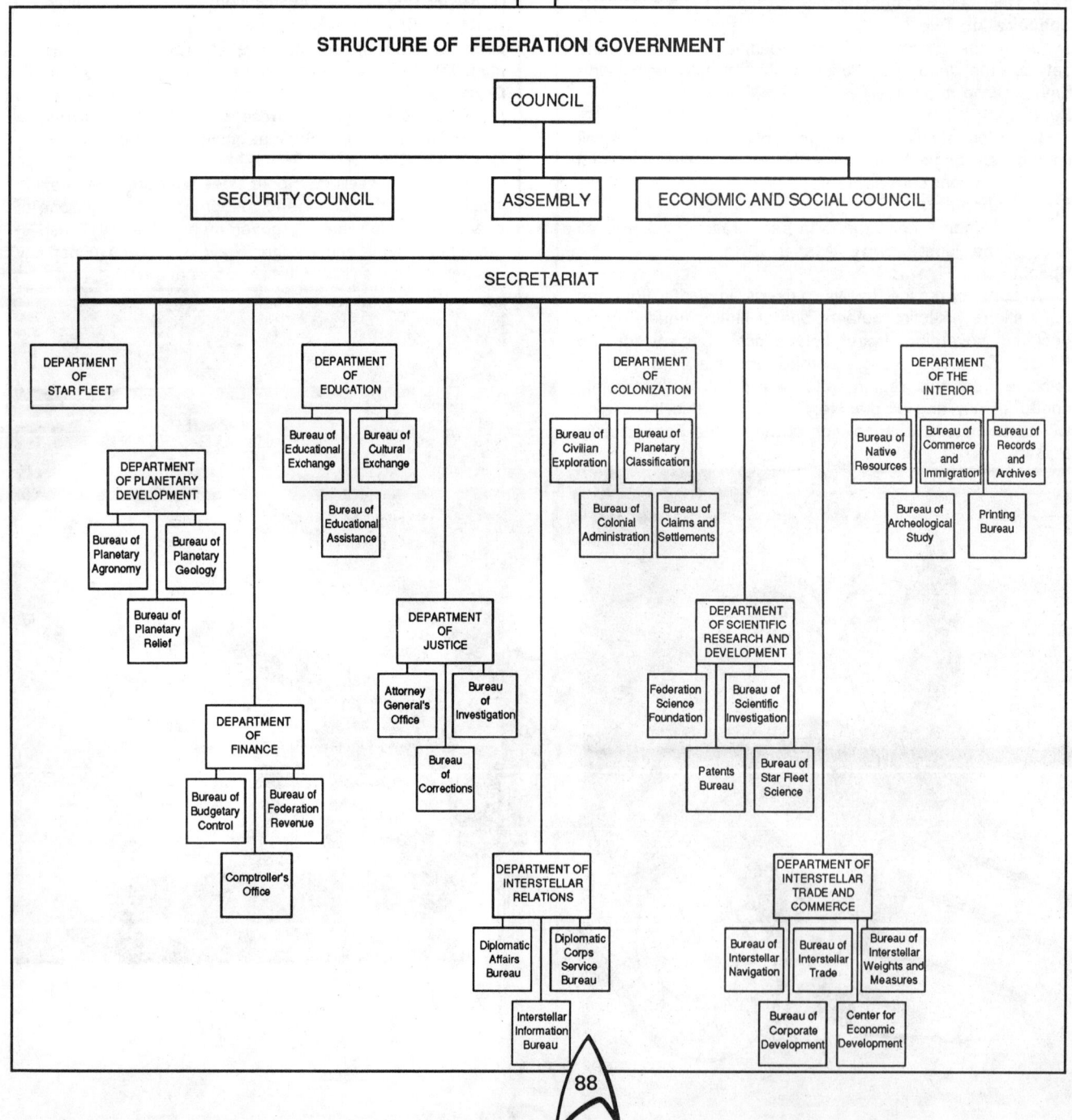

STRUCTURE OF FEDERATION GOVERNMENT

THE FEDERATION COUNCIL

The Federation Council, sometimes referred to as the High Council, is the representative body most commonly identified with the Federation. The Council is composed of one representative from each of the five founding member worlds and six planetary representatives elected by the Assembly. Council members from the five founding planets are elected by their home planet or system for a term of five years. The purpose of the Council is to ratify legislation proposed by the Assembly. Council members are the final arbiters of what policies the Federation will adopt. In addition, the Council is directly responsible for the conduct of Star Fleet in protecting and enforcing Federation interests and policy. It also nominates the various departmental Secretaries as well as members of the Federation Tribunal, subject to ratification by the Assembly. In times of emergency, the Council is empowered to act with the full authority of both bodies.

The Council is presided over by the President of the Council, who is nominated by fellow Council members and elected to a three-year term by a joint vote of the Council and the Assembly. In many respects, the President of the Council can be viewed as the most powerful individual in the Federation. He is the final arbiter of any treaties or diplomatic provisions between the Federation and other foreign governments. In the event of a tie among Council members in voting a piece of legislation, the President casts the deciding vote. In case of serious emergency, the President may act on behalf of either the Council or the Assembly, although any emergency measures he imposes require ratification by the Council at the earliest opportunity.

FEDERATION COUNCIL PRESIDENTS

Years in Office	Name	Home Planet
0/87 - 1/01	Harmon Axelrod	Terra
1/02 - 1/04	Ursula Yare	Terra
1/05 - 1/10	Cristofur Thorpe	Alpha Centauri
1/11 - 1/13	Gralless	Tellar
1/14 - 1/16	Sardix	Vulcan
1/17 - 1/19	Thortathanal	Andor
1/20 - 1/22	Barbara Einicrox	Terra
1/23 - 1/25	Suessor	Vulcan
1/26 - 1/28	Todahlahr	Andor
1/29 - 1/34	Richard Morvehl	Alpha Centauri
1/35 - 1/37	Janissa Kurvannis	Terra
1/38 - 1/43	Greshlahrigm	Tellar
1/44 - 1/52	Sutorox	Vulcan
1/53 - 1/58	Paula Christenson	Terra
1/59 - 1/64	Petra Menliss	Alpha Centauri
1/65 - 1/67	Jacob Varis	Arcturus
1/68 - 1/70	Sanara Dadari	Terra
1/71 - 1/72	Claton Mintaine	Terra
1/72 - 1/79	Sarboran	Vulcan
1/80 - 1/85	Aesanna Lithir	Cygnet XIV
1/86 - 1/89	Thomas Oromon	Izar
1/90 - 1/94	Gregory Salamorn	Terra
1/95 - 1/97	Alohk Ixan	Deneva
1/98 - 2/03	Warren Quinland	Terra
2/04 - 2/06	Sandra Eloth	Izar
2/07 - 2/12	Adam Zagrin	Deneva
2/13 - 2/18	James Abelmare	Terra
2/19 - present	Alistair Fergus	Daran V

FEDERATION COUNCIL MEMBERS

Name	Home Planet
Thostic	Andor
David Eargoss	Alpha Centauri
Gamlehiphr	Tellar
Juliana Lorress	Terra
T'triss	Vulcan
Ruzzel Tapkan	Arcturus
Mrinnix	Cait
Arova Luranas	Cygnet XIV
Simira Hahn	Deneva
Polva Trassen	Ingraham B
Christopher Ronnie	Izar

THE FEDERATION ASSEMBLY

The Assembly of Worlds is composed of representatives from every member planet in the Federation. Each planetary government with full-member status is allowed two delegates to the Assembly, and associate members are allowed one. Assembly representatives from full member worlds serve for a period of six years, and associate member representatives serve for four years. Under special circumstances, protectorate worlds may be allowed to send one non-voting member to the Assembly, though this provision requires the consent of the full Assembly. Currently, the Assembly is composed of 823 representatives; 440 from the 220 full-status members, one from each of the 382 associate members, and one protectorate representative from Coridan.

The purpose of the Assembly is to formulate legislation for ratification by the Council. It is solely responsible for originating legislation reflecting the needs of all Federation members, such as providing for the common defense and cultural advancement of sentient beings in the Federation. The Assembly is also responsible for ratifying Council nominations for both departmental Secretaries and the Federation Tribunal. A voice vote of two-thirds of the Assembly is required before a prospective nominee can assume office. In addition, Assembly members are often appointed to head various committees that deal with any special needs of the Federation.

THE FEDERATION SECURITY COUNCIL

Providing for the common defense of every member planet in the Federation is a task beyond the capabilities of a single administrative body. During the Romulan War, the Federation government was hard-pressed to meet the demands of waging a full-scale interstellar war while handling its day-to-day duties. After the Romulan War, a special provisional Assembly committee was established to examine the likelihood of renewed Romulan hostilities in the next decade. This provisional body assumed added importance when the Federation went to war with the Klingons, and eventually became the permanent organization known as the Federation Security Council.

The Security Council is an advisory body composed of 20 civilian and military specialists who report to both the Federation Council and the Assembly. The size of the Security Council may vary; members can be appointed by either the Assembly or the Federation Council. There is no fixed time for a Security Council member's term of office, though traditionally, members do not hold office for more than three to four years.

More than just a consulting agency, the Security Council can appoint special commissioners to deal with matters governing both internal and external security. Under emergency conditions, these commissioners can assume full command over local civil authorities as well as Star Fleet personnel. As the threats to Federation security have increased over the years, the Security Council has appointed more and more commissioners. Therefore, it is not unusual to find a Security Council commissioner overseeing the delivery of an important cargo shipment, such as grain deliveries to Sherman's World in the Organian Neutral Zone or plague vaccine to Macus V.

The executive head of the council, the High Commissioner, also manages the Federation Security Agency (FSA). The FSA is an intelligence gathering agency that collects and correlates political, military, and social information on foreign governments. Although these specialists typically act in an information-processing role, they have also been employed in counter-intelligence capacities.

THE FEDERATION ECONOMIC AND SOCIAL COUNCIL

Established under the provisions of the Articles of Federation, the Federation Economic and Social Council (ESC) is considered one of the primary agencies in the Federation bureaucracy. Under the guidance of the Council Director, the ESC monitors the economic and social development of all Federation member worlds. At periodic intervals, it reports to the Federation Assembly on matters relating to economic and social progress. The ESC is also concerned with observing the individual rights of Federation citizens. Given clear evidence that such rights have been violated, the ESC may make specific recommendations to the Federation Council or any other agencies aimed at correcting such conditions. This council also coordinates social and economic improvements enacted by other Federation governmental organizations.

THE FEDERATION JUDICIARY

Under the Articles of Federation, every Federation citizen is guaranteed the right of equal protection under law, without distinction for planetary origin, political affiliation, or social and cultural identification. The Federation judicial system was created to enforce this basic right and other legislation ratified by the Council. Besides the Federation Tribunal, which is roughly analogous to the ancient Terran Supreme Court, there are various lower courts located throughout the different quadrants of Federation space.

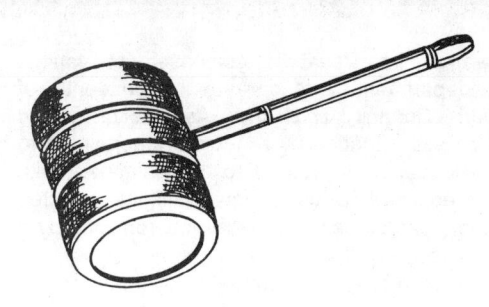

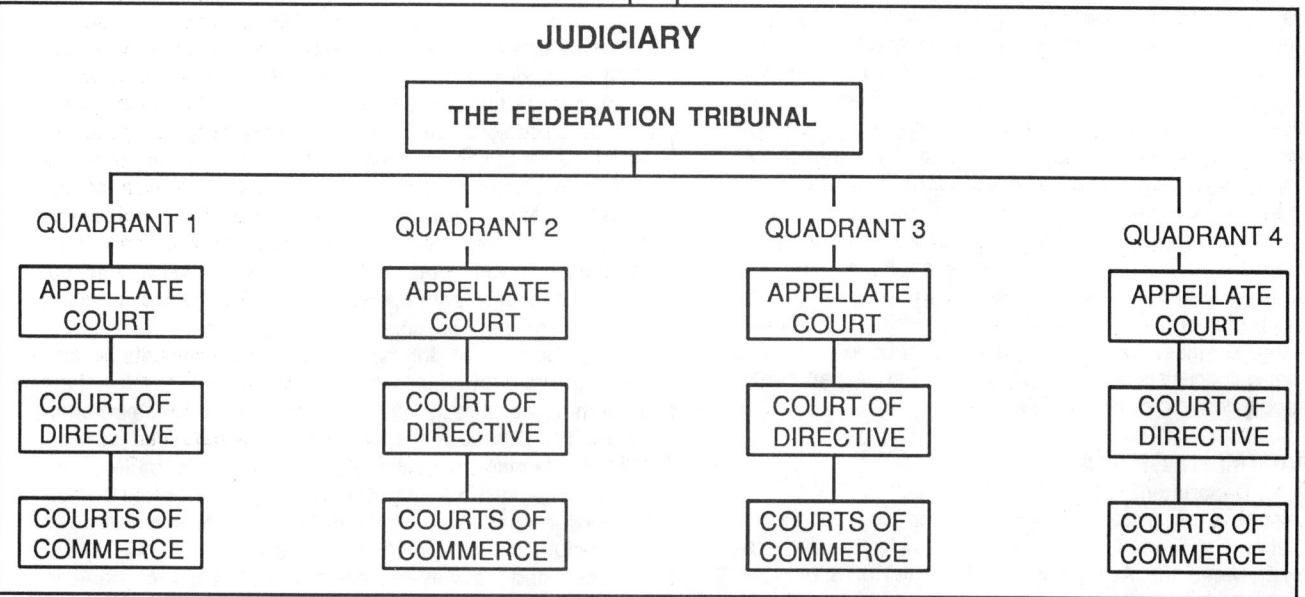

THE FEDERATION TRIBUNAL

Located on Alpha III, the Federation Tribunal consists of nine members appointed for life by the Federation Council and ratified by the Assembly. These magistrates are deemed the most experienced legal professionals in the Federation and may originate from any member planet, regardless of that government's member status. The Tribunal acts as a final court of appeal on matters pertaining to interstellar relations. It also hands down the final decisions with respect to possible violations of the Star Fleet Prime Directive. Although they lack direct enforcement powers, members of the Tribunal can request the Security Council to investigate matters of sufficient importance and to make a full report to a joint session of the Council and the Assembly.

QUADRANT COURTS

Subordinate to the Tribunal are a series of lower district courts allocated on a quadrant basis. For purposes of judicial representation, the entire expanse of Federation space is divided into four regions known as quadrants, designated one to four. Within each quadrant, the Federation judiciary maintains three key elements: Federation Courts of Commerce, Courts of Directive, and Appellate Courts. These are typically established in major star systems or on star bases.

The Federation Courts of Commerce hear cases involving such matters as smuggling, interstellar trade relations, and interstellar flight to avoid prosecution. Courts of Directive are judicial watchdogs concerned with civil cases involving the operations of Star Fleet Command. Though they primarily review cases involving possible violations of the Prime Directive, these courts also handle civilian claims against Star Fleet and Star Fleet personnel. Appellate Courts review the decisions of the lower courts. Under special circumstances, local planetary governors may appeal directly to an Appellate Court to arbitrate questions of local planetary jurisdiction.

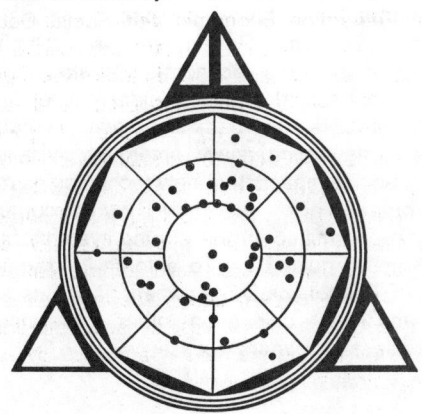

THE FEDERATION SECRETARIAT

The Federation Secretariat is composed of various administrative departments that operate independently of the Federation Council and the Assembly. These departments are each headed by a secretary appointed to office for a three-year term, subject to reappointment with the Assembly's approval. Deputy secretaries are selected by the department secretaries and serve until replaced by a designated successor.

There are currently ten governmental departments in the Federation Secretariat. These ten departments are as follows: Department of Star Fleet, Department of Interstellar Relations, Department of Interstellar Trade and Commerce, Department of Colonization, Department of Planetary Development, Department of Scientific Research and Development, Department of Justice, Department of the Interior, Department of Education, and Department of Finance. Each department is subdivided into numerous agencies headed by an undersecretary, usually a career civil servant. These agencies are responsible to their secretary for specific areas under their parent department and for the administration of their own local planetary offices. Federation Civil Service Corps personnel primarily man these offices, although independent scientific and academic specialists are also employed. The departments are listed below in order of their seniority.

DEPARTMENT OF STAR FLEET

The Department of Star Fleet is the civil and administrative organization responsible for the supervision and support of Star Fleet operations. Acting primarily as a liaison between the Assembly and the Chief of Star Fleet OperationS, this department works closely with Star Fleet personnel to coordinate long-range planning and control of Star Fleet resources and to formulate policy and civilian-Star Fleet relations. Typically, the Secretary of Star Fleet is a retired Star Fleet admiral or other high-ranking individual with intimate knowledge of Star Fleet, its objectives, and its personnel.

DEPARTMENT OF INTERSTELLAR RELATIONS

The Department of Interstellar Relations (IR) discharges all diplomatic obligations and responsibilities of the Federation. Not only does it handle the routine operations of hundreds of Federation embassies, diplomatic mission teams, and independent diplomatic corps operatives, it also coordinates all diplomatic activities between the Federation and various foreign governments. Under this department are three principal agencies: the Diplomatic Affairs Bureau, the Diplomatic Corps Service Bureau, and the Interstellar Information Bureau.

The Diplomatic Affairs Bureau assigns diplomatic corps specialists to various tasks within and without Federation space. This bureau is likewise concerned with the establishment and routine maintenance of embassies and the operation of contact teams and special envoys to other interstellar powers. In addition, this bureau decides whether a planet is to be placed under the Prime Directive. A major service agency under this bureau is the Federation Arbitration Agency, which mediates disputes between Federation members at the request of the Assembly.

The Diplomatic Corps Service Bureau is responsible for recruiting and training all diplomatic corps personnel. This bureau also handles the relocation and cultural adjustment of field operatives and their families.

The Interstellar Information Bureau provides firsthand information on all unclassified diplomatic activities for public viewing. This bureau is also responsible for providing detailed information on diplomatic activities to Council and Assembly members. The bureau's Infonet Service is responsible for the accurate and unbiased reporting of all newsworthy events within Federation space.

DEPARTMENT OF INTERSTELLAR TRADE AND COMMERCE

The Department of Interstellar Trade and Commerce (ITC) is responsible for regulating and controlling all aspects of interstellar trade between members of the Federation, Federation colony worlds, and independent civilizations within the Federation sphere of influence. This considerable task is managed through various bureaus: the Bureau of Interstellar Navigation, the Bureau of Interstellar Trade, the Bureau of Corporate Development, the Bureau of Interstellar Weights and Measures, and the Center for Economic Development, which in turn control various agencies and offices of considerable importance.

The Bureau of Interstellar Navigation maintains the safety of major interstellar shipping lanes and the free flow of commerce throughout every quadrant of Federation space. The bureau is responsible for constructing, locating, and maintaining navigational-communications beacons at specific intervals in space. Civilians must file copies of their interstellar flight plans with this office. Also, this bureau is responsible for constructing and maintaining deep-space stations used as way-centers and free ports of trade in remote regions of space.

The Bureau of Interstellar Trade administers major starports and civilian space centers throughout the Federation. In particular, this bureau enforces customs regulations and inspects commercial cargo carried between worlds. Special effort is made to prohibit the exportation of potentially dangerous life forms and contraband. No cargo may be shipped offworld from a major Federation port-of-call without the approval of local Interstellar Trade officials.

The Bureau of Corporate Development manages interstellar trade concerns among major interplanetary corporations within the Federation. This bureau's Securities and Exchange Commission is responsible for chartering newly formed Federation corporations and enforcing Federation regulations governing corporate activities. The Bureau of Corporate Development also maintains agencies that enforce Federation laws dealing with fair business practices, industrial safety, and offworld mining.

The Center for Economic Development is a watchdog bureau that supervises the economic development of planets and planetary societies placed under the conditions of the Prime Directive. In particular, this bureau is responsible for safeguarding newly emerging civilizations from the harmful social impacts that new technologies might create. This bureau also determines what corporate operations may be permitted in and around systems falling under Prime Directive guidelines. To enforce its decisions, the Center for Economic Development has its own investigators, and may call upon other governmental departments for assistance when necessary.

DEPARTMENT OF COLONIZATION

The Department of Colonization is responsible for locating, administering, and supporting new colony worlds. It is also responsible for selecting and relocating civilian settlers to newly opened colony systems. Wherever applicable, the Secretary of Colonization is authorized to appoint planetary governors to individual settlements. Since the imposition of the Organian Treaty, the Department of Colonization has also been responsible for developing colony worlds within the Organian Neutral Zone. This department also maintains ties with various settlements within the Triangle Zone on an informal, case-by-case basis. Under the control of this department are several bureaus concerned with colonial affairs: the Bureau of Civilian Exploration, the Bureau of Planetary Classification, the Bureau of Colonial Administration, and the Bureau of Claims and Settlements.

Not all galactic exploration is accomplished by Star Fleet. Independent scouts, explorers, and prospectors are locating a growing percentage of newly discovered worlds.

DEPARTMENT OF PLANETARY DEVELOPMENT

The Department of Planetary Development is concerned with the development of planetary resources, both natural and agricultural. To a greater or lesser extent, it is involved in all major planetary systems as well as new colonies with either protectorate or associate-member status. Within this department are three major bureaus. The Bureau of Planetary Agronomy is responsible for regulating and advancing efficient agricultural practices on Federation worlds. This bureau maintains research and development as well as cultural/technological exchange agencies. The Bureau of Planetary Geology specializes in regulating geological exploration and planetary mining practices on mineral-rich planets. The third important bureau, the Bureau of Planetary Relief, conducts relief efforts to member planets stricken by famine or unexpected natural disasters. When necessary, this office will work with the Federation Security Council to coordinate relief efforts on a system-wide scale.

The Bureau of Civilian Exploration acts as a liaison between the Star Fleet Office of Exploration and the civilian sector in such matters. It administers bounties to individuals for discovering Class M planets as well as funds to civilian agencies that promote further exploration.

Once a system has been identified and surveyed, the findings are submitted to the Bureau of Planetary Classification for analysis. The chief responsibility of this office is to determine whether a given planet should be opened for colonization or, whether for scientific or social reasons, it should be granted a hands-off status under the guidelines of the Prime Directive. Assuming that the newly discovered planet is deemed suitable for exploitation, the bureau then decides to what extent individual and corporate concerns may begin economic or social development of the planet.

The Bureau of Colonial Administration handles all matters involving the actions of Federation planetary governors. It reviews the qualifications of various candidates for positions as governors or assistant governors, makes recommendations to the Secretary of Colonization on the most likely candidates, and handles colonial affairs involving individual governors and colonial populaces throughout the Federation.

When Federation colonization personnel inadvertently incur damage to a population, the Bureau of Claims and Settlements is called in to settle the matter and, if necessary, to allocate a fair and equitable compensation. This office also handles any disbursements made directly to civilians as part of actual colonization efforts, such as requisitions in kind, emergency appropriations, and so on.

DEPARTMENT OF SCIENTIFIC RESEARCH AND DEVELOPMENT

This department is responsible to the Assembly for all matters related to the advancement of new sciences and technology throughout the Federation. Receiving the highest departmental budget within the Federation government, SRD administers major scientific research projects, both civilian and military. It also sets policy and determines standards governing the ethical conduct of scientific investigation throughout the Federation. Through its subordinate, the Federation Science Foundation, SRD provides research grants and loans for scientific research conducted at major universities and interstellar corporations. SRD's Patents Bureau, which maintains offices on each full-status member world, acts as the final arbiter for granting licenses for new technologies. Its Bureau of Scientific Investigation maintains permanent staff members at the Vulcan Science Academy and Terra University on Sol III to evaluate new scientific breakthroughs and inventions for civilian and military application. Finally, SRD maintains the Bureau of Star Fleet Science, a full-time advisory board that assesses the technological needs of Star Fleet Command. This board acts as a liaison with Star Fleet weaponry development teams, reporting annually to a special closed session of the Federation Security Council.

DEPARTMENT OF JUSTICE

The Department of Justice is the Federation's internal law enforcement and security arm. It deals with all criminal acts not subject to local planetary sovereignty. This includes acts of piracy within Federation space, illicit transportation of prohibited technologies or goods to foreign powers, and acts of treason against the Federation. Under the Secretary of Justice is the Federation Attorney General's Office. The Attorney General is the chief prosecutor for the United Federation of Planets, and acts as the Federation's chief legal advisor in matters involving the Federation Judiciary.

The Bureau of Corrections is responsible for maintaining the Federation penal system, appointing directors and staff for such institutions as Tantalus Colony and the Elba Correctional Facility. The bureau also manages the transfer of incorrigibles from local facilities to high-security institutions. Like its old Terran namesake, the Department of Justice's Federation Bureau of Investigation is empowered to investigate possible crimes against the Federation, and may aid in local criminal investigations whenever local resources are inadequate. The Bureau of Investigation also appoints a dozen marshals for each quadrant of the Federation. These marshals are responsible for the maintenance of civil order throughout Federation space. Their judicial authority is equal to that of planetary governors, and, under conditions of martial law, they may temporarily supersede such authority. Each marshal acts as the primary representative of the judicial system within his zone of the quadrant. He can call upon any person, civilian or military, for assistance. When necesssary, he may take extraordinary measures to maintain order and to deal with violations of Federation law that do not involve Star Fleet Command.

DEPARTMENT OF EDUCATION

The Department of Education is responsible for the free exchange of information concerning Federation cultures and the education and social integration of member cultures. To accomplish these aims, this department controls two major bureaus: the Bureau of Educational Exchange and the Bureau of Cultural Exchange. These two organizations coordinate and encourage the exchange of students and private individuals between member planets. In addition, each bureau sponsors numerous cultural programs and exhibitions involving the arts and humanities. These programs forge closer ties between member worlds through better understanding of each society's social values.

This department's Bureau of Educational Assistance helps individuals of all races to achieve higher levels of education. In addition, this office also encourages non-Humans to enter major universities, including the Star Fleet service academies.

DEPARTMENT OF FINANCE

The Department of Finance is responsible for collecting and administering all Federation finances. In the fiscal year ending on 2/2301.01, this amounted to approximately 785.5 trillion credits. Such finances are the result of levies voted by the Federation Assembly for specific projects as well as the general operative fund, to which all full-status member worlds contribute. To manage such astronomical sums, the Department of Finance has three principal bureaus: the Bureau of Budgetary Control, the Bureau of Federation Revenue, and the Federation Comptroller's Office.

The Bureau of Budgetary Control maintains the solvency of the Federation's various departments and agencies as well as the soundness of the Federation monetary system. This bureau not only regulates current monetary conditions through numerous UFP banking institutions, but also formulates policy for the future monetary security of the Federation.

The Bureau of Federation Revenue is involved in the actual collection of levies ordered by the Assembly. It collects each member's contributions in standard credit amounts or in kind, which requires local currencies to be converted into credits for the proper estimation of levy obligations.

The Federation Comptroller's Office administers the disbursement of Federation funds to departments and agencies, based on operating expenses and various special projects and discretionary funds. It also ensures that such funds are not misappropriated or otherwise misused. On behalf of the Federation, the Comptroller's Office is also authorized to make investments in businesses and corporations both within and outside Federation space.

DEPARTMENT OF THE INTERIOR

The Department of the Interior heads a collection of bureaus dedicated to the management of internal Federation affairs not assigned to other departments. For example, the Federation Bureau of Native Resources administers all major recreational areas (such as Wrigley's Pleasure Planet) and cooperates with local planetary officials to preserve areas of cultural or historic significance. The Bureau of Archeological Study works with local planetary agencies to fund and to administer private research into the location and excavation of ancient civilizations, such as the Preservers or the Triacans. The Bureau of Commerce and Immigration is responsible for issuing travel permits and visas to private citizens, with respect to local regulations and restrictions concerning alien visitations. The United Federation Printing Bureau is responsible for publishing printed, visual, and audio materials originating from the various governmental departments and bureaus. Lastly, the Federation Bureau of Records and Archives maintains the Federation archives housed at Memory Alpha and administers various UFP museums and collections at various locations on different worlds.

POLITICS

In a government the size of the Federation, the variety of conflicting political interests is mind-boggling. From its inception, the Federation has had to balance the rights of individual worlds against the necessities of collective security. Moreover, there are Federation members who seriously question whether a Federation is a good idea after all. The following section briefly examines some of these major issues as well as the current alignments in the Federation government.

ISSUES

From its beginning, the Federation has been embroiled in political debate. For example, during the first Babel Conference, the delegates debated inclusion of the Orion Colonies in the Federation. This inclusion would have profited the Federation immensely, as the Orions possess an impressive financial base and an extensive network of trade. This advantage was offset by the Orions' practice of interstellar slavery, in particular that of Green Orion females, which conflicted with Federation policy on individual rights. The matter was eventually resolved by the Orions themselves. Fearing that merging their merchant fleets with Star Fleet would diminish their corporate empire, the Orions demanded several trillion credits in 'compensation' for their admission as full-status members. This offer, viewed by some as a cleverly disguised bribe and by others as a demand for tribute, turned Federation delegates against Orion membership once and for all. However, the issue of Orion slavery would continue.

Perhaps the greatest political threat to the Federation was created not from outside pressures, but through the demands of its own citizenry. In particular, the Back-to-Earth movement of the Terra-Return League came within a narrow margin of formally dissolving the Federation over a century ago. At that time, the Federation's bureaucratic structure was not yet flexible enough to handle the growing demands of its hundreds of worlds and diverse cultures. The Archimedes Scandal reflected the need for reform, and such reform was forthcoming. The Security Council was strengthened, and various socially conscious agencies and organizations were developed to handle the growing needs of Federation citizens.

INTEREST GROUPS AND POLITICAL PARTIES

Like any other political organization, the Federation is made up of many groups working to further their own interests while supporting the common good of the majority. Many of these special-interest groups are officially recognized lobby groups while others remain largely unofficial, but nonetheless influential. Because the Federation is composed of various peoples with different points of view, it is not surprising that several political parties have developed. At present, there are over 20 recognized political parties in the Federation. The following section describes several of the more influential parties as well as selected special interest groups that have an impact on Federation politics.

THE OUTER SYSTEMS PARTY

This party consists of various member planets along the outer fringes of the Federation. It was founded in the belief that the five original members of the Federation have created an unfair power block that no new member can ever hope to overcome. On Stardate 1/7506.15, the delegation from Tiburon formed an alliance of several of the newest Federation worlds to advance local planetary interests at the expense of galactic issues. Generally conservative, the 13 members of the Outer Systems Party support a strong Star Fleet, but are against galactic expansion at the cost of neglecting planetary concerns.

THE ASSOCIATES UNION PARTY

Formed on Stardate 1/6202.06, the Associates Union Party was created by various associate Federation members to ensure the passage of their legislation over opposition from full-status members. Their main goal is the betterment of all associate member worlds. Viewed as exclusionist, even separatist, the group has lost some of its original members due to other Assembly delegates' growing animosity toward it. Moreover, many argue that the party has lost sight of its original purpose, existing today as nothing more than opposition to those supporting traditional Federation goals and objectives. However, the Associates Union Party still passes quite a bit of legislation through bargains with other parties and special-interest groups. Indeed, the AUP is often referred to as the bend party, suggesting that AUP members will vote according to the best bargain struck and will bend to the wishes of the party offering the highest bid for their vote. However, weakening membership has not stopped new member worlds from wishing to join this powerful party.

THE INDEPENDENT SYSTEMS MOVEMENT PARTY

The ISMP is a remnant of the now-defunct Terra-Return League that originated on Benecia. Following the collapse of that party after the Second Babel Conference in 1/7701, hard-line members emigrated to the new colony world of New Princeton to protest continued Federation expansion. They reorganized their remaining adherents and, within a decade, reentered politics. Today, the ISMP is a small but vocal power.

THE STAR FLEET ADVOCATES ASSEMBLY

One of the most powerful lobby groups within the Federation is the Star Fleet Advocates Assembly. This group consists of retired Star Fleet officers who have moved into political careers. Their purpose is to guarantee that Star Fleet receives enough finances to cover operating expenses, new ship construction, and advanced weapons systems research. The group's influence extends into the Federation Council itself, where recent efforts have resulted in many Council members adopting a more favorable attitude toward new projects such as the *Excelsior* starship design. The group has been less successful in influencing members of the Federation Assembly, who view the party's goals as an effort to fritter away Federation resources on military materiel.

THE AMALGAMATION OF FEDERATION SCIENTISTS

The Amalgamation of Federation Scientists is the main representative lobby for Federation scientists and engineers. Created on Stardate 1/8804.05, this lobby is one of the most respected in Federation politics and in the Federation scientific community. Some of the most famous scientists in the Federation belong to the group, including the retired Vulcan representative to the Federation Ambassador Sarek. The purpose of this elite organization is to ensure the Federation's continued commitment to scientific inquiry and research, as well as to add their support to specific research projects that are being considered for funding by the Federation Science Bureau. At the moment, the Amalgamation's major concern is the ongoing debate over the Genesis Project. They hold that the Federation should turn over any and all materials on the project to a select group of scientists for further study and evaluation. Moreover, they believe that Star Fleet should not be allowed to intervene in the research in any way.

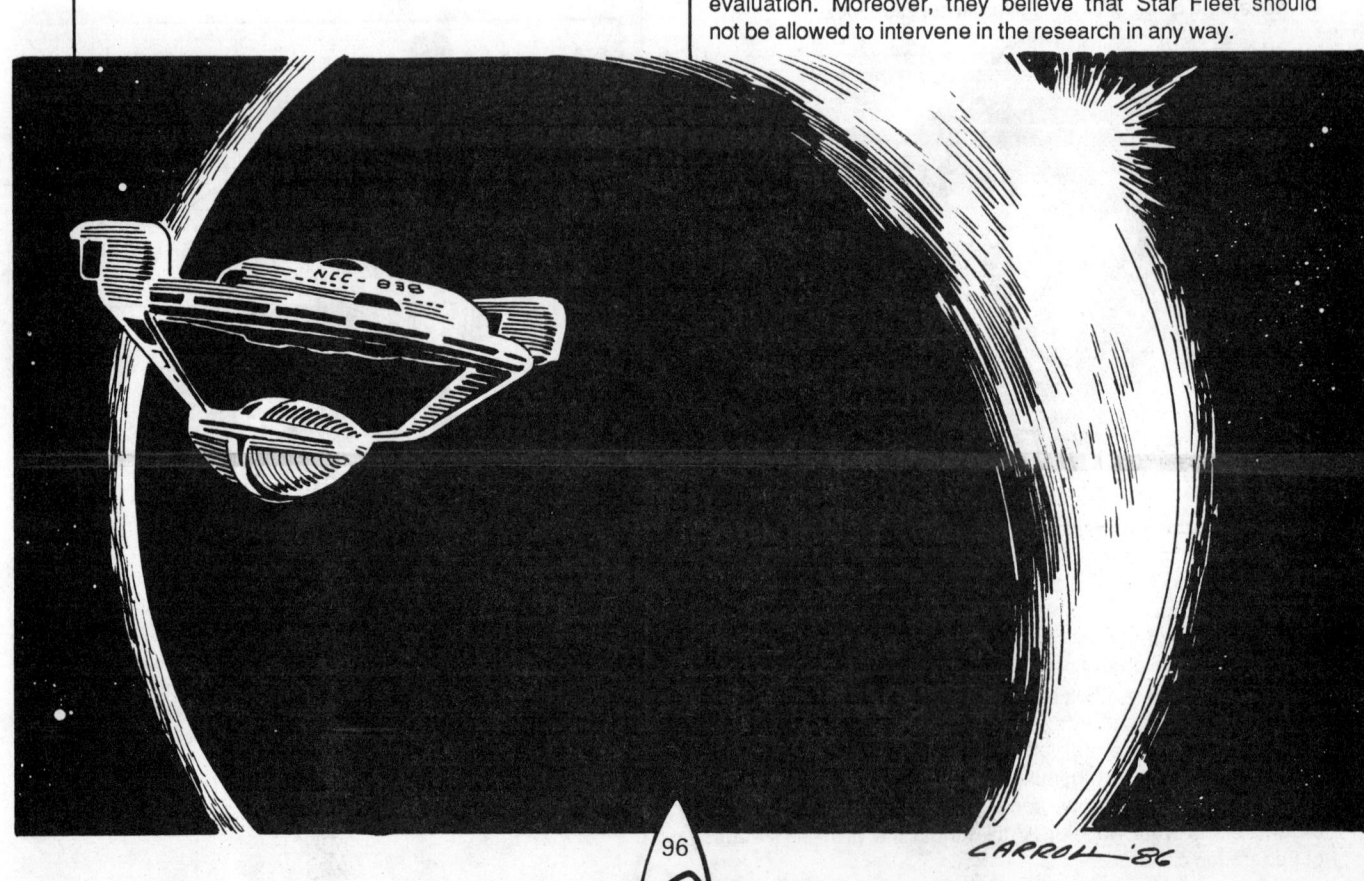

ECONOMICS

From its inception, one of the Federation's primary objectives has been free and unhindered trade among the stars. Except for those worlds under the protection of the Prime Directive or otherwise quarantined, trade between Federation members is unrestricted as long as it does not violate local or regional restrictions. The Federation encourages its members to exchange financial and commercial goods and services, and it often subsidizes programs designed to promote such exchanges. It supports efforts to colonize new worlds along the unexplored edges of the Federation, thus ensuring the growth of new markets for years to come. The UFP also maintains a galactic-wide stock exchange and commodities program for individual, governmental, and planetary investors.

This section describes how interstellar finance is regulated within the Federation. Much of the information is the direct result of policies determined by the Federation Department of Finance in conjunction with the Department of Interstellar Affairs. Present-day Federation economy represents over a century of effort to assimilate and reconcile different planetary economic systems as the Federation gains new members.

MONETARY SYSTEMS

Following is a summary of the ways Federation commercial institutions and private citizens finance monetary exchanges between member worlds.

THE FEDERATION CREDIT EXCHANGE

At the apex of the Federation's massive interstellar economic system is the credit system, which reconciles the differences in local monetary values between member worlds. Although planets and planetary systems may maintain their own monetary exchange system, all member planets also subscribe to a common monetary exchange system. Called the Federation Credit Exchange, the system also finances all Federation (and Star Fleet) personnel and associated operations. In brief, the FCE established the credit as the monetary unit used as the standard medium of exchange between member planets. Individuals (or corporations) may use the credit as a unit of exchange whenever goods or services are rated in terms of credits.

Whenever local economics require the use of local currencies, credits may be exchanged at the rate determined by the Board of Interstellar Exchange, which is under the Department of Interstellar Trade and Commerce. Visitors to such a member world may exchange local currencies for standard-issue credits prior to leaving the planet.

LETTERS OF EXCHANGE

Letters of exchange are formal drafts for specified amounts of local currency, 'paper' transactions that can be used by more than one individual over an extended period of time. When a letter of exchange is presented to a financial institution on a member world, that institution must present the bearer with the equivalent in local funds. Exchange rates between member worlds are fixed by representatives of the Board of Interstellar Exchange. These rates change every 50 days, as it takes a long time to transmit the figures via subspace radio. However, the long intervals do lend a degree of stability to interstellar transactions that would not be possible under daily changes in exchange rates.

SUBSPACE TRANSFER OF FUNDS

In star systems containing two or more planets with a common economic structure, funds can be transferred from one world's financial institution to another world's via subspace radio. Occurring in a matter of minutes, STF transactions may take place between individuals or serve as a convenience for an individual travelling between worlds. In the latter case, an STF transfer establishes a temporary holding account with the receiving institution. In most instances, STF transfers are for a limited duration only.

GUARANTEED EXCHANGES IN KIND

Funds may be physically transferred between member worlds, in kind rather than through other, more symbolic means. In short, individuals may wish to convert local currencies into physical objects of value that can be transported over vast distances and re-sold for a higher price at their destination. Unlike standard corporate trading practices that create interstellar speculation and price fluctuations, this particular practice is intended for the average citizen. To avoid price changes that could seriously devalue a certain article from one system to another, the Department of Interstellar Trade and Commerce, for a modest fee, assesses the value of a given item and guarantees its value, which can be recovered in standard credits at any Bureau of Interstellar Exchange office. This prevents losses due to local fluctuations in price.

EMERGENCY FUNDING

In a crisis situation, any Federation citizen may obtain emergency funds through a Federation embassy. The amount of the loan is subject to the discretion of the planet's ranking embassy official. Any such aid must be refunded (without interest) within one year.

MAJOR CORPORATIONS

The following information provides specifics concerning the major interstellar, multiplanetary corporations chartered by the Bureau of Corporate Development's Securities and Exchange Commission.

Name: A'ALAKON LANDISS INC.
UFPSC Symbol: AlkrLs
 Home Office Location: Divallax, Andor
 President/CEO: Sri' Lurix
 Chartering Organization: Securities and Exchange Commission
 Founding Date: 1/7503.06
Principal Divisions
 Division Name: Alakron Environmental
  Division Head: Suriv Parn
  Chief Product: Space Environmental Support Systems
Stock Profile: 3C38
 Price/Date: 23.45 Cr on 2/2306.01
 Dividend: 1.00 Cr
Balance Sheet, Year Ended: 2/2301

Cash:	Assets:	Liabilities:	Ratio:
334 MCr	145 MCr	123 MCr	1.17

Business Summary:

A long-standing contractor with Star Fleet Command and private industrial concerns, A'Alakon Landis manufactures personal and group-oriented life support systems for use in zero-gravity and thin atmospheric environments. Founded by Sri' Lurix Landis at the age of 25, the company is named in honor of Sri's father, A'Alakon Landis, who died in a spaceliner accident. A'Alakon Landis Inc. suffered initially from a lack of operating capital and managerial personnel, which almost took the firm into receivership within its first five years. High-quality standards and product performance allowed the firm to weather its growing pains, and Sri' Landis is confident that the worst years are now behind her. A'Alakon Landis currently maintains four manufacturing plants on Andor and Cygnet XIV, and plans to add two more within the next decade.

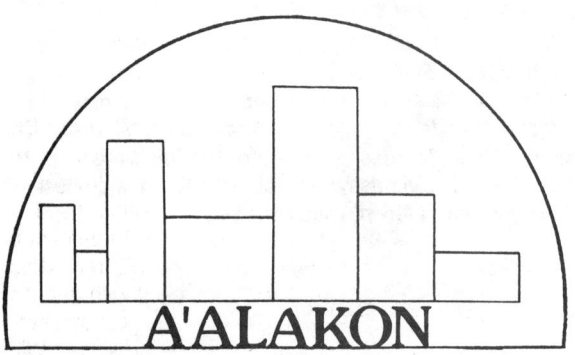

Name: ANIMATION ULTRAGRAPHICS
UFPSC Symbol: AnUgrc
 Home Office Location: Arrival, Tellar
 President/CEO: Jason d'Andrew
 Chartering Organization: Securities and Exchange Commission
 Founding Date: 1/8809.2
Principal Divisions
 Division Name: Ultra Animations
  Division Head: Samantha LaSalle
  Chief Product: Vid-cart Productions
 Division Name: Ultra Historicals
  Divison Head: Jennifer von Dame
  Chief Product: Planetary Broadcast Documentaries
Stock Profile: 2D66
 Price/Date: 77.85 Cr on 2/2306.01
 Dividend: 2.50 Cr
Balance Sheet, Year Ended: 2/2301

Cash:	Assets:	Liabilities:	Ratio:
534 MCr	953 MCr	129 MCr	7.38

Business Summary:

Founded by Jason d'Andrew of Terra and Arrv Delepphid of Tellar, Animation Ultragraphics has established itself as a leader in using vid-cart and tri-dimensional broadcasting technology as system-wide entertainment media. Animation Ultragraphics is noted for combining subliminal psychological triggering systems with the latest Cygnian holographic techniques to create extremely dramatic visual/emotional productions. Primary markets for this corporation's productions include Alpha Centauri, Cygnet XIV, Tellar, and Terra. Discussions are currently underway to establish a trade agreement that would introduce these innovative systems to the Orion Colonies as well. Animation Ultragraphics is a member of the entertainment cartel that owns and operates Wrigley's Pleasure Planet.

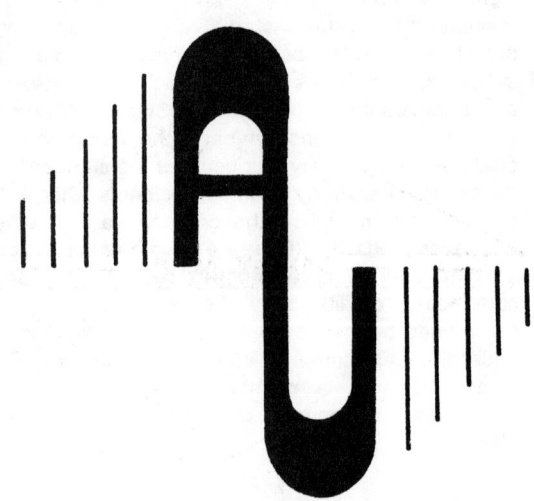

Name: BANK OF ANDOR
UFPSC Symbol: BkAnd
Home Office Location: Daldorran, Andor
President/CEO: Valtess' Uvar
Chartering Organization: Securities and Exchange Commission
Founding Date: 0/9901.1
Principal Divisions
Division Name: Andor Prime Financial
    Division Head: Milith Jargus
    Chief Product: Exclusive Financial Savings and Lending Services to the Andorian Government
Division Name: Andor Galactic Financial
    Division Head: Larex Oppora
    Chief Product: Financial Savings and Lending Services to Offworld Depositors
Division Name: Andor Universal Investments
    Division Head: Kerv Ballip
    Chief Product: Private Commercial Investment Services
Stock Profile: 1A15
Price/Date: 789.45 Cr on 2/2306.01
Dividend: 56.75 Cr
Balance Sheet, Year Ended: 2/2301

Cash:	Assets:	Liabilities:	Ratio:
4,566 BCr	6,780 BCr	150 BCr	45.2

Business Summary:
Clearly the most successful financial institution outside Orion space, the Bank of Andor serves as the financial advisor and principal lender to various planetary corporations as well as many of the Federation's governmental organizations. The Bank of Andor is also the major repository for Federation hard currency holdings.

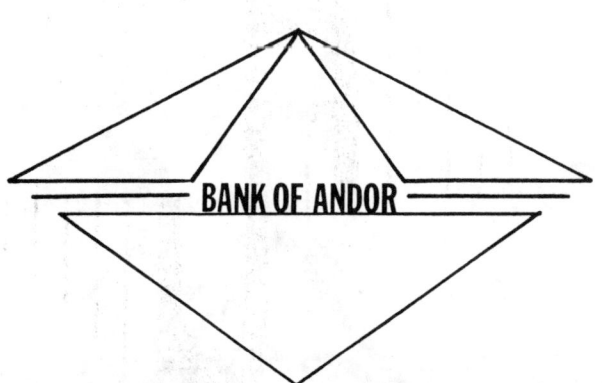

Name: BAXTER PHARMACEUTICALS, INC.
UFPSC Symbol: BxtrPh
Home Office Location: Chicago, Terra
President/CEO: Marin Ballantrye
Chartering Organization: Securities and Exchange Commission
Founding Date: 1/2304
Principal Divisions
Division Name: Baxter BioMetrics
    Division Head: Dr. Sarah Jane Forrester
    Chief Product: Prescription Drugs and Pharmaceuticals
Division Name: Baxter BioResearch
    Division Head: David MacNorman Sterling
    Chief Product: BioChemical Research
Stock Profile: 1C46
Price/Date: 54.45 Cr on 2/2306.01
Dividend: 7.00 Cr
Balance Sheet, Year Ended: 2/2301

Cash:	Assets:	Liabilities:	Ratio:
234 MCr	959 MCr	230 MCr	4.16

Business Summary:
Baxter Pharmaceuticals is one of the largest multiplanetary producers of drugs and serums to fight infectious diseases. Research at Baxter into new, experimental compounds has led to many of the major medical breakthroughs in the last century. Among its many claims to fame is the development of the first workable, mass-produced serum to combat Rigellian blood-burn fever. In addition, Baxter Pharmaceuticals remains among the leaders in manufacturing biomedical adaptive compounds as well as preventive research into numerous Federation diseases.

Name: BIO/GENETIC RESEARCH, INC.
UGPSC Symbol: BioGen
Home Office Location: London, Terra
President/CEO: Victoria Demoiselle
Chartering Organization: Securities and Exchange Commission
Founding Date: 0/0201.7
Principal Divisions
Division Name: BioGen Radionics
    Division Head: Laura Patterson-Smythe
    Chief Product: Biological Engineered Compounds
Stock Profile: 2B32
Price/Date: 34.45 Cr on 2/2306.01
Dividend: 1.25 Cr
Balance Sheet, Year Ended: 2/2301

Cash:	Assets:	Liability:	Ratio:
12 MCr	182 MCr	15 MCr	12.08

Business Summary:
Founded shortly after the Eugenics Wars on Terra, Bio/Genetic Research, Inc. began business by conducting research into radiation sickness. It is credited with developing Hydronilen, a genetically engineered compound used to retard the effects of high-level radiation. Over 90 percent of all subjects so treated experienced symptom remission. Today, Bio/Genetic Research is experimenting with genetically tailored microorganisms to manufacture new synthetic compounds for agriculture, industry, and medicine. With offices and research labs on 13 Federation planets, Bio/Genetic Research hires an estimated one out of ten Federation geneticists graduating from major planetary universities each year.

Name: CHANDLEY WORKS, LTD.
UFPSC Symbol: ChdlWk
  Home Office Location: Caravalla, Mars
  President/CEO: William Adams Chandley II
  Chartering Organization: Securities and Exchange Commission
  Founding Date: 0/6202.04
Principal Divisions
  Division Name: Chandley Armaments
    Division Head: Margaret T. Carsen
    Chief Product: Hybrid Multiple-Weapons Control Systems
  Division Name: Chandley Constructs
    Division Head: Richard Lyndon Chandley
    Chief Product: Starship Construction
  Division Name: Chandley Tactical
    Division Head: James Ballard Peterson
    Chief Product: Military Operations Research Planning
Stock Profile: 2C25
  Price/Date: 43.25 Cr on 2/2306.01
  Dividend: 5.50 Cr
Balance Sheet, Year Ended: 2/2301.01

Cash:	Assets:	Liabilities:	Ratio:
657 MCr	751 BCr	12 BCr	60.08

Business Summary:
  Founded by Rear Admiral Thomas Chandley before the Federation was formed, Chandley Works has long been a major supplier and producer of efficient combat vessel designs. In addition, many of the integrated weapons fire control systems used aboard Star Fleet and independent vessels are manufactured by Chandley. Most recently, Chandley Works has been engaged in producing the new *Chandley* Class frigate for Star Fleet. The *Chandley* is unique in that it permits large numbers of marine personnel to be aboard ship with a minimal decrease in vessel efficiency or crew performance.

Name: CHARLOTTES SHIELDS, INC.
UFPSC Symbol: ChShl
  Home Office Location: Quiberon Prime, Alpha Centauri
  President/CEO: Dr. Elizabeth Charlottes
  Chartering Organization: Securities and Exchange Commission
  Founding Date: 1/7002.07
Principal Divisions
  Division Name: Charlottes Shielding Works
    Division Head: Morgan Lethen Prin
    Chief Product: Energy Shielding Systems
  Division Name: Charlottes Energies
    Division Head: Jackson Roykirk IV
    Chief Product: Deflector Shield Technologies Research
Stock Profile: 2C68
  Price/Date: 45.35 Cr on 2/2306.01
  Dividend: None
Balance Sheet, Year Ended 2/2301

Cash:	Assets:	Liabilities:	Ratio:
567 MCr	878 MCr	150 MCr	5.85

Business Summary:
  This veteran Centauran firm is currently one of the major Federation designers and manufacturers of deflector shield systems and their associated technologies. Founded by Dr. Elizabeth Charlottes, Charlottes Shields began producing practical defense shields in Stardate 1/83. The firm has contributed significantly to defense shield engineering by designing and developing a working double-phase shift transformer, which yielded Charlottes a large share of the shielding market. Some major competitors sought to unseat this upstart firm in a series of corporate battles that raged from Stardates 1/94 to 1/99. In the final year of 'The Great Shield Wars', the Federation Fourth Quadrant Court of Commerce ruled that Wyandotte Defense Shields and Surelox Systems had acted in collusion to make Charlottes Shields the victim of price-fixing. The resulting judgement brought economic parity to these three industrial concerns.

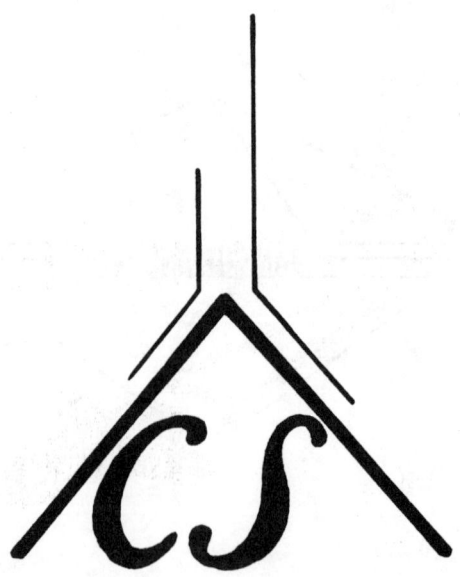

Name: CHIOKIS STARSHIP CONSTRUCTION
UFPSC Symbol: ChksSt
  Home Office Location: Thelavor, Andor
  President/CEO: Thuriyh Velm
  Chartering Organization: Securities and Exchange Commission
  Founding Date: 1/3412.1

Principal Divisions:
  Division Name: Chiokis Constructs
    Division Head: Theleva Velm
    Chief Product: Star Fleet Military Command Starship Construction
  Division Name: Chiokis Commercial Concepts
    Division Head: Raymind Harcourter
    Chief Product: Commercial Passenger and Cargo Vessel Construction
  Division Name: Chiokis Systems Technologies
    Division Head: Marian Gorond Alabastre
    Chief Product: Starship Support Systems

Stock Profile: 1B19
  Price/Date: 52,51 Cr on 2/2306.01
  Dividend: 2.50 Cr

Balance Sheet, Year Ending: 2/2301

Cash:	Assets:	Liabilities:	Ratio:
348 MCr	488 BCr	44 BCr	11.09

Business Summary:

Chiokis Starship Construction is a joint Andorian/Terran venture that has witnessed phenomenal success in starship design and construction. Chiokian employees are proud that their firm has produced more vessels and independent vessel designs than any other shipyard in Federation history. Designing both military and commercial craft, Chiokis has sometimes worked in conjuction with Ranturra Shipping and Chandley Works, Ltd. to produce ships for Star Fleet Command. This firm is noted primarily for the unique saucer-shaped design it uses to construct military and exploratory vessels. Currently, it turns out over 120 vessels of various designs for Star Fleet Command per year, a record unequalled by any other competitor.

Name: DAYSTROM DATA CONCEPTS
UFPSC Symbol: DstDC
  Home Office Location: San Francisco, Terra
  President/CEO: Richard Daystrom II
  Chartering Organization: Securities and Exchange Commission
  Founding Date: 1/9805.1

Principal Divisions:
  Division Name: Daystrom Datatronics
    Division Head: Richard Daystrom II
    Chief Product: Multitronic Computer Designs
  Division Name: Daystrom Data Storage
    Division Head: Dr. Cynthia Daystrom
    Chief Product: Mass Data Storage Systems Security

Stock Profile: 1C32
  Price/Date: 26.75 Cr on 2/2306.01
  Dividend: 1.75 Cr

Balance Sheet, Year Ending: 2/2301

Cash:	Assets:	Liabilities:	Ratio:
689 MCr	899 BCr	202 BCr	4.45

Business Summary:

Founded by Dr. Randall L. Daystrom, the inventor of the first multitronic engram-logic-enhanced computer, this family corporation is a major supplier of advanced computer systems designs. In particular, it is the sole manufacturer of the Multitronic computer series used by Star Fleet Command as well as numerous civilian and educational concerns. Replacing the older "L" series with multitronic computers (the "M" series) has led to significant breakthroughs in warp drive and weaponry systems designs. Daystrom Data Concepts also provides extremely efficient software for storing large amounts of sensitive data as well as internal and external security options for such systems. Following the death of Randall Daystrom, Dr. Richard Daystrom took control of company operations until his mental collapse required his son Richard Daystrom II to take over the position of CEO. This company supervised the restoration of Memory Alpha's main computer complex following the Lights of Zetar incident, which had massively damaged the museum's computer memory core. Dr. Cynthia Daystrom is credited with salvaging all but a minute portion of the research center's total accumulated access files. Daystrom Data Concepts is continuing research aimed at improving the Multitronic series and is expected to announce a major breakthrough within the next two to three years.

Name: DURASPORT, INC.
UFPSC Symbol: Drspt
  Home Office Location: Ursinnis, Argelius
  President/CEO: Samuel Vashin
  Chartering Organization: Securities and Exchange Commission
  Founding Date: 1/5712.2
Principal Divisions:
  Division Name: Durasport Luxuries
    Division Head: Michael Adam Christopher
    Chief Product: Gravitic Furniture Designs
Stock Profile: 3E53
  Price/Date: 61.44 Cr on 2/2306.01
  Dividend: None
Balance Sheet, Year Ending: 2/2301

Cash:	Assets:	Liabilities:	Ratio:
23 MCr	825 MCr	112 MCr	7.36

Business Summary:
Durasport manufactures and distributes a wide range of gravitic recliners, comforters, and other luxury furniture for business and private residencies. Similar designs can be found aboard all major interstellar passenger liners and private pleasure craft.

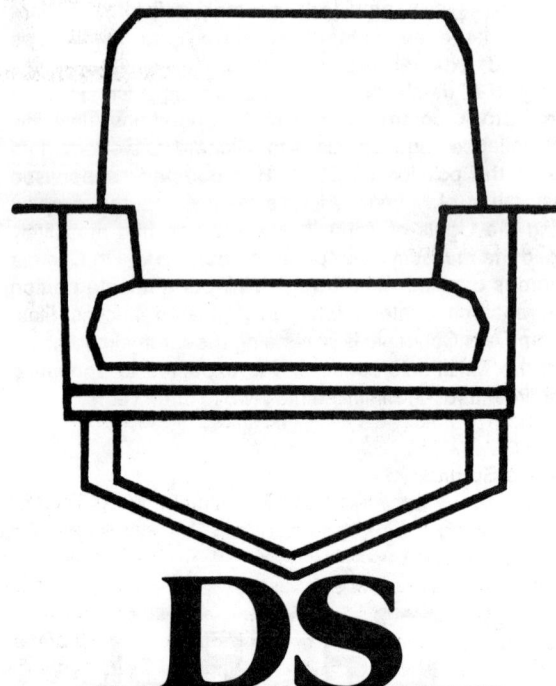

Name: GENERAL ENTERTAINMENT CONCEPTS
UFPSC Symbol: GEntCn
  Home Office Location: New Orleans, Terra
  President/CEO: Logan Barnell II
  Chartering Organization: Securities and Exchange Commission
  Founding Date: 1/3805.7
Principal Divisions:
  Division Name: General Entertainment Releases
    Division Head: James Patrick Namura
    Chief Product: Tri-dimensional Film Production
  Division Name: General Space Entertainments
    Division Head: Harrison F. Valcohr
    Chief Product: Construction Management Of Orbital Amusement Centers
  Division Name: General Entertainment Marketables
    Division Head: Jacqueline Kallus
    Chief Product: Personal Audio/Visual Equipment
Stock Profile: 2B43
  Price/Date: 45.45 Cr on 2/2306.01
  Dividend: 3.75 Cr
Balance Sheet, Year Ending: 2/2301

Cash:	Assets:	Liabilities:	Ratio:
67 MCr	948 BCr	101 BCr	9.38

Business Summary:
General Entertainments Concepts is dedicated to the idea that the universe is one never-ending adventure to be enjoyed again and again. This corporation currently has two major ventures demanding its attention. The first is the recovery, restoration, and tri-dimensional holographic release of various classic films from various cultures. Successful efforts have unearthed numerous Terran, Centauran, and Vulcan epics that have received considerable acclaim. In addition, General Entertainments Concepts has embarked on an ambitious project to turn worthless asteroids into amusement centers geared toward specific cultural tastes. In this regard, it can draw upon vast reserves of capital from its Marketables division, which produces audio- and visual-oriented holographic equipment for personal entertainment. Its most expensive project has been Wrigley's Pleasure Planet, in which it is the leading investor. Similar projects have been completed in the Cygnian and Argelian systems, and future plans include introducing even larger creations for the Tellarite and Vulcan systems.

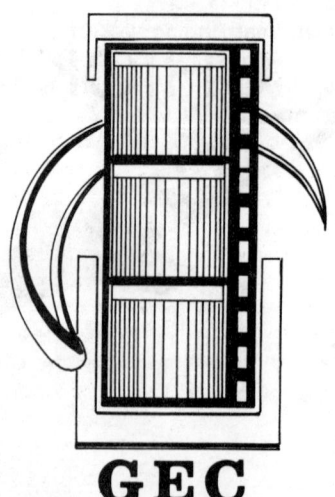

Name: GGRAMPHUD HISTO-CRYOGENICS, INC.
UFPSC Symbol: GgrHC
  Home Office Location: Tellar
  President/CEO: Arrv Ggramphud
  Chartering Organization: Securities and Exchange Commission
  Founding Date: 1/8807.7
Principal Divisions:
  Division Name: Ggramphud Developments
    Division Head: Arrv Ggramphud
    Chief Product: Cryogenic Support Systems
  Division Name: Ggramphud Research Development
    Division Head: Glunddra Ggramphud
    Chief Product: Cryogenic Research
Stock Profile: 3C36
  Price/Date: 53.10 Cr on 2/2306.01
  Dividend: None
Balance Sheet, Year Ending: 2/2301

Cash:	Assets:	Liabilities:	Ratio:
112 MCr	926 MCr	122 MCr	7.59

Business Summary:
One of the more ambitious corporate ventures in many years, this recently founded private corporation is dedicated to research concerning cryogenic techniques for life prolongation. Funded largely by the Federation Science Foundation, this Tellar-based corporation hopes to provide a practical application of cryogenic technology by the end of the century.

Name: HIBEAM ENERGIES, LTD.
UFPSC Symbol: HBEng
  Home Office Location: Luna City, Luna
  President/CEO: Patricia D. Maxim
  Chartering Organization: Securities and Exchange Commission
  Founding Date: 11/1508.23
Principal Divisions:
  Division Name: HiBeam Defense Systems
    Division Head: Yuri Gomorell
    Chief Product: Shipboard Phased-Energy Weapons Systems
  Division Name: HiBeam Research Frontiers
    Division Head: Roger Darcronn
    Chief Product: High-Energy/Plasma Research
Stock Profile: 2D63
  Price/Date: 45.50 Cr on 2/2306.01
  Dividend: 2.25 Cr
Balance Sheet, Year Ending: 2/2301

Cash:	Assets:	Liabilities:	Ratio:
12.5 BCr	987 BCr	121 BCr	8.15

Business Summary:
Formed in the early history of the Federation, HiBeam Energies has become a principal contractor to Star Fleet Command. In Stardate 1/94, HiBeam designed the first phaser weapons system, the Mark 1. The phased energy weapon replaced previous laser weapons aboard Star Fleet vessels, and by the end of the Four Years War, all such ships had the phaser system. Close association with Daystrom Data Concepts led to the Mark 3 (FH-3) design, which used the M-1 multitronic computer. Currently, HiBeam Technologies maintains no less than 17 full-scale production facilities running 24 hours a day to meet civil and defense needs.

Name: KLORATIS DRIVES
UFPSC Symbol: KlDrv
  Home Office Location: Tellar
  President/CEO: Dsdrad Wrrnes
  Chartering Organization: Securities and Exchange Commission
  Founding Date: 1/8108.1
Principal Divisions:
  Division Name: Kloratis Warp Technologies
    Division Head: Dr. Cyristal Kelvar
    Chief Product: Warp Engine Systems & Intercoolers
  Division Name: Kloratis Physics Technologies
    Division Head: Dr. Ggrhm Klorata
    Chief Product: Space Warp Physics Research
Stock Profile: 3E84
  Price/Date: 44.25 Cr on 2/2306.01
  Dividend: 4.75 Cr
Balance Sheet, Year Ending: 2/2301

Cash:	Assets:	Liabilities:	Ratio:
405 BCr	1,875 BCr	112 BCr	16.66

Business Summary:
A manufacturer of assorted warp engine technologies for Tellarite starship designs, Kloratis Drives is also a leading developer of various impulse engine designs. Kloratis researchers are presently working with Shuvinaaljis Warp Technologies to develop a new series of micro-warp engines for small transport systems.

Name: LEEDING ENGINES, LTD.
UFPSC Symbol: LdEng
  Home Office Location: Sydney, Terra
  President/CEO: Dr. Maxwell Haren
  Chartering Organization: Securities and Exchange Commission
  Founding Date: 2/0201.01
Principal Divisions:
  None
Stock Profile:
  Price/Date: 22.75 Cr on 2/2306.01
  Dividend: 1.75 Cr
Balance Sheet, Year Ending: 2/2301

Cash:	Assets:	Liabilities:	Ratio:
119 MCr	782 MCr	115 MCr	6.78

Business Summary:
Following his dismissal from Shuvinaaljis Warp Technologies, Dr. Harold S. Leedstrom took his entire research team and founded Leeding Engines, Ltd. This firm was the first manufacturer of warp drive systems capable of sustained Warp 8 speeds and emergency speeds of Warp 10. Association with Daystrom Data Concepts and Chandley Works helped Leeding create the tandem FWC-1 engine designs. Unfortunately, these dynamic successes sparked an intense corporate war with Shuvinaaljis that culminated with the death of Dr. Leedstrom himself in Stardate 2/0501. It has not been conclusively proven whether Dr. Leedstrom committed suicide or was the victim of a very elaborate plot. Presently under the direction of Dr. Maxwell Haren, Leeding Engines continues to provide Star Fleet with FWG-1 engines for the *Enterprise* Class cruiser.

Name: LEEPER-FELL UNIVERSAL, LTD.
UFPSC Symbol: LFUnv
  Home Office Location: Tritium, Sol IV
  President/CEO: Tristan Leeper II and Aurora Fell
  Chartering Organization: Securities and Exchange Commission
  Founding Date: 1/2703.04
Principal Divisions:
  Division Name: Leeper-Fell Importations
    Division Head: Federiko Comstock
    Chief Product: Multi-System Commercial Imports
  Division Name: Leeper-Fell Exportations
    Division Head: B'rintrae
    Chief Product: Multi-Systems Commercial Exports
  Division Name: Leeper-Fell Engine Dynamics
    Division Head: Dr. Tamara Uvanca
    Chief Product: Warp Engine Components
  Division Name: Leeper-Fell Shielding
    Division Head: Dr. Randolf Merriweather III
    Chief Product: Force-Field Defense Systems
  Division Name: Leeper-Fell Terraforming
    Division Head: Dr. Sara Undara
    Chief Product: Plantary Terraforming
Stock Profile: 1C24
  Price/Date: 39.75 Cr on 2/2306.01
  Dividend: None
Balance Sheet, Year Ending: 2/2301

Cash:	Assets:	Liabilities:	Ratio:
92 MCr	889 BCr	212 BCr	4.17

Business Summary:
A powerful corporate entity, Leeper-Fell Universal is one of the few corporations to reach gross revenue levels of over 100 trillion credits last year. A widely diversified firm, Leeper-Fell began its corporate existence as an import/export company dealing with merchandise ranging from Spican flamegems and Saurian cognac to tribbles and Argelian silks. Beginning in Stardate 1/30, Leeper-Fell diversified into planetary terraforming. Their initial successes on the planets Ardanna and Babel convinced several planetary concerns to contract with Leeper-Fell, which advanced corporate interests as never before. Within the last two decades, Leeper-Fell amassed enough profits from this area to branch out into direct manufacturing concerns. Using generous salary and benefits programs, the firm enlisted the abilities of hundreds of university engineers skilled in both warp drive and defense shield technology. As a result, Leeper-Fell became a powerful competitor in the manufacture of warp drive components and shielding systems. It has managed to acquire several hefty manufacturing contracts, enabling it to employ over 500,000 individuals in its Engine Dynamics division alone.

There is a sinister shadow hanging over the operation of Leeper-Fell, however. Many are convinced that the firm was involved in the recent corporate wars that almost bankrupted Charlottes Shields. In recent years, allegations of ties between Leeper-Fell and various underworld organizations have also surfaced. Although these allegations have yet to be proven, many people are concerned over the continued growth of Leeper-Fell and its dubious corporate ethics.

Name: LORAXIAL CORPORATION
UFPSC Symbol: LRxl
  Home Office Location: Andor
  President/CEO: Richard Ebossa
  Chartering Organization: Securities and Exchange Commission
  Founding Date: 0/0202.7
Principal Divisions:
  Division Name: Loraxial Magnetic Dynamics
    Division Head: Luthar Barabrin
    Chief Product: Photon Weapon Attack Systems
Stock Profile: 2D70
  Price/Date: 23.50 Cr on 2/2306.01
  Dividend: None
Balance Sheet, Year Ending: 2/2301

Cash:	Assets:	Liabilities:	Ratio:
74 MCr	990 MCr	111 MCr	8.91

Business Summary:
Though initially founded to design accelerator cannons, Loraxial experienced a drastic change near the end of the Four Years War. Priscilla Feddric created an efficient antimatter containment system, which led to the first operational photon torpedo. The FP-1 photon torpedo system was installed on front-line ships and wreaked havoc on Klingon ships before the war ended. Loraxial is responsible for several photon system designs currently on Star Fleet vessels.

Name: MARSFOODS CORPORATION
UFPSC Symbol: Mrsfd
  Home Office Location: Vandalia, Mars
  President/CEO: Elias Wintergreen
  Chartering Organization: Securities and Exchange Commission
  Founding Date: 2/0907.4
Principal Divisions:
  Division Name: Marsfoods Express Service
    Division Head: Elias Wintergreen
    Chief Product: Fast Food Products
Stock Profile: 2D89
  Price/Date: 66.75 Cr on 2/23306.01
  Dividend: 1.25 Cr
Balance Sheet, Year Ending: 2/2301

Cash:	Assets:	Liabilities:	Ratio:
124 MCr	944 MCr	219 MCr	4.31

Business Summary:
Reviving an ancient Terran business concern, founder Elias Wintergreen established Marsfoods as the Federation's most outrageous fast foods supplier. To date, this chain of planetary system concessions is estimated at well over 100,000 units. Much of Wintergreen's success is due to his imaginative advertising as well as judicious corporate arrangements with General Entertainments Concepts, which introduced Wintergreen's franchise in its numerous amusement park worlds.

Name: MORRIS MAGTRONICS
UFPSC Symbol: MrMag
Home Office Location: Palyria, Sol IV
President/CEO: Cartwright Morris
Chartering Organization: Securities and Exchange Commission
Founding Date: 1/4501.12
Principal Divisions:
Division Name: Morris Gravitics
  Division Head: Jacob Thrusher
  Chief Product: Artificial Gravity Systems and Supportive Technologies
Division Name: Morris Weapons Developments
  Division Head: Angelina Wrill
  Chief Product: Photon Torpedo Weapons Systems
Stock Profile: 3B65
Price/Date: 14.25 Cr on 2/2306.01
Dividend: None
Balance Sheet, Year Ending: 2/23301

Cash:	Assets:	Liabilities:	Ratio:
110 MCr	782 MCr	125 MCr	6.25

Business Summary:
Morris Magtronics is one of the Federation's leading producers of anti-gravity and artificial gravity systems. The Gravitics division services all gravity controls on Star Fleet and civilian vessels and life-support systems on offworld and low-gravity installations. Its success prompted corporate leaders to diversify the firm by introducing an improved photon-torpedo weapon system, the FP-4, in Stardate 2/02.

Name: MULTIPLANET METALS, INC.
UFPSC Symbol: MltiPl
Home Office Location: Gdurav, Tellar
President/CEO: Oscar Palmersen
Chartering Organization: Securities and Exchange Commission
Founding Date: 1/9902.28
Principal Divisions:
Division Name: Multiplanet Geologies
  Division Head: Oscar Palmersen
  Chief Product: Planetary Geological Exploration
Division Name: Multiplant Extractions
  Division Head: Greuniv Garj
  Chief Product: Planetary Mining
Stock Profile: 2D72
Price/Date: 30.25 Cr on 2/2306.01
Dividend: None
Balance Sheet, Year Ending: 2/2301

Cash:	Assets:	Liabilities:	Ratio:
6.25 MCr	901 MCr	227 MCr	3.96

Business Summary:
The largest Tellarite mining concern in existence, Multiplanet Metals is the result of several corporate mergers that have left Tellar with one major mining corporation. Tellarites hope that this government-supported action will cut their overhead enough to allow them to underbid rival Andorian firms for contracts to extract planetary ores.

Name: M'YENGH YARDS
UFPSC Symbol: MYnYd
Home Office Location: Shzerensohr, Cait
President/CEO: K'rissa
Chartering Organization: Securities and Exchange Commission
Founding Date: 1/3902.2
Principal Divisions
Division Name: M'Yengh Constructions
  Division Head: Trinsak
  Chief Product: Starship Construction
Division Name: M'Yengh Dynamics
  Division Head: Construction Research Development
  Chief Product: Starship Navigational Systems
Stock Profile: 1D37
Price/Date: 97.50 Cr on 2/2306.01
Dividend: 2.50 Cr
Balance Sheet, Year Ending: 2/2301

Cash:	Assets:	Liabilities:	Ratio:
697 MCr	565 BCr	118 BCr	4.78

Business Summary:
This government-owned and -sponsored starship construction firm makes bids for both Star Fleet and civilian projects. Thus, M'Yengh Yards would not be greatly affected if the Federation Council votes to reduce starship construction, which has happened on several occasions. As the majority of its revenues come from more stable, commercial requests, M'Yengh Yards can afford to invest more income into research and development.

Name: NEW AMSTERDAM GRAVITICS
UFPSC Symbol: NAmGrv
Home Office Location: New Amsterdam, Alpha III
President/CEO: Joseph Ottermen
Chartering Organization: Securities and Exchange Commission
Principal Divisions:
None
Stock Profile: 1D64
Price/Date: 38.50 Cr on 2/2306.01
Dividend: 2.25 Cr
Balance Sheet, Year Ended: 2/2301

Cash:	Assets:	Liabilities:	Ratio:
119 MCr	905 MCr	202 MCr	4.48

Business Summary:
This firm is a major supplier of commercial and industrial anti-gravity platforms and conveyors for use in high-gravity environments. New Amsterdam Gravitics is rumored to be undergoing financial distress, though this has yet to be verified. Other rumors suggest that the firm may soon be taken over by a larger competitor.

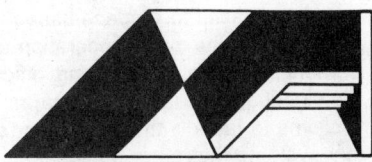
NEW AMSTERDAM GRAVITICS CO.

Name: PAN-GALACTIC PRODUCTIONS
UFPSC Symbol: PGPrd
Home Office Location: London, Terra
President/CEO: Justine Mallor
Chartering Organization: Securities and Exchange Commission
Founding Date: 1/3401.17
Principal Divisions
Division Name: Galaxy Videos
    Division Head: Houston Mallorn
    Chief Product: Tri-mensional Holographic Films
Stock Profile: 3B79
Price/Date: 12.75 Cr on 2/2306.01
Dividend: 10.45 Cr
Balance Sheet, Year Ended: 2/2301

Cash:	Assets:	Liabilities:	Ratio:
750 MCr	456 BCr	92.7 BCr	4.91

Business Summary:
A major producer of tri-dimensional films, Pan-Galactic Productions is noted for its visual techniques as well as its wide range of current and counter-culture presentations. It is also part owner in several theme parks and recreation centers on Imagination and Wrigley's Pleasure Planet, which are expected to provide a steady flow of income for decades to come.

Name: PHOENIX ENTERPRISES LIMITED
UFPSC Symbol: PEL
Home Office Location: Reynard, Salazaar
President/CEO: Cranston Issaiah McTeague
Chartering Organization: Securities and Exchange Commission
Founding Date: -1/8208.1
Principal Divisions
Division Name: Phoenix Shipping
    Division Head: Soldan
    Chief Product: Interstellar transportation of cargo
Division Name: Phoenix Commodities
    Division Head: Ian Freed
    Chief Product: Interstellar commodities speculation
Stock Profile: 2B58
Price/Date: 48.75 Cr on 2/2306.01
Dividend: 1.25 Cr
Balance Sheet, Year Ended: 2/2301

Cash:	Assets:	Liabilities:	Ratio:
63 MCr	998 BCr	225 BCr	4.43

Business Summary
Phoenix Enterprises Limited began as a Terran sea-going shipping firm operating out of Sydney, Australia in the late 20th century. Phoenix was one of the few corporations to survive the Eugenics Wars relatively intact. In the aftermath of that global catastrophe, it was instrumental in maintaining the tenuous seaborne contacts between survivors during the planet's reconstruction. With the discovery of the warp drive in the 21st century, Phoenix managed to make the transition from a sea-based to a space-based transportation firm. Today, it is one of the major Federation-wide commercial cargo carriers in space, maintaining offices in the Salazaar, Sol, Betelgeuse, Argelian, and Antaran systems. One of its major claims to fame is that it transports material to minor planetary systems that other competitors find economically unproductive to support. The common consensus is that Phoenix will carry any cargo anywhere at any time for a reasonable fee. Though suspected of transporting illegal goods, the firm's reputation remains untarnished, at least officially.

Name: RANTURA SHIPPING LINES
UFPSC Symbol: RntrSh
Home Office Location: New Daran, Deneva
President/CEO: Onto Rantura
Chartering Organization: Securities and Exchange Commission
Founding Date: 1/2127
Principal Divisions
Division Name: Denevan Shipping
    Division Head: Eloise Rantura
    Chief Product: Interstellar passenger transportation
Division Name: Rantura Shipping and Receiving
    Division Head: Felix Rantura
    Chief Product: Interstellar cargo transportation
Stock Profile: 4C28
Price/Date: 45.67 Cr on 2/2306.01
Dividend: 2.25 Cr
Balance Sheet, Year Ended: 2/2301

Cash:	Assets:	Liabilities:	Ratio:
25 BCr	715 BCr	87 BCr	8.21

Business Summary:
Rantura Shipping was founded by Esaha Rantura, a second-generation inhabitant of Deneva, as a shuttle service between Deneva and nearby Colony V. Within a single generation, Rantura Shipping expanded to handle over 80 percent of the passenger as well as cargo transport needs of both worlds. An agreement with Chiokis Starship Construction in Stardate 1/2184 further advanced Rantura's prospects by giving Rantura exclusive shipping rights to and from Chiokis corporate facilities throughout dozens of planetary systems. These two firms later collaborated to produce the highly successful *Deneva* Class Towship, which began operations in Stardate 2/0205. Rantura suffered a near disastrous setback when flying parasites from Ingraham B nearly decimated Deneva. Numerous key corporate personnel were lost in this tragic episode. However, none of the Rantura fleet were in the system at the time, and a sufficient number of competent employees were available to enable Rantura to rebuild, though slowly and with some difficulty.

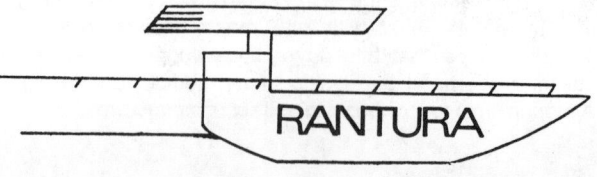

Name: SHIPUTER CORPORATION
UFPSC Symbol: ShpC
   Home Office Location: Bristol, Terra
   President/CEO: Franklin Trinikar
   Chartering Organization: Securities and Exchange Commission
   Founding Date: 1/3507.8
Principal Divisions
   Division Name: Shiputer Navigation Systems
      Division Head: Jeffrey Trinikar
      Chief Product: Starship Navigational Computers Support Systems
Stock Profile: 4F73
   Price/Date: 23.75 Cr on 2/2306.01
   Dividend: None
Balance Sheet, Year Ended: 2/2301

Cash:	Assets:	Liabilities:	Ratio:
34 BCr	588 BCr	290 BCr	2.02

Business Summary:
   A long-term supplier of starship navigational control systems, Shiputer Corporation recently exhausted much of its corporate reserves in an unsuccessful attempt to take over Daystrom Data Concepts. Presently, Shiputer is selling off many of its holdings to reduce its current liabilities resulting from the protracted Daystrom fight. Though it is expected to return to its original solvency in the near future, Shiputer will nevertheless be in an unfavorable position for some time.

Name: SHUVINAALJIS WARP TECHNOLOGIES, INC.
UFPSC Symbol: Shvalj
   Home Office Location: Shuridar, Vulcan
   President/CEO: Sintar
   Chartering Organization: Securities and Exchange Commission
   Founding Date: 1/1209.9
Principal Divisions
   Division Name: Shuvinaaljis Warp Drives
      Division Head: Urden Victa
      Chief Product: Warp Engine Construction
   Division Name: Shuvinaaljis Developments
      Division Head: Tirex
      Chief Product: Long Range Shuttle Craft
Stock Profile: 1D50
   Price/Date: 112.75 Cr on 2/2306.01
   Dividend: 33.55 Cr
Balance Sheet, Year Ended: 2/2301

Cash:	Assets:	Liabilities:	Ratio:
489 BCr	5,689 BCr	345 BCr	16.48

Business Summary:
   Begun as a manufacturer of warp engine systems, Shuvinaaljis Warp Technologies gambled in a large way on the development of a new range of micro-warp engine technologies. The firm installed the micro-warp on several advanced, long-range warp shuttles, which are expected to service both government and military needs over the next several decades. Though research and development costs have been higher than expected, contracts from the Vulcan government and from Star Fleet Command for the new vessels have bolstered confidence in this firm.

Name: S'LEK VARAN
UFPSC Symbol: SLkVn
   Home Office Location: Shuridar, Vulcan
   President/CEO: Sehrtor
   Chartering Organization: Securities and Exchange Commission
   Founding Date: 1/1212.17
Principal Divisions:
   Division Name: S'Lek Support Systems
      Division Head: Sheriv
      Chief Product: Starship Auxiliary Systems Production
Stock Profile: 3B61
   Price/Date: 105.25 Cr on 2/2306.01
   Dividend: None
Balance Sheet, Year Ended: 2/2301

Cash:	Assets:	Liabilities:	Ratio:
760 MCr	458 BCr	132.3 BCr	3.46

Business Summary:
   S'Lek Varen produces auxiliary and support systems for both commercial and military craft. It not only contracts through the Vulcan government, but also works as a sub-contractor for other, less specialized shipbuilders on cooperative projects.

Name: SMITH & SMYTHE MOTOR WORKS, LTD.
UFPSC Symbol: SSmWkL
   Home Office Location: Surleft, Andor
   Chartering Organization: Securities and Exchange Commission
   Founding Date: 1/3409.19
Principal Divisions
   Division Name: S & S Nuclears
      Division Head: Timothy Selk
      Chief Product: Starship Power Plants & Control Systems
   Division Name: S & S Engines
      Division Head: Dr. Margaret Hurn
      Chief Product: Impulse Engine Designs
Stock Profile: 2E52
   Price/Date: 21.25 Cr on 2/2306.01
   Dividend: 1.25 Cr
Balance Sheet, Year Ended: 2/2301

Cash:	Assets:	Liabilities:	Ratio:
441 MCr	567 BCr	101.5 BCr	5.58

Business Summary:
   Smith and Smythe is the principal manufacturer of auxiliary power systems and support equipment for starship designs. In Stardate 1/76, it gained recognition as the first firm to mass-produce an impulse engine system. Though contracting exclusively through the Andorian government, Smith & Smythe is not a native Andorian firm, but rather a transplanted Terran company that took over an Andorian competitor. The corporation is one of the few examples of firms that succeeded in gaining acceptance at both the governmental and public level after their takeover. Smith & Smythe researchers have also developed a new micro-impulse warp engine design, which was released in Stardate 2/09.

Name: STARWIDE MERCHANTS
UFPSC Symbol: Strwid
  Home Office Location: Grinitaine, Alpha Centauri
  President/CEO: Mortimer Trellenstone
  Chartering Organization: Securities and Exchange Commission
  Founding Date: 1/0302.2
Principal Divisions
  Division Name: Starwide Service Supply
    Division Head: Margaret Verliek
    Chief Product: Stores and Supplies for Colonial Expeditions
  Division Name: Starwide Acquisitions
    Division Head: Ingram Braddock
    Chief Product: Import-Export Trade
Stock Profile: 3B22
  Price/Date: 110.75 Cr on 2/2306.01
  Dividend: 25.25 Cr
Balance Sheet, Year Ended: 2/2301
Cash:	Assets:	Liabilities:	Ratio
458 MCr	6,788 BCr	348 BCr	19.5

Business Summary:
Starwide Merchants' appraisers are reputed to select only the finest quality items for distribution. Based on this reputation, the corporation's vast capital has also permitted it to finance and equip (sometimes with government support) colonial expeditions. Starwide Merchants agrees to outfit a given expedition—even to the extent of financing construction of an exploration vessel—in exchange for a percentage of any gross revenues in exports collected by the colony world in the future. Most of these financed expeditions have been successful, and Starwide Merchants is expected to remain profitable and financially sound for many years to come.

Name: SURELOX SYSTEMS
UFPSC Symbol: SurSys
  Home Office Location: Tybrenn, Arcturus
  President/CEO: Martin Wymann Surrex
  Chartering Organization: Securities and Exchange Commission
  Founding Date: 1/8402.05
Principal Divisions
  Division Name: Surelox Shielding
    Division Head: Dr. Fiona W. Yare
    Chief Product: Shipboard Defensive Shield Systems
Stock Profile: 2C36
  Price/Date: 23.75 Cr on 2/2306.01
  Dividend: 1.75 Cr.
Balance Sheet, Year Ended: 2/2301
Cash:	Assets:	Liabilities:	Ratio
328MCr	678MCr	239MCr	2.83

Business Profile:
A corporate subsidiary of Leeper-Fell Universal, Surelox Systems entered the interstellar marketplace in Stardate 1/84 as a manufacturer of ship defense shield systems. Financed largely by funds from Leeper-Fell, Surelox produced an inexpensive, low-power, single phase-shift transformer. Though only slightly better than other available shield systems, the product established Surelox as a major competitor in the defense shielding industry. In Stardate 1/90, Surelox upgraded its original model A by introducing new double phase-shift technology. In Stardate 1/94, the firm acquired Landauer Systech, a rival manufacturer that had previously gone into receivership. Two years later, backed by massive loans from Leeper-Fell, Surelox Systems negotiated with Wyandotte Defense Shields to wage a secret campaign of price-fixing to reduce Charlottes Shields leadership in the field. This almost proved to be Surelox's undoing when the Federation Tribunal Court settled the matter by awarding Charlottes Shields a large financial judgement. Though the judgement has greatly reduced its corporate assets, Surelox still maintains considerable holdings.

Name: SURVIVORS CORPORATION
UFPSC Symbol: SrvrCp
  Home Office Location: Tycho City, Deneva
  President/CEO: Martin Uerger
  Chartering Organization: Securities and Exchange Commission
  Founding Date: 1/8912.1
Principal Divisions
  Division Name: Survivors Protection
    Division Head: Maxwell Uerger
    Chief Product: Personal Insurance Services
Stock Profile: 2C25
  Price/Date: 27.02 Cr on 2/2306.01
  Dividend: 4.75 Cr
Balance Sheet, Year Ended: 2/2301

Cash:	Assets:	Liabilities:	Ratio:
54 BCr	447 BCr	124 BCr	3.59

Business Summary:
Formed after the Four Years War, Survivors began as a family project to provide affordable emergency/casualty insurance to veterans of that conflict and to their families. Today, it is the Federation's principal insurer of high-risk operations such as colonial exploration, starship construction, and weapons research and development. Survivors deals at all levels of business—private, corporate, and governmental.

Name: TACHYON MICROMECHANICS, LTD.
UFPSC Symbol: TcynMc
  Home Office Location: Grinidasa, Arcturus
  President/CEO: Loraine Ingressaine
  Chartering Organization: Securities and Exchange Commission
  Founding Date: 1/3809.12
Principal Divisions
  Division Name: Tachyon Industrials
    Division Head: S'bumi Thagir
    Chief Product: Sensor Detection Devices
Stock Profile: 2E80
  Price/Date: 37.33 Cr on 2/2306.01
  Dividend: 3.75 Cr
Balance Sheet, Year Ended: 2/2301

Cash:	Assets:	Liabilities:	Ratio:
149 MCr	909 MCr	387 MCr	2.34

Business Summary:
Manufacturing miniaturized sensor and recording equipment, Tachyon Micromechanics provides research and exploration operations with a wide range of computer-directed tracking and analysis systems. A relative financial newcomer, Tachyon Micromechanics is a family-owned and -operated firm whose stock is currently declining due to recent research and development failures.

Name: VULCAN MONETARY SOCIETY
UFPSC Symbol: VlcMon
  Home Office Location: Vulcan
  President/CEO: Fehashj
  Chartering Organization: Security and Exchange Commission
  Founding Date: 1/2807.30
Principal Divisions
  Division Name: Vulcan Monetary Controls
    Division Head: Sedklass
    Chief Product: Government and Corporate Financing
Stock Profile: 1B12
  Price/Date: 560.25 Cr on 2/2306.01
  Dividend: 23.50 Cr
Balance Sheet, Year Ended: 2/2301

Cash:	Assets:	Liabilities:	Ratio:
784 BCr	6580 BCr	234 BCr	28.11

Business Summary:
The principal governmental monetary control agency for the planet Vulcan, the Vulcan Monetary Society maintains all planetary and offworld financial operations involving the Vulcan government and major Vulcan corporations. Due to this firms's heavy investment on other worlds as well as the complete support of the Vulcan matriarchy, Vulcan Monetary enjoys considerable support and stability.

Name: WILSON ENERGIES LTD.
UFPSC Symbol: WlsEgy
  Home Office Location: Great Britain, Terra
  President/CEO: William Dolfius Wilson III
  Chartering Organization: Securities and Exchange Commission
  Founding Date: 1/2611.01
Principal Divisions
  Division Name: HiEnergy Corp
    Division Head: William D. Wilson IV
    Chief Product: Hand Phasers
  Division Name: Energies Research
    Division Head: Dr. James R. Wilson, Sr.
    Chief Product: Energy Weapon Research
Stock Profile: 2C29
  Price/Date: 82.73 Cr on 2/2306.01
  Dividend: 4.95 Cr
Balance Sheet, Year Ended: 2/2301

Cash:	Assets:	Liabilities:	Ratio:
444 MCr	1,908 BCr	361 BCr	5.28

Business Summary:
Following HiBeam Energies' development of the first shipboard phaser, Dr. James Wilson's skills in micro-miniaturization led to the design of the first hand-held phaser weapon and the birth of Wilson Energies. The new firm's position was secured when Star Fleet ordered an unprecedented half-million units to be supplied over the next twelve years. Not content with this coup, Wilson Energies refined the original Phaser I design, resulting in the upgraded Phaser II pistol and rifle. These advances have created a production demand that Wilson Energies is, even today, hard-pressed to match. Currently, five separate manufacturing concerns under Wilson Energies' supervision are cranking out phasers 24 hours a day.

THE FEDERATION STOCK EXCHANGE

The Federation Stock Exchange allows private and corporate financiers to invest in the corporate future of hundreds of businesses and corporations scattered throughout the stars. Actually a series of individual exchanges, it reflects the relative financial health and stability of the Federation and its various businesses.

Each quadrant of the Federation maintains a dozen separate stock exchanges that list individual companies and corporations according to their primary goods or service, i.e., shipbuilding, data processing, exporting, and so on. To become a member of one of these Quadrant Exchanges, a firm must be chartered by the Bureau of Corporate Development's Securities and Exchange Commission and be able to show net revenues of over one million credits a year for three out of the last five years.

Firms represented on the Federation Stock Exchange, known as the Big Board, are considered to be the major corporate entities within Federation space and, as a result, are prime candidates for government subsidies, "favored business status" taxation, and commerce breaks. The number of companies represented on the Big Board may vary with changing financial conditions from year to year. Admission to the Big Board requires gross revenues of over one billion credits and net worth of over 250 million credits in three years out of a six-year period. Current members of the Federation Stock Exchange and their financial condition as of 2/2306.01 are listed below.

THE FEDERATION STOCK EXCHANGE

Closing Date: 2/2306.01   **Weekly Trend:** Unchanged

	Dividend	Sales 1000s	Close	Net Change
AlkrLs	1.00	22	23.45	+ 1.00
AnUgrc	2.50	112	77.85	0.00
BkAnd	56.75	342	789.45	+ 2.25
BxtrPh	7.00	102	54.45	+ 1.05
BioGen	1.25	77	34.45	− 0.05
Chdlwk	5.50	57	43.25	+ 1.22
ChShl	0.00	11	45.35	+ 0.75
ChKsSt	2.50	25	52.51	− 0.20
DstDC	1.75	158	26.75	+ 0.75
Drspt	0.00	12	61.44	− 0.55
GEntCn	3.75	118	45.45	+ 1.10
GgrHC	0.00	43	53.10	+ 2.25
HBEng	2.25	238	45.50	− 1.00
KlDrv	4.75	193	44.25	+ 1.20
LdEng	1.75	56	22.75	− 0.55
LFUnv	0.00	117	39.75	− 0.22
LRxL	0.00	66	23.50	+ 2.30
Mrsfd	1.25	103	66.75	+ 0.57
MrMag	0.00	12	30.25	0.00
MltiPl	0.00	36	30.25	− 0.45
MYnYd	2.50	1133	97.50	+ 0.69
NAmGrv	2.25	17	38.50	− 0.67
PGPrd	10.45	100	12.75	0.00
PEL	1.25	45	48.75	− 0.50
RntrSh	2.25	1290	45.67	+ 0.10
ShpC	0.00	10	23.75	+ 1.17
Shvalj	33.55	2378	112.75	+ 0.75
SLkVn	0.00	19	105.25	+ 1.05
SSmWkl	1.25	458	21.25	+ 1.00
Strwid	25.25	3458	110.75	+ 2.25
SurSys	1.75	83	23.75	− 0.25
SrvrCp	4.75	459	27.02	0.00
TcynMc	3.75	230	37.33	0.00
VlcMon	23.50	6589	560.25	0.00
WlsEgy	4.95	788	82.73	− 0.10

FEDERATION COMMODITIES MARKET

The following items are available to investors through the Commodities Market.

Commodity	Origin	Major	Minor	Price	Availability
COMMON GOODS					
Agricultural Implements	Various		X	560 per STU	common
Foodstuffs	Various		X	100 per STU	common
GEMS AND RARE STONES					
Diamond	Various	X		349 per carat	uncommon
Emerald	Various	X		349 per carat	uncommon
Ruby	Various	X		349 per carat	uncommon
Sapphire	Various		X	300 per carat	uncommon
Spican Flamegems	Spica		X	456 per carat	uncommon
Turquoise	Various		X	150 per carat	uncommon
LUXURY ITEMS					
Air Truffles	Various		X	200 per kg	uncommon
Altair Water	Altair	X		2 per ml	common
Antarean Glow Water	Antares		X	7 per ml	common
Tribbles	Jorindas		X	60 per indiv	common
METALS AND MINERALS					
Copper	Various		X	458 per STU	common
Kevas	Vulcan		X	450 per kgm	common
Pergium	Various	X		5400 per kgm	rare
Steel	Various		X	568 per STU	common
Trillium	Vulcan		X	60 per kgm	common
Zienite	Various	X		450 per kgm	common
SPECIAL COMMODITIES					
Dilithium Crystals	Various	X		2300 per indiv	rare
Radioactives	Various	X		580 per kgm	rare

Chart Key

Availability: Common, uncommon, rare, very rare
Major: Major export Item
Minor: Minor export item
Origin: Place of origin
Price: Standard price in credits per unit
STU: Standard Trade Unit

KEEPING THE PEACE

FEDERATION-STAR FLEET RELATIONS

Star Fleet Command is the largest single military force in the history of the major interstellar powers. Established by the Articles of Federation, Star Fleet's purpose is to provide common defense and security for the Federation's member worlds, as well as to explore and investigate space. Constitutional safeguards exist to prohibit the illegal use of any Star Fleet resource against one or more members of the Federation. However, many individuals believe that the continued increase of Star Fleet's personnel, combat-ready ships, and political influence within the Federation bureaucracy may threaten the continued stability of the Federation.

Detractors of Star Fleet expansion point to the incidents surrounding the Scandal of Archimedes of Stardate 1/7201. Prior to this date, mining interests on both Andor and Tellar disputed the right to mine the resources of the planet Th'allt in the Archimedes system. The crux of the argument concerned whether or not Andor had exclusive claim to the planet's wealth. As their survey teams had discovered the planet about the same time as the Andorians, the Tellarites claimed the right of equal opportunity. Eventually, the matter was forwarded to the Department of Interstellar Trade and Commerce for adjudication. Before this agency could act, however, Andorian Star Fleet Admiral Hathari seized the initiative and began to detain forcibly Tellarite merchant ships operating out of Th'allt. He confiscated ore cargoes and fired on Tellarite vessels refusing to stop and submit to search. Although Admiral Hathari was later disciplined for his actions, and Star Fleet agreed to pay Tellar extensive reparations for damages, the incident shows what could occur if any portion of Star Fleet were ever employed irresponsibly.

Two lengthy and costly wars with the Romulan and Klingon Empires have proven the necessity of a strong defensive capability, which only Star Fleet can ensure. Moreover, the presence of independent groups such as the Orion Colonies and the Asparaxian Confederation requires that some force patrol these unstable locations. Nevertheless, many civilized societies refrain from joining the Federation because they are either philosophically or politically reluctant to contribute finances to this thinly disguised military arm of the Federation. Clearly, Star Fleet has sometimes been used to enforce Federation policy, such as the ban on Orion slave trade.

Advocates of a strong Star Fleet point to the enormous sacrifices that Star Fleet has made and continues to make for the security and well-being of the Federation. They also point out that the mix of non-Humanoid and Humanoid personnel in Star Fleet deters any single power block or interest group from gaining undue influence. Lastly, Star Fleet has always obeyed the government's efforts to economize in times of peace by cutting back fleet size, even if opposed to such measures.

Star Fleet remains a mixed blessing, viewed as either a primary peace-keeper or a potential disruptor of political and economic freedoms. It remains to be seen how the Federation government will continue to use this willing (or unwilling) instrument of its policies.

FUNDING THE FLEET

Star Fleet Command is currently responsible for over 12,000 capital ships and over 20,000 auxiliary and support vessels of various types. These craft range in size from small, fully-automated ore carriers to *Excelsior* Class battleships incorporating the latest Federation technology. In addition, Star Fleet is responsible for maintaining several star bases as well as hundreds of smaller support, repair, and construction facilities. As might be expected, the financial necessities of maintaining such a wide array of men and materiel is beyond the normal capabilities of any single agency. Star Fleet receives its annual operational funding through the sources described below.

It should be remembered that the Federation is Star Fleet's major source of revenue and, more importantly, trained manpower. When new technology or weaponry calls for new vessel designs or classes, Star Fleet must make a special request of the Federation Assembly for extraordinary funding. Likewise, whenever normal fleet size must be expanded, such as during times of war, Star Fleet is required to make a similar request to the Assembly.

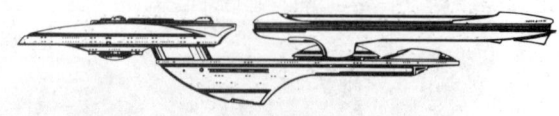

UFP BUDGETARY CONTRIBUTION

Despite the misgivings of various members, the Federation remains committed to use Star Fleet for the defense and security of its member societies. The Federation Assembly limits the amount of governmental support designated by the Federation Council. Star Fleet Command receives less than half its total funding from direct Federation contributions. In recent years, the average sum contributed by the government has amounted to between 40 and 45 percent of Star Fleet's total financial resources.

CUSTOMS DUTIES AND RELATED EXPENSES

In many parts of the Federation, there are no cargo or passenger carriers to provide transportation for local Federation members. In such cases, Star Fleet supplies such transportation for a nominal fee. Usually based on local financial need and ability to pay, these arrangements cost less than comparable civilian rates.

A private corporation or citizen may occasionally call upon Star Fleet to transport secret or extremely valuable cargoes from one star system to another. In such cases, similar customs fees are invoked. If no Federation customs or port officials exist within a system, Star Fleet will regulate cargoes between different systems, imposing local customs duties where applicable. Together, these various sources account for about ten percent of Star Fleet's annual budget.

STAR BASE PRODUCTION

Star Fleet maintains numerous star bases at critical points within Federation space to defend planetary systems and to support Star Fleet operations in the vicinity. Such star bases are self-sufficient centers of military and civilian activities. They can also be commercial centers capable of supplying the industrial needs of local planetary systems. Except in regions where major planetary trade centers already exist, Star Fleet allows star base commanders to commit base resources toward manufacturing numerous trade and commercial articles to help develop local worlds. Often, a local planetary governor will request such activities, conducting extensive trade with the star base for a certain good that his world does not possess. Star base production accounts for nearly 30 percent of Star Fleet's annual revenues.

PLANETS FOR SALE

Every year, Star Fleet survey teams discover many uncharted planets in unexplored areas of space. Following a formal geological survey by Star Fleet personnel, the survey team forwards its findings to the Department of Colonization. It sometimes happens that a newly discovered Class M world possesses no economic or industrial potential, and neither private, commercial, nor colonial interests claim it. It is Federation policy that if no one claims the planet in a year's time, jurisdiction over it falls to Star Fleet. Planet-side star bases may be constructed on such worlds, but occasionally they are sold to wealthy private citizens. (Flint's World is a case in point.) The planet then becomes the personal property of the new owner, and Star Fleet compensated accordingly. The Federation Assembly accepts this practice as a legitimate means of collecting money that would otherwise have to come from member contributions.

Within the last two decades, there have been 118 such sales, not all of which resulted in actual occupation and/or habitation of the planet. The private sale of Star Fleet-owned planets accounts for over ten percent of Star Fleet's annual budget.

COMMERCE PROTECTION

Despite the best efforts of Federation politicians and diplomats, a large number of independent and hostile planetary governments sanction pirate activities against shipping interests within the borders of Federation space. In recognition of its efforts to eradicate such marauders, the Federation permits Star Fleet to confiscate and sell any seized contraband vessel engaged in piracy against Federation civilians. The Department of Interstellar Trade and Commerce auctions off such vessels and their cargoes, then turns over the proceeds to Star Fleet Command. Revenues received in this manner account for roughly five percent of Star Fleet's annual operating budget.

PRIVATE CONTRIBUTIONS

Some planetary governments have decreed that half of all contributions made by individual corporations and private citizens to the Star Fleet general operations fund are tax-deductible. Corporations making such deductions must be chartered by the Federation's Securities and Exchange Commission. Such contributions account for about five percent of Star Fleet annual revenues.

GENERAL ORDERS TO STAR FLEET

The following section lists the general instructions for Star Fleet Command. Recommended by the Secretary of Star Fleet and established through executive order by the Federation Council, these General Orders pertain to all Star Fleet personnel. They specify the extent to which the Federation Council and Assembly maintain control over their military counterparts. Conversely, these General Orders also represent to what extent Star Fleet is capable of influencing Federation policy.

There are currently 25 general orders for the proper conduct of Star Fleet operations. The list presented below gives the General Orders as of Stardate 2/2306.01. The first six are the original orders that were established upon the founding of the Federation. The remainder list the dates on which they became law.

GENERAL ORDER 1

As the right of each sentient species to live in accordance with its normal cultural evolution is considered sacred, no Star Fleet personnel may interfere with the normal and healthy development of alien life and culture. Such interference includes introducing superior knowledge, strength, or technology to a world whose society is incapable of handling such advantages wisely. Star Fleet personnel may not violate this Prime Directive, even to save their lives and/or their ship, unless they are acting to right an earlier violation or an accidental contamination of said culture. This directive takes precedence over any and all other considerations, and carries with it the highest moral obligation.

GENERAL ORDER 2

No Star Fleet personnel shall unnecessarily use force, either collectively or individually, against members of the United Federation of Planets, their duly authorized representatives, spokespersons, or designated leaders, or members of any sentient non-member race, for any reason whatsoever.

GENERAL ORDER 3

The sovereignty of each Federation member being respected in all things, Star Fleet personnel shall observe any and all statutes, laws, ordinances, and rules of governance currently in effect within the jurisdiction of a member planet. Violators of such ordinances will be subject to such punishments or corrections as shall be determined by local governmental bodies.

GENERAL ORDER 4

If contact is made with hitherto undiscovered intelligent life-forms, under no circumstance shall Star Fleet personnel, either by word or deed, inform said life-forms that worlds other than their own or intelligent life-forms other than their own exist outside the confines of their own space.

GENERAL ORDER 5

In cases of extreme emergency, Federation special representatives are empowered to assume emergency powers to deal with a condition or circumstance that is deemed hazardous to the welfare of Federation citizenry. Within the scope of these emergency powers, duly authorized civilian personnel may assume temporary command of Star Fleet vessels and/or personnel to deal with the emergency. Star Fleet personnel must submit to their authority for the duration of the crisis.

GENERAL ORDER 6

The request for emergency assistance from Federation citizenry demands unconditional priority from Star Fleet personnel. Such personnel shall immediately respond to said request, postponing all other activities.

GENERAL ORDER 7 (STARDATE 1/9608)

No Star Fleet vessel shall visit the planet Talos IV under any circumstances, emergency or otherwise. This order supersedes General Order 6. Any transgression of this general order shall be punishable by death.

GENERAL ORDER 8 (STARDATE 1/9611)

Upon sighting a warship within Federation space and identifying it as belonging to a foreign power, the commander of the Star Fleet vessel shall determine the reason(s) for that craft's presence in the vicinity. If there is conclusive evidence that the vessel has hostile intentions, the Federation vessel may take appropriate action to safeguard the lives and property of Federation members. In such cases, the commander may use his discretion in deciding whether to use force to disable the hostile vessel. However, care should be taken to avoid unnecessary loss of sentient life.

GENERAL ORDER 9 (STARDATE 1/9701)

No commander of a Star Fleet vessel, military or auxiliary, may grant political asylum to any individual without first being given express permission to do so by a representative of the Federation government.

GENERAL ORDER 10 (STARDATE 1/9802)

If there exists eyewitness testimony by senior officers or similar verifiable evidence that an individual has violated the Prime Directive, said individual may be relieved of duty by a duly sworn representative of the Federation government and placed under immediate arrest. The governmental representative shall then take such action as he deems necessary to minimize the results of the violation.

GENERAL ORDER 11 (STARDATE 1/9903)

Star Fleet officers with the rank of captain or higher are granted full authority to negotiate conditions of agreement and/or treaties with legal representatives of non-Federation planets. In such circumstances, the acting officer carries *de facto* powers of a Federation Special Ambassador. Any and all agreements arranged in this manner are subject to approval by the Chief of Star Fleet Operations and the Secretary of Star Fleet.

GENERAL ORDER 12 (STARDATE 1/9907)
Federation officers may violate Neutral Zone areas as designated by treaty only if such action is required to save the lives of Federation citizens under conditions of extreme emergency.

GENERAL ORDER 13 (STARDATE 1/9910)
Except when orders state to the contrary, Star Fleet personnel will respect the territorial integrity of independent planetary systems and governments, and will not violate territorial space belonging to such worlds.

GENERAL ORDER 14 (STARDATE 1/9912)
Star Fleet personnel may intervene in local planetary affairs to restore general order and to secure the lives and property of Federation citizens only upon receiving a direct order to do so from a civilian official with the title of governor or higher.

GENERAL ORDER 15 (STARDATE 2/0007)
No officer of flag rank shall travel into a potentially hazardous area without suitable armed escort.

GENERAL ORDER 16 (STARDATE 2/0111)
Star Fleet personnel may extend technological, medical, or other scientific assistance to a member of a previously unrecognized sentient species only if such assistance in no way compromises the Prime Directive or the security of the Federation or Star Fleet.

GENERAL ORDER 17 (STARDATE 2/0112)
Star Fleet vessel captains are to consider the lives of their crew members as sacred. In any potentially hostile situation, the captain will place the lives of his crew above the fate of his ship.

GENERAL ORDER 18 (STARDATE 2/0202)
Upon being accused of treason against the Federation, Star Fleet personnnel may demand a trial conducted by the Federation judiciary. If the individual is acquitted, Star Fleet Command shall have no further legal recourse against the accused in said matter.

GENERAL ORDER 19 (STARDATE 2/0307)
Except in times of declared emergency, Star Fleet personnel may under no circumstances convey personnel or materiel between planets or planetary systems when there is reason to believe that said personnel or materiel may be used to conduct aggression. This order applies to independent worlds within the Federation as well as to Federation members.

GENERAL ORDER 20 (STARDATE 2/0501)
Officers and personnel of Star Fleet Command may employ whatever means necessary to prevent the possession, transportation, sale, or commercial exchange of sentient beings held against their wishes within the boundaries of Federation space.

GENERAL ORDER 21 (STARDATE 2/0712)
No Star Fleet personnel, either officer or enlisted, may offer his services to an independent foreign government without the express authorization of the Federation Assembly.

GENERAL ORDER 22 (STARDATE 2/0912)
As the rights of individual expression and free discourse are considered sacred, Star Fleet personnel may debate the policies and decisions of their governmental representatives privately at any time, to the extent that such discussions do not violate their command oath or specific duties to the Federation per these General Orders or Star Fleet regulations.

GENERAL ORDER 23 (STARDATE 2/1003)
When verifiable proof is presented to the senior commanding officer of a Star Fleet vessel or post that a Federation representative may currently be acting or have acted in the past to violate the Prime Directive, the officer may relieve said representative of office, then assume the full powers of that office pending a full investigation by governmental officials.

GENERAL ORDER 24 (STARDATE 2/1204)
If a commanding officer deems that an individual or group of individuals pose a threat to Star Fleet personnel or Federation civilians, he may take any action deemed necessary (including force) to secure the safety of those threatened.

GENERAL ORDER 25 (STARDATE 2/1507)
Civilian and military personnel taken into custody by Star Fleet personnel during times of extreme emergency shall be accorded proper treatment consistent with their rank or station, insofar as such treatment does not compromise the security of the Federation or Star Fleet.

SELECTED PERSONALITIES

The following section gives brief biographical information on individuals who, for better or worse, have left their imprint on Federation history. The entries were selected from Mixal Corodomondin's *Who's Who In The Federation, Past And Present*, Stardate 2/1402, and are used here with permission.

Name: COCHRANE, Zephram Edark
Rank/Title: Scientist
  Position: President of Driticus University, Alpha Centauri

Race: Alpha Centauri
Age: Deceased
Sex: Male

Attributes:

STR	— 45	CHA	— 47
END	— 49	LUC	— 50
INT	— 69	PSI	— 29
DEX	— 58		

Significant Skills	Rating
Administration	39
Computer Operation	58
Computer Technology	48
Electronics Technology	49
Mechanical Engineering	90
Physical Sciences	
Mathematics	86
3-D Geometry	68
Physics	78
Small Vessel Engineering	44
Small Vessel Piloting	49
Small Equipment Systems Operation	55
Medical Science	
Psychology, Alpha Centauran	48
Space Sciences	
Astrogation	64
Astronomy	75
Astrophysics	77
Warp Drive Technology	98

Distinguishing Physical Characteristics:
Cochrane was tall and muscular, with finely chiselled features. He definitely did not look like a typical scientist.

Brief Personal History:
Birthplace: Lurivala, Alpha Centauri.

Zephram Cochrane will be remembered throughout Federation history as the inventor of the warp drive system, enabling Alpha Centaurans and Humans to explore and colonize the galaxy surrounding them. Following the experimental success of his theories, Cochrane was immediately hailed as hero of the day. Similar displays of well-earned respect were showered on him during his brief visit to Terra. A quiet and unassuming individual, Cochrane showed calm and reserve in accepting the honors.

Returning to Alpha Centauri, Cochrane served as chief warp technology consultant for the Alpha Centauri Concordium of Planets until age 52, when he became president of Driticus University. During his later years, Cochrane became increasingly absorbed with interstellar navigation and piloting as an escape from the drudgery of academic administration.

At the age of 68, shortly before his retirement from Driticus University, Cochrane purchased a small interstellar transport to make one last journey to Terra. Shortly after his departure, communication with Cochrane's craft was lost, and he was never heard from again. Presumably, he died in interstellar space, though his body has never been found.

COCHRANE

Name: DANNON, Abraham Tacitus
Rank/Title: Council Member
Position: Senior Member of United Federation of Planets Council

Race: Alpha Centauran/Human Hybrid
Age: Deceased
Sex: Male

Attributes:

STR	− 61	CHA	− 75
END	− 68	LUC	− 54
INT	− 72	PSI	− 30
DEX	− 44		

Significant Skills	Rating
Administration	70
Leadership	74
Languages	
Orion	48
Tellarite	42
Andorian	40
Negotiation/Diplomacy	69
Social Sciences	
Federation Racial Culture/History	67
Federation Law	60
Orion Law	58
Orion Racial Culture/History	44
Trade and Commerce	42
Trivia, Romulan Culture	37
Value Estimation	38

Distinguishing Physical Characteristics:
Dannon had pale, blue-grey eyes and a small red birthmark on his left cheek.

Brief Personal History:
Birthplace: Ixis, Alpha Centauri.

Abraham Dannon is revered today as the Federation's most honored statesman, though he was hated and despised as an appeaser and would-be traitor in his own time. Dannon was the architect of the Federation's treaty with the Romulan Star Empire, which brought an end to that long and bloody conflict. His treaty efforts were hampered by the desire of many Council members to extract vengeance on the Romulans for the many Federation lives lost during that conflict. Realizing that a series of harsh treaty conditions would prolong the war, Dannon delivered his "Sighted Man of Peace" speech on Stardate 1/0901.20. This now-famous speech convinced the Council members to soften their conditions, which included the voluntary surrender of previously held Romulan star systems, to bring about a much-needed peace.

Though Dannon's efforts were eventually successful, he never lived to see their fruits. A dissident Andorian assassinated him four years after the ratification of the treaty bearing his name.

DANNON

Name: DAYSTROM, Richard, Ph.D.
Rank/Title: Professor Emeritus
Position: Chief Science Advisor, Daystrom Data Concepts

Race: Human
Age: 49
Sex: Male

Attributes:

STR	– 52	CHA	– 57
END	– 44	LUC	– 47
INT	– 85	PSI	– 12
DEX	– 46		

Combat Statistics:
To-Hit Numbers—
 Modern: 23
 HTH: 26
Bare-Hand Damage: 1D10+2
 AP: 8

Significant Skills	Rating
Administration	38
Computer Operation	86
Computer Technology	92
Electronics Technology	86
Physical Sciences	
Computer Science	96
Mathematics	59
Physics	48
Mechanical Engineering	55
Medical Sciences, Psychology, Human	68
Small Equipment Systems Technology	55

Distinguishing Physical Characteristics:
Daystrom is tall and slender, with fiery eyes.

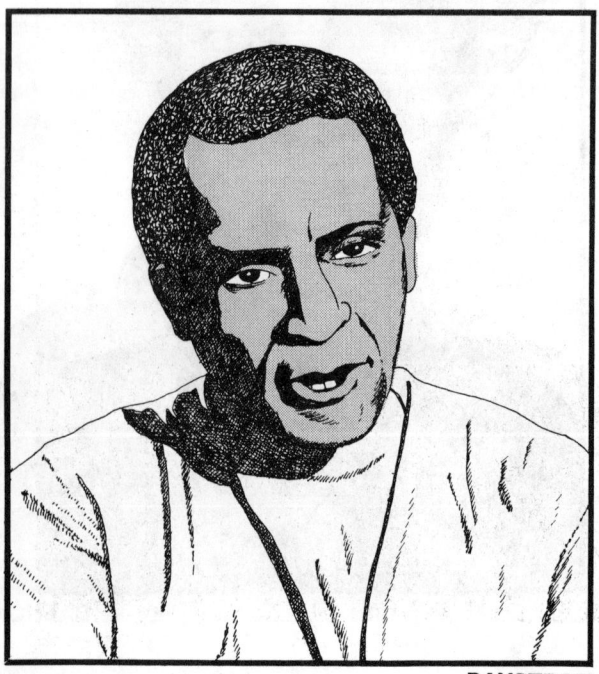

DAYSTROM

Brief Personal History:
Birthplace: New Orleans, Terra.

A true genius, Dr. Richard Daystrom exemplifies the best and the worst of Federation scientists over the last century. For the last 30 years, he has been the acknowledged leader in the field of computer science and technology. Dr. Daystrom produced the first practical mathematical study on the relationship between sub-atomic structure and data processing (now called duotronics) in Stardate 1/56 at the age of ten. Daystrom later shared the Nobel Prize with Dr. William Abramson in Stardate 1/7200 for the development of the universal translator. His pioneering work in duotronics was later supplemented by various Cygnian researchers, and represents state-of-the-art computer technology.

An overachiever and compulsive workaholic, Daystrom conducted research into the practical development of a higher-order computer with artificial intelligence capabilities. After two decades of research and development (funded by Star Fleet appropriations), he completed the M-5 multitronic unit in Stardate 1/8602. However, the strain of the last few years, combined with design flaws in the M-5, plunged him into mental breakdown.

Upon recovery, Daystrom retired to New Orleans to found Daystrom Data Concepts, a corporate think-tank, to expedite further research into multitronics and to reap commercial success from improvements on his previous work. This firm is now headed by his son Richard Daystrom II, although Dr. Daystrom continues to serve as chief science advisor.

Personality:
Motivations/Desires/Goals:
Daystrom is no longer obsessed with the need to prove his genius to the universe. He is now determined to spend the rest of his career assisting other, younger computer scientists accomplish what he was not able to do—construct a truly independent, logical thinking machine.
Manner:
Daystrom is rather quiet and reserved.

Special Knowlwdge/Powers:
None.

Name: GANDAR, Rodimus
Rank/Title: Chief Executive Officer
  Position: Operations Manager, Syntax Corporation

Race: Human
Age: 35
Sex: Male

Attributes:

STR	—	43	CHA	—	46
END	—	63	LUC	—	45
INT	—	70	PSI	—	07
DEX	—	67			

Combat Statistics:
To-Hit Numbers—   Bare-Hand Damage: 1D10+1
  Modern: 38   AP: 10
  HTH 46

Significant Skills	Rating
Administration	48
Bribery	48
Carousing	80
Computer Operation	28
Languages	
Orion	85
Romulan	47
Leadership	66
Marksmanship, Modern	69
Medical Sciences	
Psychology, Human	56
Negotiation/Diplomacy	70
Personal Combat, Unarmed	49
Social Sciences	
Federation Law	40
Orion Law	36
Orion Racial Culture/History	35
Streetwise	84
Trade and Commerce	65
Trivia, Orion Corporations	38
Value Estimation	49

Distinguishing Physical Characteristics:
  Gandar is tall and lanky, with reddish-blond hair.

Brief Personal History:
  Birthplace: Southhampton, England, Terra.
  Rodimus Gandar's story is an archetypical rags-to-riches story, though with a sinister twist. At age 27, he inherited an almost bankrupt corporation from his father, following the latter's death under mysterious circumstances. Since that time, Rodimus has managed to increase the corporation's financial base by catering to the seedier side of the Federation's citizenry. It is said he will do anything for a credit and that his company follows this motto with equal vigor. Though concrete proof is lacking, Rodimus may be an importer of Orion Green Slaves for private interests within the Federation.

Personality:
Motivations/Desires/Goals:
  Because his father blamed him for his mother's death in childbirth, Rodimus has been deprived of parental affection all his life. As an adult, he seeks to make up for this loss by pursuing material goals.
Manner:
  Rodimus has no scruples over any action, however illegal, as long as it will turn him a quick profit.

Special Knowledge/Powers:
  None.

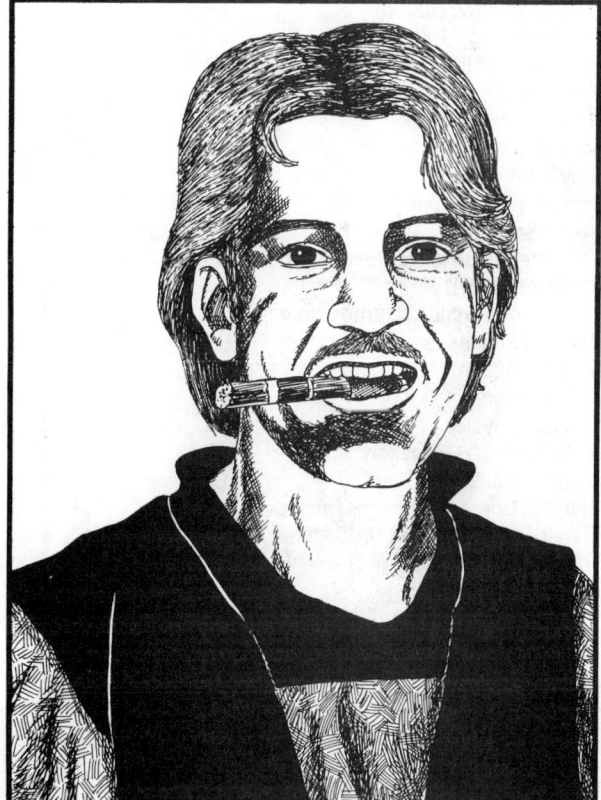

GANDAR

Name: GARTH, Kelvar
Rank/Title: Fleet Captain, Retired
   Position: None

Race: Izaran
Age: 62
Sex: Male

Attributes:

STR	– 68	CHA	– 79
END	– 42	LUC	– 49
INT	– 78	PSI	– 12
DEX	– 50		

Combat Statistics:
   To-Hit Numbers—   Bare-Hand Damage: 1D10+3
      Modern: 68   AP: 9
      HTH: 54

Significant Skills	Rating
Administration	36
Computer Operation	38
Computer Technology	33
Electronics Technology	59
Language, Klingonaase	82
Leadership	77
Marksmanship, Modern	68
Medical Sciences	
General Medicine, Human	28
Psychology, Human	68
Psychology, Klingon	58
Personal Combat, Unarmed	58
Personal Weapons Technology	12
Negotiation/Diplomacy	36
Shuttlecraft Pilot	40
Small Unit Tactics	87
Small Vessel Engineering	48
Social Sciences	
Federation Racial Culture/History	48
Federation Law	44
Klingon Racial Culture/History	47
Space Sciences	
Astrogation	38
Astronomy	53
Astrophysics	44
Starship Helm Operation	55
Starship Sensors	68
Starship Combat Strategy/Tactics	88
Transporter Operation Procedures	33
Transporter Technology	30
Warp Drive Technology	56

Distinguishing Physical Characteristics:
   Garth has steel-gray hair brushed straight back in the classic Izaran style. He has numerous scars and burns from injuries suffered during the Battles of Axanar.

Brief Personal History:
   Birthplace: Trelemarcas, Izar.
   Star Fleet Medal of Valor
   Karagite Order of Heroism
   Terran Medal of Honor
   Andor Cluster of Conspicuous Gallantry
   The leading graduate of Star Fleet Academy, class of 1/85, Garth rose to become the leading Star Fleet tactician and military expert during the Four Years War. His victories over two Klingon task forces in the Axanar star system prevented the Klingons from establishing supply lines into the heart of the Federation. Though unknown at the time, Garth received several head injuries during these battles that would eventually cause acute mental disorders.
   After the Four Years War, Garth was promoted to the rank of Fleet Captain in charge of *Constitution* Class vessels, replacing Captain Christopher Pike, and was awarded Star Fleet's highest commendations. He later received command of the *USS Lexington*. While serving as a diplomatic representative of the Federation to the planet Antos, a power plant on the planet's surface exploded, burning and disfiguring him. In the aftermath of the tragedy, Antosian experts managed to restore much of Garth's damaged tissue. During this time, Garth learned the Antosian secret of molecular metamorphosis, allowing him to alter his shape and form at will. Unfortunately, the accident accelerated Garth's mental collapse. The Captain's resulting paranoia and megalomania almost caused the destruction of the Antosian people when Garth attempted to use the *Lexington*'s firepower to destroy his benefactors.
   Garth was thereafter committed to the Federation Penal Colony on Elba II. After several years, new and revolutionary serums for treating mental disorders reversed his psychic deterioration. Eventually rehabilitated and discharged, Garth was given a seat on the Star Fleet Operating Forces Board. He has since retired from Star Fleet and returned to Izar, where he enjoys the respect he deserves as Star Fleet's finest officer.

Personality:
Motivations/Desires/Goals:
   Aside from an occasional lecture at Star Fleet Academy, Garth is content to live out his life on his home planet. He is satisfied that his contributions to the Federation have been recognized and that his military tactics are required reading at the academy.
Manner:
   Garth is humble and reserved. He does not flaunt his past exploits, remembering all too well the near disaster on Antos.

Special Knowledge/Powers:
   Garth has learned the Antosian's secret to cellular metamorphosis, which allows him to alter the physical makeup of his body at will for limited periods of time.

GARTH

GREEN

Name: GREEN, Edward Featherstone
Rank/Title: Colonel, United Nations Armed Forces
   Position: Rebel Leader

Race: Human
Age: Deceased
Sex: Male

Attributes:

STR	— 47	CHA	— 57
END	— 55	LUC	— 40
INT	— 56	PSI	— 04
DEX	— 42		

Significant Skills	Rating
Computer Operation	28
Electronics Technology	46
Leadership	76
Negotiation/Diplomacy	41
Small Equipment Systems Technology	38
Small Unit Tactics	57
Small Vessel Engineering	37
Small Vessel Piloting	43
Social Sciences, Terran History	44
Space Sciences	
Astronomy	32
Astrophysics	22

Distinguishing Physical Characteristics:
   Green has magnetic eyes, and wears his black hair slicked back.

Brief Personal History:
   Birthplace: Paris, France, Terra.
   Colonel Green is one of the most insidious leaders in Terra's long and troubled history. In Stardate 0/35, at the height of his military career, Green led a revolt against the Terran government to force its leaders to discontinue space exploration. Gaining control of the Luna military defense base, he destroyed the first fusion reactor-driven prototype vessel. Thereafter, he threatened to use Terra's remaining stockpile of nuclear weapons against selected population centers if his demands were not met. A UN task force succeeded in recapturing Luna Base, but not before Green managed to launch several nuclear missiles, incinerating two major metropolitan centers with millions of casualties. Escaping capture when Luna Base fell, Green returned to Terra, where he and his supporters conducted numerous terrorist activities in what became known as Colonel Green's War. After concerted efforts yielding over a million casualties, Colonel Green and his supporters were hunted down and killed in a missile barrage on their island fortress near Singapore.
   In the last century, Colonel Green has come to be revered by supporters of the Back-to-Earth movement, and the leaders of the Terra-Return League made him a representative of their cause.

Name: ILLISEN, Gwendolyn Daemon
Rank/Title: Planetary Governor
Position: Benecia Colony Administration

Race: Human
Age: Deceased
Sex: Female

Attributes:
STR	— 47	CHA	— 57
END	— 48	LUC	— 45
INT	— 68	PSI	— 32
DEX	— 75		

Significant Skills	Rating
Administration	69
Agricultural Technology	68
Bribery	44
Computer Operation	20
Leadership	86
Negotiation/Diplomacy	75
Streetwise	48
Value Estimation	47

Distinguishing Physical Characteristics:
Gwendolyn is a short, stout woman with a rich, deep voice.

Brief Personal History:
Birthplace: Benecia
Gwendolyn Illisen was the planetary governor of the Benecia colony between Stardates 1/5001 and 1/7802. She was also the leader of the Terra-Return League, a political group that favored the dissolution of the Federation and the emigration of all Humans back to the Sol system. The Scandal of Archimedes gave support to the movement, whose members called it inexcusable that the existing political system was incapable of controlling its own military leaders. Through Illisen's influence, a Federation-wide conference was called to discuss economic issues relating to the Th'allt system, though, in reality, the meeting was to consider the formal dissolution of the Federation. When put to a final vote, the Terra-Return League failed to achieve its objectives. There was more support for a Federation system, with all its flaws, than for numerous system-states in competition with each other.

Following her political defeat, Illisen withdrew with her remaining supporters to found the colony world of New Princeton. There, they renewed their political struggles, though with less influence than before. Illisen died on Stardate 1/7904.03.

ILLISEN

Name: JONES, Cyrano
Rank/Title: Merchant Captain
Position: Independent Trader

Race: Human
Age: 48
Sex: Male

Attributes:
STR	— 42	CHA	— 39
END	— 45	LUC	— 48
INT	— 49	PSI	— 07
DEX	— 56		

Combat Statistics:
To-Hit Numbers— Bare-Hand Damage: 1D10+2
  Modern: 38   AP: 9
  HTH: 32

Significant Skills	Rating
Administration	10
Computer Operation	22
Electrical Engineering	34
Languages:	
Klingonaase	15
Orion	12
Marksmanship, Modern	20
Mechanical Engineering	28
Personal Combat, Unarmed	22
Social Science, Federation Law	30
Small Vessel Engineering	28
Small Vessel Piloting	40
Space Sciences	
Astronomy	21
Astrophysics	10
Trade and Commerce	44
Value Estimation	55

Distinguishing Physical Characteristics:
Cyrano is a short, pudgy man with apple cheeks and a mop of gray hair.

Brief Personal History:
Birthplace: Deneva
Cyrano Jones has spent his entire life in space, acting as an independent trader and speculator among the numerous worlds near the Organian Neutral Zone. Typically staying just one step ahead of financial ruin, Cyrano is one of many free-spirited adventurers who ply the space lanes, ever eager to make a quick (though honest) profit.

Personality:
Motivations/Desires/Goals:
Cyrano has an adopted daughter, Hellena, whom he supports as best he can. His lifelong dream is to make an immensely profitable business deal that would enable him to retire and spend the rest of his life with her on Deneva. He loves her more than anything else in life.
Manner:
In hopes of getting a better deal for himself, Cyrano pretends to be a buffoon. Warm and friendly when he chooses to be, Cyrano is usually gregarious, outspoken, and eager to convince others of his sincerity and goodwill.

Special Knowledge/Powers:
None.

Name: MUDD, Harcourt Fenton (Harry)
Rank/Title: Independent Adventurer
   Position: Con Artist

Race: Human
Age: 46
Sex: Male

Attributes:

STR	— 52	CHA	— 57
END	— 55	LUC	— 39
INT	— 58	PSI	— 04
DEX	— 60		

Combat Statistics:
   To-Hit Numbers—   Bare-Hand Damage: 2D10+2
      Modern: 45   AP: 10
      HTH: 47

Significant Skills	Rating
Bribery	55
Carousing	58
Computer Operation	22
Electronics Technology	13
Forgery	66
Gaming	92
Language, Orion	57
Marksmanship, Modern	30
Personal Combat, Armed	22
Small Vessel Engineering	16
Small Vessel Piloting	43
Space Sciences	
Astronomy	41
Astrophysics	12

Distinguishing Physical Characteristics:
   A rotund, balding man, Harry has a distinctive black handlebar mustache.

Brief Personal History:
   Birthplace: St. Louis, Terra.
   Harry Mudd has spent his entire life convinced that it is unreasonable to invest an honest day's work into anything when he can get someone else to do it for him. Harry is without doubt the finest con man in Federation history, although his greed and ego often upset his plans. He has avoided incarceration by slim margins on more than one occasion. Recently, Harry managed to stumble upon the planet that has since been christened Mudd's World. There, he discovered the remains of an advanced android culture. When members of Star Fleet caught up with him, they sentenced him to remain on Mudd's World under the supervision of the android population until he became socially rehabilitated. Later, he escaped from the planet and resumed his con games. Elements from Star Fleet recaptured him while he was selling fake love potions to miners, and Mudd was sent away for rehabilitation once more.

Personality:
Motivations/Desires/Goals:
   Harry Mudd began his career of larceny and deception to get away from his shrew of a wife. His insatiable ego and desire for bigger and better con jobs keep him quite busy.
Manner:
   Not a bad sort as most of his profession go, Harry is nevertheless self-centered and given to manipulating others for his personal advantage.

Special Knowledge/Powers:
   None.

JONES

MUDD

Name: O'CONNOR, Maximus Roxin
Rank/Title: Entrepreneur/Industrialist
Position: Import-Export Dealer

Race: Human
Age: Deceased
Sex: Male

Attributes:

STR	– 47	CHA	– 55
END	– 52	LUC	– 44
INT	– 66	PSI	– 12
DEX	– 63		

Significant Skills	Rating
Administration	65
Artistic Expression, Painting	55
Computer Operation	44
Language, Orion	47
Physical Science, Chemistry	88
Social Sciences	
Federation Racial Culture/History	55
Federation Law	58
Orion Racial Culture/History	55
Orion Law	44
Trade and Commerce	70
Trivia, Orion Family Genealogies	48
Value Estimation	75

Brief Personal History:
Birthplace: Daraniss, Daran V.

Maximus O'Connor was one of the most unique individuals in Federation history. He is remembered as being the richest private individual who ever lived within Federation space. In biographical texts, he is often referred to as the "Buyer of Worlds" and as one who obtained his riches largely through illegal activities. The son of a wealthy shipping magnate, O'Connor amassed his own fortune at an early age by engaging in slave trade with the Orions before such trade was outlawed in the Federation. Building on his reputation for superior grade goods and on prices well below those of his competitors, O'Connor amassed enough wealth to permit him to purchase several planets. His undisputed control of the Federation-based slave trade ended with his marriage to Laura Deneuve Gamartine of Alpha Centauri. Renouncing his former ways, O'Connor retired with his wife to Laura's World, one of his many planets. Not long after his wife's death from Vegan choriomeningitis, he too died, of grief.

O'CONNOR

Name: SAREK
Rank/Title: Ambassador
Position: Director of Vulcan Science Academy

Race: Vulcan
Age: 117
Sex: Male

Attributes:

STR	– 77	CHA	– 57
END	– 49	LUC	– 50
INT	– 79	PSI	– 78
DEX	– 44		

Combat Statistics:
To-Hit Numbers—   Bare-Hand Damage: 2D10+2
  Modern: 48   AP: 8
  HTH: 38

Significant Skills	Rating
Administration	57
Computer Operation	58
Computer Technology	77
Leadership	88
Negotiation/Diplomacy	85
Physical Sciences	
Computer Science	85
Mathematics	88
Physics	55

Distinguishing Physical Characteristics:
Sarek has a stocky build and a hawk nose.

Brief Personal History:
Birthplace: Remsusala, Vulcan.

Sarek first gained political prominence with his stirring defense of Star Fleet Command after the disastrous Scandal of Archimedes. He openly challenged the Tellarite ambassador Gafhf's demand to reduce the size of Star Fleet to prevent misuse of its resources. Although Sarek personally dislikes diverting men and money from scientific into military avenues, his defense of Star Fleet helped avert serious cutbacks in Star Fleet's budget. During the Babel Conference of Stardate 2/09, Sarek persuaded the Federation delegates to make the planet Coridan a UFP protectorate.

Due to his near-fatal heart attack prior to the Babel Conference, Sarek returned to Vulcan. In addition to his post as Ambassadorial Representative to the Federation, he took up the position of Director of the Vulcan Science Academy. Using these two positions to his advantage, Sarek continues to influence Federation policy while enjoying (insofar as a Vulcan can "enjoy" anything) a well-deserved semi-retirement.

Personality:
Motivations/Desires/Goals:
A calm, rational individual with strong family loyalties, Sarek is a model Vulcan citizen. He exemplifies the proper application of logic and reasoning in place of emotion in political, personal, and private matters.
Manner:
Respectful of other life-forms, Sarek is tolerant of the shortcomings of others, even when such shortcomings put him at a disadvantage. Serene and proud, he is supremely confident of his own abilities.

SAREK

Name: SMITHSON, James Gunther
Rank/Title: Captain
Position: Captain

Race: Human
Age: Deceased
Sex: Male

Attributes:

STR	66	CHA	77
END	68	LUC	48
INT	55	PSI	17
DEX	57		

Significant Skills	Rating
Administration	48
Computer Operation	48
Gaming, 3-D Chess	30
Leadership	63
Medical Science	
Psychology, Human	40
Personal Weapons Technology	44
Shuttlecraft Pilot	20
Shuttlecraft Systems Technology	33
Social Sciences	
Federation Racial Culture/History	24
Federation Law	38
Space Sciences	
Astrogation	33
Astronomy	52
Astrophysics	47
Starship Sensors	40
Starship Helm Operation	32
Warp Drive Technology	27

Distinguishing Physical Characteristics:
Jim has a full, bushy beard and wild eyes.

Brief Personal History:
Birthplace: Bremanhaven, United States of Europe, Terra.

Captain Smithson holds the unenviable distinction of being the first Star Fleet officer to be court-martialed for violating the Prime Directive. In Stardate 1/2803, Captain Smithson entered orbit around Vega Proxima, where the two rival power blocs were about to start a world war. The two governments each possessed nuclear weapons and were about to unleash them when Smithson intervened. He directed his ship's lasers to intercept and neutralize the missile that would have doomed Vega Proxima. Although he only wanted to give the planet another chance to reconsider this violent choice, Smithson was relieved of his command and dishonorably discharged from Star Fleet.

Special Knowledge/Powers:
None.

THE FUTURE OF THE FEDERATION

As the federation nears its 150th anniversary, speculations on its future are fitting. Following are some of the most widely held opinions on what the next several decades hold in store for it.

CULTURAL ASSIMILATION

One of the Federation's contributions to galactic peace is that it has succeeded in preventing factionalism and chaos from dominating the galaxy. Despite the threat of the Terra-Return League, the Federation's diverse civilizations are well on their way to cultural unification. Large-scale social interactions will increase the standard of living on dozens of struggling planets, promote cultural exchanges, increase trade, and promote a greater understanding of ethical and philosophical values. Many social scientists predict that major Federation worlds will achieve thoroughly homogeneous populations within the next two generations. In particular, the concept of "Humanity" may be redefined to include all sentient life-forms adopting the tenets of peaceful coexistence, regardless of their place of origin.

THE PRICE OF FREEDOM

The protection of the Federation's internal harmony and security will continue to depend on a vigilant Star Fleet Command. Research from numerous independently commissioned groups rates the probability of hostilities between the Federation and one or more of its belligerent neighbors at 25 percent during the next two decades and 20 percent thereafter. Such considerations are based largely on recent intelligence reports suggesting that the Organians are declining to continue acting as peace-keepers between the Federation and the Klingon Empire. If Star Fleet fails to maintain a quantitative or qualitative edge over the Klingons, the *Komerex* may decide that such weakness demands exploitation. Thus, mammoth increases in Star Fleet resources and responsibilities may be in order.

Some argue that the development of transwarp drive technology, rather than the introduction of new construction projects, will grant Star Fleet the flexibility it needs to protect the Federation without risking an arms escalation with its enemies. Transwarp-driven vessels could re-deploy to critical combat zones quickly, allowing for greater concentration of forces in less time without any increase in actual fleet size. In any case, Star Fleet will continue to rely on its technology and training to offset any numerical inferiority with its enemies.

Join the Official *Star Trek* Fan Club and receive the full-color Official *Star Trek* Magazine and Newsletter for a whole year!! Send $15.00-U.S., $17.00-Canada, $25.00-Foreign for 1 year membership to:

STAR TREK
THE OFFICIAL FAN CLUB
P.O. Box 111000, Aurora, Colorado 80011, U.S.A.

HOME IS WHERE YOU MAKE IT

Cultural observers can expect to witness massive colonization efforts in every quadrant of the Federation. Anticipated advances in physical and medical sciences suggest that future colonies will boast healthier environments than many homeworld systems. In particular, breakthroughs in global disease prevention, atmospheric immunology, and planetary weather control will result from closer cooperation between medical researchers and corporate terraforming engineers. Colonies showing longer average lifespans will be a powerful inducement to continued star migration.

Faced with the possibility of renewed hostilities in the next few decades, Star Fleet is considering the establishment of a new "defense in depth" posture. This involves the construction of hundreds of forward choke points in strategic planetary systems to contain the advances of any enemy incursion. Many social scientists are predicting that the number of populated planets within the Federation's sphere of influence will double within the next two generations.

THE GRADUATING CLASS OF 2/37

One of the more interesting developments concerning Federation citizens involves the advances expected in education. The mating of multitronic computer systems with subspace radio capabilities will make it possible for students to acquire college skills without relocating to another planet for several years. Students on even the remotest Federation colony will be able to access educational and research materials as well as receive live personalized and computer-assisted instruction. Access to large data storage facilities (such as that on Memory Alpha) will further advance the extended university into more and more fields of endeavor with each passing year.

CARROLL '86

SELECTED SHIPS OF STAR FLEET COMMAND

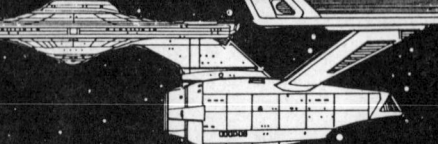
ANDOR CLASS IX CRUISER

GENSER CLASS IV ESCORT

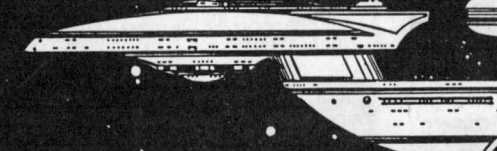
ENTERPRISE CLASS XI CRUISER

LIBERTY CLASS VII FREIGHTER

EXCELSIOR CLASS XIV BATTLESHIP

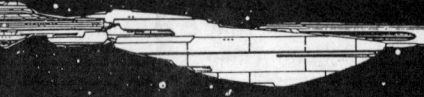
LENTHAL CLASS IX DESTROYER

CHANDLEY CLASS XI FRIGATE

RELIANT CLASS XI CRUISER

NELSON CLASS VII SCOUT

CONSTITUTION CLASS XI CRUISER

CONTINENT CLASS IX ASSAULT SHIP

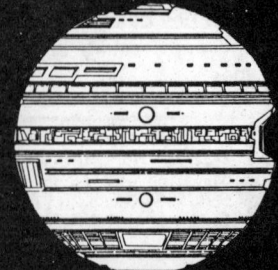
THUFIR CLASS IX DESTROYER

FENLON CLASS V MONITOR